by E. L. Doctorow

Welcome to Hard Times

Big as Life

The Book of Daniel

The Book of Daniel

The Book of Daniel

A NOVEL BY

E. L. Doctorow

Originally published in 1971 by Random House, Inc.

ISBN 0-375-50834-1

Random House website address: www.atrandom.com
Printed in the United States of America
on acid-free paper

1 2 3 4 5 6 7 8 9

Random House, Inc., 2002 Edition

for Jenny

and

Caroline

and

Richard

Then a herald cried aloud, To you it is commanded, O people, nations and languages, That at what time ye hear the sound of the cornet, flute, harp, sackbut, psaltery, dulcimer, and all kinds of music, ye fall down and worship the golden image that Nebuchadnezzar the king hath set up: And whosofalleth not down and worshippeth shall the same hour be cast into the midst of a burning fiery furnace. Therefore at that time, when all the people heard the sound of the cornet, flute, sackbut, psaltery, dulcimer, and all kinds of music, all the people, the nations, and the languages, fell down and worshipped the golden image that Nebuchadnezzar the king had set up.

Daniel, 3:4

With music strong I come, with my cornets and my
    drums,
I play not marches for accepted victors only, I play
    marches for conquer'd and slain persons.

Walt Whitman,
Song of Myself

America I've given you all and now I'm nothing. . . .
I can't stand my own mind.
America when will we end the human war?
Go fuck yourself with your atom bomb.

Allen Ginsberg,
America

Contents

Book One
MEMORIAL DAY

On Memorial Day in 1967

Daniel Lewin thumbed his way from New York to Worcester, Mass., in just under five hours. With him was his young wife, Phyllis, and their eight-month-old son, Paul, whom Daniel carried in a sling chair strapped to his shoulders like a pack. The day was hot and overcast with the threat of rain, and the early morning traffic was wondering—I mean the early morning traffic was light, but not many drivers could pass them without wondering who they were and where they were going

This is a Thinline felt tip marker, black. This is Composition Notebook 79C made in U.S.A. by Long Island Paper Products, Inc. This is Daniel trying one of the dark coves of the Browsing Room. Books for browsing are on the shelves. I sit at a table with a floor lamp at my shoulder. Outside this paneled room with its book-lined alcoves is the Periodical Room. The Periodical Room is filled with newspapers on sticks, magazines from round the world, and the droppings of learned societies. Down the hall is the Main Reading Room and the entrance to the stacks. On the floors above are the special collections of the various school libraries including the Library School Library. Downstairs there is even a branch of the Public Library. I feel encouraged to go on.

Daniel, a tall young man of twenty-five, wore his curly hair long. Steel-rimmed spectacles and a full mustache, brown, like his hair, made him look if not older than he was then more self-possessed and opinionated. Let's face it, he looked cool, deliberately cool. In fact nothing about his appearance was accidental. If he'd lived in the nineteen thirties and came on this way he would be a young commie. A cafeteria commie. He was dressed in a blue prison jacket and dungarees. His Brooklyn-born wife was nineteen, with long straight natural blond hair worn this day in braids. She came to his shoulder. She wore flower bellbottoms and a khaki rain poncho and carried a small bag with things for the baby. As a matter of principle she liked to talk to strangers and make them unafraid, and although Daniel hadn't wanted her to come along, he was glad he relented. The rides came quickly. She talked for him while he stared out the window. Cars, he noticed, were very big and wide and soft. The people who drove them were not fearful but patronizing. They were inquisitive and obviously entertained to be driving these young American kids who probably smoked marijuana even though they had a baby.

At about one o'clock they were let off at Route 9 in Worcester, a mile or so from their destination. They were looking up a long steep hill. At the crest of the hill, too far away to see, were the gates of Worcester State Hospital. Daniel had never been here but his father's directions were precise. Daniel's father was a law professor at Boston College forty miles to the east.

He didn't like my marrying Phyllis, neither did my mother, but of course they wouldn't say anything. Enlightened liberals are like that. Phyllis, a freshman dropout, has nothing for them. Liberals are like that too. They confuse character with education. They don't believe we'll live to be beautiful old people with strength in one another. Perhaps they sniff the strong erotic content of my marriage and find it distasteful. Phyllis is the kind of awkward girl with heavy thighs and heavy tits and slim lovely face whose ancestral mothers must have been bred in harems. The kind of unathletic helpless breeder to appeal to caliphs. The kind of sand dune that was made to be kicked around. Perhaps they are afraid I kick her around.

Daniel considered taking a city bus to the top of the hill but the traffic was bumper to bumper and they could almost outpace it by walking. With Phyllis beside him, her hand lightly on his arm, and with his thumbs hooked under the chest straps of the baby rig, he trudged up the hill. The road was jammed in both directions, and a blue haze of exhaust drifted through the heavy air. Daniel imagined it curling around his ankles, his waist, and finally his throat. A stone wall ran beside them separating the sidewalk from the hospital grounds. On the downhill side of the street were gas stations, dry cleaning drive-ins, car washes, package stores, pizza parlors. American flags were everywhere.

As they approached the top of the hill, they saw a stone kiosk in which a number of people waited for the bus. A bus arrived. It discharged its passengers, closed its doors with a hiss, and disappeared over the crest of the hill. Not one of the people waiting at the bus stop had attempted to board. One woman wore a sweater that was too small, a long loose skirt, white sweat socks and house slippers. One man was in his undershirt. Another man wore shoes with the toes cut out, a soiled blue serge jacket and brown pants. There was something wrong with these people. They made faces. A mouth smiled at nothing, and unsmiled, smiled and unsmiled. A head shook in vehement denial. Most of them carried brown paper bags rolled tight against their stomachs. They seemed to hold their life in those bags. Daniel took Phyllis' arm. As they reached the bus stop the weird people dispersed and flowed around them like pigeons scuttling out of their way, flowing around them and reforming behind them, stirring restlessly in the kiosk in the wake of their passing. Except for one man. One man, the one in the undershirt, ran ahead of them, looking back over his shoulder as they turned into the hospital grounds. He ran ahead of them waving his arm windmill fashion, as if trying to rid himself of the rolled up paper bag locked in his fist. Beyond him, down the tree-lined road (the fumy air clearing in the trees) was the turreted yellow-brick state hospital at Worcester, a public facility for the mentally ill.

SO THAT'S WHERE THEY'RE GOING!

From the *Dartmouth Bible*: "Daniel, a Beacon of Faith in a Time of Persecution. Few books of the Old Testament have been so full of enigmas as the Book of Daniel. Though it contains some of the most familiar stories of the Bible, nine of its twelve chapters record weird dreams and visions which have baffled readers for centuries."

The way to start may be the night before, Memorial Day Eve, when the phone rang. With Daniel and his child bride at sex in their 115th Street den. The music of the Stones pounds the air like the amplified pulse of my erection. And I have finally got her on all fours, hanging there from her youth and shame, her fallen blond hair over her eyes, tears sliding like lovebeads down the long blond hairs of her straight hair. The phone is about to ring. The thing about Phyllis is that when she's stoned all her inhibitions come out. She gets all tight and vulnerable and our lovemaking degrades her. Phyllis grew up in an apartment in Brooklyn, and her flower life is adopted, it is a principle. Her love of peace is a principle, her long hair, her love for me —all principles. Political decisions. She smokes dope on principle and that's where I have her. All her instinctive unprincipled beliefs rise to the surface and her knees lock together. She becomes a sex martyr. I think that's why I married her. So the phone is winding up to ring and here is soft Phyllis from Brooklyn suffering yet another penetration and her tormentor Daniel gently squeezing handfuls of soft ass while he probes her virtue, her motherhood, her vacuum, her vincibles, her vat, her butter tub, and explores the small geography of those distant island ranges, that geology of gland formations, Stalinites and Trotskyites, the Stalinites grow down from the top, the Trotskyites up from the bottom, or is it the other way around—and when we cannot be many moments from a very cruel come that is when the phone rings. It is the phone ringing. The phone. I believe it is the phone.

But how would I get this scene to record Phyllis' adenoidal prettiness, her sharp nose and fair skin and light Polish eyes.

Or her overassumption of life, a characteristic of teenage girls of high school culture. How would it connote the debts all husbands pay for their excesses. Already stirring in this marriage not two years old were the forms of my fearful kindness coming out like magic watercolor under her rubbing. And if the first glimpse people have of me is this, how do I establish sympathy? If I want to show disaster striking at a moment that brings least credit to me, why not begin with the stacks, Daniel roaming through the stacks, searching, too late, for a thesis.

Worcester State Hospital is situated off Route 9 in Worcester, Massachusetts, on the crest of a hill overlooking Lake Quinsigamond, a body of water so quiet that it is famous for crew races. The hospital is in fact two hospitals, an old and a new. The new hospital back toward the woods does not concern us. Lacking steps it is for older patients. The old hospital was put up around the turn of the century. It was designed with the idea that madness might be soothed in a setting of architectural beauty. It is darkly Victorian, with arched doors of oak and mullioned windows. One other fact of considerable interest is that contrary to the popular belief this is one insane asylum that is not overcrowded. In fact it is, upon Susan's arrival, half empty. That is because modern methods of therapy, including tranquilizing drugs, do away with the necessity of incarcerating every nut who happens to live in Worcester, Mass., or environs. The idea now is to commit only those patients who cannot take care of themselves on the outside, or who are murderously inclined. Even for these, there are programs of visits home on weekends if there are homes, and other such privileges. The theory is that the person's normal environment is therapeutic. The theory is that the person wants to go home.

Daniel found his sister in the Female Lounge. The walls there are yellow, ocher and tan. The ceiling is tan. The chairs are dark green imitation leather with chrome tubing arms and legs. There are two TV sets, one on either side of the room, and a rack for magazines. Susan was the only patient in the lounge. A staff attendant in a white uniform with white stockings, which tend to make the legs look fatter than they are, sat with her legs together on a straight chair by the door. She played with her hair and read Modern Screen. Does Dick Really Love Liz? Let me indicate my good faith by addressing myself to the question. I don't think he really loves her. I think he is fond of her. I think he enjoys buying her outlandishly expensive things and also an occasional tup in bed. I think he loves the life, the camera's attention, the ponderous importance of every little fart he makes. I think he loves fraud of spectacular dimension. I think if they were put on trial for their lives, he might come to love her.

They had dressed Susan in one of those beltless, collarless hospital robes, and soft slippers. They had taken away her big granny glasses that always seemed to emphasize the spaciousness of her intelligence, and the honesty of her interest in whatever she looked at. She squinted at Daniel with the lovely blue eyes of a near-sighted girl. When she saw it was he, she stopped trying to look at him and rested her head back against the chair. She sat in a green imitation leather chair with her arms resting on its tubed chrome arms and her feet flat on the floor in their slippers. She looked awful. Her dark hair was combed back off her face in a way she would never have combed it. She always parted it in the middle and tied it at the back of her neck. Her skin looked blotchy. She was not a small person but she looked physically small sitting there. Not looking at him, she lifted her arm, her fingers dipping toward him, a bored, humorous, gesture, one that made his heart leap; and he took the outraised hand in both his hands thinking Oh honey, oh my poor honey, and kissed the back of her hand, thinking It's her, it's still her, no matter what she does, and only then noticing in front of his eyes the taped bandage around her wrist. When he'd had a good look, she pulled her hand away.

For ten minutes Daniel sat next to her. He was hunched over and staring at the floor while she sat with her head back and her eyes closed, and they were like the compensating halves of a clock sculpture that would exchange positions when the chimes struck. He thought he knew what it was, that sense of being overcome. You suffocated. The calamity of it. He had had such spells. People looked at you in a funny way and spoke to you down corridors. You didn't know what to do. Something was torn, there was a coming apart of intentions, a forgetting of what you could expect from being alive. You couldn't laugh. You were in dread of yourself and it was dread so pure that one glance in the mirror scorched the heart and charred the eyes.

Daniel must have sighed. Susan reached out and patted him gently on the back. "They're still fucking us," she said. "Goodbye, Daniel. You get the picture."

He listened alertly. He was not sure if she had said goodbye or good boy. He hung around for a while after that but she didn't say another thing or even acknowledge that he was in the room. He gazed out the window, leaning his shoulder against the window frame. The window was barred. He could see Phyllis playing with the baby down on the hillside. At the top of the hill was a retaining wall of brick, and inside that wall a parking lot filled with pastel cars. Into his sight rolled a dark blue Chevrolet he recognized as the Lewins'. Then the view was cut off by the top of the brick portico sheltering the steps of the main entrance to the hospital.

Without saying much of anything, without even caring if he was there, Susan could restore in him the old cloying sense of family, and suggest that his wife was not in the same class and his child a complete irrelevance. That it was their thing, this orphan state, and that it obliterated everything else and separated them from everyone else, and always would, no matter what he did to deny it. Actually I don't try to deny it. But I reserve the right to live with it in my own way, if I can. In Susan resides the fateful family gift for having definite feelings. Always taking stands, even as a kid. A moralist, a judge. This is right, that is wrong, this is good, that is bad. Her personal life carelessly displayed, her wants unashamed, not managed discreetly like most people's. With her aggressive moral openness, with her loud and intelligent and repugnantly honest girlness. And all wrong. Always wrong. From politics back to drugs, and from drugs back to sex, and before sex, tantrums, and before tantrums, a faith in God. Here is a cheap effect: A long time ago, on an evening in June, 1954, June 22 to be exact, at exactly ten P.M., Susan gave me the word about God. It was during a night game between the Yankees and the Boston Red Sox.

Allie Reynolds was pitching for the Yanks and it was nothing–
nothing in the top of the seventh. Boston had one out and
a man on first. Jim Piersall was up and the count was three and
one. Reynolds picked up the rosin bag. Mel Allen was saying
how a base on balls is always trouble and as he spoke there was
a short beep over his voice the way it happens on television to
indicate that a new hour has begun. At that moment Susan,
age eight, and I, thirteen, could not look at each other. Allie
Reynolds dropped the rosin bag, pulled at the peak of his cap,
and leaned forward for the sign. And that's when Susan told
me there was a God.

"He'll get them all," she whispered. "He'll get every one of
them."

Ah Susy, my Susyanna, what have you done? You are a dupe
of the international moralist propagandist apparatus! They
have made a moral speed freak of you! They have wrecked your
hair and taken away your granny glasses and dressed you in the
robe of a sick person. Oh, look at what they've done, Susan,
look at what they've done to you—

THE NATURE AND FUNCTION OF GOD
AS REPRESENTED IN THE BIBLE

Actually that's what God does in the Bible—like the
little girl says, he gets people. He takes care of them. He lays on
this monumental justice. Oh the curses, the admonitions; the
plagues, the scatterings, the ruinations, the strikings dead, the
renderings unto and the tearings asunder. The floods. The fires.
It is interesting to note that God as a *character* in the Bible
seems almost always concerned with the idea of his recognition
by mankind. He is constantly declaring His Authority, with
rewards for those who recognize it and punishment for those
who don't. He performs fancy tricks. He enlists the help of
naturally righteous humans who become messengers, or carriers
of his miracles, or who deliver their people. Each age has by
trial to achieve its recognition of Him—or to put it another way,
every generation has to learn anew the lesson of His Existence.

The drama in the Bible is always in the conflict of those who
have learned with those who have not learned. Or in the testing
of those who seem that they might be able to learn. In this context it is instructive to pause for a moment over the career of
Daniel, a definitely minor, if not totally apocryphal figure (or
figures) who worked with no particular delight for a few of the
kings in the post-Alexandrine Empires. It is a bad time for
Daniel and his co-religionists, for they are second-class citizens,
in a distinctly hostile environment. But in that peculiar kind of
symbiosis of pagan kings and wise subject-Jews, Daniel is ap-
parently able to soften the worst excesses of the rulers against
his people by making himself available for interpretations of
dreams, visions or apparitions in the night. Dreams, visions and
apparitions in the night seem to be an occupational hazard of
the ancient rulers. Typically, the King (Nebuchadnezzar, or
Belshazzar, or Cyrus) suffers a dream which he cannot understand. He consults his various retainers—magicians, astrologers,
soothsayers, Chaldean wise men. Typically, they fail him. As
a last resort Daniel, a Jew, is summoned. Daniel seems to be
a modest man, brave, and more faithful to God than wise, for it
is by means of prayer and piety that he learns from God the
dream interpretations he must make to the King in order to
survive. In one case, he must even recreate the dream before
he can interpret it because the dumb King, Nebuchadnezzar, has
forgotten what it is. For this wisdom Daniel is accorded min-
isterial rank in the tradition of Joseph and Moses before him.
It is no sinecure, however. We think of Charlie Chaplin taken
home every night by the fat, wealthy drunkard and kicked out
of the drunkard's house in the sobriety of the following morning.
Like an alternating current, though quite direct. At one point,
Daniel's three brothers are accused of sacrilege by the cunning
Chaldeans and the King sentences them to death in a fiery
furnace. God sees that they survive the fire, but the strain on
Daniel has to have been considerable. Another time Daniel,
under the same indictment himself, is thrown into a pit with
lions but survives an entire night unscratched. His is a life of
confrontations, not the least of which has him putting down his
employer in front of the whole crowd: You've bought it, Kingy.
"God hath numbered thy kingdom and finished it, thou art

weighed in the balances and found wanting. . . ." This is not a job for a man sensitive to loud noises or bright light. Daniel survives three reigns but at considerable personal cost. Toward the end his insights become more diffuse, apocalyptic, hysterical. One night he suffers his own dream, a weird and awesome vision of composite beasts and seas and heavens and fire and storms and an Ancient on a throne, and ironically he doesn't know what it means: "I, Daniel, was grieved in my spirit in the midst of my body, and the vision of my head troubled me. . . . My cogitations much troubled me, and my countenance changed in me: but I kept the matter in my heart."

So much for Daniel, Beacon of Faith in a Time of Persecution. (You've got to be desperate to read the Bible.) Five grown-up people are trying to recover one twenty-year-old girl from a public insane asylum on Memorial Day. It can't be done. It is not a working day. There is no one to process her record, sign her out, check her over. There is no one there to say she can go. I am livid. "Let's just take her!" I shout. But that can't be done. Robert Lewin, a professor of law at Boston College, won't do it. Lise, his wife, tells me to be serious. And Dr. Duberstein, the infamous Dr. Alan Duberstein, makes useless phone calls in the public phone booth. Duberstein is a short, skinny man with a high voice. He was shot up during World War II and has a face annealed by plastic surgery. Straight hair that looks sewn into his scalp. Stucco skin, and no eyebrows. Into this fiasco he pokes a pipe. There are spots on his striped tie, and his brown wing-styled shoes need a shine.

"I was told there would be no problem," he insists to the admitting nurse. "We have an ambulance out there that is costing these people thirty-five dollars an hour."

"I can't help that," the admitting nurse says. She is large and cheerful. The state police brought Susan in off the turnpike and that makes her a public charge. "She has to be released," the nurse says patiently. This must be the way she talks to maniacs. With a melody in her voice. "I can't do it and you can't do it. We haven't even typed the admitting diagnosis."

I pace the lobby, pounding my fist into my palm. Phyllis sits on a bench, the baby sliding down her lap. Her earnest face tracks me, she pulls the baby back, it struggles, she pulls it back. I have no real desire to rescue Susan by force. But I wish I had her capacity to do things in a big way—that gift for causing public commotion, that family talent. Actually it's just as well that Duberstein is kept away from her. And our parents too, for that matter. She has been going to Duberstein for years; once she told me she lost her respect for Duberstein when she found out he played golf twice a week. Then why do you go, Susan? "Alleviates parental anxieties," said Susan the college girl. Alleviates parental anxieties. This makes me feel guilty for both of us. I look at the Lewins: pale, worried, under fire once again. I cannot bear the guilt. I begin to scold them. They should have called me sooner. I would have had the sense to get her out of here yesterday. "What were you trying to hide from me? What was the point!"

Lise, my mother, a tiny woman in a blouse and short skirt with low-heeled shoes and shoulder bag, is a curious combination of 1945 WAC and slightly aging Viennese charmer onto the new fashions. She sits down on the bench next to Phyllis and takes the baby, an unconscious maternal gesture which gratifies Phyllis because it brings her into the family. "Oh, Danny," Lise says, "don't be a fool. Nobody's hiding anything. You are down there. We are here. We are her parents. We cope. And if someone in the family can be spared for twenty-four hours, why not? Or should everyone stop functioning?"

She seems to be taking the whole business with more fortitude than my father. My father speaks in his soft voice to Duberstein, suggesting various alternative courses of action. There are doctors at work even on Memorial Day. Find the senior doctor in charge. Talk to him. If he's not in the building, find out where he is and call him. My father is very fond of Susan. Her excesses have always seemed to render him contemplative. This is the worst she's been, the worst thing she's done; it has occurred to him, perhaps, that the pattern of our lives is deterioration, that the movement of our lives is toward death.

With great justice he refuses to pick up my pusillanimous charge. I have long since given up rights in Susan's welfare. Who am I to tell them what to do or not to do? But he grants me my rights. "Let's go outside," he says. We all wait in the park-

ing lot while Duberstein goes off to find the medical administrator. The women and the baby sit in the Lewin car, a 1965
Impala with a regular shift, and leave the doors open; my
father and I with our backs to the hospital lean against the car
grille and look down the hill. Behind us, near the entrance, a
sleek red and grey ambulance lurks in wait, the driver asleep
behind the wheel with his cap tilted over his eyes. The hill is
dotted with patients clutching brown paper bags.

"We knew she was depressed," Robert Lewin says. "We
wanted her to come home for the weekend. But she said she had
to get away. She didn't sound so bad. She's been making her
classes. She's been doing her work." My father is looking older
by the minute. He is bound to feel that Susan's attempt at de-
fection is his fault. If my mother feels that way she won't show
it. It occurs to me that they didn't call me immediately because
they were afraid of my reaction. They weren't sure what it
would be, they weren't sure that Daniel wasn't capable of the
same thing, as if what Susan did was contagious.

Suspense is all Robert Lewin can look forward to as the father
of these children. He doesn't even have the assurance of his
own genes. I feel such sad tenderness for the guy, I put my arm
around his shoulder. He's no slouch. He works like hell, and belongs to committees, and practices law for poor people and
writes for the law journals. He is big in the ACLU. He is popular
with his classes, a thorn in the Dean's side, a demonstrator
against Dow Chemical recruiters. When he has the time, he likes
to read *The New Yorker*.

Neither of the Lewins is capable of regretting what they did
for Susan and me. As cruel as we are. And we are really terrible
low down people. I mean really low down. But they must know
we mean them no harm except the harm in our love for them.
Everyone in the family understands the mythological burden of
acts much smaller than their consequences. My sister and I can
never inflict total damage—that is the saving grace. The right
to offend irreparably is a blood right.

Suddenly Daniel was overwhelmed with a strong sweet sense
of the holiday. The sun was trying to come out, the warm slight
breezes of the overcast day played across the eyes, he was here
with everyone in his immediate family standing on this really

groovy prospect in Worcester, Massachusetts. He was thankful to Susan for relieving the dangerous tedium of his graduate life. She would be all right. In the meantime there was drama, a sweet fatality, a recharging of the weak diffused impulses of giving a shit. Robert Lewin felt his sympathy and was warmly reciprocating. Was Daniel all right? Had he or Phyllis eaten anything since leaving home that morning? He produced from the glove compartment a handful of candy bars. "Milky Ways all around," he said with a sad smile. And there was a car to take care of, Susan's car, still in the lot at the Howard Johnson's near Exit 11 on the Westbound side of the Turnpike. The two men chatted quietly, building comfort for each other in the warm afternoon while Duberstein went about his futile attempts to get the hospital authorities to release Susan. Building concern for each other and then, in a widening circle of small talk, for their wives, for the innocent fat baby, and for anybody still within their power of concern, for anybody who could be saved by concern. The afternoon grew festive—

Bukharin was no angel, of course. In the course of his trial he spoke of condoning the murder of Whites in the heat of the revolutionary struggle. Going down before Stalin, he felt obliged to make the distinction between murder that was politically necessary and factional terrorism. In 1928, ten years before his trial, he criticized Stalin's line of forced industrialization and compared Stalin personally to Genghis Khan. In September, 1936, a meeting of the Central Committee was called to consider the expulsion from the Party of Bukharin, Tomsky and Rykov for leading a Right Wing–Trotskyite conspiracy. Bukharin said that the real conspiracy was Stalin's and that to achieve unlimited power Stalin would destroy the Bolshevik Party and that therefore he, Bukharin, and others, were to be eliminated and that was the source of the charge against him. The Central Committee accepted Bukharin's defense and voted not to expel him. The conspiracy charge was dropped. Within a year, ninety-eight members of the Central Committee were arrested and shot. (We learn this from N. Khrushchev in his address to the 20th Party Congress.) Then the charges were reinstated and Bukharin was put on trial.

Actually, there are separate mysteries to be examined here.

Why do the facts of Russian national torment make Americans feel smug? Why do two state cops, finding a young girl bleeding to death in the ladies' room of a Howard Johnson's, take her not to the nearest hospital, but to the nearest public insane asylum? On second thought these mysteries may not be unrelated.

Subjects to be taken up:

1. The old picture poster that I found in Susan's Volvo, in the front seat, in a cardboard tube.

2. The terrible scene the previous Christmas in the Jewish household at 67 Winthrop Rd., Brookline, a two-family house built, in the style of that neighborhood, to look like a one-family.

3. Our mad grandma and the big black man in the cellar.

4. Fleshing out the Lewins, maybe following them to the Turnpike and then to Brookline. Remember it wasn't until you got into Susan's car that it really hit you. They're still fucking us. You get the picture. Good boy, Daniel.

5. Just as long as you don't begin to think you're doing something that has to be done. I want to make that clear, man. You are a betrayer. There is no cheap use to which you would not put your patrimony. You're the kind of betrayer who betrays for no reason. Who would sit here and write all this, playing with yourself instead of doing your work—what do you think, Professor Sukenick will come to see if you're really working? Do you think it matters to him? Or are you just looking for another father. How many fathers does one boy need? Why don't you go out and get a job? Why don't you drop something heavy? Why not something too heavy? Why not something to show Susan how it's done?

SILENCE IN THE LIBRARY: Who is this cat who starts out of his chair and bumps the reading table, and rushes into the stacks looking for anything he can find? Does Columbia University need this kind of graduate

student? Going through the shelves like a thief—
plundering whatever catches his eye, stumbling back to
his place, his arms loaded with Secondary Sources! What
is his School! What is his name!

6. The trip downtown to see Artie the Revolutionary
and the suspicion of financial shenanigans afoot.

7. The Isaacson Foundation. IS IT SO TERRIBLE
NOT TO KEEP THE MATTER IN MY HEART, TO GET
THE MATTER OUT OF MY HEART, TO EMPTY MY
HEART OF THIS MATTER? WHAT IS THE MATTER
WITH MY HEART?

The summer of 1967 was just beginning. There would be a
wave of draft-card burning. There would be riots in Newark
and Detroit. Young people in the United States would try a
form of protest originated in this century by the Buddhist monks
of South Vietnam. They would douse themselves with gasoline
and light matches to themselves. They would burn to death in
protest. But I, Daniel, was grieved, and the visions of my head
troubled me and I do not want to keep the matter in my heart.

Ascher's huge hand was like a band of steel. He was
a gentle, soft-spoken man, but when he was excited he lost control of his great strength and didn't know he was using it. Daniel
tried to pull away, to loosen the ring of pain around his wrist,
but Ascher's response was to tighten his grip and pull even
harder. "Come, children, come," the lawyer said. Laboriously
they scrambled up the steps from the subway—a steep flight
encased in black dirt and littered with gum wrappers and
flattened cigarette butts. Rising after them were the hot odors
of arcade popcorn, pizza, donuts, pretzels—all the marvels of
cheap nourishment following after them like the cries of animals in a pet store. He always imagined they wanted to be
bought.

"Come, children, come." Susan—smaller, lighter, shorter in
the leg—couldn't keep up. She dangled from Ascher's hammy
hand, her shoes banging on the steps, finding purchase only to

be hauled into the air again. "You're hurting me!" she screamed. Why was he holding them so? Did he think they'd run away?

"You're hurting her arm, Mr. Ascher," Daniel said. "If you let us go we can get up the steps faster than you."

"What? All right then, scoot," Ascher said. Rubbing their wrists they clambered up, easily outgaining the huge, heavy lawyer. "Don't fall!" he called after them. "Stay right there at the top."

Calm now, curious, they watched the great bulk straining to reach them. Where they stood, in the mouth of the precipitous entrance to the subway, two winds converged, the hot underground draft rising to caress their faces and the cold blast of the street cutting at their backs. Dust, paper, soot, swirled along the ground. It was a cold, windy day. The brightness of the sun made their eyes squint.

Ascher climbed the last two steps with his hands pushing at his knees. "I'm not going to live long," he said, trying to catch his breath. He pulled them out of the stream of people pouring down the stairs.

They stood against the building while Ascher took deep breaths and got his bearings. Across the street was Bryant Park and the Public Library. To the right was Sixth Avenue. "That way—we go west," Ascher said, and he took their wrists again and they were off. They waited for the lights, crossed Sixth, and proceeded along 42nd Street toward Broadway. The newsstand man wore earmuffs. The wind blew hard. The kids walked with their faces averted, Daniel with the nubbin brim of his wool cap down on his forehead. His nose was running and he knew the wind would chafe him. It cut right through his pants. Ascher's heavy grey overcoat moved in front of his eyes. Abruptly the hand let go of his wrist and he was thrust up against Ascher's side, contained by the hand, sheltered from the wind. "Stay in close, that way you can walk," the lawyer said. So it was like a strange six-legged beast walking down the windy range of Sixth Avenue, the two kids pressed into the man's sides.

"Like the rest of our luck," Ascher muttered into the wind. "Like the way all our luck is running." With his face buried in the man's coat Daniel was aware of sounds: horns, cars starting and stopping, the large yet soft sound of innumerable people walking, music coming out of a record store. And then a clop-clopping that made him pull back and look around the coat. Two cops on horses, straight backed, tall, manly on their really fine brown horses. And he felt guilty for admiring them, for he knew they were reactionaries.

The lawyer spoke. "Now you must stay close to me and do as I tell you to do. We are a little late. I can tell from here, a tremendous crowd, it's a great tribute. You should feel proud. When you're standing up there, keep your heads up, look proud and tall and don't slump, stand up straight. So that everyone can see you. *Vershtey*? Don't be afraid. What is it, little girl?"

"I've got something in my eye."

"We have no time now, Susan. Come."

Susan leaned back against Ascher's grip and planted her feet. "I've got something in my eye," she insisted.

"Keep your eye closed. It will come out."

"No! It hurts," she said.

Ascher let go her hand and started to yell. Daniel understood that everyone was nervous. He took his sister by the hand and led her into the doorway of a shoe store. Here they were protected from the wind. He took off his gloves and lifted the back of his mackinaw and dug into his pocket for a handkerchief. "Take your glasses off," he said. "Don't rub it. Take your hand away—that's it. Look up."

Her little red face was squinched up around the closed eye. "How can I see what it is if you don't open your eye," Daniel said.

"I can't."

Daniel laughed. "Come on, Susyanna—you should see what a funny face you're making."

"I am not!"

"Please, children, we are late. This is very important! Quickly, quickly!"

"Just a minute, Mr. Ascher," Daniel said. "She's only a little girl, you know."

The poignancy of this description so affected Susan that she began to cry. Daniel put his arms around her and said he was sorry. Ascher muttered in Yiddish and lifted his arms. Then he dropped them, with a smack, against his sides. He walked away and came back.

"Come on, Susan, let me get it out and when we get home I'll play with you. I'll play Monopoly with you." That was a treat because it was such a long game.

Susan opened the afflicted eye, blinked and blinked again. She discovered that whatever it was was gone.

"*Gottzudanken!*" Ascher said.

"Will you still play with me?" Susan wanted to know.

"Yes." Daniel wiped away her tears, wiped her nose, and then wiped his own.

"Hurry, hurry!" Ascher said.

When they reached the corner of Broadway the wind wasn't so bad because the street was filled with people. They were moving into a crowd. More police on horseback, in ranks of two, stood along the curb. Other policemen, on foot, were diverting the Broadway traffic east and west on 42nd Street, which is what made the traffic jam. Horns sounded and a policeman blew his whistle. In the surge of people Ascher held Susan and Daniel by the wrists and crossed with them through the spaces between the cars. Two entire blocks from 40th to 42nd on Broadway were cordoned off. People stood in the street. It was an amazing sight. The center of attention was down at 40th: a man on a platform was shouting through a microphone. Two loudspeakers on the tops of trucks beamed his voice at the people but it was hard to hear what he was saying. The crowd, which was attentive, seemed by its massiveness to muffle the sound. A man saying something quietly to someone next to him destroyed the amplified words. Only the echoes of the unintelligible voice bounced off the buildings. Some people in the crowd held placards aloft, and at moments in the speech when applause rattled like marbles spilling on the ground, these were poked upwards rhythmically.

Ascher led the two children into the edges of the crowd, keeping near the buildings where it was thinnest. They went single file, Ascher preceding Daniel and holding his wrist and Daniel pulling Susan behind him. "Pardon me," Ascher said. "Excuse me."

But at 41st Street the crowd became too thick for this strat-
agem. People were packed together right up to the building line.
Daniel could not see the sidewalk except where he stood. Ascher's
response was to wade right into the crowd, cutting diagonally
into the street and bulling his way through the overcoats. "Let
me through, please. One side, one side." Now it was stiflingly
hot. Daniel felt the crowd as a weight that would crush him to
death if it happened to close the path made by Ascher. An elbow
came up and knocked his hat askew. His hands occupied, he
couldn't set it right. Finally it fell. Susan squatted to retrieve the
hat and his hold on her hand was broken. Ascher was pulling
him on and Susan disappeared in the closing ranks behind him.

"Wait!" he shouted, struggling in Ascher's grasp. His wrist
burned in the steel band.

"Daniel, Daniel!" his sister called.

Panicking, he shouted and dug in his heels. The grip broke.
He fought his way back, pushing between the bodies that were
like trees, immovable boulders. "Susan!"

Faces looked down angrily. "Shhh!" People muttered to him
to keep quiet. The amplified voice filled the sky over his head:
"Is this our so-called American justice? Is this an example to
the world of American fair play and justice?"

"Those are the children!" he heard Ascher cry out. "But those
are the children!" He ran into Susan before he saw her—clutch-
ing his hat with both hands, with no more room around her than
her body made, her arms jammed against her chest. He put his
arm around her shoulder and tried to regain his sense of direction. The heat was unbearable. He looked up, saw the sky, saw
the roofline of buildings to his left. He decided if they were to
cut through to his right they would reach the sidewalk and could
follow the curb back toward the beginnings of the crowd. He
knew how to get home.

"I don't like this," Susan said. "I can't move!"

"Here they are!" A man standing next to him peered down.
"I've got them."

And then Ascher was there and they were being pulled
forward once more. "These are the children," Ascher kept saying. "Let us through, please. I've got the children." Eventually
this was understood by people in the crowd. "He's got the chil-

dren!" they called to each other. Daniel could see a banner stretched on poles across the top of the platform ahead. FREE THEM! Someone lifted him up and he found himself being passed over the heads of the people, propelled sinuously like something on the top of the sea. He was terrified. He heard Susan's voice behind him. "Let me down!" she was saying. "Help! Danny!"

And finally it was the amplified voice that was booming out over Broadway: "Here are the children!" And a great roaring filled his ears as he and Susan were raised, tottering, onto the platform. He was dizzy. He grabbed Susan's hand. Flushed and breathless, dizzied by the motion of heads and the thousands of voices in motion like the roar of the sea, they stared out at the crowd, a vast hideous being of millions of eyes that seemed to undulate in the canyon of the street, splashing life and sound and outrage in great waves up on the platform. Islanded, he felt the wind in his eyes. He felt for a moment that he and Susan had been betrayed and that the great mass would flood over them and carry them away. But the roar, though directed at them, was not meant for them; it was meant for others who dwelt in a realm so mysteriously symbolic that it defied his understanding. At the foot of the platform, at his feet, Ascher's face stared up from the street, triumphant, beatific. He was shouting something but Daniel couldn't hear. The man who had been speaking put one arm around his shoulder and one arm around Susan's, gently, but with unmistakable authority, arranging himself between them. Still they held hands. And the roaring of the crowd had become a chant, a great choir echoing against the buildings until it was continuous: Free them, free them, free them! And he and Susan were transfixed by the placards, the oversized pictures of their mother and father everywhere above the crowd, going up and down in rhythm as the crowd roared Free them, free them, free them.

Oh, baby, you know it now. We done played enough games for you, ain't we. You a smart lil fucker. You know where it's at now, don' you big daddy. You got the picture. This the story of a fucking, right? You pullin' out yo lit-er-ary map, mutha? You know where we goin', right muthafuck?

AN INTERESTING PHENOMENON

Many historians have noted an interesting phenomenon in American life in the years immediately after a war. In the councils of government fierce partisanship replaces the necessary political coalitions of wartime. In the greater arena of social relations—business, labor, the community—violence rises, fear and recrimination dominate public discussion, passion prevails over reason. Many historians have noted this phenomenon. It is attributed to the continuance beyond the end of the war of the war hysteria. Unfortunately, the necessary emotional fever for fighting a war cannot be turned off like a water faucet. Enemies must continue to be found. The mind and heart cannot be demobilized as quickly as the platoon. On the contrary, like a fiery furnace at white heat, it takes a considerable time to cool.

Take World War I. Immediately after this war, President Wilson's ideal of international community ran afoul of fierce Republican partisanship under the leadership of Senator Henry Cabot Lodge, a man who had his eye on the Presidential elections of 1920. Congress' failure to ratify Wilson's dream of a League of Nations was regrettable, to say the least, in view of the unfortunate events in Europe that were to follow. Wilson himself can be said to be a victim of this partisanship, suffering a cleaving stroke down the left side of his face and body. This is a phenomenon noted by many historians.

On the labor front in 1919 there was an unprecedented number of strikes involving many millions of workers. One of the larger strikes was mounted by the A.F. of L. against the United States Steel Corporation. At that time workers in the steel industry put in an average sixty-eight-hour week for bare subsistence wages. The strike spread to other plants, resulting in considerable violence—the death of eighteen striking workers, the calling out of troops to disperse picket lines, and so forth. By branding the strikers Bolsheviks and thereby separating them from their public support, the Corporation broke the strike. In Boston, the Police Department went on strike and Governor Calvin Coolidge replaced them. In Seattle there was a general strike which precipitated a nationwide "red scare." This was the first red scare. Sixteen bombs were found in the New York Post Office just before May Day. The bombs were addressed to men prominent in American life, including John D. Rockefeller and Attorney General Mitchell Palmer. It is not clear today who was responsible for those bombs—Red terrorists, Black anarchists, or their enemies—but the effect was the same. Other bombs popped off all spring, damaging property, killing and maiming innocent people, and the nation responded with an alarm against Reds. It was feared that as in Russia, they were about to take over the country and shove large cocks into everyone's mother. Strike that. The Press exacerbated public feeling. May Day parades in the big cities were attacked by policemen, and soldiers and sailors. The American Legion, just founded, raided I.W.W. headquarters in the State of Washington. Laws against seditious speech were passed in State Legislatures across the country and thousands of people were jailed, including a Socialist Congressman from Milwaukee who was sentenced to twenty years in prison. To say nothing of the Espionage and Sedition Acts of 1917 which took care of thousands more. To say nothing of Eugene V. Debs. On the evening of January 2, 1920, Attorney General Palmer, who had his eye on the White House, organized a Federal raid on Communist Party offices throughout the nation. With his right-hand assistant, J. Edgar Hoover, at his right hand, Palmer effected the arrest of over six thousand people, some Communist aliens, some just aliens, some just Communists, and some neither Communists nor aliens but persons visiting those who had been arrested. Property was confiscated, people chained together, handcuffed, and paraded through the streets (in Boston), or kept in corridors of Federal buildings for eight days without food or proper sanitation (in Detroit). Many historians have noted this phenomenon. The raids made an undoubted contribution to the wave of vigilantism which broke over the country. The Ku Klux Klan blossomed throughout the South and West. There were night ridings, floggings, public hangings, and burnings. Over seventy Negroes were lynched in 1919, not a few of them war veterans. There were speeches against "foreign ideologies" and much talk about "100 percent Americanism." The teaching of evolution in the schools of Tennessee was outlawed. Elsewhere textbooks were repudiated that were not sufficiently patriotic. New immigration laws made racial distinctions and set stringent quotas. Jews were charged with international conspiracy and Catholics with trying to bring the Pope to America. The country would soon go dry, thus creating large-scale, organized crime in the U.S. The White Sox threw the Series to the Cincinnati Reds. And the stage was set for the trial of two Italian-born anarchists, N. Sacco and B. Vanzetti for the alleged murder of a paymaster in South Braintree, Mass. The story of this trial is well known and often noted by historians and need not be recounted here. To say nothing of World War II—

Dr. Alan Duberstein probed the air with his ice cream spoon. It was his belief that Susan's breakdown was connected somehow to her extracurricular activities. He thought she might be in SDS, but he knew for sure she had been active in the Boston Resistance. Last winter, when he and Susan had agreed to terminate her therapy, he had warned her about becoming too involved in political activities. He was having a vanilla soda with peach ice cream. We were all five of us plus the baby stuffed in a Howard Johnson's window booth. Phyllis sat next to him and I imagined her as his wife. She fed the baby ice cream from a dish. I didn't like their baby, a fat kid with red cheeks, light hair like his mother's, and an odor of vomit.

Incredibly, we were all sitting in the Howard Johnson's restaurant near Exit 11 on the Westbound side of the Massachusetts Turnpike. Yet it was logical enough. We had come to pick up Susan's car, left by the police in the parking lot. It was mid-afternoon; everyone was hungry and thirsty. Perhaps also we were trying to see what there was about a Howard Johnson's that would make Susan want to die here. Perhaps we felt if we could only understand we could help her. Nevertheless, I was ill. I am very sensitive to inappropriateness. For instance, to weddings in catering halls. There are no decent settings for joy or suffering. All our environments are wrong. They embarrass our emotions. They make our emotions into the plastic tiger lilies in the window boxes of Howard Johnson's restaurants.

"Ordinary political expression was difficult enough for her," Duberstein said. "Dissent was traumatic. It's understandable after all. She bit off more than she could chew."

"She's a willful person," my father said quietly.

"I have great faith in her," Duberstein said, looking under his napkin for a straw.

Every table was taken. A holiday crowd stood behind the hostess stationed by the velvet rope at the entrance to the dining room. With her menus held to her breast, she swept her gaze across the tables. The hostess was in her forties with a beehive hairdo of platinum blonde. She wore an aqua crepe dress with a cowled collar and she was looking serious.

"If you're not finishing your sandwich," I said to Phyllis, "pass it over here." I was angry with her for imagining Susan's misery in the earnest compassionate way of high school girls with day-glow flowers. I strongly suspected her of having found it thrilling to marry into a notorious family. That was something I still had to look into.

"Well, listen," Duberstein said, "I'd be insulting your intelligence if I didn't admit this is a pretty serious business. There's a lot to work out. But she has tremendous resources. She's been down before."

"What did you do, put ketchup on this?"

"What?" Phyllis says.

"You put ketchup on a club sandwich."

Phyllis looks at me unhappily. She is still hoping someday to be accepted by her in-laws if not by her husband. My mother, Lise, perceives this. "Why not ketchup," she says.

"We'll get her all settled," Duberstein says to my father, "and then we can go to work."

"Yuk!"

"What's the matter, Dan," my father says. He is sitting next to me.

"Ketchup on a club sandwich. Yuk."

"Would you like something else? How about ordering something."

"No thanks, Dad. I'd still have to sit here and listen to this schmuck talk about my sister."

It is just a few volts, but enough to do the job. The thing about the Isaacson family, the thing about everyone in our family, is that we're not nice people. The issue, however, is real. I love my foster parents, but in this emergency they have chosen Duberstein. Duberstein is their man. God knows where he came from originally, I forget the circumstances, but to me he is just one of the thousands of intruders in my life, in my sister's life —one of the thousands of guides, commentators, counselors, sympathizers and holders of opinion.

"Daniel, I hope you are prepared to apologize," says my mother.

"What is it about Susan and me that makes anyone feel privileged to say anything at all to us. Why do I have to sit here and listen to this creep. Who needs him?"

"I called Dr. Duberstein because I think we need him very badly. I think Susan needs him. And I don't think you're handling yourself very well."

"Dad—"

"I would expect better of you."

"Dad, can you tell me—"

"Keep your voice down, please. You speak of privilege, but I'd like to know what gives you the privilege to be a foulmouth?"

For the Lewins, civility is the essence of being human. It is what makes communication possible. The absence of civility disturbs them because it can mean anything from rudeness at a table to suicide. Or genocide. I won't go into this now in any detail but it is bound up with Robert Lewin's love of the law. He knows the law is vulnerable to the mentality of the people who live by it, but he is concerned to see it evolve toward perfection. He is concerned to be moral. My mother too: she is a refugee, hunted by the Nazis all across Europe as a kid. Who am I to claim privilege by my suffering? After all they've done, and never once holding it up to me, why am I so quick to shame them?

"He can't even get her out of there!" I tell them. "He can't get her out of a public asylum for wards of the state and bums they pick up off the street."

"Another twenty-four hours in what happens to be one of the best facilities in the East is not going to hurt your sister," Duberstein says coolly. "I had a long talk with one of the staff people who, as it happens, took his residency at Jacobi when I was there. It's a mistake that they admitted her. But the situation is under control."

"He makes it sound like a personal triumph."

"Danny." My mother takes a handkerchief out of her pocketbook. "We're all under a strain. Please, Danny."

Duberstein says: "Why do you resent anyone who tries to help Susan?" He looks keenly at me as befits his question.

"Screw off, Doc. Go find your golf clubs and play a round with Dwight David Eisenhower." It is a witless, anachronistic retort that astonishes even me. I must be on the edge. Everyone is pale. Even the baby has felt the current. He's begun to cry. I leave the table.

Daniel leaving the Howard Johnson's dining room perceived walking ahead of him, toward the crowd of people waiting for a table, the draped aqua ass of the hostess. And a regal ass it was, well girdled, and set on a pair of still-young legs. Her golden beehive bobbed on her neck and wisps of untucked hair at its base intimated dirty times for the lucky dong who happened to be there when all that hair came down. Her arm was raised, and for a moment Daniel thought she made the peace sign with her fingers. But it was a table for two.

Daniel made his way through the hungry families standing on tiptoe. Kids swarmed in front of the candy display. Popcorn lay in the carpet. In the men's room all the crappers but two required a coin in the slot. On the other side of this wall, Susan had opened her veins and stood over the toilet until she fainted. He tried to get the picture. The sound of fountaining urinals distracted him. He noted on the wall a dispenser which, for twenty-five cents, offered the discriminating customer the choice of a pre-moistened soap-impregnated paper hanky, or a sanitized pocket comb, or a compass from Hong Kong in the form of an automobile tire, or two plastic dog magnets, one black, one white, stuck together in the pack by their magnetized feet.

He went outside. People eating ice-cream cones drifted through the parking lot. A stout woman in a housedress walked a bulldog from the tires of one car to the tires of another. At the gas pumps cars were waiting on line. The sun was out now, late in the afternoon, and the air was close and full of fumes. The thing is, Robert and Lise Lewin do not belong in highway service stops. It is misleading to show them out of their element. Especially when they are not feeling their best.

Daniel walked between the rows of parked cars. He found the Volvo. It was black and covered with a layer of grit. It was parked between an old station wagon, low on its springs with kids climbing in and out of the back, and a blue Futura convertible in which a teenage girl in shorts and halter was rolling her hair in curlers, the rear-view mirror tilted so that she could see what she was doing. Daniel took the keys out of his pocket. He felt that it would be obvious to this girl in the convertible and these children in the station wagon that he was not the owner of the Volvo. Through the window he saw on the seat beside the driver's seat a plaid suitcase. And next to it, half hidden, the celluloid and cardboard wrapping for a pack of Gillette Super Stainless blades. This describes the picture the moment before Daniel got the picture. To be just, he had started something in the restaurant so as to get to Susan's car. He had needed to see the car. The feeling that crept upon me was of being summoned. They're still fucking us. That somehow it wasn't the old pain-burn across Susan's eyes that was important, or the brand-new wreckage of someone who has tried something devastating and has failed, no, nor that grieving for her or being in agony for her agony could matter, or believing that some of the force that propelled her razor was supplied by me—none of this mattered—or imagining, even, the scene in its details—locking the stall door, taking out a fresh Gillette Super Stainless blade, slicing veins, holding the opened veins over a toilet bowl in a public bathroom, fainting from loss of blood or courage or both, perhaps hearing a scream from a stout lady in a housedress, or a child, and, in a coma, perceiving the door as it opens, the lady in the blond beehive hairdo with the master key attached to a wooden handle holding up her fingers—V for Victory, or V for Peace? Or V for the victory over peace?—an error, I say, to dwell in any of this gore or pity, or to think how bad it is now, and how much worse it is than it was, and that it is definitely worse and getting worse, remembering moments when the Lewins were still solemnly charmed by the two fresh orphans to whom they had committed their lives, and the orphans charmed by peace. And how they would take us to Boston on the Beacon Street trolley and we'd ride on the swan boats and trudge through the Commons and see where Paul Revere was buried, and Sam Adams, feeling the flesh healing, the flesh of the soul healing in peace and irony—Oh, Freedom Trail! It was better then. Hope was not tested then— all of it a mistake for being beside the point, and unimportant because Susan had communicated with me; just that; and if now in our lives only extreme and dangerous communication was possible, nevertheless the signal had been sent, discharged even, from the spasm of soul that was required—and that was the sense of summons I felt sneaking up over the afternoon like a blanket of burned space around my ears. Susan and I, we were the only ones left. And all my life I have been trying to escape from my relatives and I have been intricate in my run, but one way or another they are what you come upon around the corner, and the Lord God who is so frantic for recognition says you have to ask how they are and would they like something cool to drink, and what is it you can do for them this time.

FIRE SALE! EVERYTHING MUST GO!

One picture poster, 36 × 24, used in demonstrations. Like new! Black and white double portrait depicts Isaacsons two faces   historical curiosity   cheap   very cheap worthless   comes in its own up-yours tube   corners slightly deteriorated   weighted with pieces of plaster   amuse your friends with this historical curio   free them. I remember his cock. Face it, if I do, I do. Always shaved without clothes. She, too, shameless by design. I remember the hair around her slit, sparse and uneven. One of the theories of aspiring modernity. Treat the body without shame. Let the kid see it, let him learn to be natural and uninhibited. They didn't go so far as to let me watch them fucking, but I did that too one way or another—I was a small criminal of perception; and that doesn't mean just to see them or hear them, which is the same as seeing, but knowing when they had and sometimes even when they were going to. But everything was theory. Everything was done for a reason, and was usually not the way the rest of the world did it. All the more reason. All part of the plan. The idea I had was of life as training. We were all training for something. There was some kind of moral, intellectual and physical award that would be available to those who worked for it, and were worthy of it. The State of Perfection Award. And I was not to be amazed that we were serious candidates, or that our pursuit of this perfection never brought us any closer. And I wasn't, I bought it all. Why shouldn't I? We were us.

Like those trips to the beach. My God. Late Sunday morning, Dr. Mindish would come by in his car; I remember it, a 1942 Chrysler New Yorker, high off the ground, with small windows, the upholstery torn. And we'd all pile in and go down the Concourse, across the Triborough Bridge, to the Grand Central Parkway, on toward Jones Beach (named for the common man), and the traffic would stack up, and maybe by three in the afternoon we'd get to the huge parking lot packed with baking cars and buses fourteen miles from any beach, and they'd all be sweating, and grumbling and arguing with each other and shushing each other, Dr. Mindish and his dumb wife and their cretin daughter, almost six feet tall, and Mom and Pop and me and the baby, Susan, all stuck in that stuffy car, sick with the fumes, and no, my father would say, this lot is too far away and we'd angle around, and sneak past the attendants, and bickering and sweating, complaining, and swearing never to do it again, my mother declaring my father a torturer, the Mindishes mad now because they wanted to park and walk the damn five hundred miles from the lot to the beach, with the sun baking the roof of that car and the baby spitting up like mushed bananas, and little carsick bastard Daniel complaining too (Mindish drove cruelly, starting and stopping, a jerk driver too), and then my father, leaping out of the car and guarding a parking space, miraculously found near the beach itself, with horns blowing and another driver threatening, he, Paul Isaacson, sweating and triumphant, guiding, like a cop, the big dented Chrysler into the space; and then a long enough walk to the beach through odd grass gardens for the common man: planted with tiger lilies and geraniums unbelievably ugly in the hot sun; to the beach so crowded that it seemed impossible to find room to put down a blanket. And following Paul, our safari of babies and towels and blankets, large paper bags with sandwiches, thermoses, the *Sunday Worker,* the week's *Workers,* the Sunday *Times,* bottles of baby food, through the sand that burned your feet; and then finally to Paul's mystical spot, the best spot inevitably and all the fussing and grunting and exchange of directions as the rented umbrella went up and the blankets went down, and the goods were arranged, and the shoes off, and the clothes, and finally, sweating, unbelievably, hours since the first good idea had occurred to go to the beach this Sunday, I stood at the shore of the ocean and looked out at the waves.

And my father said, "Some things are worth the effort."

So if they walked around nude or shopped for the best meat at the lowest price, or joined the Party, it was to know the truth, to be up on it; it was the refusal to be victim; and it would justify them—their poverty, their failure, their unhappiness, and the really third-rate families they came from. They rushed after self-esteem. If you could recognize a Humphrey Bogart movie for the cheap trash it was, you had culture. If you discovered the working class you found the roots of democracy. In social justice you discovered your own virtue. To desire social justice was a way of living without envy, which is the emotion of a loser. It was a way of transforming envy into constructive outgoing hate.

But they stuck to it, didn't they, Daniel? When the call came they answered. They offered up those genitals, didn't they, Dandan? Yes, they did. There were moments when I thought he would crack, I had my doubts about him. But I knew she would take it finally, to the last volt, in absolute selfishness, in unbelievably rigid fury. But with Paul you couldn't help feeling that the final connection was impossible for him to make between what he believed and how the world reacted. He couldn't quite make that violent connection. Rochelle was the realist. Her politics was the politics of want, the things she never got, the

chances she never had. If my mother had been anything but
poor, I don't think she would have been a Red. I can't say that
about him. He had that analytic cool; he claimed to believe in
the insignificance of personal experience within the pattern of
history. He even wrote that when he was in jail. The electric
chair as methodology of capitalist economics. But he didn't fool
me. He was scared. He was without real resources of character,
like most intellectuals. He was a brash, untested young man
who walked out of CCNY into the nineteen forties, and found no
one following him. No one followed my papa where he went.
He was a selfish man. Or maybe no, merely so physically rude
that he appeared selfish. Whatever he did had such personal
force that it seemed offensive. Like sticking his tongue out to
examine it in the mirror. Like shaving in front of me, talking all
the while, while my eyes followed his razor through the thin
spread of brushless cream. And when he was through, his jaw
was as blue as before. That was offensive. That was selfishness
of a profound sort. He didn't keep his razor clean. He left
blotches of gloppy shaving cream in the sink. He left the shower
faucet dripping. He left towels wadded up. You knew he'd been
there. He had a way of being conspicuous. Nothing he did was
obscure—how beautiful that is to contemplate. Even his breathing was noisy. Bending over those radios. You could hear the
concentration of the job in his release of breath, as if assuring
himself that he was working hard and that something considerable was at stake. I would stand at his worktable and listen to
him breathe, the twist of a screw or the soldering of a wire
allowing him to reward himself with another exhalation. It was
just the way he existed in the space he occupied. Right out to
the edges. He didn't dig me for a long time. He found it odd
that he was my father. Why would I think that if it wasn't so?
Smoking one of those cigars that didn't go with his face, he
studied his son like a psychologist through a pane of glass. He
didn't understand what I meant when I flirted with him like a
woman, as all little boys flirt with their fathers, or my angers,
or what I wanted when I pleased him. With his long legs
crossed at the knees and his large rude eyes magnified by his
glasses. Like Susan's eyes. And his skinniness, and the same
face I have with the big lips and big teeth, and round bulb

Russian nose. And the sleeves of his blue work shirt rolled up to the elbows—to just below the elbows. I remember his thin arms, with then jet-black hair, and the sinews moving under the skin. The hair grew right down over the backs of his hands to his knuckles. He was skinnier than I am. His hair was like wire.

But this describes just a moment's oversensitive perception by the little criminal of perception. He was warm and affectionate. What I remember is the lectures. He wanted me to grow up right. He wrestled society for my soul. He worked on me to counteract the bad influences of my culture. That was our relationship—his teaching me how to be a psychic alien. That was part of the training. He had to exorcize the influences, the bad spirits. Did I ever wonder why my radio programs had commercials? He'd find me reading the back of the cereal box at breakfast, and break the ad down and show what it appealed to, how it was intended to make me believe something that wasn't—that eating the cereal would make me an athlete. There were foods one didn't eat, like bananas, because they were the fruit of some notorious exploitation. There were companies whose products we boycotted because of their politics or labor history. Like National Biscuit Company cookies. He didn't like National Biscuit Company. He didn't like Standard Oil. He didn't like General Motors—not that we were ever in a position to buy a car. He didn't like General Motors because they were owned by Du Pont, and Du Pont had had cartel agreements with I. G. Farben of Nazi Germany.

My mother was impatient with all of this. She was a pragmatist. She probably thought he wasted too much of himself, and me, on what should be accepted as a matter of course. It was nonsense to distinguish one capitalist perfidy from another. She put them all down and that was the end of it. But my father dwelled because he couldn't help it in the abuses of justice and truth which offended his natural innocence. He couldn't get them out of his mind. He took a peculiar kind of bitter joy from them. He gave me pamphlets with titles like *Who Owns America* or *Rulers of the American Press*. When I could barely read. He told me things I could never find in my American History about Andrew Carnegie's Coal and Iron police, and Jay Gould's outrages, and John D. Rockefeller. He told me about using imported Chinese labor like cattle to build the West, and of breeding Negroes and working them to death in the South. Of their torture. Of John Brown and Nat Turner. Of Thomas Paine, whose atheism made him an embarrassment to the leaders of the American Revolution. I heard about the framing of Tom Mooney and the execution of Joe Hill, and all the maimed and dead labor heroes of the early labor movement. The incredibly brutal fate of anyone who tried to help the worker. He described to me the working conditions and wages of the steelworkers, and coal miners, in the days before the unions—how men would be crippled for life or buried alive because the owners were so busy draining every last penny from their work that they wouldn't even put the most primitive safety measures into effect. He told me about Henry Ford and Harry Bennett's goons and the sit-down strikes, and the Depression which came like a blight over capitalist America at the very same time Socialist Russia was feeding every one of her citizens and providing each of them a fair share of the country's wealth. He told me about Sacco and Vanzetti. About the Scottsboro boys. He ran up and down history like a pianist playing his scales. Reading to me the facts and figures of economic exploitation, of slavery in the eighteenth, nineteenth, and twentieth centuries. Putting together all the historic injustices and showing me the pattern and how everything that had happened was inevitable according to the Marxian analysis. Putting it all together. Everything was accounted for: even my comic books which he studied with me, teaching me to recognize and isolate the insidious stereotypes of yellow villains, Semitic villains, Russian villains. Even the function of public games like baseball. What its *real* purpose was. The economic class of baseball fans. Why they needed baseball. What would happen to the game if people had enough money, enough freedom. I listened because that was the price I paid for his attention. "And it's still going on, Danny," a famous remark. "In today's newspaper it's still going on. Right outside the door of this house it's going on. In this house." He said Williams, the janitor in the cellar, was a man destroyed by American Society because of his skin and never allowed to develop according to his inner worth. "The battle is not finished, the struggle of the working class is still going on. Never forget that, Danny." And it seemed to me then that I was marked. Because *they* had a lot more power than *we* had. And it seemed to be even in the clouds which blew up through the sky over the schoolyard, that power of theirs to destroy and put down and take vengeance on the ideas in my head, on the dangerous information put in my head by my reckless father.

But I was a smart-ass kid, I wasn't that innocent. I took what he gave to have him. On Sunday morning I went with him from door to door to sell subscriptions to the *Worker*. This was the Sunday Mobilization. It was arduous—he talked a lot to everyone, not just me. How much of it didn't I hear except for the sound of the voice itself? A quality difficult to remember now, except that it was nasal, sing-songy, a voice I associate with the expression on his face of complete self-absorption. Yes, that is how I remember him: talking, developing some dialectic with great relish, the words very liquid; he spoke with a wet mouth, as if, sometimes, his tongue lay in bubbles, that type of speaker who in his excitement sometimes sprays his listener; developing some idea, overdeveloping it tiresomely, I could tell by my mother's face, although I may have personally found it interesting. He was tendentious! Yes! A word he loved to apply to others. Tendentious. Also indiscriminate in his attention to ideas, problems, from the most mundane to the most serious, giving them equal time in his tireless broadcast, high or low, serious or stupid. It was Rochelle who worried about having enough to eat. *Was there one like him on the Black Tennis Court?* She wanted him to make more money. The family mythology was that in practical matters of the world, Paul Isaacson was a more or less irresponsible child. He couldn't be trusted. He couldn't be trusted to make a living, to find his glasses, to remember to come home for lunch, to take the garbage out, to wear his rubbers when it rained. There was between my mother and Aunt Frieda and Aunt Ruthie a maternal rivalry for his irresponsible heart. Frieda and Ruth, his older sisters and his only living relatives, felt that he was a genius; and that his genius had never been given a chance because he had married too early and been overcome by family responsibilities. Rochelle was bitter about that. She had to prove to them that she could take care of him better than they had. That the girl he met at City before the war, and married during the war, the girl who went down to live with him in Washington, D.C. *before* they were even married, was good for him and would help him fulfill himself. In this, though a Com- *Mm* munist, she was totally bourgeois, wasn't she. Tacitly I know she accepted their judgment of Paul as a failure; but who was to blame—that was the real issue. There was a degree in engineering that was never taken. Unlike Rochelle, Paul had never completed college. He'd gone off to war and come back a married man, a father, a provider—their Pauly! They never forgave her for Paul Isaacson's fate as a radio repairman or for his political views. They believed he would have outgrown his radicalism if not for her.

I cooperated in this myth of my irresponsible father. I enjoyed it. It pushed him into childhood with me. Sometimes I felt as if Rochelle was mother to us both. Sometimes I felt that in practical knowledge of what had to be done for the moment, I was his older brother. I imagined my father subject to Rochelle's discipline, to Williams' wrath as he threw the garbage pails around the cellar, to Grandma's curses. Just like me. There was truth in it and I'd laugh.

But when he was in the back of his store the natural order of things was recovered. My father was skinny, nervous, selfish, unreliable, full of hot radical passion; insolent in his faith, loyal to Marxism-Leninism, rude-eyed and tendentious. He scared me. But when he repaired radios, I was released. The pressure was off me and I was free in his concentration. I loved him in that lousy store. I always wanted to go there. On rainy days when I got on my mother's nerves, she sent me there. Or at lunchtime when he hadn't come home, she'd give me his sandwich in a bag and his coffee in a thermos and send me to the store before I went back to school. Or sometimes I'd have to go bring him home for dinner. I went along the school fence to 174th Street, then down 174th Street still along the school fence, to Eastburn Avenue; across Eastburn; and another block past the shoemaker, the dairy, Irving's Fish Market, Spotless Cleaner, to Morris Avenue; across Morris; and in the middle of that block right between the candy store I didn't like, and Berger's Barber Shop, was Isaacson Radio, Sales and Repair.

In the window an advertising cutout faded from the sun: a modern housewife, smartly turned out in a dress that reaches almost to her ankles. She has her hand on the knob of a radio and does not look at it but out at you, as she turns it on. She is smiling and wears a hairdo of the time. She is not bad looking, with nice straight teeth, and she obviously has a pair though not trying to jam them in your face. She is in green, faded green. Her dress, her face, her smile, all green. Her radio is orange. The table it is on is orange. She is a slim, green woman for whom the act of turning on an orange radio is enormous pleasure. Maybe it was a defective radio and gave her a jolt. Maybe she was turning it off. I never thought of that. On the bed of the window, resting on old curled crepe paper, bleached grey, are two display radios—a table model and a console with cloth-covered doors and a combination automatic record changer. When you go inside you see that the two window display radios have nothing inside them. They are empty cabinets. Not many people buy radios here. Mostly they have their old ones fixed. There is no irony in Paul Isaacson's owning his own business, because he makes no profit. He employs no one and, therefore, exploits no one. Isaacson Radio, Sales and Repair, is not a good business. There were lots of poor or lower middle class people in that neighborhood. They all knew someone who could sell cheaper. And they did not support big repair bills. He was honest and he never overcharged. Rochelle, who kept the books at home, was supposed to figure out how to pay the rent each month.

Most of the store was used for the shop behind the counter. Behind the counter were boxed display shelves of unpainted plywood. There was an opening with an old living room drape of Rochelle's hung from a rod. Then you were in the shop. Here were the racks of tubes with their numbers. And on the worktable the dusty radios, each with its tag. A patterned ceiling that drooped in the middle. I loved it there. It was a place to feel safe. It was all enclosed. And if he was busy, he didn't talk. And I'd be engrossed with the mystery of the problem, the tracking down of the trouble inside the guts of a machine.

It would hum, or beep, or sputter, or wouldn't light, or make no sound at all. And he'd fix it. With his elaborate breathing he'd fix it. Sometimes he'd let me vacuum out the insides, clear the dust of years out of a chassis with a small powerful vacuum that was like a flashlight. And completely occupied with the problem he wouldn't talk. History had no pattern in those moments. I didn't have to worry. Imperialism, the last phase of capitalism, did not exist. There were tubes and condensers, and speakers and soldering irons and wires—a technology that was neutral and had no ideological significance. No, that's wrong. He merely relented in noting it. When he was busy, I could secretly feel about him as other boys felt all the time about their fathers. And I didn't have to worry about the Forces set against us in our struggle.

But sometimes he would listen to the radio while he worked on it. And he liked to listen to the commentators—it didn't matter which one. They talked for fifteen minutes at a time. John W. Vandercook, Raymond Gram Swing, H. V. Kaltenborn, Johannes Steel, Frank Kingdon, Quincy Howe, Gabriel Heatter, Fulton Lewis, Jr. They were carry-overs from the Second World War when people really wanted to know what was going on. They were an industry. My father listened as he worked. He shook his head. He poked his soldering iron into the heart of the radio as if trying to repair the voice, trying to fix the errors of analysis and interpretation. He stabbed it in the tubes, like a primitive again, as if the machine was talking, as if trying to re-program the lie box. I remember Radio Town Meeting of the Air. He used to turn that on at home. It would make him furious. The question to be debated was always loaded. The strong speaker was always a right-winger. The town crier would ring the bell and announce the program and he'd sit and listen until he couldn't bear it any longer. It was the ritual of eating your heart out. That was my mother's phrase for these things: "What are you eating your heart out for? Pauly. You know who owns the stations. You know it's all rigged. Why must you eat your heart out?" Her contribution to his self-esteem was in warning him that his sensitivity could ruin his health. Who owns the airwaves? Who owns the American Press? Who rules America? Like Du Pont dealing with I. G. Farben. Evidence, there was never enough evidence. He swam in it. That was it—physical training, it was the way he stayed in shape. That has to be it. You ate your heart out to keep the revolutionary tension. But Rochelle didn't have to do that. She didn't have to go through the primer again and again. She knew the lesson. She was truer to the idea. In her way she was the more committed radical. Because, look, the implication of all the things he used to flagellate himself was that American democracy wasn't democratic enough. He continued to be astonished, insulted, outraged, that it wasn't purer, freer, finer, more ideal. Finding proof of it over and over again—the struggle is still going on, Pop!—like a guy looking for confirmation. How much confirmation did he need? Why did he expect so much of a system he knew by definition could never satisfy his standards of justice? A system he was committed to opposing because he had a better one in mind. It's screwy. Lots of them were like that. They were Stalinists and every instance of Capitalist America fucking up drove them wild. My country! Why aren't you what you claim to be? If they were put on trial, they didn't say *Of course, what else could we expect*, they said *You are making a mockery of American justice!* And it was more than strategy, it was more than Lenin's advice to use the reactionary apparatus to defend yourself, it was passion.

My father never really believed it would happen. My mother wasn't to be surprised from the day they were indicted. But he never believed it was possible. He believed in the beneficence of his ideas, and could not appreciate that anyone would find them offensive enough, threatening enough to do—that. His ideas were an extension of himself, and he meant only well. Because the other side of finding confirmation over and over again, of dwelling in evidence, was that he would never believe any of it. He would never believe that America was not the cafeteria at City College; and as often as it was proved to him he forgot it.

Pauly. Sometimes he used to cut my mother's hair. I don't remember her ever cutting his. She would put a towel around her shoulders and spread newspaper on the floor in the kitchen and sit on a kitchen chair in the middle of the floor, and he would go to work; holding a scissors and a comb in his long hands, he would comb through her hair, get a short bunch of it off the comb and between his fingers, and with the comb like a harmonica in his mouth, pick up the scissors and slice off the hair. He was very deft. She had thick hair that tended to curl and she liked to keep it short. I wouldn't say she enjoyed saving money, I would say it gave her satisfaction. I would say it was a righteous pleasure. She wore plain clothes that were bought to last. All our clothes were bought to last. She always bought things that were too big. "She wanted us to get use out of them," I once explained to Susan when we were talking about this. "She wanted us to grow into them." But Susan said: "She bought Daddy's things too big, and her own things too. She dressed us all like bags. Why must you always think she was perfect? Why can't you admit she just didn't know how to buy clothes?"

I think she was a sexy woman, despite her austerity, her home-cut hair, her baggy clothes, her no make-up except for very red lipstick on her small, prim mouth in the full cheeks. Her grim appreciation of life. She was full-breasted and heavy-hocked and wore corsets, which I would see her pull on or off while she said something like "Danny, go turn the light out under the coffee." She was exacting about cleanliness and kept us all cleaner than we thought was necessary. When she was working, before Susan was born, she would clean the house late at night and on weekends. That miserable little house. In my bed, when she came to fix the covers, I smelled her after her bath—she smelled of the steam of cleanliness, of powdered redness. She made curtains and tacked down linoleum and found bargains at the Salvation Army, and hammered and tacked and waxed and polished and scrubbed. She washed our clothes on a washboard in the deep half of the kitchen sink. She had enormous energy. The whole thing with Rochelle was defending herself against the vicious double-crossing trick that life was. Income was defense. A clean house. A developed political mind. Children. Her weaknesses were not as obvious to me as Paul's. If someone claims to deal with life so as to survive, you grant him soundness of character. But she was as unstable as he was. In her grim expectations. In her refusal to have illusions. In her cold, dogmatic rage. As if there was some profound missed thing in her life which she could never forget.

Some betrayal of promise. It wasn't sex. It couldn't have been
sex. They used to make the whole house rock. They really went
at it, they balled all the time.

In prison, she began to write.

Her politics was not theoretical or abstract. She had no
difficulty making connections. Her politics was like Grandma's
religion—some purchase on the future against the terrible life
of the present. Grandma lit candles on Friday night, with a
shawl over her head and her hands covering her face while she
said her prayer. When she lowered her hands, her eyes, her
blue eyes, were filled with tears, and devastation was in her
face. That was my mother's communism. It was something
whose promise was so strong that you endured much for it.
Like a woman suffering pregnancy and childbirth to get the
child. The child would make it worthwhile. The coming of
socialism would sanctify those who had suffered. You went out
and took your stand, and did what had to be done, not because you expected anything from it, but because someday
there would be retribution and you wanted just a little of it to
bear your name. If she had been religious like her Mama, she
would have conceived this as a memorial plaque on the back of
one of the pews in the Synagogue. But she was enlightened, in-
dependent, a college graduate, a girl who read and understood,
who had joined the radical set at school, had scandalized her
mother, had gone to live with her boyfriend when he was
drafted and stationed in another city. She was a modern
woman.

"Rochelle!" I hear my grandma's taunt. "Imagine Rochelle!"
And then in Yiddish: "Rachel is not good enough for her."

But this isn't the couple in the poster. That couple got away.
Well funded, and supplied with false passports, they went either
to New Zealand or Australia. Or Heaven. In any event, my
mother and father, standing in for them, went to their deaths
for crimes they did not commit. Or maybe they did commit
them. Or maybe my mother and father got away with false
passports for crimes they didn't committ. How do you spell
comit? Of one thing we are sure. Everything is elusive. God
is elusive. Revolutionary morality is elusive. Justice is elusive.
Human character. Quarters for the cigarette machine. You've

got these two people in the poster, Daniel, now how you going to get them out? And you've got a grandma you mention once or twice, but we don't know anything about her. And some colored man in the basement—what is that all about? What has that got to do with anything?

PEEKSKILL

It is Sunday, a warm Sunday morning in September. Everyone is up early. The phone is ringing. I am admonishhed to hurry up and wash and get dressed. I have to feed stupid Susan while the grownups get dressed. We are into that efficient co-operative use of time, by which it is saved, like money. I hate it when something like this is going on. My mother directs us all like a military commander. Susan takes the bowl of the spoon into her fat cheeks and clutches the shaft of it in her fat hand. She won't let go. The phone rings again. I am directed to answer the phone. It is someone wanting to know the schedule. Everyone is meeting at our house. At nine-thirty they begin to arrive. The first, of course, is Dr. Mindish, and his wife and giant daughter. I hate Mindish. He seems to me an insincere man. I never believe anything he says. He is my father's closest friend and the whole family's dentist. He's a tall man, balding, with a fat nose and a perpetually unshaved face. His eyes are small and colorless. He speaks with a foreign intonation. His daughter looks just like him, is as tall, has as big a nose, but with long hair hanging down each side of her face. His wife seems like an intruder in their family. "Well," Mindish says when I answer the door, "they've got a new butler." He's really funny. As Linda Mindish, the daughter, walks by me, she pokes me in the ribs. Despising myself I smile at Mindish's lousy wit and flinch from Linda's hand. She is twelve or thirteen, and very strong.

A while later, the rest of them begin to troop in. Nate Silverstein, and his wife who teaches school downtown. Silverstein is a furrier, a florid man with a hoarse voice. And then Henry Bergman who is a professional musician, primarily a fiddler, although good enough on the French horn to play one season with Toscanini's NBC Symphony. My favorite of my parents' friends, Ben Cohen, a thin, gentle man with a mustache and an aromatic pipe. If my father died, I would want my mother to marry Ben Cohen. He always speaks softly when he speaks, which is not often. He never patronizes me. He is quiet and contemplative, and I like what he does too: he works for the City in the subway system, in a change booth. This seems to me a really fine job. You're underground in a stronghold that has barred windows, and a heavy steel door that locks from the inside. It's a very safe, secure place to be. You can eat your lunch in there, and read when the work is slow. All you have to do is make change, which is easy. If a bomb drops, you probably won't even feel it. If there's a storm, you don't get wet. The only thing wrong about this job is that Ben Cohen never stays in one place. He's always switching around. If I had the job, I'd want to have the booth in our station, 174th Street. Then I'd be close to home.

And then the Kantrowitz sisters who work for Welfare, the light one, and the dark one, both unmarried. And then other people besides the regulars—people I don't know too well, people at the edges of my parents' close friendships. There are about two dozen in all and a few of them have kids, and one couple has an infant in arms. They have all brought their lunch in brown paper bags.

The house is heavy with people, and they are all talking. Every once in a while Grandma comes out of her room and curses loudly from the top of the stairs. They all seem to know she is crazy and try to pay no attention. Rochelle is making our lunch in the kitchen, egg salad sandwiches. The eggs smell warm and visceral. Mindish is there, looking in the refrigerator, his own idea and one that annoys my mother as I can tell from the expression on her face. I have never liked the way Mindish looks at my mother.

My father is calling up the bus company to make sure they have dispatched the bus as they said they would. It is to arrive in front of our house. Our house is the meeting point, a fact which makes me proud. I go out on the porch to see if it is coming. One of the kids follows me. I ham it up for him, holding onto the porch rails as I lean out and peer down to the corner. "I'm going," he says. "Are you?"

I hadn't thought there was any question about it. My Aunt Frieda has been enlisted to sit with Susan. Across the street, in the sunken schoolyard, the big guys are playing baseball. Home plate is a block away at the other end of the yard—in the corner at Eastburn Avenue. Sometimes, very rarely, a ball hits the Weeks Avenue fence. Even more rarely it comes over and lands in the street in front of my house. Now a ball is rising over the schoolyard over the roof lines of the buildings into the sky, a figure is running around the bases; the ball clears the fence and clunks into the street, and bounces up on the sidewalk in front of the porch. A softball, miraculously whole and in shape after having traveled that fantastic distance.

I grab it and run halfway across the street. In the school-yard they are all frozen still, and facing backwards looking at me, as if the National Anthem was being played. I heave the ball back over the fence. It drops out of sight. There is silence for a moment; and then I see the ball streaking back to the in-field, propelled by the hidden left fielder who caught my toss. I feel a thrill, an electric connection to that ball, also a sharp sense of having let the mightly athletes know that I am alive.

In the meantime a yellow school bus has turned into the block. The driver is hunched over the wheel, peering at house numbers. There are people already in the bus. It passes our house, screeches to a stop, backs up.

I want to announce the bus's arrival, but by the time I get to our door it is open and people are coming outside. I find my mother in the kitchen and ask her if I'm going. I ask for con-firmation. I expect her to say of course, and my heart sinks when she prims her mouth and says, "Your father's in charge."

"Please, Rochelle," he says, "don't start that." Whenever my mother says my father is in charge he gets very upset. He is packing the egg salad sandwiches in their wax paper into a khaki rucksack. He likes to carry things camping-style to keep his hands free to read a newspaper or a book. He settles his glasses with the back of his hand. "Don't you want your child to hear one of the great voices of our time? Don't you want your son to have that to remember? I don't see that it's such a terrible thing to inflict on a child—that he sees Robeson, a great people's artist."

"Pauly, I told you my feelings. You do what you want."

"There's a problem?" Mindish says, nibbling a piece of cheese.

"There's no problem," my mother says. She puts the mayonnaise in the icebox, wipes the table, walks out of the room.

"Am I going?" I ask my father.

"Yes, yes," he says irritably. Nothing is really official without my mother's endorsement. It makes us both uneasy to have something decided without her approval. My father follows her upstairs. "Get ready," he calls to me, one of those vague orders demonstrating his lack of authority. Its real meaning is that I shouldn't follow him upstairs.

I wait in the hall. And though the front door is open and people are spilling out of the door onto the porch, and friends like Mindish are milling about, and everyone is talking and anticipating the trip, I hear enough of what's being said upstairs to understand the issue. It's a small house.

"There is nothing to be afraid of, Rochelle! If I thought there was the slightest chance of violence, do you think I would allow you to go, let alone the kid? Be sensible."

"Don't speak to me of being sensible," my mother says. "He's seven years old."

"Well, let's just go," Paul says. "Mindish is taking his daughter. There's a dozen kids downstairs. There's a court order protecting the thing, for God's sake."

"Court orders," Rochelle says bitterly.

There is silence for a moment. "And you call yourself a progressive," my father says, a change in tack. He commences a speech about the forces of reaction and what they thrive on. My mother says wearily, "Oh, Pauly, you're such a fool sometimes."

People are calling from the front door. "Let's go! Come on, let's go!"

I am really more interested in this conflict of wills than in whether or not I go to the concert. The truth is the prospect bored me; now that some mystery is attached to it, I'm more inclined to put up a fuss if I can't go.

Somewhere in the silences of their conversation upstairs, my mother relents. "Danny," she says, coming down the stairs. "Go get your thin blue jacket. And tie your shoelaces, and pull up your socks. And go to the bathroom even if you don't have to." She is frowning, looking grim. She has reddened her mouth with lipstick. My father descends behind her, lighting a cigar.

A week before Paul Robeson was supposed to have sung at the Lakeland Picnic Grounds in Peekskill, New York. A local mob blocked the approaches, burned up the camp chairs, attacked the audience that was there, and the concert never came off. After a week of protest meetings, and a court order, Robeson was going to try again to sing in Peekskill. Robeson was a Communist, a proud black Communist. Thousands of people were going to sit in the open air, in the country, and testify by their presence Robeson's right to sing and their right to listen. Governor Dewey had called out the State Troopers to guard the grounds. In this age of witch hunts, when men were being sent to jail for their political beliefs (like Foster, like Gene Dennis), it was going to be a triumphant affirmation of the right of free assembly, it was going to be a great moment for the forces of progressivism and civilization.

I learn all this on the bus. My father tells me. He is exhilarated, happy. Everyone sings Robeson's songs in anticipation of hearing him. It is very nice. I'm glad my mother let me come. The bus roars along through the Bronx, heading north across Van Cortlandt Park to the Saw Mill River Parkway, and everyone is singing *Peat Bog Soldiers*. We are the Peat Bog soldiers, marching with our spades to the bog. Only my mother doesn't sing. I sit on her lap at the window. Next to me my father sings. The whole bus sings. The bus seems to surge along in rhythm. The window of the bus is streaked with dried rain.

It is a long ride. My eyes grow heavy with the backward-moving scenery. Before we get to Peekskill, the singing has stopped. The people in the bus are quiet. In Peekskill, I see men standing on the road shouting and waving their fists. There is a line of police holding them back. "Go home kikes!" someone yells at our bus. I hear the sound of military music. I did not know there was a band at the Robeson Concert. But my father, standing up to peer back through the rear window of the bus, says it is an American Legion Band. They are parading to protest the concert.

It is hot and unpleasant in the concert grounds, and a long time goes by without any concert. I have long since finished my egg salad sandwich and I'm hungry again. The crowd is immense. I sit between my parents. They are surrounded by their friends. Around the friends sit thousands of people. If something bad was going to happen, it would have happened already, everyone reasons. I can't imagine what harm could come to us here in this friendly crowd. They are like an army. Our own people are cool. They are relaxed. They kid around. My father reads something aloud from a book, something funny, and everyone laughs and comments on it. My mother is smiling. She sits cross-legged on the grass, with her long, pleated skirt billowed over her legs so you can't see them. She holds me against her side. My father waves his cigar as he talks. He talks constantly. Every once in a while he settles his eyeglasses firmly on the bridge of his nose. Ben Cohen, lying on his side on the grass, holds his pipe and listens to him. Dr. Mindish listens. Nate Silverstein, the furrier, listens. It is clear they all have respect for him. No, not so much respect as fondness. Fondness for him and respect for his energy. He seems tireless, full of electricity, restless, constantly speaking his thoughts and postulating his ideas.

Finally, a long distance off, there is a shout, a cheer, and then a massive roar as Robeson appears. I can't make him out too well. His voice comes to me larger than his small figure in the distance, but it is a deep voice, an incredibly deep resounding voice, and it reminds me of Williams who lives in our cellar. They are both black. I wonder why Williams did not come with us. Robeson sings spirituals. He sings *Old Man River*. He sings *Peat Bog Soldiers*. He sings I dreamed I saw Joe Hill last night, alive as you and me. He is accompanied by a pianist. I wonder if he lives in the cellar of his house.

We are all cheering wildly when the concert is over. Everyone talks busily as we walk to the bus. It has turned into a happy day. There have been ennobling sentiments. But in the parking lot my mother grasps my hand and I find that we are hurrying.

The bus moves off in a line of buses and cars. Peekskill policemen direct the traffic. "This is not the way we came," Mindish says, leaning forward from his seat behind my father's. My father rises wonderingly, in a sitting position. We are going uphill on a winding, narrow road through some woods. The buses are in low gear, the gear of pain, the sound that makes an engine human. I notice something odd—three or four grown men running along the edge of the woods. They run faster than the bus. I lean forward to see where they are running, and see more men coming out of the woods. They are throwing things toward the road. "Look out," my father screams. At this moment the bus jerks to a stop, stalling in gear. The driver throws up his arms. There is the sound of shattering glass. A cry goes through the bus, the involuntary leaping out from throats of perception. My father sits back down, holding the railing of the seat in front of him. We all sit dumbfounded as if it was a show that had nothing to do with us. The driver's face is decorated in blood. From the front to the back of the bus, people are ducking, like dominoes going down in a row, a beautiful pattern of shatter appears on the window alongside my mother's head, and in the moment before I feel my head being forced down to the seat, I see a man with a boulder, heaving it into the rear window of the bus in front of us.

People are shouting to get the bus moving. But the driver is out of his seat, and even if he weren't, there is no place to go. There are buses in front, and buses behind. The thunking of rocks on the sides and roof of the bus punctures the ears. Glass breaks like music. People cry out. "What is this," demands my father's voice, above me. "What is this!"

Flying in with the rocks, like notes tied to them with string, the words kike, commie bastard, jew commie, red. I listen carefully. Jew. Commie. Red. Nigger. Bastard. Kike. Nigger-lover. Red. Jew bastard. These words are shouted. The rocks, some of them as big as my head, are propelled by the motives of education. "We'll teach you!" the enraged voices cry. "This will teach you, you commie bastard kikes!"

My mother and I are squeezed down between our seat and the back of the seat in front. We are kneeling. Every rattle, every crash operates like a simple machine for the tightening of her hold upon me. I imagine some kind of system of pulleys activated by shouts, pounding rocks, shattering glass. Inch by inch I am buried more firmly under her, until my head rests on her folded leg, and her breasts and arms cover the curve of my back, and her hands hold me by the bones of my ass. I feel through the cloth of her skirt her thigh muscle twitching under my mouth and chin, quivering in what—fear? rage? exertion? —and she is laying her head on my back and muttering into my backbone. Murderers. Dogs. Scum. It is the muttering epithet of my grandma, but in English. Fascist scum. Nazi pigs. Murderers.

I am in an intoxication of fear. The thought of my grandma has suggested a new meaning of her famous curses—not as the rantings of an old madwoman, but the exact and potent introjection of measures of doom into our lives. The bus is rocking. We are all going to die. My heart beats furiously but I am aware of the material of my mother's skirt—a rough, wool cloth, which will leave a rashlike sensitivity on my cheek.

I hear Mindish yelling at my father to get down. "Pauly!" my mother cries over my back. "What are you doing! Paul!"

My father, crouching in the aisle, has seen something through the window. He steps over people and around them, making his way tortuously to the front of the bus. "Officer!" he shouts. "Officer!"

My spindly father, spinning his way to the front. To the war. This mustn't be permitted. "This mustn't be permitted," he calls back in explanation. Then he is at the door commanding the driver to open it. The bus is rocking. He holds the overhead bar, insisting that the driver open the door of the bus. But the others yell to keep the door shut. "We can't permit this," he turns around to say. "We cannot permit this outrage."

Mindish has followed him forward. The big dentist is smiling. "Get down, Paul. What are you doing! Get back here!" My father has sighted the policeman again, and is trying to pry open the double door with his hands. He shouts through the opening in the rubber guards of the door, shouts through the opening he makes with his hands. "Officer! Why do you permit this!" He struggles to fold back the doors, straining like Samson between the pillars, with his thin arms. He has attracted the attention of the commandos outside, and they are trying to help him open the door. We are at a moment of great insanity. My father's entire left arm disappears through the doors. He leans at a crazy tilt. He is like one of my knotted shoelaces pulled up tight to its knot. How do I know this? If I was crouched behind a seat, how do I remember this? Calmly, with his right hand, my father removes his glasses, folds them against his chest and hands them up to Mindish. The deliberateness of this act terrifies me. I see something I don't recognize, something I never knew with my child's confidence in my perception of my parents. I am stunned. Now the bus stops rocking. The patriots have zeroed in on their target. They are all up at the front, outside the door. We stare in silence as my father silently experiences the breaking of his arm. Sweat pops up on his forehead. His face contorts. "Open the door!" my mother screams. "Open the door before they break him in half!" When the door opens with a hiss, my father flies from our view. A roar goes up. Two men who have been holding him in the insane tug of war tumble out after him. It is a comic sight to see them all go flying out the door, connected like sausages. I cannot see what is happening outside. There are frightening sounds. "Stop them!" my mother cries, pushing into the aisle. I am slammed against the seat. People are surging out to do battle, or to run, I can't tell which. Above the heads, at the front of the bus, I see Mindish holding aloft my father's folded glasses. He is a tall man and has this weird, embarrassed expression on his face, a smile for the ridiculous idea of being at someone's mercy.

I don't remember how we got home. There were police sirens, there was groaning and crying on this road through the woods. There was an ambulance. But I remember my father lying on the old couch in the living room. His arm was in splints, the whole top of his head was wrapped in a bandage, like an odd hat. There were scratches on his face. But he looked at me through glasses that were unbroken. He tried to smile through his cracked, swollen mouth. He couldn't talk. I stared at him and I was frightened. There were tears in his eyes. My mother sat on the floor beside him, looking at the floor, and she held his hand. Their heads were close. They looked so desolate that I began to cry. I had not cried at all before this, but I cried now, and my mother pulled me over to her and sat me on her lap, and held me against her breast, and held my father's hand and kissed it.

So there were limits to his failure. There were times when this passionately unreliable, naïve childish being found the world perfectly disposed. My mother was right about the Robeson Concert, but my father was headstrong. I began to appreciate the mystery in the dark intercourse of adults. The phone kept ringing—that night, the next day. Everyone said that if Pauly had not done what he had done, the bus would have been turned over and God knows how many crushed to death. It was true that in that whole bus, he was the only man who did anything. Nobody else could move. I thought about it a lot. That was something to be proud of, that he got up to do something. But *what* he did was mysterious and complicated and not anything like what people were saying. I thought about it for a long time. I decided he was trying to get the attention of the cop because he really thought the cop would help. The Law would arrest the Fascist hoodlums. That is what put him at the door and made him vulnerable.

Long after everyone stopped talking about it, I tried to work out this mystery in my mind. Rochelle was nervous because he wasn't going to work. It was disturbing to have him around the house all day. No money was coming in. He complained of headaches. The doctor bills were criminally high. My father didn't go back to the store until the cast on his arm was dirty. But I could not forget the calm ferocity of his decision, folding his glasses against his chest and handing them to Mindish. I could not forget the commitment in his absurdly naked eyes; or in his act, the quality of calmly experienced, planned revolutionary sacrifice—

Bukharin provided the most interesting defense of the Purge Trial of 1938. He pleaded guilty and went out of his way on several occasions to affirm his responsibility for the sum total of crimes committed by the defendant block of "rightists and Trotskyites," of which he was considered a leader. He vehemently agreed that he was guilty of conspiracy, treason, and counterrevolution. And having agreed, he took exception during the trial to every specific charge brought against him. Under duress to testify on cue, he nevertheless contrived to indicate with the peculiar kind of overtone characteristic of Soviet voices under Stalin, that he and Russia as well were being victimized. And what good did it do him except that he became a hero in a novel and an image of sorrowful nobility to Sovietologists. We may say of Stalin, in turn, that the show trials of 1936 to 1938 as well as the thousands of less structured exterminations carried out under his aegis reflected his determination to make an ally out of Hitler. Kennan says Stalin had to make sure there would be no opposition to fault him in his unpopular move known to the world as the Non-Aggression Treaty of 1939. Bukharin and many of the other defendants were anti-Fascists. Whatever Stalin's reasons for wanting to make an ally of Hitler—whether in despair of promoting Russian interests with the Western countries, or out of a keen impulse toward a Fascist-Soviet hegemony, or because he needed time to prepare his country for war with Hitler which he knew was imminent (but if this was so, why did he kill his ranking army officers?), it can be said that this, like every major 1930's policy move of Soviet Russia the Great Socialist Experiment, was predicated on the primacy of the nation-state, the postponement of Marxist dreams, and the expendability of the individual. E. H. Carr suggests that the genius of Stalin was in his recovery of Russian nationalism, dormant under the westernized, internationalist Lenin. "Socialism in one country" was Stalin's affirmation of his country's fierce, inferiority-hounded pride in the face of the historic, tragic, western hostility to backwoods Russia.

"International Marxism and international socialism, planted in Russian soil and left to themselves, found their international character exposed to the constant sapping and mining of the Russian national tradition which they had supposedly vanquished in 1917. Ten years later, when Lenin was dead, the leaders who had most conspicuously represented the international and western elements in Bolshevism—Trotsky, Zinoviev, and Kamenev, not to mention minor figures like Radek, Krasin, and Rakovsky—had all disappeared; the mild and pliable Bukharin was soon to follow. The hidden forces of the Russian past —autocracy, bureaucracy, political and cultural conformity— took their revenge not by destroying the revolution, but by harnessing it to themselves in order to fulfill it in a narrow national framework. . . ."

This insight of Carr's is useful in understanding such moments of agony to world-wide socialism as the Soviet refusal to support the Communist-left coalition in Germany that might have prevented Hitler's rise to power; the Soviet betrayal of the Republican cause in Spain (many of the purge victims were veterans of the Spanish campaign); the cynical use of the popular front and collective security as elements in Soviet diplomacy; and the non-aggression pact. Thus, to those critics who see in Stalin the "Genghis Khan" he was called by Bukharin, or the extreme paranoid he is sorrowfully admitted to have been by today's Soviet leadership, we must say: no revolution is betrayed, only fulfilled.

Thermidor.

Daniel Thermidor found considerable play in the Volvo's steering

and what about Kronstadt—we mustn't forget KRONSTADT! And Gorky, too, with his untimely thoughts.

A NOTE TO THE READER

Reader, this is a note to you. If it seems to you elementary, if it seems after all this time elementary . . . If it *is* elementary and seems to you at this late date to be pathetically elementary, like picking up some torn bits of cloth and tearing them again . . . If it is that elementary, then reader, I am reading you. And together we may rend our clothes in mourning.

On Memorial Day in 1967, Daniel Lewin drove his new black Volvo onto the Massachusetts Turnpike and headed east, toward Boston. Sitting beside him was his wife, Phyllis, a throbbingly sad blond flower-child with light blue, Polish eyes that turned grey on days of rain. And behind them, wedged not too comfortably between a large suitcase and some other junk, was their baby son, Paul.

Daniel had never driven this car before, and he passed the first few miles working with the four-speed stick shift and feeling his way with his spine into the springs and with his arms into the steering.

There was a wobble in the wheels, a small thrump-thrump at sixty-five. There was considerable play in the steering. Also a slight pull to the left when he touched the brakes. There were certain loosenesses in the car. It was a less than well-tuned, well-maintained car. It had a leathery smell. Daniel imagined its career in Boston and Cambridge, the collegiate recklessness. His sister Susan had bought it cheap from a guy dropping out of Harvard. And whom had he bought it from? A reckless car. A car in character reckless.

"It's raining," Phyllis said. So it was. Shattered raindrops appeared on the windshield. Daniel's eyes focused on the surface of the windshield, trying to anticipate the small explosions of rain. This was too difficult, so he fixed on one drop and followed its career. The idea was that his attention made it different from the other drops. It arrived, head busted, with one water bead as a nucleus and six or seven clusters in a circle around it. It was like a melted snowflake. Each of the mini-drop clusters combined and became elongated and pulled away in the direction of its own weight. As he accelerated the car, so did they increase their rate of going away from the center.

"Shouldn't you put on the wipers?" Phyllis said.

The sky was darkening rapidly. Headlights of oncoming traffic multiplied in the drops of water on the windshield. The tires hissed on the wet road.

Daniel groped for the wiper switch. The car veered for a moment, and a horn blew behind them. Then the wipers were thumping away. But Daniel had noticed in the moment of the car's veering that Phyllis clutched the armrest of the door with her right hand and extended her left back over the seat to protect the baby.

She glanced at him to see if he had seen.

"I like the rain," Daniel said.

"I love rain," Phyllis said. "I especially love warm rain in the summer when there's no lightning or thunder."

"No, I mean now, in this car," Daniel said. "The rain has the effect of a cocoon, it encapsulates us."

"Yes," she said looking ahead. She was unbraiding her hair. Her eyes were fixed on his father's Chevrolet directly ahead of them with the silhouettes of three heads in the front seat.

"Oh, Daniel, I wish I could hold Susan and hug her and kiss her and be her friend."

He nodded.

"Maybe when she's better she should come and live with us for a while. We would really love her and make her happy. The baby would love her. Do you think she would?"

"I don't know."

"Maybe she was coming to see us. Do you think she was coming to New York?"

"Yes."

"Do you think she was coming to visit us?"

"No."

"She's so beautiful," Phyllis said, and she sighed.

I met my wife at a Central Park Be-In. In the Sheep Meadow. She was there with two other girls from her neighborhood who weren't cool. They gaped at the genuine hippies. They broke down and giggled like Brooklyn high school girls. She was embarrassed by them. She was very lovely. Someone had solemnly offered her a daffodil and solemnly she had accepted it. Solemnly with a spiritual smile, she walked with her flower, taking those too large, slightly awkward strides of hers. She was avid for spiritual experience. I took her home to 115th Street and put on some Bartók. She was amazed by the numbers of books. I suggested to her that fucking was a philosophical act of considerable importance. I knew that in deference to this possibility she would allow herself to be fucked.

Phyllis's parents are young and recently into money. Not wealthy, well-off. Her father sells carpet at a discount. He is a partner with another man, a World War II buddy of his, and they have one store in Brooklyn and one in Queens. He is one of the Young Turks in the Brooklyn Reform Jewish Center. He takes Phyllis's mother to Florida for two weeks every winter. In the afternoon they play golf and in the evening they go to one of the night clubs and listen to a comedian. In their apartment in a new high-rise in Brooklyn are porcelain lamps of nymphs. Over the stuffed, buttoned sofa in the living room is an original imitation Hudson River School painting in an elaborate gilt frame and with its own spotlight.

There is a younger child, a boy, twelve, Scott. He despises and hates and fears me only a little less than the mother and father do. They are appalled at Phyllis's marriage, and we see them less and less frequently. They send gifts for the baby. When we were still talking, the father tried to bring himself to ask me about the bruises his wife saw on his daughter's upper legs; he mumbled and cleared his throat, but I pretended not to understand, and he gave it up. I think they call her during the day.

This is no day to be in the library. It is too beautiful and warm and you can hear a bird or two. I will go back and take them to the park and we'll see if there are any boats on the river—

A few minutes later Phyllis unbuckled her seat belt and turned around to see to the baby, who was stirring fretfully. "I have only one diaper left," she said. Clumsily she got to her knees and leaned over the back of the seat to change Paul. Her ass wiggled as she moved her arms. Her long hair hung down. The rain was coming down, rattling the roof and streaming over the windshield. Daniel checked his rear-view mirror and swung into the left lane. A moment later with Phyllis still occupied, he passed his father's car, then another, then another.

"There," Phyllis said. "You take a nap now. And soon we'll be at your grandma and grandpa's house. All right now, close your eyes." She turned, and tucking one leg under the other, she slid heavily into a sitting position. "Oh," she said. "It makes me dizzy to do that." She opened her window a crack. "It's very close in here."

Daniel said, "Will you do me a favor?"

"What?"

"Take your bells off."

She looked at him and laughed. Perhaps she was pleased that he could joke this way and come up from being so far down. Perhaps she was cheered by this expression of the Life Force on such a deadening day. "Very funny," she said. But she was appreciative.

"I'm not being funny. I mean it."

She studied his face.

"Come on, Phyllis. Right now."

"Daniel—"

"Take them off."

"I don't think that's right. I don't want to do that."

"But I want you to, Phyllis."

She was looking for the lights of the Chevrolet, but the road immediately ahead was empty. She noticed that the car was going faster.

"Oh, Daniel, why are you doing this? It's so foolish. It's so unnecessary."

"Move it, Phyllis."

"I don't know what you want me to do."

"I want you to take your pants off."

"And then what? You can't do anything while you're driving. All you'll do is get us crashed."

Daniel gently depressed the accelerator and said nothing.

"This is a kind of sick kidding around, Daniel. It frightens me. You have no right to freak out driving a car with your own baby in it."

Daniel pressed down further on the accelerator. Phyllis was sitting straight in the seat now with both feet on the floor and her arms folded across her breasts. Daniel quietly explained to her the mechanical problems of the car: there was considerable play in the steering, the front wheels were unaligned, the brakes were worn and the tires slick. He glanced at the speedometer and informed Phyllis that they were doing eighty-five miles an hour.

"When we get to Brookline I'll do whatever you want," Phyllis said. "I know I bore you, Danny, I know your family thinks you married someone not as good as you. But you gotta gimme credit for trying, don't you?"

Daniel said nothing.

"You're all such big deals," Phyllis said. "You're all such big deals of suffering."

Daniel was pleased with this formulation. She wouldn't have been capable of it six months before. He thought of complimenting her. Instead he leaned forward and turned off the windshield wipers.

The rain poured down the windshield now in such torrents that the visibility, though slightly distorted, was good. Phyllis, not a driver, was hardly comforted. She was gazing at a light screen with white and red lights enlarging, shrinking, wavering, scattering, and pouring off her sight like water. Her impression was of not being able to see where the car was going. For the first time there was the sound of thunder rumbling over the sounds of the engine and the slick tires creaming the water. The thunder seemed to buffet the car, which swayed gently at the rear, left to right, right to left.

"You're going to kill us!" Phyllis screamed.

"All you have to do is take off your pants."

"I'll do it, I'll do it, but first slow down!"

"First do it!"

Phyllis unbuckled her belt and unzipped her fly and arching her back off the seat pulled her bellbottoms down. "I'm going to tell them," she said. "I'll tell them what you do to me and they'll put you right in there with your sister. The both of you!"

"All the way off, please."

Lifting her knees, she put the heels of her boots on the seat, unzipped her boots, pulled them off, dropped them on the floor, and pulled the pants over her ankles, and threw them down on top of the boots. Then she looked at him and pulled her underpants off and threw them into the pile at her feet. Then she held her hands over her ears and closed her eyes and bent her head.

Daniel took his foot off the gas pedal and turned on the windshield wipers. Phyllis was crying. She ran her fingers up through her hair and held her ears and cried. Daniel moved into the right-hand lane. A clap of thunder struck directly overhead. Daniel instructed Phyllis to kneel on the seat facing her side of the car, and to bend over as far as she could, kneeled and curled up like a penitent, a worshiper, an abject devotionalist. Weeping, she complained that the car was too small and she too big to get comfortable that way. Daniel gently urged her to try.

"Like this?" she said, her voice muffled by her hair.

"That's fine."

"Everyone will see me."

"No one can see you."

"The baby."

"The baby is asleep."

"Don't hurt me. Just don't hurt me, Daniel."

He ran his right hand over her buttocks. The small of her back was dewy with sweat. She shivered and the flesh of her backside trembled under his hand. He tracked the cleft downward. Triangulated by her position it yielded a slightly sour smell of excrement. He teased the small hairs of her tiny anus. Then, with the back of his hand, he rubbed her labia lying plump in their nest between the upturned soles of her feet.

The rain drummed down. The thunder was fierce. Cars were passing on the left. The sky was black. Daniel leaned forward and pressed the cigarette lighter. His hand remained poised. Do you believe it? Shall I continue? Do you want to know the effect of three concentric circles of heating element glowing orange in a black night of rain upon the tender white girlflesh of my wife's ass? Who are you anyway? Who told you you could read this? Is nothing sacred?

On the other hand the only thing worse than telling what happened is to leave it to the imagination. There is a classic surrealist silent film by Buñuel and Dali. It is a film about a live hand in a box, and a man dragging the carcass of a cow through his living room at the end of a rope; and the cow turns into a grand piano; and the hand is thrown into a sewer, and a crowd gathers and someone driving away from this fear in a taxi finds the hand in its box in the taxi—and if I recall these images inaccurately that is just as good. But the central event of the picture is this: a hefty and darkly handsome man in a tight-fitting ribbed undershirt stands in a room sharpening a straight razor. A lady sits on a wooden chair in the room with him. She too is half-dressed. Her face is controlled. Through the window we see that it is a moonlit night and that there are clouds moving through the bright moonlit sky. The man comes over to the woman, large eyed, bow mouthed, and impassive in her straight-backed chair, and with his thumb and forefinger spreads her eyelids as far apart as they will go. Then he brings his straight razor down toward her face and her eyeball. The film cuts to the night sky outside the window. A thin, knifelike cloud is seen gliding across the bright orb of the moon. And just as you, the audience, have settled for this symbolic mutilation of the woman's eye, the camera cuts back to the scene, and in close-up, shows the razor slicing into the eyeball.

They never talked about Paul and Rochelle. While they grew up with the Lewins there was no need to. They had shared an experience so evenly that to have spoken about it would have diminished what they knew and understood. Share and share alike, the cardinal point of justice for children driven home to them with vicious exactitude. (Do not strike, this is rhetorical but true. Only a son of Rochelle's could say this line. In our house there could be a laying on of words like lightning. Dispensed outrage, the smell of burning in the mouths of our mother and father. Once she said, "Let our death be his bar mitzvah.") So at the beginning at least, there was no need to talk about it. When the brother and the sister went somewhere, or did something together; when he tightened her skate or helped her with her homework, or took her to the movies; the way they moved, physically moved, in a convalescence of suffering spoke about it. The way he would hold her arm as they ran across the street in front of traffic spoke about it. The way his muscles tensed when she wasn't where she was supposed to be at any given time of the day, that spoke of it as well.

But they grew. He had taught her how to play casino and all the chords he knew on the guitar, he had taught her to ride a two-wheeler and to do the crawl, and one day she appeared to him suddenly past the age of being taught and taken care of. There were certain needs and expectations for life that could not properly be filled by your brother or sister. That was normal. And she must have come to feel, as he did, bored or unfairly burdened by the habits of a relationship that were drying up into sentimental gestures. And added to that was what he supposed was the normal inevitable loathing for the people who look like you and smell the same as you. That experience of total dissatisfaction with the closely related: who are not smart enough, good-looking enough, cool enough, to get through a day without boring you or shaming you. Except with their parents not available for that kind of self-honing, that sharpening of independence, he was the strop; the mother, the father, the brother, the family. And it was painful and they had some terrible fights.

Embarrassingly, Daniel and Susan adjusted to the rise in their fortunes. The life provided by an assistant professor of law was, by comparison, one of spectacular wealth. At the time there was no mention of the Trust. Each child had a room of his own. Lise bought them clothes that fit. It was life in the middle class and it was unbelievably good. Bob Lewin with his kind smile and his gentle sense of humor, came on in a way that seemed to suggest it might be possible to live comfortably and yet with honor. Their new parents never shouted, life didn't beat out that rhythm of crisis and training for crisis. There was an absence of ideology and relentless moral sentiment. They had a new name, which was like being high. The streets were new, the house was new. It was quiet. There were no intruders. There was a daily routine of school, play, practice, homework. There was a weekend routine of a planned activity or outing. There was an assumption that constantly surprised Daniel, that took getting used to: It was all right every now and then to enjoy yourself and have a good time. It really was all right.

Less and less did my heart bound in erratic dysynchronous jumps, like the rubber band balls I used to make.

And so Susan and Daniel Lewin slipped into the indolent rituals of the teenage middle class. In order for them to do this, there had to be a dialectic of breaking free: you asked yourself why live in faith or memorial to the people who had betrayed you. For obvious reasons this too was unspoken between them. There were at least a couple of years, a couple of good years, when none of it had happened. Or if it had happened, neither of them could have cared less. They had their own bodies, their own friends, they had lives of their own.

But it was all a counterrevolutionary illusion. It seemed so easy to break free because it was what the world wanted of you. The world wanted you to forget who you had been and what had happened to you. The world did not want to visit the sins of the fathers. If, in their proud, snotty, tormented adolescence he and his sister tacitly came to the conclusion that Paul and Rochelle Isaacson were not worth their loyalty, there was, however, nothing they could do to squander it. The decision was out of their hands. Whatever they did, whatever view they took, it was merely historical process operating. And even faithlessness in their hearts, real genuine bitter-brewed carelessness of spirit, could not dissolve that. Under one guise or another they were still the Isaacson kids. "You poor kids," all the comrades used to say. They were like figures in a myth who suffer the same fate no matter what version is told; who remain in eternal relationship no matter how their names are spelled. Or they were like those two horses in that experiment you learned about in high school who were hitched up to pull apart two hemispheres that had been fastened by vacuum; who heaved and strained, one pulling one way, the other the other way, to prove that nothing is more powerful than a vacuum.

Still, they did not talk. And when he was eighteen he went off to school and took an apartment in Cambridge, and for two or three years she might as well not have existed. And when he came to his senses, and the real life of his childhood, that had become a dream, became real again, he tried to make contact with Susan. But Susan was now a commanding presence: too bright, too loud, too hysterically self-occupied. She gave him glimpses of herself in her underwear. She let him know that she had been laid more than once. She was very busy with her life. And he mourned the little kid sister and he thought We should have talked, we should always have talked.

BINTEL BRIEF

My dear Mr. Editor, you who hear the troubles of so many, and share the common misery, permit me to say what I have to say if my heart is not to burst. Surely I do not have to tell you what my life has been: first the terrible fear of flight from the Czarist maniacs who would not let us live, and who killed us in his pogroms, and conscripted our young Jewish men for twenty-five years of slavery in the Army—from this terrible animal oppression I fled by paying the same torturers money under the table to slip across the border with only the rags on my back, from the Pale, the Pale with my poor old mother and father who felt too old to go kissing my head and blessing me and calling on YHVH to protect me, Mr. Editor, and I knew I would never see them again because I was their life and with me to America, their only reason for enduring this suffering on earth, just to know I was safe, a little piece of themselves going to live in America before they would lay down and smile under the Cossacks' horses; I kept their brown picture; across in the filth of steerage, a boat for cattle, and we were cattle, and then the terror of the Immigration Officers who would or would not let us be Americans—the woman right next to me with her trachomatous eyes not going in, staying on the island in seclusion, in America, and yet never to be in America, and to her I had to say goodbye my own good fortune being my health and my youth and my strength. And a boy from the same town with me came on the boat behind the old man who couldn't remember the name his sons told him to say, one that the American inspectors could pronounce, and the poor old man so bewildered said piteously in Yiddish, I forget, *ich ver-*

gessin, and named like a newborn babe, this old man, Ike Fergusson, oh I could tell you stories . . . But this boy and I went right away for the license and with no further ado we became married and the next day went looking for work and began our life with needle and thread, my stout young protector and me in our paid room as boarders on Stanton Street, a couple neither smart nor dumb, neither fair nor dark, neither short nor tall or ugly or beautiful, but hard-working folks and for thousands of years my people stumbling through the world in their suffering looking for paradise on earth, righteous in our adoration of YHVH, trying to find a home on earth, an earth habitable in reason and peace and humanity, somewhere. And I tell you, Mr. Editor, for children who have seen the bottom of the pagan Cossack horseshoe and the drunken grin of the Czarist bureaucrat, to sew sixteen hours a day for pennies, in bad light, and to live in a one-room, with the children bathing in the laundry sink in the kitchen and the dead rat floating in the common toilet at the end of the dark stinking hall—it can be done. And you think you can stitch a life together, penny by penny, with the small muscles in your fingers drive the metal needle through the cloth a million nimble moments each day —it can be done. And anything can be endured with hope: My eldest runs into the street and is crushed under a wagon. My two younger sisters who I have brought to this country with my pennies are destroyed in the Triangle Fire, a hundred and fifty of them burned to death in that sweatshop. And my second son, Jacob, who wanted to be called Jack, and who loved to swim in the East River, he does not survive the terrible flu epidemic in 1918. And in this country, fifteen years, twenty, my old man and me, I recognize us one day cleaning ourselves for the Sabbath: we are my mother and father, and life, terrible life, has nailed us to the ground. Oh, Mr. Editor, there have been such sweetnesses though, and God remains pure and shining over Hester Street with the peddlers selling the fish for the Sabbath and the pushcarts with their notions, and the men in dirty vests and derbies bartering in their musical voices. And I think of the children running to school and learning English and reading in the library in such great thirst. And there are everywhere lectures and meetings of an intellectual nature and I, an ignorant woman, even I, understand the pride in common workingmen slowly admitting to themselves that their dreams are for their children. Yet nevertheless seeking in their nights or on their days of leisure the betterment of their minds, the satisfaction of mental exercise, the understanding of the universe. And that play that brought such tears to all of us of the greenhorn who came to America and had such hard lessons to learn, before, blessed G_D, our lessons, he was reunited with his mama and papa. And a glass of tea at the window with the cube of sugar in your teeth and if you listen someone will be singing a song in the alley, under the clotheslines. But what I cannot forgive, Mr. Editor, is the thankless child who becomes ashamed of his mother and father, and forsakes their ways, and blasphemes and violates the Sabbath to be a modern American; and is attracted to godless ideas in the street like a fly to flypaper. And who tells you to speak English. And who cries only when her father, my husband, finally totters to his knees like an old horse who has no more strength—*mamaneu*—under his pack of clothes, America, on the street to his knees under the day's piecework going to his knees and he coughs and drops of his blood spatter the sidewalk and someone calls me Mrs! Mrs! your husband is dying, and his friend tuberculosis, which is bits of thread on the lungs, my young man from the same town where the truth is we were married for safety by our parents before we crossed the border, my young man who has never lifted a hand against me and who bore all his sorrow in the Synagogue, is at this moment old enough to die. And he dies. And I am alone in America with only my daughter, Rachele, born 1919, and the terror of my life is yet to begin—

> A thin, small, caved-in woman dry to the touch,
> Grandma gave me pennies and called me a good boy
> Snapping open the tarnished brass clasps
> Of a flat and ancient purse of cracked leather
> And withdrawing one penny with her thumb and fore-
> finger

You get the picture. Good boy, Daniel. I tried not to offend her by giving any sign that she offended me, because she really smelled bad, my skinny mad little grandma, she smelled of her asthma grass which she burned like incense in a blue tin in her room. The sour smell, always with her, like a stink shadow —peeyouwee!—was on her fingers, in her change purse, in her black dress, in her wavy grey hair. She lifted my hand and pressed the penny into it, and then while I took a deep breath and held it, she leaned forward, about my height, and by the back of my neck pulled me forward for the dry kiss on the forehead. Daniel is a good boy, she said. That is for a good boy. I thought she meant the penny, the kiss being for her— her reward for having a good boy for a grandson. The very words she pronounced not as a judgment but as if good boy was a category of being, a species in nature which she was privileged in her old age to have living in the same house. There was a generation between us which we never discussed.

My grandma had spells. She used to accuse my mother, her very own daughter, of trying to poison her. My mother always had to taste the food she put on the table before the old woman would eat it. So my mother got into the habit of tasting everything, even a glass of milk for me, before she put it down. Grandma was the neighborhood crazywoman. When she went into one of these things, she would put a shawl over her head and run away. She would stomp down from the porch, bringing her high lace shoes together on one step before the next step was taken. And on the sidewalk, before rushing off, she would turn and shake her fist at the house and curse it in Yiddish, calling down cholera and Cossacks and typhoid and wholesale terrors of the burning fiery furnace, and if someone passed in the street she would curse him too. Suppose little Daniel was out there minding his baby sister in her carriage: Grandma would curse him out too, her eyes burning, lacking all recognition, her grey hair all uncombed, undone, the waves of it sticking out from her shawl, shockingly, like electric wire. Then she'd scurry away, describing with gestures toward the sidewalk the extent of her bitterness. Daniel was always glad to see her go. What worried him was when, a half-block away, she would turn with a raised fist for a parting blast, and it would become a very rhetorically involved curse, and she would forget in what direction she had been going and come back toward him and the house and the whole thing would start all over again. She ran away all the time. To Claremont Park. Down the hill to the New York Central tracks. In her black dress telling the world all the mad family secrets. Sometimes she went around the corner to her one friend, Mrs. Bittelman, also a widow, but a younger woman, perhaps in her late fifties, a kindly red-faced woman who seemed to Daniel to be the only person who liked Grandma and who had the patience to take seriously the stream of imprecations coming out of Grandma's mouth, and to sit with her and nod solemnly and with sighs, until the spell was over. And to bring her home. Mrs. Bittelman had, beside her kindness, impeccable credentials: her only son, Jerome, had been killed in the war. Mrs. Bittelman's apartment was on the ground floor of the apartment house around the corner on 173rd Street. The venetian blinds were always drawn shut. In one window was one of those service stars. During the war a blue star in a window meant that that family had a soldier serving somewhere in the Army. A gold star meant that the boy had been killed. Mrs. Bittelman's star was blue, but the boy had been killed. She had never had the heart to set the matter straight. She was an old Jewish lady, though not as old as my grandma, and the faded blue star on a shield of white cloth with a red border and gold tassels hung from a stick in her window years after the war was over.

Sometimes Grandma went the other way. Then, in a few hours the phone would ring. Or sometimes a police car—a police car!—would pull up to the curb in front of the house, a green and white police car, and Grandma would emerge with great dignity, contemptuous of the cops who tried to help her out of their car. A green and white police car would pull up. Here is Grandma furiously shaking off the patronizing grip of the Bronx cop as she struggles out of their car.

SEVERAL EXPLANATIONS

In my life as Daniel, I heard several explanations for Grandma's plunges into the pit. Susan, age fifteen, in her new ivy-league cool: "I never knew Grandmother, but from what you say, I suspect it was menopause." My mother, during a particularly bad spell—I have stopped by the door to watch my father holding the thrashing old woman down on her bed so that the Doctor can give her a shot; small and frail, she is putting up a terrific struggle; and my mother stands at the foot of the bed shouting "Mama, stop it. Stop this nonsense, stop it, Mama!" and then, seeing me stricken pale in the doorway, my mother leads me downstairs and explains why, at the age of five or six or whatever I am, I am subjected to such things . . . It is simple: Grandma goes mad when she can no longer consider the torment of her life. My mother's catalogue of the old lady's misfortunes—the abandoned parents whose brown picture she still keeps in her drawer, the death of her first-born in the street, the death of her two sisters in the big fire, the death of her second-born from the flu, the death of her husband, my grandfather who would have loved me if he'd lived. "What killed him was not tuberculosis, what killed him and killed them all was poverty and exploitation, and that means being poor and being kept poor by people who grow fat and rich from your labor. It's not fair, is it?"

"No, Ma."

"Your grandma slaved all her life. To end up with nothing."

Ignore the reverberations of that remark. Ignore the reverberations. Ignore them. Ignore . . . My father believed that a life committed to superstition could have no other end than madness, because madness was the disease of fantasy and fantasy of God, or superstition, was itself madness, a predictably abnormal expression of impoverished life. The most enormous problem faced by the Bolsheviks, he said, was education of the peasants. The Russian peasants had been kept in ignorance and illiteracy for so many generations that they were not much more than animals. God was an instrument of the Czar. And Grandma grew up, of course, in the *shtetl* of a provincial Russian town, a Jew, but also a Russian peasant. My father always gives you more of an answer than you bargained for.

And now let me put down what Grandma herself said about her tunings in and out. Occasionally, after her death, she liked to visit me and press a penny into my palm and bless my head, and call me a good boy. And once I asked her why she felt it necessary to blow her mind in a way so frightening to children. And Grandma said:

"In any one day, it is possible to derive joy from your being and be nourished by it. In a filthy room with cold, broken windows and the clatter of your oppression in the streets, it is possible. And starving, with your teeth rotting in your mouth, and age like lead in your bones, and your eyes shattered with the horror of what you have seen—all together, and with the madness of your children thrown in, I call it God. And there is a traditional liturgy which is lovely in itself, but which reminds you too that others born and died know this feeling also. So I sing to myself in that language. And my curses are my love for them whom I curse for existing at the mercy of life and God and for the dust they will allow themselves to become for having been born. And my complicity in their being, the fruit of my womb, that I could have tricked them this way outrages me. Unable to stay in their presence for my love of them which they do not understand, and my terrible fear of their blasphemy, and their tampering with all the deep, intricate solderings of the universe. Do you begin to understand? I am speaking of the only form of ecstasy allowed to old ladies. It begins with the fear of not being able to breathe. And they inherit that from me, too, as you do, that excess of passion that shimmering fullness of stored life which always marks the victim. What we have, too much life in each of us, is what the world hates most. We offend. We stink with life. Our hearts make love to the world not gently. We are brutal with life and our brutality is called suffering. We scream into our pillows when we come.

"You are a good boy, Daniel. What I mean by that is perhaps only that you have compassion, and that however much I scared you, or however bad I smelled from my asthma, you trusted me enough to accept my pennies and let me call you a good boy. Or perhaps it is that I recognized in you the strength and innocence that will reclaim us all from defeat. That will exonerate our having lived and justify our suffering."

"Now that scares me more than anything, Grandma."

"You're fuckin' right, Dan. Just remember, though, this placing of the burden on the children is a family tradition. But only your crazy grandma had the grace to make a ritual of it. Ritual being an artful transfer of knowledge. And pennies being the sum of her life's value."

A medical textbook. On the white and shining pages are photographs of three female bodies. Little, withered Grandma with her head of wildly twisted grey hair. Rochelle, strong, breasty, stocky, prim mouthed. And Susan in her thin gold granny glasses. They stand in a row across the double-page spread, palms turned slightly out, feet turned slightly out, nothing hidden. They could be standing up or lying down. Grandma looks like the wrinkled matriarch of an aboriginal tribe. Rochelle's got the bosoms, but Susan is taller and more feminine. They all have triangles, but move your gaze upward. This is a medical textbook. The meaning of the picture is in the thin, diagrammatic arrow line, colored red, that runs from Grandma's breast through your mama's and into your sister's. The red line describes the progress of madness inherited through the heart.

cottage cheese, tomatoes if they are good, a pound of hamburger, something gooey for dessert.

On the theory that what occurs is right. Any action is correct because it happens. What of that theory? Only if it works. I worry about images. Images are what things mean. Take the word image. It connotes soft, sheer flesh shimmering on the air, like the rainbowed slick of a bubble. Image connotes images, the multiplicity being an image. Images break with a small ping, their destruction is as wonderful as their being, they are essentially instruments of torture exploding through the individual's calloused capacity to feel powerful undifferentiated emotions full of longing and dissatisfaction and monumentality. They serve no social purpose.

You are going to have to shoot straight with Professor Sukenick. He thinks you are not applying for an NDEA fellowship because you refuse on principle to sign a loyalty oath. Why is shooting straight a metaphor for honesty? I am not applying for a fellowship because if I sign a hundred loyalty oaths, I still won't get it. I should tell him who I am. Not that I've attempted to hide this information, but it is difficult to work it into any kind of small talk. Sukenick is a youth-sympathetic liberal, very sharp. He would be intrigued by my story. He would not believe that the government checks me out once or twice a year. My own father doesn't believe it. Of course, this is not an assignment any FBI man, even the most callow, could consider without yawning. Nevertheless, my dossier is up to date. I live in constant and degrading relationship to the society that has destroyed my mother and father. I will never be drafted. If I left school today my classification would still be 2-A, which covers any situation not in the national interest. Listen, Professor, I could burn my draft card on the steps of the Pentagon and nothing would happen. Nothing I do will result in anything but an additional entry in my file. My file. I am deprived of the chance of resisting my government. They have no discoveries to make about me. They will not regard anything I do as provocative, disruptive or insulting. Nobody in the Federal police will ever say to a colleague: Who *is* this guy! No matter what political or symbolic act I perform in protest or disobedience, no harm will befall me. I have worked this out. It's true. I am totally deprived of the right to be dangerous. If I were to assassinate the President, the criminality of my family, its genetic criminality, would be established. There is nothing I can do, mild or extreme, that they cannot have planned for. In the meantime, they have only to make sure that I am in no way involved with the United States Government, either as a social beneficiary, or as a servitor, however humble. They will give me no money. They will force me into no uniform. No administration will ever be connected to me in any way to make itself vulnerable to the opportunism of congressmen.

If, on the other hand, I were to become publically militant Daniel Isaacson all their precautions would have been justified. And probably whatever cause I lent myself to could be more easily discredited.

The final existential condition is citizenship. Every man is the enemy of his own country. EVERY MAN IS THE ENEMY OF HIS OWN COUNTRY. Every country is the enemy of its own citizens. Here are some places in the world I don't have to look out for: Switzerland, Finland, Bolivia, Uruguay, Sweden, Red China, Taiwan, Soviet Russia, England, France, Italy, Germany, Australia, Canada, the entire continent of Africa, the entire continent of Antarctica, Japan, Mexico, India, Pakistan, Vietnam, Burma, Israel, Egypt, South America, Cuba, Haiti, Aukland, all the little stamps in the stamp album, the Free Port of Shannon. All these places have relationships with my country not with me. My relationship is with my country. In the film *Paths of Glory*, a French regiment is shown in the trenches during World War I. They are ordered to attack with their rifles and bayonets an impregnable German position called The Pimple. They physically are not able to bring themselves to leap out of their trenches to commit this mass suicide. In a rage, their General behind the lines orders his own artillery to fire upon them. The artillery balks. The General withdraws this regiment from the lines and punishes it for rank disobedience by executing three enlisted men who have been picked by straw lot. Their own comrades are the firing squad. In war the soldier's destruction is accomplished by his own Commanders. It is his government which places a rifle in his hands, puts him up on the front, and tells him his mission is to survive. All societies are armed societies. All citizens are soldiers. All Governments stand ready to commit their citizens to death in the interest of their government.

Drawing and Quartering. This particular form of execution was favored by English monarchic government against all except the aristocratic inner circle which was allowed the dignity of simple beheading. For everyone else the method worked like this: the transgressor was hanged and cut down before he was dead. Then he was emasculated, disemboweled, and his entrails were set on fire in front of his eyes. If the executioner was merciful the heart was then removed from the body, but in any case, the final act of the ritual was then performed, a hacking of the body into four parts, the quarters then being thrown to the dogs. Treason was the usual crime for this punishment, its definition being determined by the King's courts for the King's convenience.

In 1954, Robert Lewin accepted an appointment as Assistant Professor of Law at Boston College, a Jesuit institution in Newton, Massachusetts. Making a modest down payment, he bought an old house in nearby Brookline, and with his wife and two children, Daniel, fourteen, and Susan, nine, took possession one warm September afternoon a week or so before classes began. The three-story house, grey stucco with maroon trim and a roof of slate, was situated on Winthrop Road. This was a quiet residential avenue that curved up the hill from Beacon Street with its stores and trolley tracks. It wound through facing ranks of attached redstones, apartment buildings and cumbersome old houses set close to one another on small lots. The best feature of the new house as far as the Lewins were concerned was that it produced income to pay for itself. Inside the front door, with its clear, plastic louvers, was a small entranceway to two doors, two mailboxes, two bells. Like many of the houses in the neighborhood, number 67 was built for two families and designed to look as if it contained only one. The Lewins occupied the ground floor, and half of the second. Their tenants occupied half of the second floor and all of the third. Each apartment had a downstairs and an upstairs, and each was a mirror version of the other.

The two-family house was just an odd fact in the Lewin children's odd life. Every sound had echoes, every image bore another. The very first full day in the house, before anything was unpacked, the new family went exploring, running down the one hundred forty-seven wood steps of Winthrop Path (always to be that number, the same each time, a source of great satisfaction) between the tiers of backyards on this terraced hill with the backs of houses resting on stilts, Brookline being built on hills; and catching the Beacon Street trolley to downtown Boston. There, in their explorations—all of them being

New Yorkers—they came upon the street signs of the Freedom Trail.

It is possible that the law professor and his wife were facing it squarely, right off the bat. It is possible they had decided to begin immediately to describe alternatives. Yet, according to one criminal of perception who watched them rather closely, they did not easily adjust to the presence of the ghosts in the lives of their children. These ghosts were not strange sounds in the attic, nor were they mists who moaned in the midnight garden. These ghosts were ironies. These ghosts were slips of the tongue. They were the brutal meanings in innocent remarks. They were the necessity to remain sensitive to your own words and gestures. These ghosts clung to the roof of your mouth, they hovered in your brain like fear, they resided in your muscles like nerves.

Sit up straight, Danny. You're always squirming. This particular dinnertable remark of Lise's put her to bed with a white hankie crumpled in her fist. I recreate an evening of over a dozen years ago. My new mother is really upset. My new father, sucking his pipe, tunes his fine mind to the problem, runs his fingers through his then brown hair, already sparse from running his fingers through it as he thinks. He sits by the bed, ignoring the sound of his wife's weeping. He thinks the problem through and reaches something like the intellectual translation of his children's feelings.

Honey, *we* are ironies to them, this *house* is ironic, if it *rains* it's ironic. You're crying about a condition of their lives that is irrevocable. Please allow us to live as normally and imperfectly as all people live. Let's go to sleep. We'll do what we can. We will all go to bed at night and we'll all get up in the morning. Just like the rest of the world.

I have no more of them than the present of their lives. Of course, it was more complicated, but the image that returns to me is of a young couple reading about it in the newspapers and rushing downtown on the subway. Before that I know that Lise, with some other Jewish children, went from country to country, in front of the Nazis, from cellar to cellar, until she reached England. I don't know how she got from England to America. I don't know who took care of her. She met Robert Lewin at a summer camp in New Jersey where they both waited table. Another image is of Robert and Lise standing in front of a Rabbi with Robert in his Army uniform. There are some distant cousins. An old aunt or two. It is too late for me now to find out who they are or where they came from. And I don't have the heart for it. Ascher chose them. They made a good home for us and provided examples for our lives of sanity and stability. We have repaid them by treating them as poorly as children treat their real parents. They are liberal Jews who live comfortably in a Christian world. Their home reflects idiosyncrasy that is valuable to me. Lise's taste in furniture is distinctly old-fashioned and runs to middle European mahogany; her cuisine is Viennese. Robert years ago got into the habit of doing his work in the dining room—perhaps because he didn't want his work to put him off from his family. From the dining room he can see through the center hall to the living room. And he can hear what is going on in the kitchen. So it is a dining room with a typewriter, and blue exam books and law journals and letters strewn about, and a meal prepared for by clearing all the detritus of the legal profession from the table to the buffet.

On the evening of that Memorial Day, 1967, Daniel pulled up in front of the Lewin home on Winthrop and turned off the motor. The rain had stopped. The streetlights shone on the wet street. Daniel's wife immediately got out of the car, pushed the back of the seat forward, and lifted out her baby. Then she walked away in the direction of Beacon Street.

The Lewin house was a complete absurdity. It had Tudor-style bay windows on the second floor. But a Greek revival portico with plaster columns framed the front door. On the right-hand pillar, the number 67 gleamed in raised hemispheres of reflecting glass. Daniel turned off the car lights.

The house was dark. He thought he was about fifteen minutes ahead of the Lewins, although they might be longer if they had to drop Duberstein somewhere. Daniel got out of the car and stretched his legs. The rain had cooled things off. The air was fresh and the breeze moist and cool.

The mailbox alongside the door Daniel found stuffed with mail. This was a measure of the Lewins' distraction. How else could you explain mail on Memorial Day. Among the letters was

a small blue envelope addressed to Daniel Isaacson Lewin. It
was a girl's handwriting. The postmark was Cambridge.

Daniel took the letter back to the car. He was a naturally
graceful fellow, and an old woman shuffling by in house slippers
behind her Alaskan malamute could not help remark on the
insolent long-legged grace of youth as it reads its letters by the
light of a dashboard, one foot in the wet street, and the other
planted in the car. She had written him here. He was terrified.
He had decided when he sat with her that she was not mad,
she was inconsolable. But she was mad.

This is the text of the letter.

Dear Daniel,

I have been thinking about last Christmas. Of course
I'm going ahead with my plans but that's not the point.
You couldn't have come on that way unless you believe
the Isaacsons are guilty. That's what I didn't want to
understand at the time. You think they are guilty. It's
enough to take someone's life away.

Someday, Daniel, following your pathetic demons,
you are going to disappear up your own asshole. To
cover the time until then, I'm writing you out of my
mind. You no longer exist.

S. I.

Annotation of Susan's Letter. 1. The address on the envelope,
67 Winthrop, indicates no recognition of Daniel's New York
residence, or, by implication, the last five years of his life. This
is deliberate but not malicious. For Susan there are still issues.
For Susan the issues must be preserved. Everything about
Daniel's recent life is irrelevant—except as it confirms his loss
to the cause. The funny thing is, however, that he got the letter
where it was mailed. And after no particular delay.

2. The Christmas referred to was
the Christmas previous in the winter previous in a previous
phase of the world. At that time, the peace movement had not
yet peaked. People who marched were called doves. The previous
spring there had been a great big march of the doves down to
the UN. Martin Luther King was alive. Bobby Kennedy was

alive. The student left had not yet come to the attention of *Time* magazine. Newark and Detroit and Cleveland would not burn till the summer. The great Pentagon rush would not occur till the following October. Everyone was defining Black Power. You remember? It was an innocent world then with the old-timey simple sadnesses. The Beatles were not yet political. And Walt Disney had just died. At the Lewin home on Winthrop Road, Lise's face red from checking the holiday turkey roasting in the oven, Robert serving one too many drinks, an altercation occurred of some magnitude between the children, and Christmas, boldly celebrated in this Jewish home as American-Family Day with the Kids Home, was not merry.

        3. The plans referred to were the apparent subject of the bitterness, the elder orphan child, Daniel, having not received word of them with sufficient respect. The plans for a Foundation for Revolution were offered up by the younger orphan child, Susan, a Radcliffe student, flushed with the triumphs of the Boston Resistance, a loosely confederated group of middle-class boys and girls who were returning draft cards to Washington and demonstrating in front of draft boards to indicate their opposition to the war in Vietnam. It bothered Daniel that his sister was so shining and bold as she spoke of their most recent demonstration, routed by the cops with clubs. She had been carrying a sign that read Girls Say Yes to Boys Who Say No, and she was knocked down and a cop had tried to hit her between the legs. Susan unbuttoned the sleeves of her blouse and displayed her swollen and discolored wrists. Phyllis gasped. Daniel noticed the Lewins look at each other with paling apprehension. Robert Lewin was amazed no bones had been broken. Susan was radiant. She wore an old-fashioned blouse with a high ruffled collar and puffy sleeves; she wore a dark skirt of velvet that came down to the tops of a pair of high lace boots. She was a lean attractive girl wearing old clothes picked up in an old clothes boutique, and naturally they looked like the latest thing. With her hair parted in the middle and pulled tight over her ears and clamped behind her neck, she was Rosa Luxemburg glancing at Daniel through her granny glasses of thin gold as if from the gates of another city, her fearless blue eyes striking his heart like the tolling of a

bell. Daniel felt in this situation a poverty in his choice of wife. He suspected the Lewins of that sentimentality for radical action to which liberals are vulnerable—an abstract respect for the dangerous politics they themselves are incapable of practicing. I'm being unfair. They were disturbed by what she had done, just as they had been unnerved when, for a time, her thing had been to drop acid. And she had been a forthright head with the same idealism, with the same passionate embrace for that liberation as for this.

Susan fended off the worries of her parents. She put them down for their cautiousness. She lectured on the moral and tactical differences between those who believed in going to prison and those who preferred Canada. Daniel drank his drink. The Foundation was to be named after Paul and Rochelle Isaacson. The Paul and Rochelle Isaacson Foundation for Revolution. The money would come from the trust when it came due to them. She was already talking to people in New York. In the coming year, on their respective birthdays, his twenty-fifth, her twenty-first, they would come into possession of the trust fund set up in their name by Ascher a dozen years before, and administered with great skill since by their foster father. Half and half. Susan suggested that she would welcome Daniel's participation in the Foundation, not only for the money that was his, but because it would indicate, as well, a unanimity of family feeling, a proper assumption of their legacy by the Isaacson children. Indicate to whom, Daniel wanted to know. Why to the world, Susan said, her eyebrows lifting in surprise. Daniel asked Robert Lewin his opinion of the idea. Robert Lewin said Susan had been thinking about it for a while and had asked him if it was technically feasible, which it was. Daniel said sitting in front of draft boards or going to jail for refusing to be inducted was not his idea of how to make revolution. Susan nodded as if this was a point she had expected to come up. She herself thought resistance was an early phase, a stage in political development, and that other things were going on, new things were beginning to happen, and didn't he keep his ears open at Columbia because she was sure Cambridge didn't have a monopoly on New Left dialectic. She herself went through changes every day, and she would think the proper position now was not to stand outside and criticize but to get inside and help create. "What the movement needs is money, Daniel. The Foundation can have a fantastic stabilizing effect. It can be really great. It can be something out of which other things happen."

"Susan, how is it whenever you present me with an idea, or ask me to do something, it's in a way calculated to turn me off."

She lowered her eyes. "I guess, Daniel, because not much is required to turn you off."

"Let's keep the discussion on a reasonably high plane," Robert Lewin said.

"I try to, Daddy," Susan said, "but anything that comes from me is automatically suspect. Right, Daniel?"

"No, it's just that I hear about it as a privilege, after the decisions are made."

"But nothing has happened yet. We're just talking."

"Who's just talking."

"You're unbelievable. We're just talking, now, you and me. Us."

"No, you said you were talking to people in New York."

"Oh, right, I have, I'm talking to a lot of people. I talk to whoever listens."

"Who?"

Susan nimbly rebuttoned her sleeves. "Forget it. Forget I said a thing. You do as you like." She turned to our father. "It makes me sad, it really does. We're in this horrible imperialist war, we're burning people, and the issue is how I happen to talk."

"No, I'll tell you what the issue is. The issue is if you want to give your money away why not just do it, why do you have to put a family tag on it? Why do you have to advertise?"

"That's a Rightist question. It's not advertising. The name Isaacson has meaning. What happened to the Isaacsons is a lesson to this generation. I suppose you can't understand that."

"There it is, the fucking family gift for self-objectification. You hear that? She calls her own mother and father the Isaacsons!"

"Listen, you two," Robert Lewin said. "If you can't conduct a civil discussion I'd prefer no discussion at all."

"I'm not ashamed of the name. I'm proud of who I am. Unlike you. If you could only see the schmucky way you come on in this world!"

"That may be. But I don't think starting a Foundation is necessarily a good idea just because it has the name Isaacson on it. How will it work? Who is it for? What will it do?"

"WHY NOT LET'S TRY IT AND SEE!" She had stood up, and her fists were clenched at her sides. "You cop out with this phony cynicism bag that conveniently saves you from doing anything. Well, you tell me what to do. You give me a better idea what to do with this blood money."

"This blood money has bought you an education, skiing lessons and records."

"Why don't you just admit you're a selfish prick!"

"On the contrary, I don't want the bread. I thought we'd give it to our parents."

Robert Lewin said, "That is the one alternative that as guardian I won't permit."

"Well, I think you ought to reconsider. Your just due for all the bullshit you've put up with."

"Don't worry, Daniel. You can forget the Foundation. It doesn't need you. You have all the political development of a retardate. Go back to your life. Take this milk cow of yours and go home."

"If this doesn't stop right now," Lise said, "I'm not going to serve dinner."

"Go back to the stacks, Daniel. The world needs another graduate student."

"Well, I don't have to go out and get beat up to justify my existence."

"No, you'd rather jerk off behind a book."

"This must stop," the mother said. "You are ruining my dinner."

"Susan, I don't think you're handling this very well."

"Oh yes she is, she really is. She's a Revolutionary! She's got all the answers. She's been to the barricades!"

"Oh Jesus," Susan said, beginning to cry. "And you know I blame you," she said to Robert Lewin. "I blame you all for the piece of shit this brother of mine—"

"Susan—"

"I mean what did they do it for? What did they die for? For this piece of shit?"

"Susan—"

"Leave me alone, Daddy. You let him sit there and twist everything I say. My mother and father were murdered—why do you let him sit here and do it again!"

4. *You no longer exist.* This curse, for that is its literary form, actually has two stages. The first is a prophecy of the final outcome, a disappearance of Daniel into his own asshole, which is the only appropriate destination for his egocentricity. Until that happens, however, another act is required to get him immediately out of the human community. He is "written" out of mind. Why in this complicated construction is Daniel not ready *now* to disappear up his own asshole? Because he has not used up all the chances? Because he is not yet beyond redemption? Someday is not today. Nevertheless he must be purged. There is some indication that this was easier said than done. There is some evidence that she was driven finally to eradicate him from her consciousness by the radical means of eradicating her consciousness.

1947

A certain importance had come to the household. It was not bad at all. It was almost exciting. He wore his good white shirt with the clip-on bow tie. And his new trousers. He was told to stay clean. And nobody bothered him much. On the kitchen table was a fantastic treasure of cakes and candy: sponge cake, honey cake with thinly sliced nuts in the crust, home-baked layer cake with pink icing. The sponge and honey cake came in paper containers with the edges slightly browned. You peeled the crinkly paper from the slice and then at the end licked the cake stuck to the paper. There were also white cardboard boxes of cookies from the bakery—those little crumbly cookies with dabs of chocolate in the center or sticky maraschino cherries, or green dots. There were boxes of candy still wrapped; he stacked these boxes in tiers behind the cakes. He played store.

On the stove was a glass pot of coffee with a small light under it. Cups and saucers were arranged on the counter. Every once in a while someone, some woman with a whiff of the street, would come in and smile falsely, cutely, at him and say something stupid and pour a cup of coffee and return with it to the front of the house. Sometimes they would notice the memory glass on top of the icebox, and they would try to look sad. Voices which bothered him filled the house. The chattering flew back into the kitchen like birds. Nevertheless he had to admit it was exciting. The excitement shook the house into harmony. The house, heavy with people, the air made heavy with the voices of people, seemed to sit everything more firmly on the ground. If, for instance, a great storm came up, the house would be less likely to blow away with so many people. A great wind, crying and straining and cursing, would have to work much harder to carry away so many people. These people were like heavy stones to hold the house down. Perhaps a great wind would leave the house alone altogether because it wasn't just him and his family, but all those other people who had nothing to do with it. Who had nothing to do with it.

Every now and then a man would come into the kitchen and pour whiskey from the open bottle that stood on the counter with three or four tiny glasses around it. He would pour the whiskey into one of the little glasses and gulp the whiskey down and smack his lips or drink a glass of water from the tap. It did not matter to any of these men if the glasses were used. They put the glasses down without washing them, and used them again that way. But they did not immediately become drunk, which was encouraging. They drank whiskey and went back to the front of the house and weren't drunk, which was a relief. So the bitter volatile smell was endurable. The smell of the coffee was good, and the scent of baking that came out of the cakes was very good—warm and lemony. Like the visitors, all the smells were new, busy smells. They meant that when someone dies, not everyone dies. It was very encouraging to know this. Just because someone you know dies doesn't mean you have to die too. It does not mean it is your turn to die right then. He was grateful for this. He was happy. He wondered if all the laughter and chatter from the front of the house meant everyone else was feeling as good as he was. He had noticed when he was answering the door that every person came in with a very sad look on his face, but after a few minutes inside was talking away merrily, chatting and laughing. Maybe they were simply glad his grandma was dead. Because Grandma had died instead of them. Because maybe by dying she used up all the dying for a while so that nobody else would die for a long time. Or maybe everyone was talking and laughing but only pretending to be happy. And only trying to cheer his mother up. And make her not so sad. He went down the hall to the living room to see her. There were ladies from the neighborhood sitting around her and talking merrily, but she was sitting on a little wooden bench and she had no shoes on. That bothered him. She had no shoes on and her hair was not neat. She was sitting in a hunched-over position with her arms across her knees, as if she was on the potty. Her face was all swollen and puffy around her eyes. He stared at her mournfully. She saw him and sat up, holding out her arms. "Here's my happiness," she said, smiling through her unfamiliar, puffy face.

He hadn't wanted to be seen. "Look at that doll," one of the women said. "He's getting so big!"

"He's a good boy," his mother said. "He's a very good boy." She pulled him onto her lap, her skirt rising above her knees as she took him into her arms. She held him tightly.

"Well, that's something," another of the women said. "At least she had the blessing of grandchildren."

"She loved them," his mother said in an unnaturally soft voice. "For all her troubles she always had time to smile when Danny came into the room. He was her favorite. She never really got to know the baby, but Danny? Danny could do no wrong in her eyes. She was crazy about him."

"He's bigger than my Philip," one of the women said.

He stopped listening. Gradually he loosened his mother's grip until he judged he could slip away without attracting her attention.

In the front of the living room his father was talking to

some men. His sleeves were rolled up and his tie was pulled down a little and his collar was open. He was smoking a cigar and moving it in the air with his hand as he talked. The afternoon sun was coming through the windows; it shone on his glasses. When the smoke from the cigar came into the sunlight, it became a blue-white color. He tried to watch one segment of smoke as it rippled up from the tip of the cigar and then burst into brilliant blue whiteness and then turned dim, even seeming to disappear as it rose, spreading out, above the planes of sunlight.

"It is unbelievable to me," his father said, "that the Congress of the United States could pass such an insane bill. It is simple insanity. If the Communist Party doesn't register it breaks the law. If it does register, it admits to the status of conspiracy to overthrow the United States. It is damned if it does, and damned if it doesn't. Only insane men could make such a law. Only insane men could expect it to survive in the Courts." His father laughed in a kind of fake astonishment. His father's face was flushed and his eyes were bright. He looked very happy and excited.

A man said, "But my dear Isaacson, that this should be unbelievable to you! Do you have a lingering respect for the United States Congress that you are so astonished? Do you expect more from these atavars? Half of them are criminals; and the other half are petty bourgeois profiteers. Every southern Congressman is in office illegally, and each session they all vote to increase the appropriation of the Un-American Activities Committee. What is so unbelievable?"

His father laughed again. The man who spoke sat in the big chair with the edges that came out; so that if you sat back your face couldn't be seen from the side. He sat with his arms folded across his chest and his feet crossed at the ankles. Daniel had never seen him before.

"The fact is," the man said, "the politicians are quite aware that the Mundt-Nixon bill is unconstitutional. Furthermore, they know it will not go to a vote in the Senate before the end of the legislative session. Their intent is not to pass a simple bill making the American Communist an outlaw; they are not in a position to do that—yet. Their intent is to stifle and intimidate the forces of progressivism in this country, to turn back the tide of history, which is, of course, futile. But things will get worse before they get better—the deportations, the contempt proceedings, the blacklists, the jailings—it is all part of the Wall Street conspiracy, it is the reflex of capitalist imperialism trying to shore up its rotting foundations. That is the whole purpose of the so-called "cold war." That is the whole purpose of our foreign policy since the death of Roosevelt. American capitalism conceives, quite correctly, that it can only survive in opposition to socialist democracy; that is the real meaning of the Truman Doctrine. That is why we ring our socialist ally who won the war in the East and thereby prevented Fascism from engulfing the West—that is why we ring her borders with military bases. That is what you do to a man who does you a favor. You cannot admit your debt, so you find a way to hate him. We made love with Soviet Russia during the war because we needed her. Now we jilt her once again and resume the great conspiracy that has gone on since the very days of the Revolution when American troops occupied Siberia in hopes of restoring Czarist tyranny."

"A drink?" his father said. "Some coffee?"

"Nothing, thank you. But you see, the domestic aspects of the cold war, all the counterrevolutionary harassment, will have just the opposite effect of what they want. It will only unify and strengthen and broaden the progressive movement in this country. It will open the eyes and politically develop all those who may have otherwise believed that imperialist capitalism is reasonable, and that there are other less radical answers than Marxism-Leninism for the social transformation of America."

"He speaks so well," a voice whispered behind Daniel. This was not a judgment he would have made himself. He didn't like the man. The man was show-offy. He thought he was a big shot. Yet looking at his father, Daniel could tell that his father would agree with the whisper behind him. His father had looked around proudly while the man talked, glad to show the man off to the people in the room. His father sucked on the cigar, his eyes glittering behind the glasses that enlarged them. His face was red under the heavy beard-shadow. He really liked this show-off man.

"Tell me, Isaacson. Surely this is nothing you don't already know."

"Yes, in my mind. Of course, I understand what the issues are. But I cannot help being shocked by Fascistic insanity in this country. It bothers me, I cannot help it. Whenever it exhibits itself, it shocks me."

"And you find it unbelievable . . . You are still a young man, Isaacson. You are not fully matured. You have a good heart, but it deceives you. If you cannot recognize the forces of reaction and their dialectical inevitability, they become twice as dangerous. It is a terrible mistake to expect any enlightenment from them. Of such errors was the Browder heresy composed. One forgets how young you are."

His father was blushing wildly. "He only looks old," said Dr. Mindish, the dentist, who always thought he was so funny. Everyone laughed.

Daniel went outside. He stood on the narrow porch and played his ship game. He was the captain on the bridge of his sailing ship—the house was the ship—and a great storm blew. He held onto the porch railing and squinted his eyes, and swayed slowly as the great storm attacked the ship. He made the sound effect, marvelously real in his own ears, of the mainmast cracking, splintering, and crashing to the deck in a tangle of lines and torn sheets.

It was Sunday afternoon, and the street was empty. He walked down the front steps. At the curb he stepped between two parked cars and looked both ways and then ran across the street to the schoolyard fence. At this end, Weeks Avenue, there was a drop of thirty to forty feet from the street to the schoolyard. The schoolyard was built into the hill that rose from Eastburn Avenue to Weeks Avenue. It was a full city block long, and half a block wide. At the other end, Eastburn Avenue, the schoolyard was level with the street. Once, playing on the porch he had seen a woman walking along the fence right here, coming home past the school. In her arms she had two bags with groceries. As he looked up and saw her, a car skidded up on the sidewalk and smashed her right through the schoolyard fence, and she disappeared. The front end of the car was stuck through the fence, and the wheels turned in the air. The police came, and there were a lot of people, and when he went across the street to look, the woman was lying down in the schoolyard; she had been carrying bottles of milk in her grocery bags, and the bottles had broken and the milk was mixed with her blood, and glass was in it. She was dead and they carried her to the Eastburn Avenue end in a stretcher, with a blanket over her, and her arm hung over the edge of the stretcher, bobbing up and down as if she was still alive.

His mother said she knew the woman's daughter. That had been a long time ago. Then they had pulled the car out and washed the schoolyard down below with hoses. A policeman stood by the hole. Then, a few days later, they came and put in a new section of fence that even now was brighter and shinier and more silvery than the rest of the fence. Although not as much as when it was new.

The schoolyard was empty. There had been a grownup softball game this morning, but now in the afternoon, it was so hot no one wanted to be in the sun. There was a long flight of stone steps going up from the yard to the school. That was the entrance for kindergarten to second grade. The school was like a castle. It was purple. It had rows and rows of long windows. It was the largest building he had ever seen. Standing where he was, he could see his classroom which looked over the schoolyard. Sometimes in class he leaned over the big radiator, if it wasn't hot, and hoisted himself up to the window when the teacher wasn't looking, so he could see his house.

He turned around. On the porch his mother and father were saying goodbye to the man who was such a big shot. The man shook his father's hand, tipped his hat to his mother, and went down the steps. His parents watched the man until he disappeared around the corner.

He wondered where the man lived. The man talked the way his father talked, but he was no friend of his father's. Fathers talked to each other in big words. Of course, he understood that it was about ways of making things better for working people. But what did the talk do to all the houses—it seemed to him that the talk should do something to the houses, but it never did. The houses remained unmoved. The apartment houses rising like steps along 173rd Street from Eastburn Avenue up to

Weeks. The private red-brick houses along Eastburn. The hills of houses all around. Only the schoolyard, like a big square pit, had no houses.

Daniel waited for his mother and father to see him and call to him. His father's sleeves were rolled up and his mother was in her stocking feet. They turned, and went back in, his hand on her shoulder. Daniel climbed the fence as high as he could, which wasn't very high. Not even a jump from the ground. It was a chain link fence, and the mesh made diamond-shaped holes. In these holes you had to place the toes of your shoes—he knew the technique all right, but he couldn't do it yet. Hanging on the fence, he looked back across the street. He had an odd house. It was the only house on the whole street unattached to any other. There was an apartment house on one side, and a row of private houses on the other. All the other houses were made of brick, but his was dark green asphalt siding, notched in squares to make it look like brick, but which fooled nobody. You could pick at it and pieces would snap off like linoleum. At the corners of the house it curled up.

It was the way the wind could sweep up the hill over the schoolyard right at his house and, during a storm, actually make the inside wall near the front door wet, that alarmed him sometimes. The sky here offered no protection, it was too open. There was an unguarded feeling, a sense of vulnerability to the sky around your shoulders and the back of your neck.

And if the house was no protection, that was truly terrifying. Except now with Grandma dead, it would be better. She would not be grabbing him around the neck to give him a penny. She would not have her fits and curse at him. He didn't have to wonder whether today would be a day she would love him, or a day she would hate him. The baby would have her room now; and he would have his room all for himself. There would not be that dying madwoman old grandma who the day she died he saw naked. She was very white and her hair was combed out on the pillow, and she did not look like an old lady. Lying on the bed naked while the doctor listened to her heart. He saw it just for a second as he walked by her door into his room. A whiteness.

He thought of Williams. Crossing the street, he went around to the side of the house, down the alley to the side door where Williams lived in the cellar. He was being brave, but really he didn't think Williams was there. When he opened the door, his eyes were not used to the darkness, and by the time he saw Williams, the super had already observed him. And in that voice of murder and menace, so deep that it sounded like singing, Williams said, "What you want?"

The cellar smelled of ashes, of dust, of garbage, and of the green poison in the corners for the mice and roaches. There was also the smell of Williams which filled the basement like its weather, which terrified him—an overwhelming burning smell which proved that Williams ruled in the cellar, that even though his family lived in the house, the cellar belonged to Williams. It was the smell of his constant anger.

I was fascinated by everything he did. He could fix anything. I didn't know whether he was an old man or a young man. I couldn't tell. He was very tall and strong, but his fuzzy hair was grey. He was powerful, but he walked slowly, with an effort. Whatever he did was monumental. Shoveling coal—I remember him shoveling coal. It would be summertime. He wore no shirt under his overalls. The coal truck with its chain wheels would back up to the curb in front of the house; the driver would leave the motor on to power the uptilting bed, and climb over the back gate of the truck and sit astride it as it tilted more and more dangerously. Then he'd pull a lever and out would spill the coal with a fearful clattering to the sidewalk, where Williams waited with his shovel. Williams would begin his work while the truck was still there, and would be at it long after the truck had left: diminishing that gigantic mountain of coal shovelful by shovelful, heaving the coal from the pile into the wheelbarrow. When the wheelbarrow was full, he'd plant the shovel in the coalpile and take the barrow down the alley in his slow, torturous, gigantic way. And a few minutes later, bring it back empty and grab the shovel again. Scrape and rattle—that was the sound. The scrape of the shovel on the sidewalk, the momentous silence as the coal flew through the air, and then the rattle of the coal in the wheelbarrow. Williams always shoveled from the bottom, a technique puzzling to a child also puzzled by the transfer of flame from the bottom of one candlewick to the top of another.

"My grandma died," Daniel said, standing by the door. Williams rose from his cot, so incredibly gigantic that he had to stoop slightly to avoid bumping his head on the pipes running along the ceiling. He lumbered toward Daniel, and Daniel tensed himself to run. But Williams grabbed two empty garbage cans near the door and carried them to the darkness of the cellar back near the coalbin. Then he came back and took two more of the cans, lifting them by the rim as if they weighed no more than paper cups. When Williams tended to the garbage cans, they rattled and crashed as loud as thunder. In his own room upstairs, Daniel sometimes heard the cans crashing around under his feet like a storm under the earth, like a storm that would raise the foundations of the house. Now he held his hands over his ears.

Williams slept on a cot without sheets. Next to his bed was an orange crate on its end, with an old wooden radio, shaped like a wishbone, on top of it. Daniel's father had given Williams the radio. The radio was connected by a cord to the light fixture in the ceiling. The light was on. Inside the crate were Williams' clothes, except for his suit which hung on a hanger from a pipe. Also Daniel saw a bottle of whiskey. Williams drank whiskey and got drunk. As he looked at the bottle with his hands over his ears, Williams passed into his vision and sat down on the cot, and took a drink from the bottle.

Williams stared at the floor. "This one trip she ain't comin' back," he said. "She really run away this time."

"She was crazy," Daniel said boldly.

Williams looked at him out of his red, murderous eyes. "Not crazy as some." Daniel understood he meant his mother and father. Now he could hear the footsteps, the murmuring voices of the people visiting upstairs. "She was God-crazy," Williams said. "Nobody believed like she did. Nobody." He took a cigarette butt from behind his ear and lit it with a kitchen match struck with his thumbnail. He did this with great deliberation.

"You don't know nothin'," Williams said. He looked at the ground between his big feet, spread apart. "Wasn't so crazy that she didn't live longer than I goan. You know all those times she

run away? Sometime it was just to stand inside that door there,"
Williams said pointing right at Daniel. "They go chasin' up and
down the blocks, and she standin' right where you are." He
began to laugh, a deep laugh that leaped over its long silences,
jumping in slow motion from one sound to another. "Sometime
she swept up around me. Took a broom and swept the dust,"
Williams said. "Sometime she brought me tea in a glass."

Daniel could see that: she drank tea from a glass. She boiled
the water herself so that no one could poison her. The glass, an
old memory glass of which there were many, was set in a saucer.
She broke a cube of sugar with her fingers (she had strong fingers—he couldn't snap a sugar cube that way), put half of it in
her mouth and sipped the tea through the sugar. Sometimes she
put jelly in the bottom of the glass and stirred it around. Her
pale blue eyes would squint as she sipped the hot tea. At such
times, if she found him watching her, she regarded him with
equal curiosity, a shrewd, keen judging look, neither mad in her
anger, nor mad with her love. She would just look back at him.

"You pretty dumb," Williams said.

"I am not."

"Afraid of that poor old Jew lady."

"I am not."

"She the class in the house," he said, making a motion
toward the ceiling with his head. "Yessuh. I believe I'd gone to
her funeral if it was up to her."

"But she's dead."

"She'd have the super to her funeral."

"But she's dead."

"G'wan!" Williams suddenly roared. He raised himself from
the cot. "Get outta heah!"

Daniel ran, his heart in his throat. He ran up the alley, the
bright sun hurting his eyes. He looked back to see if Williams
was chasing him. He ran into the house, past all the people in
the living room, and he ran upstairs. He passed her door to get
to his room. He stopped. Her room was unchanged. A mahogany
bed and matching bureau. Her cedar hope chest, and her tin of
asthma grass half burned away. He could still smell her. Down
in the kitchen was a memory glass flickering like the kind she

used to light. If she was dead, why could he still smell her? Why was the light still burning?

He ran into his room and slammed the door.

The baby woke and began to cry.

I could never have appreciated how obscure we were. A poor family in the Bronx, too hot in the summer, and too cold in the winter. I thought we were big time. I thought we were important people. I thought the world really revolved around my family. We had this way of understanding everything. There was nothing my father could not explain. And even if it was bad, we always knew what was happening. It was a terrible strain, but I began to understand that it was worth it. We had no modesty, any of us. We were fierce in our self-importance. We were really important to ourselves. Our lives were important and what happened to us was important. The day's small plans and obligations engrossed us. Going to school. To work. Shopping. To the meetings at night, to the recurrent meetings. It was all terribly important. And so when they were taken away, one after the other, and I next saw them on television or a moment of their faces in the newspaper, it was like the world had finally agreed to what I always knew—that we were important people. Recognition was just. It was more than just, it was unsurprising.

But where we lived always seemed to me the essence of obscurity. In the Bronx connected apartment houses fill each city block. Six or seven stories high they line the streets mile after mile. Kids grow up around doorways, on stoops, in courtyards. And in the dark lobbies with their tile floors, and maybe a brass elevator door and a fake old English chair. One block after another. Miles of apartment houses with their halls of cooking smells and their armament of garbage cans at the curb. From the prominence of our little wooden house on Weeks Avenue I could see around the amphitheatrical schoolyard ranks of apartment houses. Beyond my sight I knew there were more Bronx hills, more apartment houses interspersed every fifteen or twenty blocks with a purple castle of a school just like mine.

It was a kind of comfort. Because our vulnerability in this un-usual rotting wooden house on the precipice of this schoolyard street was not so great then. We were different enough not to suffer the obscurity of Bronx architecture. But surrounded by it, we were protected from worse things—storms, fireballs, the marches of ants, floods from the sky—nothing in this part of the world being worth such energy, such destruction. I had it all worked out. The people of the Bronx were beaten. So why bother to destroy them. So why bother with us who lived among them, telltale crimsoning life in our cheeks and life in our eyes. My mother lighted the façades of these houses with her personality. As we walked past them, they were lit in her revulsion. Clutch-ing my hand and pushing the carriage, hurrying up past the stacked tombs of those houses whose sight she bore in hatred and in fear—as if by not walking fast enough we would be contaminated by the life inside them. Rochelle had a profound distaste for the common man. Her life was a matter of taking pains to distinguish herself from her neighbors. Maybe that's why we lived where we did. Who chooses the home, the wife or the husband? We faced no apartment house but only the sky over the schoolyard. The only neighbors were to either side of us and so it was a half-populated street to begin with, and with half-neighbors who faced the same way and at whom we did not have to look. I knew a few of them. My parents were known to all and friends to none. Maybe it was partly the shame of Grandma spinning out of there at odd moments of the day or night, with her wild hair and Yiddish curses, but I doubt it. The public spectacle did not bother Paul that much, I remember him laughing one time as Grandma went by the store on 174th Street and shook her fist at him as she walked past the window. And there was a customer in there, too. Besides, in those days, just after the war, people were still familiar with untranquilized misery. There were more freaks on the streets than you see today. I remember one guy named Iggy who was a macrocephalic and staggered along with the kids following him, staggered along smiling under the weight of his head. He was reputed to be a mathematical genius and nobody knew his age. He was said to be older than he looked.

The fact was Paul and Rochelle did not choose their friends

by accident. People did not become friends simply because they were neighbors. My parents associated only with interesting people. That was her phrase. Respect was to say of someone that he was an interesting person. The dentist was interesting. The furrier. The subway change clerk. The fiddler. The teacher. The welfare worker. These people were interesting. They were not doomed by their shabby apartment buildings. They were not imprisoned by their miserable wages. They were not conditioned to accept slavery. Their minds were free. They had ideas. They met and discussed and contributed money to a dream future. Together like a flock of soft-throated birds they were beautiful to one another, strutting around each other, displaying the plumage of their species, trilling out the key word-cries of this very articulate race of birds that were like the ritual wisdom of their ancestors. They kept each other warm.

Oh yes, Lawd. Oh yes, complacent lawd.

Let's see, what other David Copperfield kind of crap.

So the Trustees of Ohio State were right in 1956 when they canned the English instructor for assigning *Catcher in the Rye* to his freshman class. They knew there is no qualitative difference between the kid who thinks it's funny to fart in chapel, and Che Guevara. They knew then Holden Caulfield would found SDS.

I was born in Washington, D.C., but I remember no home before Weeks Avenue in the Bronx. We moved there in 1945 when I was four years old. Or maybe in 1944 when I was five years old. Of the war I remember some tin cans flattened for a "scrap drive." The idea that bacon fat could be turned into bullets. An old man in a white helmet who was an air-raid warden. Seabees. I remember thick arrows with curving shanks stamped on maps in the newspapers and magazines. I remember the Four Freedoms. I remember what ration stamps looked like, and the stickers A, B or C on the windows of automobiles. I remember In Seventy-Six the Sky Was Red, The Bombs Were Bursting Overhead, and Old King George Couldn't Sleep in His Bed, and on That Stormy Morn—Old Uncle Sam Was Born. I remember President Roosevelt riding up the Grand Concourse in an open car without a hat although the day was chill, and that he looked right at me in the crowd and we waved at each other. I remember the Red Army Chorus singing *Meadow-land,* a virile hypnotic song simulating the canter of horses. I remember studying the picture of the Red Army Chorus on the 78-rpm album, the smiling, deep-throated soldiers of a valiant ally. I remember the horses coming out of the distance bolder and bolder in a rising crescendo of militant brotherhood, storming my heart with their cantering nobility. I remember standing on the porch of our house on Weeks Avenue. It was a warm afternoon and I had scraped my knee on the sidewalk. My mother came out to tell me that an atom bomb had been dropped on Japan. I looked up in the sky over the schoolyard, but the sky was clear. I listened for the sound of the bomb, but the sky was quiet.

Book Two

HALLOWEEN

July–August, 1967,

I was very careful with Phyllis. We lived in a state of convalescence, waking up each morning to find the marriage somewhat stronger but still in need of hugs and kisses and tender lovemaking. A self-conscious period of serious talks showed signs of coming to an end. In these talks she looked for a rationale to forgive me and I was able to help her find one. We tried to share responsibility for my actions. We considered me as our mutual problem. I was shameless. We did our family shopping together on Broadway, and some evenings that were particularly hot I took her to the movies and I held Paul in my lap as he slept and we watched the flick. Our apartment was unlivable on hot days. I spent thirty dollars american for a hassock fan. We live in two rooms on 115th between Broadway and Riverside Drive, right off the breezy Hudson, but you can't tell if you look out the window. We're in the back and we face the back of another apartment house. There are no breezes. You can hear rats in the walls. Phyllis in this time started to dream about moving out of New York. In the morning she walked me over to the library, holding my arm as I carried Paul. She would leave me at the front door of Butler and take Paul and walk off thinking happily about another day's progress on my dissertation and how it would earn me the degree that would free us from New York. She imagined a small college out west where I would be willing to teach and she might even enroll as a student. It would be nothing like Columbia. No soot in the grass. I didn't disabuse her. Perhaps she could summon up my dissertation, actually create it, just by imagining me here in the library. Why not, if her imagination was good enough?

One autumn day, with the wind slicing through the chain link fence around the schoolyard, and heavy grey clouds racking into each other over the rooftops of apartment houses, Rochelle went shopping with her son, Daniel, and her baby daughter, Susan. Daniel, as he was instructed, held onto the white wicker stroller his mother was pushing. It was an old summer stroller, with small, solid wheels and streamlined raindrop fenders like the wheelcovers on racing planes of the 1930's, and a top that could swing back to let the sun in. Daniel himself had ridden in it when he was a baby. Now it was Susan's. Rochelle had wrapped a blanket about the legs of the little girl and snugged it up to her chin. Daniel wore his mackinaw and a hunter's cap with the earflaps pulled down. They were going to the butcher's and then to the Daitch Dairy and maybe they'd stop in and say hello to their father in his store. I think this was in 1949 or 1950. I was seven or eight. Susan was about four. As we came down alongside the purple castle of a school and crossed Eastburn Avenue on 174th Street, and passed the shoemaker, Rochelle suddenly began to walk very fast, going past the Daitch Dairy, Daniel running to catch up with his hand.

"My God," his mother said. "My God, it's happened."

The carriage bounced off the curb into the street at Morris Avenue and Susan cried out in fright. Up ahead, in the middle of the next block, a crowd stood in front of Isaacson Radio, Sales and Repair. Rochelle had no time for amenities, raising the front wheels of the stroller and bringing them down hard on the sidewalk, then the rear wheels. She ran the last half block, her long black coat flapping around her legs. It's happened. That is what she said. Daniel running with his hunter's leather cap flopping around on his head, the peak turning annoyingly off center toward his left ear; Susan, holding on with both hands, peering ahead with her tremulous upper lip ready to yield the potent bawl of outrage.

This street, 174th Street, was just in this time undergoing the shock of the supermarket. An A&P had opened, the size of three or four normal stores; a Safeway would soon follow. Nevertheless, a woman could still shop for meat at a butcher's, and butter and eggs in a dairy, and fish in a fish store, and bread in a bakery. There still in this time came along the street in front of your house a horse-drawn open wagon with vegetables and fruit displayed in their wooden shipping boxes, the vegetable man crying out his prices also written in crayon on brown paper bags stuck on slats between the boxes—the whole store on wooden steelbound wheels, arranged to rise up from the wagon bed at an angle so the lady could see everything available. The man would twirl his reins around the wheel brake, urge the horse into parking position between the cars, and set up shop for his particular customers, engaging in debates concerning the quality of his fruits and vegetables relative to their prices, clambering all over his wagon for pounds of this or bunches of that at the command of the customer, exchanging philosophical ideas of great gloom with great cheerfulness. When the vegetable man with his broken old horse clattered along past my house, he knew he was the last. A decade before there were scissors sharpeners, and knife grinders, and peddlers with bundles on their backs crying "I cash clothes!" and vendors of homemade ices in the summer and hot sweet potatoes in the winter, themselves relics of the teeming market streets of the Lower East Side at the beginning of the century. At one time, the Bronx had been an escape. In 1900 you beat the Lower East Side by moving to the Bronx. Only remorselessly does history catch up. And all your secret dreams are rooted open to the light. It is History, that pig, biting into the heart's secrets.

I was not doing well in school that year. I was in the third grade. I would not fold my hands at the edge of my desk. I went to the bathroom without raising my hand. I talked when I felt like talking. There were periodic drills in the event of nuclear bombs falling. We marched into the hallways where there were no windows, and sat hunched against the wall, knees up, arms around knees, head down. I suppose it was 1949. All the schools were very big on air-raid drills. The Russians had exploded an atom bomb. Truman was said to be soft on Communism. The Chinese Reds had booted out Chiang Kai-shek. American Communist leaders were on trial for conspiracy to advocate and teach the violent overthrow of the Government. There were lots of air-raid drills in my school. The little girls preferred to kneel with their heads down, and their hands linked in back of their heads. In that way the little boys across the hall couldn't see up their dresses. We drilled in the event of atom bombs falling. My father told me not to sit with my head on my knees, nor to comply with the request to pretend that bombs were falling from the sky. My father cursed all schoolteachers who would train their classes to accept the imminence of war. I was not doing well in school that year.

But one other thing I will have to work on is the feeling of Daniel at that age in his own loose clothes not quite synchronized to the rhythm of discontent-and-crisis, discontent-and-crisis, by which, weirdly, his parents lived in simultaneous fear and hope, defeat and victory. So that running toward his father's store with the crowd in front of it on this windy, autumn afternoon, he is cool enough to perceive that nothing is the matter; that the crowd is amiable, and cops or ambulances are nowhere to be seen. There is no tension in the scene. It is a social occasion. It is the first television set to come to 174th Street, and it is sitting there in the window of Isaacson Radio, Sales and Repair, a great brown console, beaming its tiny moving pictures to the curious crowd.

I should have watched my mother's face at the moment she understood this. But I was pushing forward for a glimpse of Faye Emerson. I doubt if her face softened with relief. I doubt if she smiled at the foolishness of her foreboding.

My father came out of the store and worked his way through the group of people standing there, and ignoring him as he jostled through them. He did not have a coat on, only his shirt with the sleeves rolled up and his work apron with its pockets for tools. He took my mother's arm and together they walked a few feet away from the edge of the gathering, she still pushing the stroller.

"Where did you get that?" Rochelle said.

"It was on order. Listen—"

"Can we take it home?" I asked him.

"Just a minute, Danny. Let me talk to your mother. Mindish has been arrested."

"What!"

"Keep your voice down. Early this morning while he was eating breakfast. The FBI came and took him downtown."

"Oh, my God—"

"Don't say anything to anyone. Go about your business and let everyting remain the same. I'll be home for supper, and then we'll talk."

"How do you know?"

"His wife called me. It was a stupid thing to do. I don't understand the brains of some people. She said Mindish wanted me to know, and told her to call me."

"Oh, Pauly—"

I looked first to my mother's face, then to my father's, riding the current between them which I imagine now as blue television light, a rare element of heavy sorrow and blinding dread.

"What did he do?" I tugged my father's arm.

"You've got to keep calm and control your feelings," my father said to my mother. She was frowning and biting her knuckles. My father picked up Susan and played with her for a moment, pretending to be jolly. "How's my honey," he said to the solemn little girl. "How's my honeybun?"

"Why did they arrest him?"

"I don't know, Danny. They think he's done something. If they didn't arrest people, there would be nothing for them to do. So they decide someone does something he shouldn't and they arrest him."

"Are they going to arrest you?"

My father forced a laugh. "Don't worry."

"What's going to happen," my mother whispers.

"I've told you everything I know. Do me a favor, Rochelle. Get what you need, and go home. I'll be home at the usual time. It's only the coming of Fascism so why should we be surprised."

I associated Dr. Mindish with the smell of plaster and dental paste—a medicinal pungency emanated from him like the taste of a wintergreen Lifesaver. It wasn't unpleasant. Only when he was in his office did you not smell this. When he wore his starched, white tunic, and fussed around his chest of pencil-thin drawers with all their drill bits and instruments, and when he turned on the water jet that went around the bowl, and shoved the cotton in your mouth, and pressed his stomach against your arm, and lowered his hulk over your face, he didn't smell that way. At these times he smelled of salami.

I hated Mindish. He always patronized me. He was a large, bulky man with small eyes and a foreign intonation in his speech, and I had always known that he lacked integrity. He was an opportunist in his conversation, never providing the idea to drive it forward, but always picking up its scraps and litter, like a fat, quick-eyed wolf, I thought, with the humorous smile of a wolf. It was a matter of sorrow to me that my parents regarded him as a friend. He was the family dentist and he always hurt me when I went there. There was about him some vicious eroticism. He was always looking at Rochelle's tits or ass, a fact which she didn't seem to notice. He was always treating Paul with his clumsy humor like a ridiculous child, with shards of envy perhaps for Paul's mind or youth, or energy. Mindish was much older than my mother and father. I think he was in his fifties when he was arrested.

I was pleased by the news. I thought if the G-men had to arrest someone, as my father said because if they didn't they would have nothing to do, then they had made a wise choice in arresting Mindish. I felt that if it had been my job to arrest someone, I would have chosen Mindish too.

Early the next morning, as I was leaving for school, the doorbell rang and I opened the door and two men were standing on the porch. They were dressed neatly, and did not appear to be of the neighborhood. They had thin, neat faces and small noses, and crew-cut hair. They held their hats in their hands and wore nice overcoats. I thought maybe they were from one of those

Christian religions that sent people from door to door to sell their religious magazines.

"Sonny," said one, "is your mother or father home?"

"Yes," I said. "They're both home."

My mother did not allow me to delay going to school just because the FBI had come to the door. I don't know what happened on that first visit. The men went inside and, going down the splintery front steps, I turned and caught a glimpse of Paul coming out of the kitchen to meet them just as the door closed. My mother was holding the door and my father was coming forward in his ribbed undershirt, looking much skinnier than the two men who rang the bell.

When the FBI knocks on your door and wants only to ask a few questions, you do not have to consent to be asked questions. You are not required to talk to them just because they would like to talk to you. You don't have to go with them to their office. You don't have to do anything if you are not subpoenaed or arrested. But you only learn the law as you go along.

"They don't know what they want," Paul says to Rochelle. "It's routine. If you don't talk to them, they have nothing to pin their lies on. They are clumsy, obvious people."

"I'm frightened," my mother says. "*Polizei* don't have to be smart."

"Don't worry," Paul says. "Mindish won't suffer from anything we said." He is walking back and forth in the kitchen and he is pounding his fist into his palm. "We have done nothing wrong. There is nothing to be afraid of."

It develops that all of Mindish's friends are being questioned. Nobody knows what he is being held for. There has been no announcement on the radio, there has been no story in the newspaper. Sadie Mindish is in a state of hysterical collapse. Her apartment has been searched. Her daughter has stayed home from school. Nobody knows if they even have a lawyer.

The next day the same two FBI men come back again, this time in the early evening. They sit on the stuffed, sprung couch in the living room parlor with their knees together and their hats in their hands. They are very soft-spoken and friendly. Their strange names are Tom Davis and John Bradley. They smile at me while my mother goes to the phone to call my father.

"What grade are you in, young fellow?"

I don't answer. I have never seen a real FBI man this close before. I peer at them, looking for superhuman powers, but there is no evidence that they have any. They look neither as handsome as in the movies nor as ugly as my parents' revulsion makes them. I search their faces for a clue to their real nature. But their faces do not give clues.

When Paul comes home, he is very nervous.

"My lawyer has advised me that I don't have to talk to you if I don't want to," my father said. "That particular fact you neglected yesterday to mention."

"Well, yes sir, Mr. Isaacson, but we were hoping you would be cooperative. We're only looking for information. It's nothing mysterious. We thought you were a friend of Doctor Mindish. As his friend, you may be in a position to help him."

"I will be glad to answer any questions in a court of law."

"Do you deny now that you know him?"

"I will answer any questions in a court of law."

The two men leave after a few minutes, and then they sit in their car, double-parked in front of the house, for ten or fifteen minutes more. They appear to be writing on clipboards or on pads, I can't tell exactly. It is dark and they have turned on the interior car light. I am reminded of a patrol man writing a parking ticket. But the sense is of serious and irrevocable paperwork, and I find it frightening. There is some small, grey light in the dark sky over the schoolyard. The wind is making whistling noises at the edges of the window.

"Danny!" Rochelle says sharply. "Get away from there."

My father takes my place at the curtains. "That is outrageous," he says. "Don't you see, it is part of the treatment. They are trying to shake us up. But we're too smart for them. We're onto them. They can sit out there all night for all I care."

The next day is worse. At lunch my father tells my mother he is sure someone has searched the shop. When he unlocked the door this morning, he felt that things were slightly out of place. It wasn't anything he could pinpoint exactly. Maybe the tubes in the trash barrel. Maybe the customer tickets. It was more like a sense of things having been disturbed.

Our lunch is muenster cheese sandwiches on pumpernickel

and canned tomato soup. My father doesn't eat. He sits with his elbow on the table and his hand to his head. He nods, as if he agrees with something he has decided.

"That's it. That's why they came here and asked you to call me home. They could just as easily have come to the store, couldn't they? But they didn't. They wanted to make sure I was home when they wanted to search my store."

My mother discounts this. She says they could have waited until late at night and achieved the same thing. I understand that she is deliberately minimizing the situation. She suggests that perhaps my father is imagining the whole thing about the store being searched. As the pressure increases, she seems to be calming down. Her own hysteria has passed. She is worried about Paul. She is into the mental process which in the next three years will harden into a fortitude many people will find repugnant.

"Did you have your test, Danny?"

"This afternoon."

"Do you know all the words?"

"Yes."

But there are dark circles under her eyes. When I come home from school, the FBI men are sitting outside again in their car. My mother is lying down on the couch with a washcloth across her head. Her left forearm is bandaged. While ironing she gave herself a terrible burn. The edges of our existence seem to be crumbling. The house is cold and Williams has come up from the cellar to say in his deepest voice of menace that the furnace is not working properly and has to be cleaned. He will get to it when he can. I understand this means he will get to it when he does not feel abused by the situation. All my senses are in a state of magnification. I hang around the house feeling the different lights of the day. I drink the air. I taste the food I eat. Every moment of my waking life is intensified and I know exactly what is happening. A giant eye machine, like the mysterious black apparatus at the Hayden Planetarium with the two diving helmet heads and the black rivets and its insect legs, is turning its planetary beam slowly in our direction. And that is what is bringing on the dark skies and the cold weather. And when it reaches us, like the prison searchlight in the Nazi concentration camp, it will stop. And we will be pinned, like the lady jammed through the schoolyard fence with her blood mixed with the milk and broken bottles. And our blood will hurt as if it had glass in it. And it will be hot in that beam and our house will smell and smoke and turn brown at the edges and flare up in a great, sucking floop of flame.

And that is exactly what happens.

If they had something on them before Mindish was arraigned, why didn't they pick them up? If they were suspects before Mindish made his deal, why were they given four weeks to run away, or destroy incriminating evidence, or otherwise damage the case against them? The only answer is FBI stupidity or inefficiency, and that is a reasonable answer but not a good one.

Smoking. In Japan in the 16th century, Christians were winnowed out by having the entire population of a village walk across an image of Christ painted on rice paper and placed on the ground. Those who refused to step on Christ's face were immediately taken out of the procession and hanged upside down over a slow-burning sulfur fire. This is one of the slowest and most painful forms of execution known to civilization: the victim's eyes hemorrhage and his flesh is slowly smoked. His blood boils, and his brain roasts in its own juices. Death may come as late as the second week, without the victim's previous loss of consciousness.

First the strangulation of the phone. There are fewer calls each day. Then a period during which the phone rings once, twice, and is silent. Or I pick it up in time, but there is no answer. Finally, the phone stops ringing altogether. It is a dead thing. My father takes to making his outgoing calls in candy stores up and down 174th Street. I enjoy negotiating with him for nickels I happen to have. He needs lots of change, and during the day in school I make a point of trading off quarters for the small stuff. I like to be useful for his evening trips to the phone booth. I make no profit, I merely want to be a help to him. He travels farther and farther from the house, using up phone booths the way he uses up change.

Meanwhile, the newspapers have been reporting a chain action of arrests around the world. An English scientist. An American engineer. A half-dozen immigrants in Canada. Secrets have been stolen. The FBI has been finding these people, and convicting them in the same press release. A chain reaction. My father comes home, not only with the *Daily Worker*, the *Times*, and the *Post*, but the *Telegram*, the *Tribune*, and even the *News*, *Mirror* and *Journal-American*. He is reading everything. He speaks of auto-da-fé, and I see a Nazi demagogue, Otto Duffy, a sinister European whose Fascist ideas are sweeping over the United States. And it is not just spy arrests, but political trials like Foster and Dennis, and the other Party leaders. It is the defamation of New Dealers like Alger Hiss. It is the Un-American Activities Committee investigations of Hollywood writers. It is the Attorney General's list of subversive organizations. My father paints a picture: our house is completely surrounded by an army of madmen.

One night he reads aloud a *New York Times* story in which it is said that political discussion of any kind has virtually disappeared from college campuses. The *Times* has done a survey. Professors are afraid of being misinterpreted. It is becoming necessary in state universities to sign loyalty oaths.

"You hear, Rochelle? What does it tell you? You know where it ends, Rochelle."

"Shhh, Pauly. You'll wake the children."

I was afraid to go to sleep. I had terrible nightmares which I couldn't remember except in waking from them in terror and suffocation. I was terrified that if I went to sleep, the house would burn down, or that my parents would go away somewhere without telling us. For some reason, the second of these possibilities came to seem more likely. I would lie in the dark and think that I couldn't fall asleep because the minute I did, they would leave me and Susan and go somewhere they had never told me about. A secret place. It's the same thing when you catch them fucking, the same terror of exclusion. Flopping about, completely out of control, these people who control you.

Grunting and moaning and gasping, who have told you to tie your shoelaces and drink your juice. I could feel now in everything since Mindish's arrest, a coming to stay in our lives of the worst possible expectations. The world was arranging itself to suit my mother and father, like some mystical alignment of forces in the air; so that frictionless and in physical harmony, all bodies and objects were secreting the one sentiment that was their Passion, that would take them from me.

Where they might run off to did not occur to me as jail. I thought of it as a harmonic state of being. Gradually, I recognized the location. It was somewhere near Peekskill, when Paul got beaten up. He lay for days on the living room couch-bed with his headaches and puffed mouth, and his broken arm, and Rochelle took care of him. Her ministrations were devoted but practical, like an army nurse in a field hospital. She was as grimly involved as he in what he had done. They didn't seem to notice me. I understood the universe stood in proper relation at last to the family ego.

OH PAULY, OH MY POP, IT'S ALL RIGHT, IT REALLY IS ALL RIGHT. BUT WHY DID YOU HAVE TO GIVE YOUR GLASSES TO MINDISH?

One morning Daniel heard a knock on the door. He recognized the hour. You have to know the house to see what happened. The front door was on the left side of the house as you faced it from the inside. It opened onto a short hall, and on the right-hand side of the hall was the entrance to the living room. Halfway down this short, dark hall was the narrow stairs that went up to the two bedrooms. Under the stairs was the place we kept the carriage and also old newspapers. Just beyond this area was the doorway to the kitchen which was behind the living room in location. I tell you this (who?) so that you may record in clarity one of the Great Moments of the American Left. The American Left is in this great moment artfully reduced to the shabby conspiracies of a couple named Paul and Rochelle Isaacson. They sleep in a foldaway couch-bed in the living room. They bought it from Pauly's older sister, Frieda, my Aunt Frieda, with the mole with one hair coming out of it just above her upper lip, when she moved into a smaller apartment, after her husband died. The front hall is linoleum. A little side table, just out of range of the door when it opens, holds the phone and the Bronx phone book.

When Daniel opened the door, there stood the two FBI agents, Tom Davis and John Bradley. Behind them, across the street, frost in the crotches of the chain link fence of the school-yard shone in the early morning sun like stars in Daniel's eyes.

"Hi, Danny. Is your Dad at home?"

"What is it, Daniel?" his mother called from the living room.

"It's those two men," Daniel replied.

Daniel and the FBI men listened to the sounds of his mother waking up his father. Daniel still held the doorknob. He was ready to close the door the second he was told to.

"What time is it?" said his father in a drugged voice.

"Oh my God, it's six-thirty," his mother said.

She came into the hallway, pulling on her robe. Her long nightgown was thin cotton and Daniel panicked for a second because you could see the tips of her breasts through the material until she wrapped the robe around her and tied the belt. He glanced at the two men in the door to see if they saw, but there was nothing in their faces.

"Morning, Mrs. Isaacson. Can we come in?"

His mother was combing back her thick hair with her fingers. She turned her attention to the two men at the door, who by this time had become acquaintances of a sort. They had cultivated a we're-all-in-this-thing-together kind of approach. The idea in their exaggeratedly wry suffering of my father's verbal abuse and stubbornness was that they preferred having no part of this messy situation, but as long as they were assigned to this job, perhaps some mutual kindness and even a bit of humor would make it easier for everyone concerned. Once they even alluded to the pressure on them from their "higher-ups."

"Who are these higher-ups?" my father had said.

"Now, Paul, we're supposed to ask you the questions."

"So you're not getting enough out of me," my father said, not without pride.

"You're a tough nut, all right," one of them said. "Next thing we know, you'll be trying to indoctrinate us."

"Well, I'll tell you something. I have answered your questions about me. I have told you my biographical details. I have not answered questions about anyone else."

"You mean like Doctor Mindish?"

"I have said what I mean. But I am curious about you. I am curious that a man of reasonable intelligence like yourself would choose to become a tool of the ruling class. I would like to know what makes you do it? What is your motivation? What are you saying to all the poor and sick and exploited individuals in this country when you join this Federal Bureau of Inquisition?"

"Well now, we don't see things just the way you commies do, Paul."

Either my mother nodded that they could come in, or they took her silence as permission. I know she would have been anxious to keep the cold out. They walked through the door and immediately there was an electric charge of life just outside, and right behind them came another man, then two more, then a few more, all warmly dressed and well tailored for the harsh autumn morning, a dozen FBI men, all told, bringing into our little splintery house all the chill of the outdoors on their bulky shoulders. They poured through the front door like an avalanche of snow.

"What is it now!" my mother shouted.

"Rochelle!" my father called.

I looked outside. Five or six sedans were double-parked along the street. Another car was pulling up. Two more of the G-men stood on the sidewalk. Another was going down the alley to come in through the basement. In my ears was the crackle of a turned-up police radio.

My father was shown the warrant for his arrest as he sat on his hide-a-bed with his bare feet on the floor. He groped around for his glasses. He told my mother he felt suddenly nauseous, and she had him bend over with his head between his knees till the feeling went away. She was furious.

"What are these men doing here?" she said to Bradley and Davis. "Do you think you've got John Dillinger? What are you doing?" Men were going through the bookshelves, the bedclothes, the mahogany wardrobe closet. Men were marching upstairs.

My mother stood with Susan in her arms and tears coming down her cheeks. Every piece of furniture in the house had been, in some moment of her life, her utmost concern. She had made every curtain, she had scrubbed and polished every inch of floor. This old, leaky, wooden shack we lived in—and what newspaperman who wrote about the trial ever said a thing about the Isaacsons' poverty, the shabbiness of their home with its broken-down Salvation Army furniture and castoffs, and amateur paint jobs, its stained wallpaper where the rain soaked through the front door.

"Murderers!" my mother cried. "Maniacs! Haven't you hounded us enough? Can't you leave us alone?"

She did not appear to realize that my father had been arrested.

I ran upstairs. Two of them were in my room. They examined my dinosaur book, the model airplane I was working on, and the cigar box I used to hold my marbles. They looked under the mattress on my cot, they lifted the linoleum on the floor, they looked in the closet and went through the blankets and sheets my mother kept there, flapping out each one and then throwing it on the floor. They took the crystal radio my father had helped me make, and the table radio, an old metal Edison that I listened to my programs on, pulling out the plug and wrapping the cord around the radio and tucking it under his arm. And in Susan's room one of them opened the belly of her monkey doll with a penknife and stuck his finger in it and pulled out the stuffing. In Susan's room was my grandma's shiny hope chest, and they were going through that, tossing out Grandma's brown picture of her mother and father, and a *siddur,* two down pillows, and some old clothes of hers, and a lace tablecloth with fringe. Mothballs rattled on the floor. Down at the bottom of the chest was a blue, oblong tin with rounded corners. It was my grandma's last tin of asthma grass. One of them picked it up, opened it slowly, sniffed it, replaced the lid, and wrapped the tin in his handkerchief and put it in his pocket.

Daniel ran back to his own room. His own blue tin filled with pennies of peculiar existence had been opened and the pennies scattered on the floor.

Downstairs the place was a shambles. Broken dishes in the

kitchen. The newspapers from under the stairs strewn about. One of them was picking out copies of the *Daily Worker,* and issues of other papers with stories about ATOM SPIES arrested in England, Canada and New Jersey. A terrible draft swept through the house now, the front door having been propped open. I looked outside. Williams stood on the sidewalk. He was wearing his overalls over a grey sweat shirt. He was wearing slippers. He was looking down the alley. And from under my feet came the thunder of the garbage cans crashing around the cellar.

I don't know how long this went on. There appeared across the street, along the schoolyard fence, growing numbers of children not interested in going to school. People were hanging out of the windows of the apartment houses on 173rd Street. At each corner of our block a regular police patrol car was parked across the intersection. The FBI radio sputtered like my grandma's asthma grass. Teachers were watching. The FBI men were taking all these valuable things to their cars. I stood at the door and watched, and this is what they took: My crystal radio and my radio for listening. A stack of selected newspapers. My father's International Workers' Order insurance policy for five thousand dollars. A toolbox. A year's issues of *Masses and Mainstream.* And the following books: JEWS WITHOUT MONEY by Mike Gold, THE IRON HEEL by Jack London, STATE AND REVOLUTION by V. Lenin, GENE DEBS, THE STORY OF A FIGHTING AMERICAN by Herbert Marais and William Cahn, THE PRICE OF FREE WORLD VICTORY by Henry A. Wallace, Vice President of the United States, THE GREAT CONSPIRACY by Michael Sayers and Albert E. Kahn, WHO OWNS AMERICA by James S. Allen (the cover shows a fat capitalist with a top hat and a dollar sign inscribed on his belly, sitting in front of a factory on top of a big bag marked *profits*—oh, Red cartoons! Oh, Robert Minor with your sexy goddess of freedom lying raped and bleeding, and your workingmen of the giant arms, and the clasped hands of your black and white brothers, and your ranks of workers advancing toward the cringing capitalist bosses, I salute you! I salute you, Creator of the anti-comic strip! In such bold strokes of the charcoal pencil is my childhood forever rubbed into my subversive brain, oh, Robert Minor, oh, William Gropper, geniuses of the pencil stroke, precision tools of working-class dreams, agitators, symbol-makers, vanguard of the vanguard with your unremitting proprietorship of the public outrage) and THE STORY OF THE FIVE YEAR PLAN by M. Ilin. This last book is from my room. It is a translation of a primer for Russian children. My father gave it to me and said to keep it in my room until I was old enough to read it. I am old enough, but have not gotten around to reading past the first chapter.

> On the bank of a large river, great cliffs are being broken into bits. Fierce machines resembling prehistoric monsters clamber clumsily up the steps of a gigantic ladder hewed out of the mountain . . . A river appears where none existed before, a river one hundred kilometers long . . . A swamp is suddenly transformed into a broad lake . . . On the steppe, where formerly only feather grass and redtop grew, thousands of acres of wheat wave in the breeze . . . Airplanes fly above the Siberian taiga, where in little cabins live people with squinting eyes clad in strange dress made of animal skins . . . In the Kalmik region, in the middle of the naked steppe, grow buildings of steel and concrete alongside the felt tents of the nomads . . . Steel masts rise over the whole country: each mast has four legs and many arms, and each arm grasps metal wires . . . Through these wires runs a current, runs the power and the might of rivers and waterfalls, of peat swamps and coal beds. All this . . . is called the Five Year Plan.

Daniel stood in the entrance to the living room. He was still in his pajamas. The cold of the morning had driven itself into his chest. It filled his chest and his throat. It pressed at the backs of his eyes. He was frightened of the way he felt. The cold hung like ice from his heart. His little balls were encased in ice. His knees shifted in ice. He shivered and ice fell from his spine. His father was dressed now, standing in his good suit of grey glen plaid with the wide lapels and square shoulders hanging in slopes off his shoulders and the wide green-forest tie and the white shirt already turning up at the collars, buttoning his two-button jacket with one hand, and his face, unshaven, turned in a moment's attitude of trying to remember something, trying to remember as if it was on the floor, this sadness, this awful sadness of trying to remember, so unaccustomedly dressed up in his over-large suit with the pleated trousers and cuffs almost covering his brown wing-tipped shoes, and his other hand rises limply from the wrist, his arm rises, and he doesn't seem to care, attached to a handcuff as the man who holds him captured lifts his hands to light his cigarette, my father's hand going along in tow, the agent cupping his match and lighting his cigarette, and my father's hand dangling, having moved just as far as the other man moved it.

I remember that Susan was crying, "Why they do that to Daddy? Why they do that to Daddy?" over and over, "Why they do that to Daddy?" and that my mother was rocking her, holding her tightly, and swaying with Susan in her arms saying shhhh, shhh . . . But Susan was hysterical, sobbing with great gasps for air. We have none of us ever had enough to breathe. I kicked the FBI in the shins and I butted them in the groin, and I screamed and raged, and swung my fists at them. I know I hurt a couple of them. But I was shoved aside. And when I came back, I was lifted by the hands and feet, and flopping and squirming like a snake, and You leave my pop alone! I'll kill you, I'll kill you! I was dropped behind the stairs in the pile of papers. My father was hustled out the door. I was on my knees, warmed by my own tears, thawed in my rage, and I saw his face as he turned for one brief moment and yelled over his shoulder: "Ascher!"

And then it was terribly quiet. And all the cars were gone, and the gaping people were gone, and the door was closed, and I looked at my weeping mother, and I held her baby daughter for her as she dialed the phone. And I realized my father was really gone.

The Isaacsons are arrested for conspiring to give the secret of television to the Soviet Union. . .

So Ascher came into our lives, the first Surrogate. Ascher was not a left-wing lawyer. He had spent his professional life practicing in the Bronx, primarily in civil law. He was what my Aunt Frieda called a Jewish gentleman. Ascher was the kind of lawyer who quietly handles all the legal affairs of his Synagogue for years without compensation. He was in his sixties when I first saw him, the large features of his face showing the signs of his emphysema. His mouth was stretched wide, his eyes deep-set and slightly bulging. I felt the weight of my grief when Ascher was around because, like a doctor, he would not have been there unless something was wrong. But I didn't dislike him. He had enormous hands, and a gruff condescension to children that I did not find inappropriate or offensive.

Ascher was a pillar of the Bronx bar. He was not brilliant, but his law was sound, and his honor as a man, as a religious man, was unquestionable. He was an honest lawyer, and was dogged for his clients. I picture him on Yom Kippur standing in the pew with his homburg on his head, and a tallis around his shoulders. Ascher could wear a homburg and a tallis at the same time.

He was not my parents' first choice. My parents were not accustomed to dealing with lawyers, or accountants, or bank tellers. I think now my father must have called a half-dozen lawyers on the recommendations of his friends, before he found Ascher. Lawyers were not anxious to handle any case involving the FBI, even left-wing lawyers. When my father was trying to find a lawyer while fending off the FBI visits, the case was open-ended, as any sharp lawyer understood. Maybe Ascher understood this too. He certainly understood that this was a bad time in history for anyone whom the law turned its eye on who was a Red, or a "progressive" as Communists had come to characterize themselves. Since 1946, indecent things had happened in the country. He lectured Rochelle as if she might not know. The Democrats under Harry Truman competed with the Republicans in Congress to see who could be rougher on the Left. People were losing their jobs and their careers for things they said or appeals they had supported fifteen years before. People were accused, investigated and fired from their jobs without knowing what the charges were, or who made them. People were blacklisted in their professions. Public confessions of error had become a national rite, just as in Russia. Witnesses naming friends and acquaintances seen at meetings twenty years before were praised by Congressmen. Informing was the new ethic. Ex-Communists who would testify about Party methods, and who would write confessionals, made lots of money. The measure of their success was the magnitude of their sin. It was the time of the Red Menace. The fear of Communists taking over the PTA and Community Chest affected the lives of ordinary people in ordinary towns. Anyone who knew anyone who was a Communist felt tainted. Everything that could be connected to the Communists took on taint. People who defended their civil liberties on principle. The First, Fifth and Fourteenth Amendments to the Constitution. Pablo Picasso, because he had attended the Communists' World Peace Congress in Paris and painted doves for peace. Doves. Peace. There was a new immigration control bill and alien deportation bill, and a control of American citizens abroad bill. And there was an internal security bill providing for concentration camps for anyone who might be expected to commit espionage. And there were now people who couldn't get passports, and there were now people who couldn't find jobs, and there were now people jailed for contempt, and there were now people who couldn't find Mark Twain in the library because the Russians liked him and he was a best seller over there.

Ascher said: "And the Soviets have not helped matters with their bomb. They are now as dangerous as we are. That is intolerable. And the Communists in China now run the show there. We find that intolerable too. It is not a period that our historians will be proud of us. We are in the mood that someone should pay for what we find intolerable. If you are not Robert Taft, watch out."

This was hardly the kind of talk my mother could find comforting. Ascher was not a tactful man. He lacked a bedside manner. You accepted the way he was because of his obvious integrity, and because you had no choice. Ascher was not a political man, you could imagine him voting for anyone he found morally recognizable, no matter what the party. If anything, he was conservative. He perceived in the law a codification of the religious sense of life. He was said to have worked for years on a still unfinished book demonstrating the contributions of the Old Testament to American law. For Ascher witchhunting was paganism. Irrationality was a sin. He came to our cold house and sat without taking off his coat, and with his homburg shoved back on his head, he asked a few questions and answered a few questions, and nodded and sighed, and shook his head. For Ascher, my parents' communism was easily condoned because it was pathetic and gutsy at the same time. One of the people who wrote about Paul and Rochelle, a Jewish literary critic, said that they were so crass and hypocritical that they even called on their Jewish faith to sustain sympathy for themselves in their last months. This writer could not have understood Ascher. Or the large arms of ethical sanctity he could wrap around an atheistic Communist when in the person of a misfit Jew as ignorant as my father of the real practical world of men and power. Ascher understood how someone could forswear his Jewish heritage and take for his own the perfectionist dream of heaven on earth, and in spite of that, or perhaps because of it, still consider himself a Jew.

THE EDUCATION OF A LAWYER

We will watch this well-meaning but outclassed man as he goes downtown on the subway and learns the law as it is administered by highly motivated Federal prosecuting agencies.

After the FBI had been through the store, my mother opened it up so that customers could recover whatever was fixed, and so that we could collect whatever money my father had earned. We needed every dollar. We hadn't enough for the rent, and while Ascher had said not to think about his fee, there was now a big, new expense to worry about in addition to everything else.

I took to my mother my blue tin of pennies and gave them to her: there was about eighty cents. She cried and hugged me as I had known she would. I wanted to see her cry. I wanted her to hug me. I wanted her to experience the poignancy of the moment I had planned.

Very few people came to the store. Those who did kept their faces averted, as if by looking my mother in the eye they would contract her misfortune. Somehow I knew there was gossip to the effect that Rochelle had gall to stand in the store with her children where everyone could see her in her shame. Nobody wanted to come near us. In this Jewish neighborhood Paul Isaacson was bad for the Jews. Had not McCarthy made a speech describing the great battle between international atheistic communism and Christianity? There was no question in anyone's mind where the Jews belonged according to Joe McCarthy.

My mother was embittered by the reaction of the neighborhood. She thought about calling up those who had not picked up their radios, but decided against it. "We could be living in a peasant village," she told Ascher. "The fear, the ignorance. No one, not even the few who are sympathetic, has considered that my husband might be innocent."

"Even among the educated," Ascher said. "That is the effect of a Federal Grand Jury indictment. It strains the presumption of innocence. But don't worry, a court is still a court, and that is where it will be decided. Not on 174th Street, but in the courtroom."

My father had been indicted along with Selig Mindish and unnamed others for conspiring to violate the Espionage Act of 1917. His bail had been set at one hundred thousand dollars. That meant he would be in jail until his trial, which Ascher said was months away. Ascher had pleaded that the bail was excessive, but his plea was rejected. The Korean War was going badly, the papers were speculating on the physical damage one atom bomb could do to the City of New York. So many hundreds of thousands dead; so many millions dying of radiation sickness; so many familiar streets turned into rubble.

The store was closed.

Here do the scene of Rochelle and her two children and Williams, the colored man who lives in the cellar, carrying radio parts, tools, boxes of tubes, etc., home from the Radio Store. Cleaning out the store over a period of a few cold, wintry days and marching home with tons of junk, even Susan in her pudgy little hands carrying radio parts. Williams pushing the TV console on a dolly, in that lumbering slow-motion walk, glowering Williams in his faded blue overalls pushing the TV set up 174th Street. Behind him the store is now empty. The windows are empty. The landlord has put a lock on the door, and a painter on a ladder is very quickly blanking out Isaacson Radio, Sales and Repair.

Our lives are shrinking. The Isaacson family exists now only to the edges of its own domesticity. For my father substitute a rubber-handled screwdriver which I have taken to cherishing, along with some empty red tube boxes which I stack like cells of a hierarchic structure, or like modules of a dramatic new city. Also, a heavy, old diamond-shaped microphone from a real radio station. It broadcasts on a secret frequency directly to my father in his jail cell. I whisper instructions as to what he should do when he hears the hoot of an owl outside his cell window tonight. It will be our rescue team coming to get him. I advise him to be ready and to wait further instructions. Roger, he radios back to me. Roger and out, I reply.

In the papers I hear his voice. He tells reporters that the charge against him is insane. I have his picture in handcuffs down at Foley Square. He does not know the English scientist, the Canadian immigrants, the New Jersey engineer. He knows Mindish only as a friend. While our life is shrinking, another existence, another dimension, expands its image and amplifies its voices. The picture I save of my mother shows her walking down the front steps of our house, holding her arm up to shield her face from the camera. Or is her arm held out in the threatening gesture the caption claims? She tells a reporter her husband is innocent, and that the FBI took things from her house without a search warrant. The story describes her attitude as defiant.

In this new dimension of life we are spread into headlines and news broadcasts. Our troops are being captured and killed.

My mother reads of some hill in Korea, and says to me, "We shall bear the brunt." She is pale and her face is thin. She eats very little. She is composed but often, with no warning, grabs me and hugs me too tight or studies Susan's face or combs Susan's hair with inordinate pleasure in the texture of the dark, silken hair, or the smell of its cleanliness after she washes it. I feel sometimes she studies me as if gauging the amount of my father in me, and the amount of Rochelle.

For a week or two only Ascher or the reporters came to our door. Then one evening there was a knock and it was one of the interesting people, Ben Cohen, the gentle friend, always so quiet. He had come directly from work from the subway where it was his job to make change and which protects him from the atom bomb.

The sight of him causes my mother to weep. Awkwardly, he pats her on the shoulder.

"It's not smart to come here, Ben. It isn't a smart thing to do. You're a foolish man," she says in gratitude.

He frowns, shakes his head. They have a cup of tea in the kitchen. He combs his mustache with his fingers. He lights his pipe. He hangs one skinny leg over the other. He listens to my mother.

"What possessed him to do it? Can you tell me? All these years . . . If you cannot expect civilized behavior, simple decency from your friends, of whom can you expect it? I think about it and I think about it, and I cannot make heads or tails of it. I just can't understand what possesses a man to do something so terrible. To ruin a family, the lives of children."

Ben, mute, shakes his head.

"And I cannot forgive his wife, either. There has never been any love lost between Sadie Mindish and me. God knows what they have concocted between them."

Ben Cohen says, "I want you to tell your lawyer that I will make myself useful in any way I can. I will testify as your witness. Anything."

"Paul has already discussed this with Ascher. Paul told Ascher he doesn't want to implicate anyone, he doesn't want any of our friends to get involved. With the way things are, anyone who associates with us is himself made suspect. He says he could not bear the responsibility, it would weigh too heavily on him. And on me too, Ben. It's enough to know you have offered it."

There is something in her behavior, a regality of suffering, that is not lost on me. Perhaps the way she measures out her words keeps her emotions under control.

"Some financial help," Ben Cohen pleads in his quiet voice. My mother cries. "I miss him so. Ascher says he is fine. His letter says he is fine. But how can a man in jail be fine? He is locked up like some common criminal."

Ben is the first of a thin trickle of friends who came to see us. Nate Silverstein, the furrier with the hoarse voice and the red face. Henry Bergman, the fiddler. I forget who else. It was a very small number. In fact they were braving not only the FBI, but the downtown hierarchy of the Communist Party. I know that within twenty-four hours of my father's arrest, both he and my mother were written out of the Party. They were erased from the records. The Party did not want to be associated with anyone up on an espionage rap. Quickly and quietly erased out of existence.

But of the people who came, not one came without leaving a few dollars, or a cake, or a pound of cookies from the bakery, or a box of candy from Krum's near Fordham Road. Susan said to me: "Is my daddy dead?" I felt the same way. It was like when Grandma died and people came. It was like we were sitting *shivah* for my father.

I asked my mother what was going to happen. She told me there would be a trial to decide if my father was guilty. "Your dad," she called him. "The trial will determine if your dad is guilty."

"Guilty of what?"

"Guilty of being a spy, of giving secrets. But really guilty of wanting a new world of socialism without want."

I knew he was guilty of that, and I began to cry. "What will happen to him? What will happen to my father? What will they do to him? Will they kill him? Will he be dead?"

"Now, Daniel. Come here. Come here. I always forget how young you are. Isn't that funny? Let me hug you. Let me hug my Danny. He's such a big brave boy, I keep forgetting he's not old at all. He takes such good care of his baby sister, I forget that he's a baby too."

"I'm not a baby."

"He's my baby."

My lips were touching her cheek. "And then they'll get you," I sobbed.

"No, no, honey."

"Dr. Mindish will kill you, too."

"Don't be afraid of Mindish. Feel sorry for him. Don't be afraid of the Mindishes of this world. Pity them." She pulled away from me. Her mood was changing. "Nobody can hurt them worse than they hurt themselves. Nobody can be hurt by them as badly as they hurt themselves. The treachery of that man will haunt him for as long as he lives. His treachery will haunt his children. Mindish will live forever in hell for the terrible thing he has done. He has exiled himself from the community of man."

I couldn't control the sobs that racked me.

"Stop crying, Daniel. Don't cry. Nobody can hurt us. Hold your head up. Hold your shoulders back. Don't be afraid. Nobody will take your daddy away from you. No one can take us away from our babies."

Rochelle attempted to preserve the remnants of normal routine. Every morning I was packed off to school. I hated to go. I felt that if I wasn't home, the FBI would kidnap her. I was terrified of their coming back. I ran home for lunch and I ran home at three o'clock.

I never told her, but in school things were hardly normal. One day the principal came into our room and spoke to the teacher up at the board so that no one could hear him. After he left, I was asked by my teacher to go to another room for a few minutes. It was an empty room and I sat there the rest of the day. The next day I spent in the school library—the whole morning, and the whole afternoon. The day after that, when I was admitted back into my class, I was placed in the first seat of the row next to the window. I wondered about the change. I understood that this new position left me in proximity to the least number of other kids. It didn't bother me that much. In fact it was convenient because every few minutes I had to jump up to hoist myself on the radiators for a look out the window to my house—to see if anything was different. The teacher, with a fake smile, treated me with too much courtesy. As if she was afraid I would break. I was allowed to look out as many times as I wanted to. Her inability to hold to our previous relationship made me feel lonely. In trying to act as if nothing was different she phonied up the whole room. The kids all felt it. They felt it when she overpraised me, as if I was in kindergarten, for the answer I gave to some shitty little question. They wanted to talk about my father, but she wouldn't let them.

"Is Daniel's father a spy?"

"We won't talk about that now, dear."

I compared to my mother, uncharacteristically thin and pale, with the skin of her face so white it had become almost colorless, as something to see through to her flesh or bone—this opaque teacher with red lipstick and red fingernails, and shiny white teeth, all glazed porcelain, and smelling of flower water, who called me "dear."

I was told by kids in my class that in prison they pull your fingernails out with a pliers, and they chain you to the wall, and it's always dark, and the rats eat you, and that you have only bread and water to eat, and the bread has worms. I was told that the Army had already shot my father because he was a Russian. I was told that General MacArthur flew all the way from Japan to cut off my father's prick with a scissors.

I asked Rochelle what prison was like. She told me that during the War she had been a Volunteer for the Blood Donor program, and one day they took blood from men in prison in downtown Manhattan. Maybe it was the very same prison. She said it was very clean. In each cell was a cot, a chair, and a window. And it was true that the window had bars, and the cell had bars, and that the walls were tile, and the floors were cement, and it was hardly cozy; but it was clean. And the prisoners were allowed to read. And they went to a dining room to eat three times a day. And there was a small yard where they could get fresh air. And they had blankets to keep them warm at night.

"Really," my mother smiled at me. "It's not so bad."

One morning she told me she had to go downtown to testify before the Grand Jury. By the time I was ready to leave for school, Grandma's old friend, Mrs. Bittelman, had arrived to sit with Susan. For Mrs. Bittelman the community of misery had no politics. My mother had been desperate after being served the summons because she did not know who would take care of Susan while she was gone. She had no money to pay anyone. My father's two sisters, Frieda and Ruth, both worked, and besides that neither of them had come to see us or called since Paul had been put in jail. I suppose they felt they were the ones who ought to be consoled. Then my mother remembered Grandma's friend, around the corner, and she went to knock on Mrs. Bittelman's door and the kind woman said she would stay with Susan.

"I should be back before you're out of school, Danny. But in case not, have some milk and cookies when you get home. And take Susan to the park. For lunch I left you a peanut butter sandwich and an apple in the icebox."

I didn't want her to go.

"I have to go, Daniel."

"They're going to put you in jail, too."

"No, they're not. They want to ask me questions, that's all. That's what a Grand Jury is. You are asked questions and they listen to your answers. The government lawyers want to ask me about Daddy, and I'm going to tell them what a terrible thing they're doing and make them understand he's innocent."

She was taking the subway and was meeting Ascher at the 161st Street stop, and then they would go downtown together. She was wearing her black coat that was almost down to her ankles in the fashion of that day. She had let the hem down to make it longer. She was wearing her blue dress with the white high-necked collar. She wore her tiny wrist watch that my father gave her before they were married. She was wearing on the back of her head a little black hat she called a pillbox.

She was last seen in her black cloth coat with the hem let down and a black pillbox hat. My mother was last seen with her tiny watch on her wrist, a fine thin wrist with a prominent wristbone and lovely thin blue veins. She left behind a clean house, and in the icebox a peanut butter sandwich and an apple for lunch. In the afternoon, I had my milk and cookies. And she never came home.

My mother left me in her long, black coat, and although she never wore hats, she wore a hat that day, also black, and almost invisible in her thick curly black hair. At lunchtime I ate the peanut butter sandwich and the apple from the icebox. Mrs. Bittelman smiled at me and told me I was a *shayneh boychik*. At three o'clock I came home and had a glass of milk and two sugar cookies. My mother had still not come home. I waited for her. I played with Susan. Mrs. Bittelman kept going to the front door and looking outside. I waited. It got dark. Mrs. Bittelman began to moan softly to herself and shake her head as if some chronic pain had returned with the nightfall. She was a stout, old woman with swollen ankles and she liked to stay off her feet. It was suppertime, and after looking in our kitchen, she decided to go home to her house and cook Susan and me a meal in her own kitchen. She wanted us to go with her. I wouldn't. I told her to go and Susan and I would wait in our own house. Mrs. Bittelman went home. Susan and I waited for our mother. The house was cold. We sat in the kitchen. The rest of the house was dark. Every few minutes I went into the dark hall and opened the front door to see if she was coming. It was beginning to snow, and the snow was sticking. I turned on the light in the hall. I sat in the kitchen and played with Susan. She wanted to know where her mommy was. She was cranky. She fell asleep with her head on the kitchen table. I waited. I sat straight in my chair. I kept my head up. I tried to hear if Williams was home downstairs in the cellar. I thought I heard his radio playing. I couldn't hear him. I was afraid to leave the kitchen to find out if Williams was really home. I would have to go outside to do that, or down the dark stairs to the basement.

Then I heard him coming up the basement stairs and there was a knock on the dark door from the basement and then he shook the door. I turned the key and opened it and ran back to the table. He appeared in the doorway. I was frightened. He reached almost to the ceiling. He stood there looking at us with his murderous anger. He brought with him his menacing whiskey smell. His eyes were red. "Your momma leave you here alone?"

"No, she left us with Mrs. Bittelman. But she went home to cook supper."

"Ain't no one told you?"

"What?"

"Dear Jesus. It on the radio."

At that moment the phone began to ring.

DIDN'T MY LORD DELIVER DANIEL? —Paul Robeson

Knouting. Knouting was the primary means of punishment for capital offenses in Czarist Russia until the latter part of the nineteenth century. It was applied exclusively to serfs. Before the entire community assembled in an open field, the serf designated for this punishment was stripped of his shirt and bound to a wooden block by his arms and neck and knees. The knout was a leather thonged whip which, in the hands of a stout executioner, tore away flesh down to the bone. Sir Robert Porter, in TRAVELING SKETCHES IN SWEDEN AND RUSSIA (London, 1809), witnesses the knouting of a serf coachman accused of killing his master. Speaks of the "bloody splash of the knout" on the senseless body of the victim. In this case over two hundred strokes were applied. Afterwards the victim unaccountably not yet dead was ceremoniously disfigured in the event he managed to live on, pincers being driven up his nose and then manipulated in a sudden manner so as to tear his nostrils from his face. A law passed in 1807 specified that minors were to receive no more than thirty blows of the knout. Shall we call this an enlightened law? But in the famous case of the murder of the mistress of Count Arakcheev, Minister of War in the reign of Alexander, a brother and a sister, each under eighteen, died after seventy blows of the knout. According to Michael Jenkins, author of ARAKCHEEV, GRAND VIZIER OF THE RUSSIAN EMPIRE (Dial Press), the entire system of serfdom turned on the principle of savage corporal punishment, especially after the peasant uprising of 1774 during Catherine's reign. Shackles, knouts, stocks, birches, cages, were common equipment, like horse collars, on Russian estates. The serf had little or no recourse to justice, his master having virtually unrestrained privilege over his life. In this he was brother to servitors in the English merchant fleets and English military institutions who were commonly flogged and for the same class principles and with the same barbarity, and with equally unlikely chance of redress. Cf. the American Negro slaves.

Burning at the Stake. A practice known to all European nations until the 19th century. Clerical fondness for. Known also to Indians of North America. Used into 20th century only in the American South, often with castration. Performed on lower classes. No accident that Joan of Arc, burned at the stake, was a peasant.

Explore the history of corporal punishment as a class distinction. There is always exemption for the designated upper class of a society. In England, highborn nobles were never drawn and quartered. In Russia only serfs were flogged. For the same or similar crime, the upper class received relatively painless and non-humiliating punishment. If death, swift death. Never desecration. Where it is necessary for one reason or another to apply the torturous practice to the upper-class victim, certain rituals of transvaluation are performed which expel him from his class before he is executed. Religious excommunication, tribal excommunication. An infidel or an enemy, like a slave, can be executed with abandon.

In the French Revolution for the first time the class of the offender did not determine the kind of punishment he received. Everyone, from the King to Danton, got the guillotine.

We may say that the basis of all class distinctions in society is corporal punishment. Classes are created by corporal punishment, and maintained by corporal punishment. The authoritarian head of a society derives his power from the support not of the masses but of the upper classes or privileged bureaucracy which funds his government and divides its rewards. By contrast the loyalty of the masses is maintained only by constant physical intimidation. As societies endure in history they symbolize complex systems of corporal punishment in economic terms. That is why Marx used the word "slavery" to define the role of the working class under capitalism. Slavery is the state of absolute submission to corporal punishment. In times of challenge, however, the ruling classes restore their literal, un-symbolized right of corporal punishment upon the lower classes, usually in the name of law and order. The crime of someone in the lower class is never against another human being but always against the order and authority of the state.

I have put down everything I can remember of their actions and conversations in this period prior to their arrests. Or I think I have. Sifted it through my hands. I find no clues either to their guilt or innocence. Perhaps they are neither guilty nor innocent. Of course, there is a slight oddness in the way they reacted to the knock on the door—as if they knew what was coming. But they did know what was coming. And so did everyone else who lived with some awareness into that time. There were certain convictions that American democracy would no longer permit you to hold. If you were a Jewish Communist, anti-Fascist; if you cried Peace! and cheered Vito Marcantonio at the Progressive Party rally in Yankee Stadium; if you were poor; if you were all of these things, you knew what was coming. You might even have been relieved not to have to wait any longer. You might even have demanded of society that you not be forced to wait any longer.

A TOUR OF THE CITY

Riverside Park. It was a Saturday morning, already September, very hot, and Phyllis asked me not to go to the library but to take a break, just this once, and walk down to Riverside Park with her and the baby and maybe find a river breeze. All through this bad heat, riots on the tube every night, and people burning, we had been coming out of the Memorial Day separation a little stronger, with more understanding be-tween us, and we both wore that New York summer dragged-out look, and we were tight. In the park I threw Paul in the air and caught him, and he laughed. Phyllis smiled and out of the corner of my eye I could see an old lady with a cane stopping for a moment in her walk to smile at the attractive young family. I threw my son in the air a little higher and he screeched a little louder as I caught him. We were walking in the park. I tossed my son higher and higher, and now he laughed no longer but cried out. Still I did not stop and I threw him higher and caught him closer to the ground. Then Phyllis was begging me to stop. The baby now shut his mouth, concentrating on his fear, his small face, my Isaacson face, locked in absolute dumb dread of the breath-taking flight into the sky and the even more terrifying fall toward earth. I can't bear to think about this murderous feeling. Phyllis was pulling at my arm and trying to keep me from throwing my son high in the air and daring us all with the failure of missing him on the way down. I can't remember my thoughts. I think his weight, the heft of his little body, freaked me. I enjoyed the moment it left my hands and hated the moment it returned, with a shock to all the muscles in my arms. I enjoyed the fear in his mother. When I finally stopped she grabbed Paul and sat down on a bench and hugged him and sat hugging him. He was white. I looked around and saw some people across the street staring at me. I took off.

Fourteenth Street. Daniel Lewin boarded the West Side subway and rode downtown to 42nd, and then took the shuttle to Lexington Avenue and continued downtown on the Lex. He came up into the late summer evening of pizza and peanuts and hot dogs lying heavy in the neon of S. Klein on the Square. Despite the looming up of the red Avenue B bus he chose to walk. He walked past the record joints and the cheap goods stores, and past Luchows, and the Spanish movie house, and the keymaker, and the porno bookstore. Fourteenth Street was the most dismal street in the world. Everything about it was cheap and hopeless, perhaps because it touched Union Square, all the stores of cheap shoes and cheap clothes going past Union Square like an assembly line of cheap hopes in lights of red and yellow and green; and the shoppers with their single dollar bills folded carefully in change purses, the almond-eyed Slavic mothers with their daughters slightly mustached looking for the outfit to get married in, to get carried away in, and black people shining in their pastel cottons and in hopelessness which makes a person glow like a burning ember, and the Spanish spoken like the pigeons pecking the crumbs off the hot sidewalk—all of it shuttling past Union Square without looking, the way you don't look at a graveyard as you pass. He was walking east, away from the Square. Ahead the smokestacks of Con Edison lay against the windless evening sky like smoking cannon. When Daniel turned into Avenue B, a narrow street, the evening immediately darkened. He began to feel better.

Tompkins Square Park. The Park is crowded. This is not 14th Street, this is the community. There is a music phenomenon coming out of hundreds of transistor radios. There is a mambo phenomenon. There is a dog phenomenon—there are dogs in the dog run taking craps, dogs on the leash, dogs roaming free in packs. Men and girls play handball in the fenced-in handball courts. The girls are good. They shout in Spanish. Dogs jump for the ball in the handball courts. On the benches of the park sit old Ukrainian ladies with babushkas. The old ladies have small yapping dogs on leashes. Old men play chess at the stone tables. The old dogs of the old men lie under the stone tables with their tongues hanging. On the big dirt hill in the center of the park, a kid and a dog roll over each other. A burned-out head drifts by, barefoot with his feet red and swollen. A dog growls at him. Down the path from the old ladies in babushkas sits one blond-haired girl on the pipe fence. Her ass, in jeans, hangs over the pipe fence. Four black guys surround her. One talks to her earnestly. She stares straight ahead. Her radio plays Aretha. Her dog sleeps at the end of its leash. In the center of the park is the open paved area with its movable benches and its bandshell protected by a steel mesh curtain. There is no performance tonight. Benches are turned over, a group of hippies huddles around the guitar, dogs streak back and forth under the bandshell with the zigzag propulsion of pinballs. Two cop cars are parked on 10th Street. Mambo, mambo. A thousand radios play rock.

    Avenue B. "Yeah, I know your sister. How is your sister."

"She's sick."

"Yeah, well I'm sick too. I got hepatitis, don't get too close."

Five people are in the room, including a girl interviewer doing a story for *Cosmopolitan*. The girl interviewer moves back and her photographer moves back.

"He's just shitting," Artie's girl says. "He's been out of the hospital for two weeks."

"My liver's bad," Artie says flopping down on his mattress. "I'm yellow. I'm yellow-livered. I'm chicken." Everyone laughs because of Artie Sternlicht's reputation. "Chicken liver. Hey, baby, why don't you ever make me chicken liver."

"I will, baby." She kneels at his side and holds his hand in her lap. "He got hepatitis because of me."

"How is that?" the girl interviewer says.

"The best pigs are very creative," Artie says. "This new thing they laid on me was a blood test. I said to them, 'You don't give *me* a blood test. I've been busted fifty times and nobody's ever taken my blood. You touch me with that needle and I'll kick your balls in. My friends have instructions, unless they hear otherwise from me in twenty-four hours they are going to raid this station. Then they are going to bomb Murphy's.' Murphy's is the bar they all go to after work. So they laugh and this pig says, 'Artie, we're going to take some of your blood or we'll bust your girl friend. We'll get her for possession. We'll put her in Women's Detention in a cell with all bull dikes. You want that to happen?' So I let the fuckers stick their dirty needle in my arm and that's what they want, that's all they want. I mean what do police have to know about blood. That it's red? Fucking vampires—if they got lucky maybe I'd die."

"You're saying the police deliberately gave you hepatitis?"

Sternlicht doesn't answer but turns his head and looks at me. "Sit down, man. I'll talk to you but come down here to my level. Get down here with the proles."

Sternlicht wears dungaree shorts and sandals. No shirt. He

has a long foxlike chin and sly good looks. He may be sick but his body looks strong and supple. His nose is flat and wide and his mouth is wide and his teeth are bad. He wears a beaded headband that bunches his shoulder-length hair and makes him look like an American Indian. His eyes are light grey, like Daniel's wife's, and they're a shock because they're so vivid and clean-looking in the impression of dirtiness that Sternlicht conveys. He is stretched out on this bare mattress on the floor, lying on his side with his head propped in his hand. The photographer walks around the room shooting him from every angle.

"What is the future for the Lower East Side? What's happening?" the girl writer says.

"Well, the hippie thing turned bad and the whole community is uptight. The spics don't like the heads. Nobody likes the pigs. I don't know—what is it like, Baby? You've got PLP down here, and a W. E. B. Du Bois, and the neighborhood reformers, and Diggers like me, and some black destruct groups, and every freak thing you can think of. Eventually we'll put it together, we'll get all our shit together. All the freaks will get it together. Then we won't be freaks anymore. Then we'll be a clear and present danger."

"Yes?" The girl waits for him to continue.

Sternlicht looks at her. "The first thing we're going after is women's magazines," he says. "Liberate those girls who write about sex and dating. We're gonna pull off their pants and place daisies in their genitals."

"Oh sure," the reporter says. "Is that the kind of remark that makes people say the peace movement can't afford you?"

"What people? The question is can the revolution afford the peace movement. You mean these dudes who march down the street and think they're changing something? Peace marches are for the middle class to get its rocks off. The peace movement is part of the war. Heads or tails it's the same coin. The Indian or the buffalo, it's the same fucking nickel. Right? And they're both extinct."

"Not so fast, I don't have shorthand," the girl says. She's a honey-haired blond, very skinny, in false eyelashes and a jumpsuit. While she bends over her pad, Artie looks at his friends who sit on the floor near the windows. He draws a whistling breath and shakes his hand in the air as if he's burned his fingers. They laugh.

"Hey," the photographer says, "do you have the strength to stand up? I want to shoot you against this wall."

Sternlicht immediately jumps up and spreads his arms against the wall, like Christ, and lets his head fall to the side. His eyes bug and his tongue lolls from the corner of his mouth.

"Great," the photographer says, and shoots.

"Up against the wall!" one of the friends calls out. Artie slips his headband over his eyes and stands with his arms stiffly at his sides. His girl sticks a cigarette between his lips.

"Great," the photographer says, and shoots kneeling, standing, close up, and across the room.

The wall is interesting. It is completely covered with a collage of pictures, movie stills, posters, and real objects. Babe Ruth running around the bases, Marlon Brando on his bike, Shirley Temple in her dancing shoes, FDR, a bikini sprayed with gold paint, Marilyn Monroe on her calendar, Mickey Mouse, Gilbert Stuart's Washington with a mustache penciled on, a real American Legion cap, Fred Allen in front of a microphone, pinch-mouthed Susan B. Anthony, Paul Robeson, Sammy Baugh throwing a jump pass, Calvin Coolidge in Indian feathers, a World War One dogfight, a chain gang working on the road, an antique doll, a girl making it with a donkey, browned book jackets of *Gone with the Wind* and *One World* by Wendell Willkie, a diaphragm sprayed with silver paint, a cluster of cigarette butts, a *Death of a Salesman* poster, a young Elvis, a black man hanging from a tree, a white man selling apples for 5 cents—

"It's marvelous!" the reporter says.

"You hear that?" Sternlicht says to his girl. It develops that she is the artist.

The reporter is really impressed. "You're fantastic! How long did it take to do this?"

Sternlicht's girl says, "Well, actually I haven't finished yet. I go on a, y'know, collecting binge, and when I have a lot of stuff I plaster it up there. There's stuff underneath you can't even see anymore. I'm thinking of covering, y'know, everything, the whole house. See?" She has picked up a handful of clippings and pictures from a table in the corner. She lets them drift out of her hands, through her fingers, and they flutter and swoop all over the place. Everyone laughs.

"You're very casual about your work," the reporter says, "but I think it shows immense talent. Have you ever had formal study?"

"Well see," the girl looks at Sternlicht and starts to laugh, "actually if anyone deserves credit for my art it's Mr. Magruder."

Sternlicht breaks up.

"Mr. Magruder is our landlord, and that's how I, y'know, started. Just to cover some holes in the wall. Paper is very good insulation."

Sternlicht drops to the mattress, pulls the girl down into his lap and they laugh and hug each other. The photographer shoots.

"She's not shittin'," Sternlicht says. "You know how cold it gets here in the winter? All revolutions begin with tenants. All revolution begins with tenants freezing their asses off in the winter."

"It's marvelous," the reporter insists, gazing at the wall. "It should have a name. What do you call it?"

Artie Sternlicht and his girl look into each other's eyes. They answer in unison, and their friends chime in: "EVERYTHING THAT CAME BEFORE IS ALL THE SAME!"

The reporter looks at the photographer, and you know she has her lead now, the piece is writing itself. Everyone gets happy.

STERNLICHT RAPPING

He talks fast in a gravel voice that breaks appealingly on punch lines. He jumps around as he raps, gesturing, acting out his words.

"Like you said the movement couldn't afford us. OK. I went to this coalition meeting uptown to plan for the Convention next year? And these are good kids, New Left kids who know the score. And you should hear them spin out this shit: Participatory democracy. Co-optation. Restructure. Counter-institutional. Man, those aren't words. Those are substitutes for being alive. I got up and I said, 'What the fuck are you all talking about. What is this with resolutions and committees? What kind of shit is this, man? I mean you don't need the establishment to *co-opt* you, man. You are *co-opting* yourself. You see this chair? This is a chair, man.' And I break this fucking chair to splinters —I smash it to the floor and I stomp on it and I really make a mess of the goddamn chair. And all the while I'm shouting, 'See Sternlicht break the chair! I'm breaking this chair!' And I hold up the pieces. 'Let's fuck. Let's fight. Let's blow up the Pentagon! A revolutionary is someone who makes the revolution. If you want to sit here and beat your meat, all right, but don't call it revolution.' Well, I started a riot! It was a gas! Everyone was mad as hell and that meeting came alive. You've got to put down anything that's less than revolution. You put down theorizing about it, dreaming about it, waiting for it, preparing for it, demonstrating for it. All that is less than being it and therefore not it, and therefore never will be it. A revolution *happens*. It's a happening! It's a change on the earth. It's a new animal. A new consciousness! It's me! I am Revolution!"

"But even Fidel has a plan," the reporter says. This remark is greeted with absolute silence. Sternlicht looks over at his friends sitting in the corner. One, a fat kid with a bushy beard, says, "That's right, Mr. Sternlicht, what do you say to that?" They all laugh. The journalist flushes red.

"No, listen," Artie says holding up his hands. "It's a legitimate question. OK. Like in Cuba they find out what their revolution is by working it. They're a bunch of crazy spics who try it first and then see what it is. If something's no good they change it. But say Fidel has a plan. The lesson is not that our revolution must be like Fidel's. The lesson is that it must be our own revolution. Dig? I'm gonna answer your question. Your question is tactical. Fidel bounced his revolution off some fifth-rate spic gangster and the United Fruit Company. But we are in revolution from this—" He points at the collage. "Corporate liberalism, and George Washington and the fag peace movement, and big money and hardware systems, and astronauts. We are in revolution from something with a pretty fair momentum of its own.

And you're not going to bring it down by going into the hills with some rifles. OK? The only people in the U.S. who know they're slaves are the black people. The spade kids today don't have to be organized. I mean they are born with absolutely no tolerance for shit, they are born willing to die. And the white dropout children, the derelict kids, the whole hippie thing, the free store, is a runaway slave movement. It really is. So maybe they know it. But the rest—the kids who go to school for careers and the blue-collar sellouts and all the suburban hustlers in the land who make the hustle system work, who carry it on their backs and think they're its beneficiaries—I mean it's a double-think system, it is not ordinary repression, right? My country knees you in the neck and you think you're standing upright. It presses your face in the muck and you think you're looking at the sky. I mean you cannot make connections between what you do and why they hate you in Chile. You are hung up on identity crises. You think you are a good guy. You're not prejudiced. You believe in making money honestly. You believe in free speech. You have allergies. You have strokes. You have mortgages. Your lungs are garbage pails. Your eyes go blind with the architecture. You think the white folks are learning. You think the black folks are lifting themselves up. YOU THINK THERE'S PROGRESS. YOU THINK YOUR CHILDREN HAVE IT BETTER. YOU THINK YOU ARE DOING IT FOR YOUR CHILDREN!"

"Hey Sternlicht, shut the fuck up!"

"Hey Artie, blow it out your ass!"

"Sternlicht sucks!"

The voices come from the street. Sternlicht rushes to the window and climbs out on the fire escape. He raises his fist and jumps up on the railing. "EVERYONE IN THIS BLOCK IS UNDER ARREST!" There is laughter from outside. The people in the room crowd onto the fire escape. Badinage between the friends one flight up and the friends on the sidewalk. Avenue B is humming. Cars come through the narrow street, people are out in the hot night. Two blocks away is the park at Tompkins Square and from it emanates a pulse of energy composed of music and shouting and the heat of many people. The world came to America down Avenue B. The bar across the street is crowded and Daniel can see through its window the old polished wood and tarnished mirrors, and the light of the TV screen. He suddenly sees the Lower East Side with Sternlicht's vision: It is a hatchery, a fish and wildlife preserve. It seems created for him. *With the poor people of this earth I want to share my fate.*

I tried to distinguish the sound from any one radio or record player, near or far. It was impossible. Music came from everywhere, it was like an electrification of the air, a burning up of it.

amazing grace, amazing grace, there is still in this evening on the fire escape floating in the potsmoke like an iron cloud over Avenue B someone who knows what he says or does is important With importance his life or self concerned, and the surroundings are suddenly not obscure and the voice is amplified and a million people hear and every paint chip of the rusted fire escape its particular configuration and archaeology is truly important

The friends leave and Artie picks up his rap as we stand at the fire escape railing in the hot September night. "So how do you bring change to something this powerful. How do you make revolution. The same way a skinny little judo freak throws a cat three times his size. You don't preach. You don't talk about poverty and injustice and imperialism and racism. That's like trying to make people read Shakespeare, it can't be done. Look there, what do you see? Little blue squares in every window. Right? Everyone digging the commercials. That is today's school, man. In less than a minute a TV commercial can carry you through a lifetime. It tells the story from the date to the wedding. It shows you the baby, the home, the car, the graduation. It makes you laugh and makes your eyes water with nostalgia. You see a girl more beautiful than any girl you've ever seen. Giants, and midgets, and girls coming in convertibles, and knights and ladies, and love on the beach, and jets fucking the sky, and delicious food steaming on the table, and living voices of cool telling you how cool you are, how cool you can be. Commercials are learning units. So like when the brothers walk into the draft board down in Baltimore and pour blood all over the induction records—that's the lesson. And the Yippies throwing money away at the stock exchange. And marching in the parade on Flag Day and getting the Legionnaires to chase you and the pigs to chase you and tearing up your flags, American flags, on Flag Day! You dig? Society is a put-on so we put on the put-on. Authority is momentum. Break the momentum. Legitimacy is illegitimate. Make it show its ass. Hit and run. You got forty seconds, man. The media need material? Give them material. Like Abbie says, anyone who does anything in this country is a celebrity. Do something and be a celebrity. Next month we're going to Washington and exorcizing the Pentagon. We're gonna levitate the Pentagon by prayer and incantation and blowing horns and throwing magic invisibilities at the Pentagon walls. We're gonna lift it up and let it down. We're gonna kill it with flowers. Be there! We'll be on television. We're gonna overthrow the United States with images!"

I have an idea for an article. If I write it maybe I can sell it and see my name in print. The idea is the dynamics of radical thinking. With each cycle of radical thought there is a stage of genuine creative excitement during which the connections are made. The radical discovers connections between available data and the root responsibility. Finally he connects everything. At this point he begins to lose his following. It is not that he has incorrectly connected everything, it is that he has connected everything. Nothing is left outside the connections. At this point society becomes bored with the radical. Fully connected in his characterization it has achieved the counterinsurgent rationale that allows it to destroy him. The radical is given the occasion for one last discovery—the connection between society and his death. After the radical is dead his early music haunts his persecutors. And the liberals use this to achieve power. I have searched and searched for one story from history that is invulnerable to radical interpretation. I mean it is harder than it sounds and if you think not give it a try. Here is one from the AMERICAN HERITAGE HISTORY OF FLIGHT—I found it today and it might just stand up: In 1897 three Swedes decided that the way to get to the North Pole was by means of a free balloon flight. They set off from Spitzbergen, floating up in a northerly direction, and they were never heard from again. Then, thirty-three years later, in 1930, a party of Norwegian explorers came upon a camp in the frozen Arctic wastes and there were the three ice-cake bodies of the Swedish balloonists. Also in the camp was a camera and in the camera was film. The thirty-three-year-old film was developed and yielded snapshots of the balloonists in their last camp standing over a bear they had hunted, raising a flag, etc.—

Ascher's homburg was pushed back on his head like a cowboy hat, and his overcoat was open. His hands were clasped behind his back under the overcoat. He tilted back on his heels and forward again, while the children's Aunt Frieda sat on the couch weeping.

"I'm a widow, I have no one," Aunt Frieda said. "It's too much of a burden. I live in three rooms. Where can I put them? I stand on my feet twelve hours a day. I get up at six-thirty every morning. On my day off I haven't got the strength to get out of bed. How can I afford to do what you're asking me!"

"Mrs. Cohn, I'm not asking you to do anything. Paul is your brother, not mine. I am the lawyer. Whatever you decide, that determines what I will do."

"And what does my sister Ruth say?"

"I have discussed the problem with her only on the phone."

"Listen, don't waste your time. Selfish? The word wasn't invented till Ruthie." Aunt Frieda dismissed her sister with a wave of the hand. The gesture caught Daniel's eye. His Aunt Frieda sat with her feet planted on the floor in lace-up shoes with thick heels. He turned quickly back to the TV set, having seen more than he wanted to of Aunt Frieda's stocking above the knee. He found her repulsive. She had that hairy mole over the corner of her mouth. She looked like his father around the jaw, the mouth. She wore thick horn-rimmed glasses.

"I understand her husband is a diabetic, a very sick man. In any case I somehow feel that you would know better how to handle the situation than your sister."

Aunt Frieda nodded. "God help me, I was always the responsible one. From the time we were children. If you didn't watch Paul he would destroy himself. He never learned how to cross the street. If you didn't put the food in front of him he wouldn't eat. If you didn't hold his money he would lose it or let someone take it from him. I couldn't count on Ruthie. Ruthie was always a lazy thing. It was Frieda who solved the problems. It was Frieda, that good-natured slob, who was always there to get them out of trouble."

"You are the oldest?"

"By eight years. And when I was twenty my father followed my mother to the grave and I was now the mother and father. It ruined my life. I'm telling you, Mr. Ascher, my life was never my own."

Her tears flowed. Ascher turned his attention to the television console shining in the corner. The children were sitting on the floor, too close he thought. Too close. He made no move to interrupt their attention. If they could get inside the television they would be better off still. On the screen that Hopalong Cassidy threw his lasso through the air. Hopalong's horse reared up and braked to a stop. The lasso pulled the crook off his horse. The crook looked up sullenly from the dust with his arms pinned to his sides by the rope. From his white horse Hopalong laughed down at him. Ascher thought: We are a primitive people.

"They seem to enjoy the television," Ascher said. "Maybe we should make an exception. Do you have a television, Mrs. Cohn?"

"What? No, no—who can afford a television?"

"It is an expensive appliance," Ascher said. "The man will be here soon to assess the belongings. I will tell him not to include the television."

The children's Aunt Frieda opened her pocketbook and brought forth a handkerchief. She took off her glasses and wiped her eyes. She wiped her nose. "I'm sorry," she said. "I have always had such luck. My husband, God rest his soul, didn't last. Ruthie, poor Ruthie, has her hands full with an invalid. And Paul—can there be a greater tragedy? To turn into a Red. My Pauly, a Commonist! And you know there was no more religious man than my father. Are you a religious man, Mr. Ascher?"

Ascher shrugged. "I go to temple."

"My father is turning over in his grave. That his son became a Red. And worse!"

"What do you mean worse?"

"God only knows. I will be lucky to keep my store. If someone should make the connection with my maiden name. If my neighbors find out."

"What are you saying?"

"Nothing, nothing. But how do I explain who these children are. How do I explain where their parents are."

"Their parents are in jail. They are in jail because their bail bond is prohibitive. Their bail bond is prohibitive because in the current climate it helps the government to establish how guilty they must be and how dangerous they must be. If the shame of that is too much for you then you can lie. You can say they are in Florida. You can say they are traveling in Europe. Isaacson is not an uncommon name."

Aunt Frieda put her handkerchief in her pocketbook and snapped the clasps. "I don't blame him," she said. "He could not help himself. I blame her. She's the one. She was his ruination. He was putty in her hands from the very beginning. When he was in the Army in the war she went to Washington to live with him. Before they were married she lived with him! In sin she lived with him. In school as a boy Paul never got less than A's. On all his Regents in high school, ninety-nine in this, a hundred in that. He had a ninety-six average in Townsend Harris high school which was nothing but brilliant children. And then to get these crazy ideas—all right, so you join a club in college, it's the thing to do. But he would have outgrown all that craziness. But she was like that, too. And she drove him. It was she who did this!"

"Mrs. Cohn—"

"I will never forgive her for what she has done to my Pauly. For what she has done to all of us. To all our lives. She is the one. No one else."

"Mrs. Cohn, do you really want the children to hear this?"

"Don't worry, they know how I feel. Besides, they are not listening. Mmmmm, what is going to happen to them." Aunt Frieda held her hand to her cheek as if she had a toothache.

"So what do I understand from your answer?"

"I don't know," Aunt Frieda said. "I don't know."

"They can't stay here," Ascher said. "The black man can't

take care of them. The neighbor woman can't take care of them. I can't take care of them. There is no money for the rent, there is no money for this house, do you understand, Mrs. Cohn?"

Aunt Frieda moaned with her hand to her face.

"A man is going to come and make an offer for the furniture. A hundred, a hundred fifty dollars at the most is what we'll get. Tomorrow in court I am filing a pauper's oath for your brother. Do you know what that means?"

"Vey iss mir, vey iss mir . . ."

"It means the court will appoint me the attorney and the court will pay my fees so that I can continue to represent your brother and his wife. *Vershtey?* It means also that these children are the children of paupers and have no place to go. If you will not take them in, Mrs. Cohn, your flesh and blood, they will be out on the street. *Vershteyen zie?* They will be wards of the state."

"Babies!" Aunt Frieda wailed. "What do I know from babies!"

"Now what I suggest is that you get their belongings together—maybe the boy can help you—and get them ready to leave."

"Now? This minute?"

"It is imperative." Ascher looked at his watch. "The man will be here to give me a price for the furniture. I don't think it is good for children to see that. I don't want them to watch their house dismantled."

"I got to lug baggage to Brooklyn? I can't lift things."

"Don't worry, they have little enough. I will send you in a cab."

"Where will I put them? What do they eat?"

"Lady," Ascher shouted. "They are your brother's children. They are not animals from the zoo. What is the matter with you? *Vas iss der mair mit dein kopf?* Have you no pity? Don't you know what trouble is? Don't you know what terrible trouble these people are in?"

Abruptly Ascher sat down. He sat like a king with his arms on the arms of the chair, cooling off in his rage while Aunt Frieda smiled placatingly and wept at the same time.

Her apartment had an indescribable smell. It was the smell

of a withering, unloved body. It was the smell of dust and of Brooklyn air-shaft darkness. It was the smell of slipcovers on the furniture and double locks on the doors. It was the smell of lights that couldn't be turned on because it was a waste of money. It was the smell of no pleasure to be found around any corner, down any hall, in any closet. It was the smell of a stranger's drab home, where I didn't belong. It was the smell of a life of no account to anyone.

"Daniel," Ascher said, "I want to talk to you a minute. Come in here."

Daniel rose from the floor and followed the lawyer into the kitchen. Ascher sat down at the kitchen table and turned to face him. Ascher saw Susan in the doorway. "No no, little girl, I didn't mean to interrupt you. You may go back and watch the program."

In answer Susan sidled just inside the doorway, with her back to the wall. She stared at Ascher gravely.

"Very well," the lawyer said. "You can listen too. Children, your Aunt Frieda has consented to take you into her home until your parents are free again. This may be a month or two. Maybe three. But I have spoken to your parents, each of them, and they have decided that under the circumstances, that would be the best thing. In the meantime the house will be closed up here."

"We heard you," Daniel said. "We know."

"Yes. Well, I cannot pretend this is a happy adventure. But your mother and father are most worried about you and want to make sure that you are cared for and not neglected while they are away from you. You know she has a candy store downstairs in the same house where she lives."

"Yes," Daniel said. "But she doesn't let you touch anything. She's a stupid woman."

"Shhh." Ascher put a finger to his lips. "She may be hard to understand. People who are afraid are sometimes hard to understand. Being afraid makes people say things they don't mean. Can you appreciate that?"

"I suppose."

"She'll learn how to be good from you, Daniel. She's not a

mean person. She'll learn how to be strong from your example. You're a wonderful boy. Both you children are fine children," Ascher said, turning his eyes toward Susan.

"Where is Mommy?" Susan said.

Ascher sighed. "In jail. She's in jail."

"What is jail?"

"Jail is a place people stay instead of home. Like a hotel. Like a school. They are other places to stay instead of home."

"Jail is worse," Daniel said to Susan. "You can't come home if you want to."

"All right," Ascher said. "All right."

"Will they put me in jail?" Susan said.

"No, don't worry."

"Is my mommy coming home?"

"Daniel, I cannot go on explaining these things to her."

"Is my mommy dead?"

Ascher stood up and raised his arms in exasperation. "Please, little girl! Enough. Your mommy is not dead!" The gesture startled Susan. She burst into tears. Daniel went to her and put his arm around her. "She misses our mother and father," Daniel explained over his shoulder.

"What is wrong, what is the matter?" Aunt Frieda called from upstairs.

"Nothing," Ascher yelled. "Nothing is the matter. Now children," he said lowering his voice, "there are things to be done. Shhh, don't cry, Susan. Your aunt is packing up your clothes. I want you to help her so she'll know what to take. Any of your toys and things like that, you will have to show her what is important to you. And you both look—unkempt. Can't you wash yourselves a little bit? Can't you make yourselves clean?"

"I'll wash her," Daniel said. "And there are things like our toothbrushes. We'll have to take those."

"That's right."

Daniel patted Susan till she was no longer crying. Her body shook with sobs that were like hiccups. He said to Ascher: "Why can't we go see them? The guards can search me and they can search her and they'll see that we don't have guns or anything like that."

"Well, it is not a matter of guards, Daniel. Your mother and father both feel that it would upset you to see them in the jail."

"Why?"

"Because when the time came to leave they wouldn't be able to leave with you. And you and especially your sister might not understand and be upset."

"Maybe they would be upset too," Daniel reflected.

"That's right. And so it would be worse than not seeing you at all."

"Well, how will they know where we are?" Daniel said.

"They asked me to ask your aunt if you could stay with her. I will report to them that you are with her."

"Do they know the address?"

"They know it."

"If we write to them from there will they get the letter?"

"I have arranged it so they will."

"I got the letter they sent," Daniel said. "When you see them tell them to write more often."

"But you see I told you, Daniel, they are allowed to write just one letter a week. So you can get no more than one letter a week. They also have to write each other."

"You mean they aren't in the same place?"

"Your father is in one jail and your mother is in another jail which is for women. They haven't seen each other since your father was arrested."

What God hath joined let no man tear asunder —FATHER OF THE BRIDE, with Spencer Tracy and Elizabeth Taylor

Who wrote that Russian story, was it Babel or maybe Yuri Olesha, about a man dying in his bed. His death is described as a progressive deterioration of possibilities, a methodical constriction of options available to him. First he cannot leave the room, so that a railroad ticket, for instance, has no more meaning for his life. Then he cannot get out of bed. Then he cannot lift his head. Then he cannot see out the window. Then he cannot see his hand in front of him. Life moves inward, the sensations close in, the horizons diminish to point zero. And that is his death. A kind of prison cell concept of death, the man being locked in smaller and smaller cells, his own consciousness depleted of sensations being the last and smallest cell. It is a point of light. If this is true of death, then a real prison is death's metaphor and when you put a man in prison you are suggesting to him the degrees of death that are possible before life is actually gone. You are forcing him to begin his dying. All constraints on freedom enforce conditions of death. The punishment of prison inflicts the corruption of death on life

"You mean they are by themselves?"

"Yes."

"They're alone?"

"Yes."

"Are they unhappy?"

"They are not too happy."

"Are they frightened?"

"No, they are not frightened. They are innocent so they have nothing to be frightened of. They know they will be released after their trial. We shall prove that they are not guilty. And then you will all be together again. You hear that, Susele? Your mommy and daddy will return to you and hug you and kiss you and you will all be living together again." (So you must be a good girl and do what your brother tells you. So go now both of you and help your aunt.)

Ascher took out a big handkerchief, gave it a flap, and jammed it to his nose. We stood and watched him. He turned his back to us and blew his nose loudly, a ridiculous sound as if in antic celebration of the day my parents would be let out of jail.

Just two or three images left from this period of our life. Aunt Frieda's long, hard, change-picking fingers folding a five and two ones given her by Ascher in half, in half again, and pressing the pellet of bills into her change purse, snapping it shut, snapping her pocketbook shut. The cab driver yawning behind his wheel. On his dashboard, in a shallow cigar box with no lid, a fascicle of pencil nubbins bound in rubber bands. In times of crisis I am always sensitive to the people on the periphery. The cab driver was named Henry Lichtenstein, and his number was 45930. He wore a tan beret at a hundred-eighty-degree angle on his head. He had a toothbrush mustache and a gold tooth that flashed in his rear-view mirror when he yawned.

"I'm not making any promises," Aunt Frieda told Ascher through the window. "I'll do my best, but that's all."

I'LL DO MY BEST BUT THAT'S ALL.

In those days the cabs were still limousines, with jump seats in the back. This was a big yellow De Soto. Our bundles were piled on the floor at our feet. Susan sat in the middle between me and the bird woman. Ascher said goodbye and moved away from the window. I had perhaps eight seconds for a last look before the cabbie put down his clipboard, put the De Soto into gear, and drove us away from our home. Up from the alley rose Williams embracing an ashcan. Riding his great flat feet with an eagle's grace, floating his body through the air like a song. Stops, puts down his burden. I watch his breath steam out of him. He looks at the taxi. I stare into his red eyes of menace. He dips his head and points his arm at me, the cab lurches, and he is gone. In front of Aunt Frieda's head, on the other side of the seat, the diamond interstices of the schoolyard fence become blurred. I have not once mentioned school to Ascher or my aunt. I have not mentioned leaving school, or transferring to another school, or anything about school. They have either forgotten or don't care. But no school is what I have worked out with myself as a justification for going with Aunt Frieda. It will turn out to be not enough. Somewhere in the Bronx she orders the cabbie to the IRT. She will save most of the seven dollars by dragging us up the stairs, valises, bundles and all, and standing us with her on the elevated all the way to Brooklyn.

They're all gone—the friends, the girl who writes for *Cosmopolitan*, the photographer. Artie Sternlicht is on his back on the mattress with his hands behind his head. "I have no energy," he says. His voice is soft now. "I'm sick. I can't get up off my ass."

Daniel wants to leave but both Artie and his girl insist that he stay for dinner. She is in the cubicle kitchen just inside the front door, where boards lie across a sink-bathtub to make the table, and the icebox is half-sized so that you stoop down to open it, and the blackened two-burner stove has curved legs. The whole apartment is this front alcove converted to a kitchen, a closet bathroom with a water tank and pull chain hanging from the wall, and the bedroom furnished with a mattress, a table, a color TV set and a collage.

"Your sister mentioned you only once," Artie says. "She said she had a brother who was politically undeveloped. She made it sound like undescended testicles."

A Japanese paper lantern around a hanging bulb provides the light in the room.

"She's beautiful," Baby says from the kitchen. "I really like her. I didn't figure her to freak out. I mean, y'know, she's not the kind."

"I think she was coming here, she was on her way here," I tell them. "I think she was bringing you material for your collage."

Baby stands in the doorway. "Save the Isaacsons," she says. "That poster."

I nod. Artie sits up and folds his legs. "Oh Christ," he says. He folds his arms.

"You discussed it with her?"

"Ah shit. I wish I could drink some wine. I wish I could turn on. When do we eat, Baby?"

"I'm making whole-wheat spaghetti."

"It's too fucking hot," Artie says. "This fucking city is like an oven." He stands up and starts to pace the room. "You want to know what was wrong with the old American Communists? They were into the system. They wore ties. They held down jobs. They put people up for President. They thought politics is something you do at a meeting. When they got busted they called it tyranny. They were Russian tit suckers. Russia! Who's free in Russia? All the Russians want is steel up everyone's ass. Where's the Revolution in Russia?"

He looks at me as if he really expects an answer. He paces. "The American Communist Party set the Left back fifty years. I think they worked for the FBI. That's the only explanation. They were conspiratorial. They were invented by J. Edgar Hoover. They were his greatest invention."

"How do you know Susan?"

"Baby, how do we know Susan? I think we met her in Boston when I was up there to rap."

"That's when it was," Baby calls in.

"She was into this thing about your parents," Sternlicht says.

"Right."

"Well, man, I mean can I tell it to you straight or are you gonna trip out the minute I open my mouth?"

"Go ahead."

"Your folks didn't know shit. The way they handled themselves at their trial was pathetic. I mean they played it by *their* rules. The government's rules. You know what I mean? Instead of standing up and saying fuck you, do what you want, I can't get an honest trial anyway with you fuckers—they made motions, they pleaded innocent, they spoke only when spoken to, they played the game. All right? The whole frame of reference brought them down because they acted like defendants at a trial. You dig?"

"Yeah."

"I mean someday they're gonna really off me. When the Federales wake up and they see I'm not just some crazy acidhead, when they see that all the freaks are together and putting it together we will be set up for the big hit or the big bust or both, which is all right because I don't give a shit about dying, when you're into revolution you have to die, and you can't be a revolution unless you're willing to die. But man, if they ever put me on trial my action will be to show them up for the corrupt fuckers they really are. That trial will be my chance. I will turn that courtroom on, and what I say and do in that courtroom will go out on the wire, and the teletype, and kids all over the world will be at that trial and say, 'Man, who is that dude, dig the way he's got his shit together!' And if they find me guilty I will find them guilty, and if they find me innocent I will still find them guilty. And I won't come on except as a judge of them, a new man, like a new nation with new laws of life. And they will be on trial, not me. You see? They blew the whole goddamn thing!"

"And Susan disagreed."

"Yeah."

"She said nevertheless they were martyrs," Baby said from the kitchen.

"Sure they were martyrs. But the revolution has more martyrs than it needs. Like all the spades you never heard of murdered in their beds, and in every jail in the world, and like the millions of kids murdered in their schools, and like the people starved to death or shot or burned in Vietnam. We've got martyrs up the ass."

"You can't disagree with Artie," the girl says. Sternlicht sinks back down on his mattress. "We'll have to go see her," he says.

"I'm not sure it's a good idea. She's way down. She doesn't like to talk to anyone."

When we eat there is silence in the room. Our table is the floor. The lights of Avenue B shine on the curtainless raised windows translucent with dirt. The sounds of Avenue B flow in like heat. I am thinking if Phyllis had met him she would have gone with him and made the right choice, all her rhythm liberated, and this revolutionary stud would fuck her and afterwards they would both laugh and feel good. And she would not be hung up, a child all form and empty heart, with a man who didn't fill the form of all her impulses and fashion copies and make them come true. I am glad my wife never met Sternlicht. He is probably a champion fucker. He does not put a woman in bondage.

I look at Baby who wears a halter and short shorts, and has long hair pulled back in a ponytail. She is a thin girl, not really pretty but sexy, with a thin sexy life force in her skinniness that I find attractive, and that I understand in the sense of understanding what Sternlicht goes for, as she pokes a forkful of spaghetti into her open mouth.

"It would've been good if your sister had managed to get the picture here," Sternlicht says. "It would have been good for her. We would slap it up there on the wall, right Baby? And she would have done it, and she would have been done with it. Everything is significant, every small act changes the world."

"Did she ever talk to you about her trust money?"

"Yeah."

"The Foundation for Revolution?"

"Yeah."

"What do you think of the idea?"

Sternlicht smiles. He drinks off a glass of milk that has left a ring on the floor. He wipes his mouth. "I told your sister if she had all that bread to pass on for a bail fund or a free university or any good shit like that, that I would change every opinion I have about the Isaacsons, and I would gladly become a beneficiary of her Foundation. Fuck me if I'm ever consistent. I told her if there's bread for the Movement I don't care if it's in the name of Ronald Reagan. I told her for thirty-five thousand dollars' worth of soupbones for the diggers' pots I would kiss the ass of every pig in the city of noo yawk. That's what I said. Are you satisfied with my answer?"

"It's OK."

"Of all the questions you've asked," Artie says, "that is the one you shouldn't have asked."

"Maybe so," I admit.

"And I've been pretty easy on you, too."

"I know."

"Why did you come here? How did you make the connection?"

"She wrote your name on the container that the poster was in."

THEY'RE STILL FUCKING US. She didn't mean Paul and Rochelle. That's what I would have meant. What she meant was first everyone else and now the Left. The Isaacsons are nothing to the New Left. And if they can't make it with them who else is there? YOU GET THE PICTURE. GOODBYE, DANIEL.

Later Sternlicht and Baby invited me up to the roof for some air. We smoked dope. They sang me a song up there, on the sooty roof smelling of dead air and tar, with the night close and hot and starless and the lights cast up from the street making me feel as if I was on a stove. The song was called *Which Side Are You On.*

They say in Harlan County
There are no neutrals there
You either are a union man
Or a thug for J. H. Blair.

Oh workers can you stand it
Oh tell me how you can
Will you be a lousy scab
Or will you be a man.

Which side are you on?
Which side are you on?
WHICH side ARE you ON?
WHICH SIDE ARE YOU ON?

They ended up singing the chorus right in my face. They broke themselves up. And I went home reacquainted with the merciless radical temperament.

In September 1967 Daniel I Lewin wrote a letter to his foster father, Robert Lewin, a professor of law. I don't have a copy and I hope he didn't file it. It was a shameful letter. Artie Sternlicht, let this be my apology.

Save this space for the letter my father wrote back:

October 4, 1967

Dear Dan,

Sorry it has taken me this long to answer your letter. You gave me some interesting homework. I won't cite the precedents for you but it seems highly unlikely that a court would approve the termination of the trust if Susan so petitioned while she was under psychiatric care. Although she attains her majority this year, Lise and I remain her guardians until such time as she recovers.

However, as you know you are entitled now and have been since your twenty-fifth birthday to assume your pro rata share of the corpus. Susan's illness does not impinge on that. If you were to decide to become her guardian in our stead and apply to the court for that purpose on the grounds that as Susan's sibling you would be more likely than we to dispose of her share as she sees fit, you might get the court to agree. I, of course, would not contest such an application.

There remains one other exception. A third party might have grounds for suit in Susan's behalf by claiming her mental health would be improved were she to assume control of her share of the corpus. I cannot predict what success he would have. But assuming that "the Isaacson Foundation" as endowed by her trust money would have a salutary effect on her condition, a court could conceivably find merit in this argument.

Needless to say I was fascinated by your questions. What have you found out? I don't recall Susan's mentioning any Artie Sternlicht, nor does your mother. Of course there was a period of a month or six weeks when she was not going to class, and there is no telling what she did during that time or where she went or whom she saw. In any event I am encouraged by the drift of your thinking—by the thought that you may be reconsidering your stand not to relieve me of the responsibility of your share of the trust. Please let us know what's on your mind.

> Love from us both,
> Dad

That ends this part of the story. It is interesting to note, aside from everything else, the operating pressure of fatherhood in Robert Lewin's letter. He wants to stabilize me with responsibility. That is a true blue american puritan idea. In that idea is the fusion of the Jew and America, both of them heirs of the ancient seafarers: you ride the sea best with lead in your keel. My lawyer father is no accident, and it is no accident that he loves American Law, an institution that constantly fails and that he constantly loves, like a bad child who someday in his love will not fail, stabilized with responsibility.

While my parents were in jail awaiting their trial General of the Armies was called home, Douglas MacArthur, who cut such a fine figure with his corncob pipe, his aviator shades, and the rakish block of his garrison cap. He had tried to make policy in opposition to Washington's and he had propagandized against his own commander in chief. For his disobedience, his Neanderthal ego and his general failure to step smartly to the orders of an amateur captain of artillery, he was relieved as Supreme Commander of Everything and ordered home to a tumultuous reception. America had not forgotten her hero. In Washington, in New York, the streets were massed with shouting, screaming worshipers. There were parades. There was a mawkish address to both houses of Congress. There was talk of impeaching the President. There was talk of MacArthur for President. I watched these obscenities on Aunt Frieda's magic new television in the afternoons when she was down in her store and unable to tell me not to waste electricity. MacArthur came closer to overthrowing the government of the U.S. than any person in modern times. He was acclaimed throughout the land. I noticed he combed his hair across the top of his head to hide his baldness. How could the country trust a man of such pathetic vanity? I began to wonder if he had been that good a general. What is a good general anyway? What are the criteria? At night Susan and I slept in the same bed, Aunt Frieda's, while she slept on the couch in the living room. It was not a good arrangement. Under the sheet was a sheet of rubber. Susan was regressing and could not wake up to go to the bathroom. In the middle of the night a tide of urine gently lapped at my pajamas. I awoke in the urine mists of dawn.

I was desolate. It is an in-chest feeling of vacuum. I remembered the joy of traveling downtown on the subway with my mother and father, one on either side of me. We were going to hear the New York Philharmonic in an engagement at the Roxy. There was also a technicolor movie. Another time they took me to the Stanley Theater on 8th Avenue near 42nd Street and we saw *Alexander Nevsky*. What was life come to as I lay now with my leaky sister in the staleness of Aunt Frieda's bed in Brooklyn, a loveless bed, and looked forward the next day to possibly another sentimental speech by a killer general.

As I work out the chronology I believe this period at Frieda's coincides with the first of the government's superseding indictments. There were a total of three as the U.S. Attorney and the FBI gradually perfected the scenario. First there were eight overt acts. Then there were nine Overt Acts. Then there were TEN OVERT ACTS.

FRYING, a play in ten overt acts

Monday the 5th

Hi, my dearest Danny, what do you think of Brooklyn? Is it interesting? Have you made any friends yet? I know it's probably boring to you to be out of school, my honey, but all of this—the not being together, the disruption of the routine—is only temporary. In the meantime you should get Aunt Frieda to take you to the library and get lots of books to read. Mr. Ascher, "Uncle Jacob," is trying to get you into the public school there, but that may take a few more days. My beloved little Susan will go to a nursery school.

Listen, my dear sweetheart, I have a surprise for you: "Uncle Jacob" will be bringing a present for each of you from us. I hope you enjoy it. Your father and I discussed what we would get you in our letters and we have asked him to bring it home to you from the store. That is to make you feel not so lonely, because it is from us—and also so that you will have the best possible time!

Please write to me again, my sweet angel boy, I enjoyed your letter so much. Tell me what is on your mind. You are such a comfort to me!

And please don't worry about us! We all miss each other, but cooperate with your Aunt and take care of your sister—I know you do that without my even asking, my honey—and before you know it we'll all be together again.

With lots and lots of love,
Your "Mom."

It was two presents, an Erector set, which bored me, and a drawing pad and colored pencils. I was alarmed by the tone of the letter. I was hurt because it contained no information. Susan got a tea set of tin and a coloring book and crayons. I had to play house with her—an endless distracted game of house that began always with our sitting down to breakfast in front of the tea set. She was the mother and I was the father. After breakfast we drew pictures in our house. I was finding it increasingly difficult to breathe in Aunt Frieda's apartment. She kept the windows locked. When Ascher came with the presents he tried to open the living room window but he couldn't. The apartment was dark and airless. I was finding it more difficult to sleep. I had seen a 1930's prison movie on television: the man was shaking the bars of his cell shouting I'm innocent! I'm innocent I tell ya! I'm innocent! breaking down in sobs because no one is there to hear him and he slides to the floor in a heap, still holding onto the bars of the cell door. All night my parents rose and fell on the bars, like the horses in a merry-go-round, pulling themselves up and sliding down with their hands attached to the bars.

Susan used the cushions of Aunt Frieda's sofa to make the walls of the house. We moved over an armchair for the fourth wall. We accidentally stepped on some of the crayons and ground them into the rug. I didn't put the Erector set away and Aunt Frieda nearly tripped on some of the screws in the dark hall rolling under her foot and scratching the floor.

She was terribly neat, but not clean. She wanted nothing moved in her dusty house. I tried to read the papers in her candy store and she screamed if I lifted one off the counter. If I messed it up how could she sell it? I learned how to steal the paper from her to see if there was anything in it about Paul and Rochelle. Neighborhood kids stole things from her all the time. When her back was turned. When the light hit her eyeglasses. I could have helped her but she didn't ask for my help. I saw the same kind of coloring book on her shelves that Susan had. I saw the same kind of drawing pad and box of colored pencils I had. I realized these were Ascher's presents and that he had probably bought them from Aunt Frieda. I put the newspapers I stole into the garbage. I often had spells of difficult breathing. These frightened me. I found that if I ran around and waved my arms like a windmill, I could breathe better for a moment. I knocked over a lamp and broke it. I could not make friends in the neighborhood because I belonged to Aunt Frieda who was intolerant of children and not popular. She had warned me not to dare say who I was other than her nephew. Susan told a little girl one day that our parents were in jail. This was a lower middle class tenement neighborhood. There were a lot of smart poor people in this neighborhood. One day somebody's older brother was reported missing in Korea. There were incidents.

I found that when I couldn't breathe well I became manically active. I did not speak, I screamed. I did not walk, I ran. I couldn't keep still. I made a game of spying on Aunt Frieda. I peeked through the keyhole to watch her in the bathroom. When she walked to work down the three flights of stairs I followed one flight behind. I stole candy from her counter. I memorized the phone number in her booth and called it from her phone in the apartment. When she answered I hung up. Susan and I did acrobatics on the bed: I held Susan at full arm's length over my head. I dangled her upside down over the side of the bed. She shrieked merrily. We used the bed as a trampoline.

There is nothing in this time that is valuable to me. I feel sorry now for Aunt Frieda who was merely a limited person too tried by her brother Paul, too tried by his shitting and pissing children who tortured her, too tried by the life she was forced to lead. She was not mean, neurotic, self-serving, insensitive or miserly. She was limited. We lasted, or she lasted, five weeks. We never did get to school in Brooklyn. There are no clues in this five weeks. If she were alive today I would not go see her because she would have nothing to tell me that I could use.

Every night for supper we had elbow macaroni mixed with cottage cheese. When Ascher transferred us to the Shelter, Frieda testified that she could not afford to keep us and could not physically contain us. These were only half-truths. One day I was caught spying on her in the bathroom: her eyes were shut and her head was tilted back and her teeth were bared as she sat on the pot with her bloomers around her knees arching her back in an ecstasy of defecation; something that sounded like a rock fell into the water beneath her. A moment later I bumped my head against the doorknob and the door, not quite shut, swung slowly open. Frieda would never forgive me.

I remember nothing of our trip to the Shelter in the Bronx. Ascher probably took us. Perhaps Frieda came along to help effect it. Perhaps there were two trips, one for interviews. I remember some sort of interview. It was a weird time. The newspapers were constantly trying my parents in releases from the Justice Department. There was never in any announcement from J. Edgar Hoover a presumption of innocence. An image grew of my father as a master spy. As a master spy and ringleader. Over a period of a few weeks he became more and more prominent in any discussion of various spy arrests. Dr. Mindish was portrayed as one of those who carried out his orders. I was becoming confused. If my father was a ringleader was I in his ring? How could I be in his ring if I didn't know about it before I read it in the newspaper? Was this the Paul Isaacson who was my father? If it wasn't where was my father? I found many of the words difficult. I missed my father's voice analyzing, endlessly analyzing and exposing the lies in the newspaper, on the radio and television, in the air; I missed his truth, I missed his power to tell me the real meaning of what was presented to me. When I received a letter from him it was as uninformative and strange as the one from my mother. It didn't sound like him. I tried to work things out the way he used to but I couldn't do it. I couldn't summon up that power. He was being transformed before my eyes and he wasn't there to stop it from happening. If he was in jail maybe he *was* an atomic ringleader.

The operations of my mind tried to conform my life and my relationship with my father to the words of the newspaper.

It was Ascher's grim face which always brought me back. Looking at this overburdened man sinking deeper and deeper into the responsibilities of my parents' fate, there could be no question about the semantics of disaster. They were fucking us. Each new indictment handed down by the Grand Jury perfecting the conspiracy, expanding it, adding to its overt acts, drove it in deeper.

I felt guilty. Truman had to order the scientists to develop a super bomb. Although he had worked for the atom bomb, J. Robert Oppenheimer opposed the development of the super bomb and so would be declared a security risk. Although he liked the A-bomb he didn't like the H-bomb and so would be thought of as a traitor.

ALONE IN THE COLD WAR
with Franny and Zooey

Each boy had an army bunk bed with khaki blankets which he was expected to make every morning, a cubby next to the bed, and a footlocker at the foot of the bed. Your laundry bag was supposed to be tied to the foot of the bed. You were not supposed to paste anything on the walls. The walls were a kind of brown tile. The floor was vinyl tile, also brown. The windows were tinted safety windows imbedded with diamond cross-hatching, like filamented chain link fence. All the surfaces were hard and the din was often unbelievable. To quiet us down he blew a whistle which left points of pain in my ears. He blew a whistle to wake us up in the morning. There were always thirty to forty boys in the room, ages five to twelve. They tried to assign little guys to big guys, a kind of big brother system, but it didn't always work. Some of the kids there were obviously sick: it was commonly thought they were retarded but I know now at least a couple of them were autistic. One kid never got off his bed of his own free will. If he was stood up near his bed he stood there until he was moved. They called him the

Inertia Kid. Someone always had to arrange the Inertia Kid in the position he was supposed to be in in that moment. Another boy, a swarthy little hysteric, did not speak in recognizable sentences or with emotions that had anything to do with what was going on. He had a habit of walking around the edges of the gym whenever we went there to play. Or the outdoor yard. This kid would run around the circumference of whatever enclosure we were in, and after the first few times you didn't even notice him. He was always chattering to himself and walking around the edges of places. All the oddballs were put down at the end of the room. At the other end, near the doors, were the transient beds. Boys who came to the Shelter for only a few days or a week or two stayed there near the doors. So the sense you had of the community was of a hard core in the middle with eroded borders of nuts and temporaries. After the first month I was moved from temporary status to hardcore.

We were on the third floor of the Shelter. The girls' section was on the second floor. Sometimes at night I lay after Lights Out and in the dark quiet heard the screams of rage of my sister coming up through the walls.

Once a week we had Fire Drill. Once a week we had Bomb Drill. For Fire Drill you went out on the sidewalk. For Bomb Drill you stayed in.

The first floor was for the offices of the staff, the lunchroom and the kitchen. The fourth and top floor was completely taken up by the indoor gym. The name of the place was East Bronx Children's Welfare Shelter, City of New York (Hon. William O'Dwyer, Mayor. Hon. Edward J. Flynn, Bronx Borough President). It is located off Tremont Avenue near Crotona Park in a cluster of municipal buildings.

A bus took the hardcores to school everyday. I don't know why we were taken to one public school rather than another. There was one within walking distance to which we did not go. The big purple school we did go to was as far away, although in a different direction, as what I thought of as my real purple school, P.S. 70. It made little impression on me and I don't remember the number of it today. Nobody cared whether you did the work or not. It was an old school with tired, grim teachers and a lot of black kids.

At the Shelter the big game was softball. The quality of athletics was very high. Kids played intensely and they played well. The best games were on Sunday. In the morning we'd all sit on our beds in our best clothes and wait for relatives or guardians or whatever to take us out for the day. By noon it was clear who was not going to be taken out. There would be a choose-up game in the yard or, if it was cold, in the gym, and usually it was unsupervised. The Sunday games were played fiercely. Everyone played like hell. I learned the game on Sundays. Someone always ripped up his best pants sliding on the concrete, or tore the sole off his shoe. The girls watched and taunted and it was a completely self-contained, totally populated society with nobody of any importance missing.

Most of the children wore clothes that didn't fit. Socks bunched up around the ankles. Flowered dresses of older sisters. Pants from Goodwill that had to be folded at the waist and stuffed under the belt.

In the lunchroom they served lukewarm frankfurters from big pots of water covered with an amber slick. They served vegetable soup. They served half-pint containers of milk. They served creamed corn and mashed potatoes. I will never forget the smell of that lunchroom: it was a warm good smell, far better than the food. I suppose it was the smell of the vegetable soup which, since it eventually incorporated everything else, out-smelled everything else. I connect that smell with impoverishment. I think of vegetable soup as disenfranchisement. When Phyllis makes vegetable soup she keeps adding things in hopes of recapturing that smell for me. She's never touched it. I think you need tile walls. You need high ceilings with lights hanging down on chains and cafeteria trays of maroon-colored plastic.

The other big smell in the Shelter was the smell of vomit. There was always a lot of vomiting. Kids were always getting sick and throwing up. The janitor came around with his cart, a big broom, a shovel, and a bucket of sawdust. He covered the vomit with sawdust, and when it was all soaked up, swept up the gloppy mess with his broom and shovel. Then he'd mop around with a solution of ammonia. The ammonia smell would drown out the vomit smell for five minutes or so. But for the rest of the day the area smelled faintly of vomit. In its fainter essence it was mysterious and frightening. The smell of the insides of bodies.

Maybe it was the smell of vomit which did something for the vegetable soup.

Some of the older boys were into puberty and had hair. There was a lot of homo wrestling. One kid liked to jerk off in the middle of the room where everyone could see him. Once there was an attempted sodomizing. There were always violent confrontations and some kid or other would be discovered with a knife he shouldn't have had. Punishment was an instantaneous clout on the head. Mr. Levinson, the boys' supervisor, didn't stand for any crap. At night his assistant came on, an older man named Clancy, a flabby dried-out alcoholic with no teeth for whom this job was reclamation. Clancy went to sleep when we did.

Whenever I saw Susan it was on the way somewhere, on the run, usually, when the boys and girls brushed past each other's schedules. She always clung to me. One day I realized it was her birthday and I told Mr. Levinson, who wrote a note to the girls' supervisor. At supper they had a cupcake in her place with one candle on it, and the girls at her table sang Happy Birthday. But she had no present that day. Two days later a card came from jail. Both of them had signed it. In my mother's handwriting it said Happy Birthday to our blessed little girl. Next birthday we'll make up for this one. Love, Mommy and Daddy. Susan was five. Because she was small you would expect her to have been popular—like a pet for everyone. But she did not ingratiate herself. She was not cute. She was terrified. Her hair was black and dirty and her blue eyes had sunk into her cheeks. She looked like a D.P. She bit the girls' supervisor's hand one day and was slapped. Then she kicked the supervisor. She was a problem down there. Whenever we saw each other she clung to me.

One day Mr. Levinson told me to go downstairs to the Psychologist's Office. The psychologist was Mr. Guglielmi. He was younger than Mr. Levinson. He worked in the Shelter part-time. He wore a jacket and a tie and Mr. Levinson wore only a shirt. He wore shiny brown shoes with thick soles. He talked to each kid once a month for ten or fifteen minutes.

"Come in, Dan, have a seat."

The psychologist lit a cigarette and leaned back in a wooden swivel chair that squeaked. "Dan," he said, "I need your help."

Daniel stared at him.

"I don't know what to do about your kid sister. We're trying to make her feel at home. We're trying to make friends with her. But she's giving us a very hard time. Let me ask you: Did she throw tantrums when you still lived at home?"

Daniel shook his head.

"She doesn't eat properly. She keeps the other kids awake. If someone says something to her or even looks at her the wrong way she starts in to scream. She won't cooperate with anyone."

Daniel smiled. He couldn't help it.

Mr. Guglielmi said, "I'm asking you what you think we ought to do."

"She thinks this is jail," Daniel said.

The psychologist wrote something down. Then he leaned forward. "But that's foolish," he said softly. "There are no bars on the windows. No locks on the doors. She can go out to the play yard at playtime."

"You won't let her sleep in the bed with me," Daniel said.

The psychologist wrote something down. Then he said, "And that makes her think she's in jail?"

"In jail people are kept apart. Then they're killed." Daniel couldn't help smiling.

"Oh now, hold on a minute. That's not what happens in jail. People do something wrong, they have a trial. If they're found guilty they go to jail for a certain time and then they're released. They're not killed. Very few people do something serious enough for that."

"My mother and father are in jail and they haven't had a trial."

"Well, that's just a technicality. They're waiting for their trial."

"Why can't they wait home with us?"

"I don't know, Dan, I'm not a lawyer. Maybe the government is afraid they would try to run away."

"Well, they wouldn't feel afraid if they weren't going to kill them."

The psychologist shook his head. He put out his cigarette. "Have you discussed this with Susan?"

"No, it would make her cry."

"Would you like to sleep with her, too?"

"No, she wets the bed."

The psychologist wrote something down. He said, "Well, what are we going to do? Supposing we gave you more time with her during the day. Would that help?"

Daniel shrugged.

"You see, we have rules here. We have a certain way of doing things. The boys are in one section, and the girls are in another section. Those are the rules."

"So that's like jail," Daniel said smiling.

"Daniel, this is the East Bronx Children's Shelter. This is not jail! Hey, look at me when I talk to you: did I tell you you had to come here?"

"No."

"No. Did I tell Susan she had to come here?"

"No."

"No! Well, then how can it be jail? Your parents asked the City if you could stay here. They asked their lawyer to put your names in application. Are you saying then that your own parents would put you in jail?"

Daniel shrugged. "I don't know."

"I don't know! Would a mother and father put their own children in jail?"

"I don't know."

"I don't know! Well, they wouldn't. You know they wouldn't."

Daniel ran his finger along the edge of the desk. Supposing the letters he got from his mother and father were really written by the FBI imitating their handwriting. Or supposing the FBI made them say they wanted the children put in the Shelter. He didn't really believe it, but if it happened to be true he must be on guard. Because if they did put him and Susan in here they would have a reason, and the reason would be to make them hate their mother and father and then maybe to make up lies about them.

violin spiders

Mr. Guglielmi had come around to the front of the desk and sat
one leg down upon it. "Besides," he said, "if this was a jail you
wouldn't be allowed to have any fun. And you do have fun,
don't you, Dan?"

Daniel shrugged. "Yes."

"Are you making friends?"

Daniel shrugged. He nodded.

"Good. Is there anything bothering you that you'd like to talk
to me about?"

"No."

"OK. I think what we'll do is let Susan eat with you. And
maybe at bedtime we'll let you sit with her a few minutes
while she gets sleepy. Let's try that, OK?"

"OK," Daniel said.

"If we didn't have rules, Dan," the psychologist said, "then
we couldn't get our work done. You can see that, can't you?
There are just too many of us to get by without rules."

(when we first walked in there and sat with our things in
the office downstairs everyone on the staff checked us out. Sur-
reptitiously, of course. Quite a stir. Celebrities. Took the edge
off that soon enough, didn't we, Susy. Made them rue the day)

TREASON the only crime defined in the Constitution. Tyranny as under the Stuart and Tudor kings characterized by the
elimination of political dissent under the laws of treason. Treason statutes which were many and unending, the instrument by
which the monarch eliminated his opposition and also added to
his wealth. The property of the executed traitor forfeited by his
heirs because of the loathsomeness of his crime. The prosecution
of treason, like witchcraft, an industry. Founding Fathers extremely sensitive to the establishment of a tyranny in this country by means of ambiguous treason law. Themselves traitors
under British law. Under their formulation it became possible
to be guilty of treason only against the nation, not the individual
ruler or party. Treason was defined as an action rather than
thought or speech. "Treason against the U.S. shall consist only
in levying war against them, or in adhering to their Enemies,
giving them Aid & Comfort. . . . No person shall be convicted
of treason unless on the testimony of two witnesses to the same

Overt Act, or on Confession in Open Court." This definition, by members of the constitutional convention, intended that T. could not be otherwise defined short of constitutional amendment. "The decision to impose constitutional safeguards on treason prosecutions formed part of a broad emerging American tradition of liberalism. . . . No American has ever been executed for treason against his country," says Nathaniel Weyl, TREASON: THE STORY OF DISLOYALTY AND BETRAYAL IN AMERICAN HISTORY, published in the year 1950. I say IF THIS BE TREASON MAKE THE MOST OF IT!

> If this bee is tristante make the mort of it
> If this be the reason make a mulch of it
> If this brie is in season drink some milk with it
> If this bitch is teasing make her post on it
> If this boy is breathing make a ghost of him

My wife came back while I was ill with the flu and she took care of me. I wanted to cry when I heard the front door open. I fought down my urge to show gratitude. My helplessness released in her the tenderest passions, as the novelists used to say. Since I was incapacitated she and her baby had nothing to fear from me. Foul-smelling and stale and unshaven, yellowishly weak, I stared at her from the bedclothes as she went about cleaning the bedroom. I was waiting for her to make one false move of solicitation, but she fed me and changed the bed.

The timing of her return relieved us of the dreary rituals of reconciliation. Forgiving me turns her on, I have no other explanation for the fact that she keeps returning. Phyllis likes to forgive me. Small premature age lines have appeared at the corners of her eyes. Her face has thinned out and her thighs have got slimmer. Suffering does fine work with the chisel. I am finding her admirable, which disturbs me.

Today, as I left the apartment for the first time in two weeks, I noticed that she was way down. There is a gesture she has with her long light hair, taking the loose strands falling past her cheek and tucking them behind her ear. This morning, while feeding the baby, she did that with such deliberation that I felt she had to concentrate to get it done. To make it all perfect, from where I stood her head was just under the poster of the Isaacsons which is pasted on the kitchen wall. Yet since she's come back I have not worked on her. And our life has been friendly.

In our last reconciliation I did something that I thought did not take. I wish I knew how education works. I wish I knew the secret workings in the soul of education. It has nothing to do with time as we measure it. Small secret chemical switches are thrown in the dark. Tiny courses are hung through the electric passages of the tissues. Silken sequences of atoms which have no property other than self-knowledge.

What happened was we went to bed, as reconcilers do. She happened to be just past her period, which is a very hot time for Phyllis, and she was ahead of me. Not at her pitch I noted it as a self-concern, an inward attention that seemed to exclude me. Yet she called out my name. Her fingers were mindless digging into my back. She wound up tighter and tighter, making smaller and quicker movements. I did not break my rhythm, which was insolently slow. Her heart pounded against me, her breasts were wet on my chest, her breath chased my ears, and then she pursed her lips and the effort was as if she were half whistling in pain or amazement. All this was having its effect and I was losing my cool. She was shivering her way through one come after another. Each one was stronger than the last. She was biting my mouth. She was going for the big bang. At this point I did the cruel thing, I pulled back. This forced her to rise after it. I stirred the froth of her honey. She hung from my neck whimpering into my mouth. At the peak of her distraction I slowly sank it back in, and this was the stroke that took her beyond her limits of character and physical integrity.

She told me later it had never before been so good. She couldn't move for an hour. But leaning over her sleepy smiling eyes I could not find there the education recorded, no impression of the cruel thing, the cruel thing, and that it is always the cruel thing that mixes the tears of our eyes, the breath of our lungs, the creams of our comes. . . .

When I was in bed I remembered something that had happened at the Shelter. You needed a fever to remember this: I was under some kind of compulsion to prove myself to the other unreclaimed kids in the hardcore. I had this tremendous urge to make it so thoroughly as a Shelter kid that I would become one of the leaders. Leaders are the only ones who ever feel at home. The rest are displaced by the anxiety of trying to make it with the leaders. I wasn't the best athlete. I mean I did all right but some of those kids were unbelievable stars. One black kid named Roy did everything better than most big guys could: every time up was a hit, he could run like the wind, he could jump higher, catch better, make impossible shots—he could even make the old dead lunk volleyball work, he could make it soar like a kite. Everything he touched was gifted. And he was just the best. There were others there with specialty bags. So my chances as an athlete were not good. But I thought I had as good a mind and tongue as anyone there. I thought I could get there with my mind, which is a tough way to make it in a kid society. A mind without the right attitude, without the right tone, is disastrous in that situation—you end up as some kind of over-articulate fag intellect and you're out in the cold. So it was a challenge. I'm trying to account for the reasoning, if there was reasoning, that led me to do my imitation of the Inertia Kid. Maybe the ultimate extension of intellect is clowning. In the sitting position Inertia Kid has this hunch in his shoulders, and his head sat crooked as if one of his neckbones was out of socket. His tongue protruded and his eyes saw nothing. His hands lay as if broken at the wrists, the thumb of one in the palm of the other. Without having to think about it, I was able to do a perfect takeoff. I could do his walk, which was a pigeon-toed shuffle. I could do him asleep, which was always on his back with his eyes open. He never closed his eyes to sleep. Only his breathing changed when he was asleep. I did all these routines, becoming in one moment popular for them, a new thing in the society, a wit, a mime of affliction, a priest. And I was able to do my routines without ever having really consciously observed the Inertia Kid. In fact I found it difficult to look at him.

This is the only time in my life I have ever performed. I haven't got a performing nature. There are some for whom the turn-on of performing is so total that they must never perform or risk obliteration. I found myself doing the Inertia Kid when nobody was looking. In order to do like he did you had to disconnect your heart muscle, you had to give up your heart, just give it up to its own weight, you had to lift all the rubber bands off the wheels, and slack off the tuning pegs and let the heart lie there in you with disconnected eyes, and unconnected tongue, and limbs lying in their own slackened strings. I could even get the saliva to dribble out of the corner of my mouth. There was for a few days a steady demand, the routine got longer and longer, the cruelty of my observation of the Inertia Kid soon beyond cruelty, a fascinating trip of its own for the wonder of the others, and each time it got harder and harder to stop.

Oh little big brother, pull out, pull out, my wing commander shouts as his grinning and best pilot goes too deep into the stunt. Pull out before the sound plunges into the earth and from one moment to the next there is stillness. I even forgot to breathe. I listened for my heart to stop. My guts strained for air while I tried to remember how to breathe. I was blacking out trying to remember what the light was for.

Why do we need it? What do you do in it? What is it you're supposed to use it for? What is so valuable after all? What is it that is worth desiring?

A foundation. I desire a Foundation.

"Do you want to go home?"

"Yes."

"If I take you will you be a big girl and do what I say?"

"Yes."

"Because we have to do it so that no one sees us. And so you have to listen to me and do what I tell you to do. All right?"

"All right."

"OK, now, that's a promise."

"Yes."

"Say I promise, Daniel."

"I promise, Daniel."

"All right. Now today is Thursday. We're going to escape Saturday. That's not today and that's not tomorrow, but the next day."

"I want to escape now."

"Susan, you just made a promise. You better listen to me or we won't do it at all. If we escape before then it will be easier for them to catch us. You don't want them to catch us, do you?"

"No."

"All right. All you have to do in the meantime is what they tell you. Go to sleep when they tell you and eat when they tell you. I'm not going to wait for you if you're tired so you better not be tired. And if you eat something you won't be hungry when we go. Once we escape I don't know when we'll eat. So you've got to eat all your food and go to sleep. All right?"

"Yes."

"And on Saturday we'll go."

"Yes."

"And listen, you can't tell anyone."

"I won't. I hate them."

Saturday the discipline relaxed. Some of the kids were taken home for the weekend. There was no school. There was more free time. After breakfast there was a free period in the yard. There were a lot of kids in the yard all running around. On Saturday no one would stop you in the street to ask why you weren't in school.

It was a chilly morning. I looked up into the grey sky of swiftly moving clouds and my heart turned over. I was wearing my mackinaw and my leather hunter's cap. Susan had on her snow jacket with the hood. I had my sneakers but she only had her shiny black ankle-strap shoes. "All right now, sit down here at the fence. That's it. Now when I say you lie down. I'll lift up the fence and you roll under it."

"All right."

"Then I'll crawl under. Then run. Run as fast as you can."

I had this idea that if we went home to Williams, somehow that would have the effect of getting our mother and father home too. I felt that as long as we were in the Shelter, they would be in jail. I felt that they would have no chance of reaching home unless we were there. I wanted to put it all back to-

gether. My reasoning seemed logical at the time. I had no sense
of faith or belief. It merely seemed logical that if Susan and I
went home, it would be restored. Paul and Rochelle might even
precede us. We would meet them.

"All right now, get ready. Do you have to go to the bathroom?"

"No."

"I don't know where to find any bathroom, so you better go
now if you have to. I'll wait for you."

"I don't."

Alone in the Cold War, Daniel and Susan run down Tremont
Avenue. It is a busy, curving cobblestone avenue lined with
stores and delicatessens, movies and automobile showrooms and
bars and Chinese restaurants. From west to east it snakes over
the hills of the Bronx, a major artery. Trolley tracks, no longer
used, flow down its center. It bleats with traffic. Daniel has
some knowledge: he knows that the Shelter is in the East Bronx
and that his home is in the West Bronx. But he doesn't know
which way is west. He looks for signs on the front of the buses
nosing past. He looks for the sun but there is no sun. They
scurry along, the little girl pulled by her brother, hurrying
along the storefronts, darting past doorways, weaving through
the people walking, shopping, waiting for lights at corners.
Daniel's side hurts. Each step brings him pain. He is sweating.
"No so fast," his sister whines. "You're going to make me fall."

Every few minutes she has to stop and pull her socks off her
heels; her white cotton socks slip down into her shoes, and she
has to tug them up.

Ahead the Third Avenue El crosses over Tremont Avenue,
leaving a tunnel of shadow, a premonition of long distances. In
this darkness of black steel beams that shimmy when the trains
roar overhead, the green traffic light shines cool and bright. A
newsstand nestles under the stairs leading up to the trains. The
smell of hot dogs and juicy fruit gum and popcorn. The sugges-
tion of being lost in the city.

You can't ask anyone the way because nobody gets more
sympathy than a child who has lost his way. People don't forget
that. That is like leaving a trail of bread crumbs. Worse, they
take you in hand, you are captured. So you walk in dumb panic,

hoping to be right, looking for signs, prodding your intuition, walking as if you knew where you were going. Decisively, you cross the street and turn left.

"How much more? Are we going to be there soon?"

"Be quiet."

"Is it soon?"

"Soon. Just be quiet."

The small warm hand in my hand. The imprint is permanent. The small warm hand in my hand. It is given to me and not withdrawn. The small warm hand in my hand. Every few steps I hear in the traffic and movement of the city a soft *hiss hiss,* like a signal from a doorway, like static from a secret radio. I am ever on the alert for secret signals. But it is Susan sniffing in the privacy of my ear, measuring our progress with intakes from her runny nose. Occasionally she draws a sleeve across her face.

"What are you crying about?"

"I'm not."

"Am I going too fast?"

"Yes."

I check to see if anyone is following. We are off the rumbling avenue and walking down a tenement street of the East Bronx. It's a poor neighborhood. Occasionally we pass small porch houses with asphalt shingles just like ours. No one appears to be following. I slow up but we won't stop. Kids stare at us from their stoops and doorways. I can't pretend to be doing anything but passing through. There rises in me a feeling for the Shelter. I think of the lunch hour, the Saturday noon frankfurters. Nostalgia. A slight smear of homesick in the chest. Is that possible? Is it possible for feelings to be that indiscriminate?

Behind us is my vision of the Inertia Kid lying on his bunk. I am sorry for my routines. They were a failure. He knew I made fun of him. He knew what I was doing. I feel terrible. I feel the sickness of someone who has sold out. Occasionally in certain lights the idiocy of his expression was momentarily erased. His face was comely. I knew he was handsome and wise. I was afraid to look at him. I adored him. If I had stayed at the

Shelter I could have taken care of him and protected him from impersonations. Could Roy hit a ball, jump as high?

In the afternoon Daniel and Susan had come to the section of Bathgate Avenue between 173rd Street and Claremont Parkway that was an open market of fruit and vegetable stalls and peddlers' pushcarts at the curbs. The sidewalks were crowded with shoppers and the merchants in their full-length white aprons over their coats cried out their prices to passersby. Pyramids of apples and dark grapes, oranges and pumpkins, rose from the stalls. Prices written on brown paper bags impaled on wooden slats. Two pounds for nineteen cents! Six for thirty-three! Fresh! Sweet! Juicy! Bushels of green peppers. Boxes of carrots in bunches, and the green topping is wrung off upon purchase. Dates poured into a bag from a metal scoop. Indian nuts. Rock candy. They stood in front of an open Appetizing store magnetized by the slabs of lox, and the pickle barrels and the nut trays and the herring in cream. Who's next! How much, lady! The women elbowed past, their shopping bags crammed. The smell of warm fresh bread floated out of a white bakery. The butcher's freezer door slammed shut with a great clank. And here, with sawdust on the floor, was a store just like Irving's Fish Market, with the live fish swimming in a tank and waiting for Irving's rolling pin to stun them just before the knife sliced off their heads. How much, lady! And along the curbs were the pushcarts of notions and buttons and thread, of a selection of ladies' panties, of factory-second shoes and sneakers tied by the laces, of bananas, just bananas, a pushcart piled with bananas, the peddler a specialist in bananas. With all those bananas he had to move them cheaper than the next guy. How much, lady! They're rotten, a lady tells her friend. And everywhere were the cries of life and commerce, and the smells of the oranges and warm bread and fish and cheap new shoes. Cars inched through the narrow street. Mothers and children shouted back and forth from the street to the fire escapes. With Susan in tow Daniel slowly drifted in the eddying currents of shoppers. Loaded shopping bags swung into him. Old men pushed him out of the way. It was a dangerous passage but his heart was lifted because he had recognized Bathgate Avenue and knew it. Bathgate was spoken of with approval by his mother and father, who regretted only that it was too far to go to shop every day. But the food was best there, and the prices cheapest, and on special occasions, like with Mindish driving them in his old Chrysler, the Isaacsons would stock up from the rich markets of Bathgate Avenue. Shopping on Bathgate was a skill. One took satisfaction from one's judgments and one's purchases. Daniel also knew that when he came to Claremont Avenue he would be able to see the hills of Claremont Park, and that by climbing up the steps from Webster Avenue into Claremont Park he would inevitably come to Weeks Avenue not two blocks from his home.

"We'll be there soon, Susan."

He knew she was hungry. He considered stealing something; he had already seen two different kids filching fruit, but he was afraid. He didn't mind getting shoved around in the street because he felt virtually invisible. Who could tell that he and Susan didn't belong to someone walking right in front of them or right behind them? But if he stole something and was caught he would no longer be invisible. "We'll be home soon," he said over his shoulder.

And then tell of that last leg of the journey, the most frightening and dangerous. Claremont Avenue was a wide, dangerous street of traffic. Then you had to cross Webster, a confusing, doubly wide street of tracks and buses and cars going two ways, and lights that didn't seem to allow the opportunity to cross. It didn't seem like a street that was meant to be crossed. Also with the steep walls of the park on the other side this was an area open under the sky. One's head and shoulders were vulnerable in the open spaces of the city. Crossing Webster and climbing the steep stone flights to the park, I became sensitive to the extreme danger of what I was doing. We were becoming exhausted. Also, now that we were leaving the depths of the East Bronx for the heights of Claremont, I remembered the Brookies, a gang of East Bronx terrorists who came up off Brook Avenue like a wind and raided the softer, barely better-off neighborhoods around this park and beat up the little kids and cut them and took their money. The closer we got to our neighborhood the more frightened we became. Susan began to cry. The tears flowed, the snot flowed. She wanted to sit down on a bench and rest. She wanted to pull up her socks which had disappeared into her shoes. Her shoes were blistering the backs of her heels.

The park was empty. A bitter wind was blowing through the bare trees, and piles of leaves whirled around our feet and stuck to our knees. Dirt stung my eyes. We turned our backs to the wind, and with our hands to our eyes, whirled and turned and spun our way toward home.

Here are the names of some traitors. Benedict Arnold, of course, along with his wife Peggy; General Charles Lee, a trusted aide of Washington's; Burr, Burr's daughter and son-in-law, the double traitor Wilkerson. The names also of Federalists too prominent to mention who secretly gave the British aid and comfort and entered negotiations with them that looked to a Federalist coup after a British victory. Robert E. Lee fits the definition, and also the Mormons who mounted war against the U.S. Govt. Examples abound. But historians of early America fail to mention the archetype traitor, the master subversive Poe, who wore a hole into the parchment and let the darkness pour through. This is how he did it: First he spilled a few drops of whiskey just below the Preamble. To this he added the blood of his thirteen-year-old cousin Virginia, whom he had married and who hemorrhaged from the throat. He stirred these fluids in a small, elliptically stressed circle with the extracted tooth of the dead Ligeia. Then added some raven droppings. A small powerful odor arose from the Constitution; there was a wisp of smoke which exploded and quickly turned mustard yellow in color. When Poe blew this away through the resulting aperture in the parchment the darkness of the depths rose, and rises still from that small hole all these years incessantly pouring its dark hellish gases like soot, like smog, like the poisonous effulgence of combustion engines over Thrift and Virtue and Reason and Natural Law and the Rights of Man. It's Poe, not those other guys. He and he alone. It's Poe who ruined us, that scream from the smiling face of America.

We looked from the porch through the windows. A silver light reflected through our faces the silver sky racing over the schoolyard. The sky of silver raced through our eyes, through our house. The wind came up and pressed us to the windows. Gradually the wind carried over the schoolyard from the soot hills of apartment houses in the west a last few crushed granules of daylight that fused the windowpane to the room: The living room was empty. The walls were stained with crushed grey light. The floorboards were bare. The room was empty. The window lacked curtains. The house was empty. I moved to the other window on the porch. The room was bare. The walls bare, the floor bare. I tried the door. The door was locked. I ran down the porch steps, around to the alley. I knocked on Williams' cellar door. I put my ear to the door. I hoisted myself up to look through the window of the cellar door. In the darkness I saw the light of my own eyes. The door was locked. I ran around to the back of the house. I ran around to the front of the house. I looked through the porch window. There was no sound from the house. The only sound was the wind. Susan stood like an A in the middle of the porch, a darkening stain spreading under her foot. I was numb with cold. My face stung, my hands stung. We watched the stain expand in all directions around Susan's shoe on the wooden porch.

According to Evans, observers in New Zealand report that mosquitoes there land on the floating pupae of females, slit them open with their genitals, and mate with the females before they can emerge.

Ascher held each of us under his arm, under a giant hand pressing us into his sides, into the bulky nap of his overcoat. We were walking down Tremont Avenue. My leather hunter's cap with the earflaps was pushed awry by Ascher's coat. He never knew his strength. Susan's face was red with the cold. We looked at each other across Ascher's girth. "*Mamaneu*," Ascher said. He sighed. "If you children knew what you were doing to me. I cannot tell your mother and father. But how can I not tell them? What can I do? What can I do? I'm not going to live long."

It was Sunday. The traffic on Tremont Avenue was light. Down at the Polo Grounds the Giants were playing the Pittsburgh Steelers. One of the kids in the Shelter had gone to the game with his uncle, but Ascher only came to take us for a walk. The Giants had Charlie Conerly. The Steelers had Bobby Layne.

In our hands were Ascher's gifts: plastic orange jack-o'-lanterns and black cardboard skeletons with white bones fastened at the knees and the pelvis and at the shoulders with metal grommets.

"What can I tell you," Ascher said. "Some people are singled out. The world lacks civilization. Men do not respect God. You are only children and you can't understand—it's natural, I would run away too. Thank God I knew where to look. Oh, my children. What can I tell you? Soon, soon we will be in court. We shall have our trial."

Book Three

STARFISH

Elected silence sing to me.

The guard sees him pace his cell. His arm rises, his finger points. Occasionally a sound escapes his pantomime, some release of anguish whose diction is unclear.

He associates with Big Bill Haywood, and with Debs and with Mooney and Billings. All these fighters. The Scottsboro Boys. Their stars illuminate the walls, burn away the humiliation. Debs' cell was enormous, as big as the world. That is what the rulers never learn. The properties of steel and stone are subject to moral law.

Nor is death what it seems to be. When the ruling class inflicts death upon those they fear they discover that death itself can live. It is a paradox. Ma Ludlow is alive. Joe Hill is alive. Crispus Attucks is alive. Even Leo Frank, why do I think of Frank swinging from his tree in Georgia, but all right, Frank.

The two Italians speak and stir and smile and raise their fists in the mind of history. I am their comrade, they talk to *me*, Sacco makes his statement to *me*.

Socrates was tried. He was found guilty. He was forced to drink hemlock. By this act his persecutors raised him to eternal life and consigned themselves to the real death and total obscurity of persecutors everywhere.

Jesus was tried. He was found guilty. He was tortured and executed. If Jesus had not been tried, if he had not been put to death, how would his teachings have endured? The Christians themselves celebrate this fact in their idea of resurrection: He returns and lives with men, in the imaginations of men hundreds of generations later. Of course this doesn't touch the question of how his ideas, which were completely Jewish, were perverted by institutions which spoke in his name.

The difference between Socrates and Jesus is that no one has ever been put to death in Socrates' name. And that is because Socrates' ideas were never made law.

Law, in whatever name, protects privilege. I speak of the law of any state that has not achieved socialism. The sole authority of the law is in its capacity to enforce itself. That capacity expresses itself in Trial. There could be no law without trial. Trial is the point of the law. And punishment is the point of the trial—you can't try someone unless you assume the power to punish him. All the corruption and hypocritical self-service of the law is brought to the point of the point in the verdict of the court. It is a sharp point, an unbelievably sharp point. But there is fascination for the race in the agony of the condemned. That is a law, a real law, that rulers can never overcome—it is fixed and immutable as a law of physics.

Therefore the radical wastes his opportunity if he seriously considers the issues of his trial. If he is found guilty it is the ruling power's decision that he cannot be tolerated. If he is found innocent it is the ruling power's decision that he need not be feared. The radical must not argue his innocence, for the trial is not of his making; he must argue his ideas.

His trial is held in a large, shadowed hall. Voices echo. Gestures are solemn, oratorical. In attendance are all the world's history of dead heroes of the Left.

But a small elevator brings him up from the basement lockup and with one marshal in front of him and one holding his arm, he steps through the door into the courtroom and the raised judge's bench is off his right eye. He sees a large square room, but a room, not a hall, and the raked jury box has leather chairs of green. The walls are wood-paneled in the same dark wood of the balustrade which separates the trial area from the spectators' pews. The floors are marble. The back doors look padded, and have porthole windows. As he enters no one seems to notice. He sits and he waits. Ascher touches his arm and speaks quietly into his ear. On the other side of Ascher, Rochelle writes on a pad. He is bewildered, his own visions have made him vulnerable. Ordinary people move about the room on obscure business. There are few spectators. He turns in his chair and cannot tell who is press. Everyone looks the same. Everyone is sallow in the light of the courtroom which is a mixture of daylight and the incandescence of weak bulbs. At the same time voices seem metallic, the acoustics of the room are not good. He is reminded of what—a library, a legitimate theater with the fire curtain down, a doctor's office, an indoor swimming pool. He feels slightly ill. He recognizes the feeling, a cavern opening inside him, a cavern of fear, and closing his eyes he sees into its darkness and it has no bottom.

When the Judge comes in from his own door on the other side of the bench and quickly takes his seat, Paul, having been gently suffered to stand on his feet, takes a deep breath. It is to seal the cavern of his nauseating fear. Everyone sits and the Judge, like a businessman starting his day, commences the trial in an efficient, quiet, conversational voice. He does not look down at Paul. He addresses only the lawyers. It is Judge Hirsch. Not having known of his existence even a few short months ago, Paul knows a good deal more about him now, including Hirsch's most intimate professional secret, that he hopes to be appointed to the Supreme Court. All the lawyers in the corridor know this. Hirsch has heard more cases brought by the government in the field of subversive activities than anyone else. He is Jewish. He wears a striped, ivy league tie, the knot of which can be seen under his judicial robe.

Paul realizes that he has to adjust to the reality of the situation. Howard "Red" Feuerman, the Chief U.S. Attorney, is a thin, boyish fellow with freckles, and thin sandy red hair and a tenor voice. He is younger than Paul expected, perhaps his own age, and he too wears a glen plaid suit, of brownish tone, although his fits him better. Feuerman is a war hero. He commanded a destroyer. His career has been meteoric. He is a graduate of St. John's, and is married to an Irish girl and has seven children. Paul runs his hand through his hair. He quickly tightens the knot at his collar. He wishes at this moment, and it is unbelievable to him, and it shames him, but he wishes at this moment he could be back in his cell. On the window ledge, under the bars, he keeps the shoebox with his letters from Rochelle and the children, and his hairbrush, and his toilet articles, and the cigar box with his collection. He has a very good way of folding the extra blanket at the foot of his cot. He might be having a chat now with Doyle, the day guard, a very decent man who has had much sorrow in his life.

But you can see that is part of it too, the enforced isolation, the sapping of confidence so that being with other people in a room without bars is suddenly a terrifying thing. They are counting on just the feelings I am feeling now. I will show them they can count on nothing.

Nevertheless he feels he's lost something even in the few minutes he's been here. A run scored for the other team. Ascher is now up at the bench with Feuerman, and he looks to his left across Ascher's empty chair and catches Rochelle studying him worriedly. Behind them, filing in through the rear doors of the court, are the people from whose numbers a jury will be chosen. Surely it is ridiculous to suppose that even one Communist is among them. He wants to reach out, to touch Rochelle's hand. He puts down the urge. They have agreed to be calm and dignified and under no circumstances make of themselves spectacles for the watching eyes of the press. To show no emotion, to give no satisfaction, to provide no hearts with occasion for scorn or pity. Not pity but justice is what they will have, and not by groveling for it but by demanding it. They have worked it all out—Rochelle has been very emphatic on this point.

He must clear his head and keep cool. What matters is that he maintain his faculties. To analyze the situation and assess it correctly and do what has to be done on the basis of that assessment. He understands that the trial will be held in recognizable New York accents. His adversaries are human beings with jobs to do. They will do their jobs feeling that they honor the standards of justice. An American flag, a beautiful flag with gold fringe, hangs from a pole which is socketed in a stand behind the judge's bench. I am to be presented as an enemy of this flag. Yet Mrs. Goldstein, my fourth-grade teacher, told me of all the children in the class, I had the finest straightest salute, and I was commended to the notice of the other children: "The way Paul stands, children, that is the way to stand, nice and tall and with a straight back when you say the pledge of allegiance." The marvelous Mrs. Goldstein. The marvelous smell of the classroom on rainy days, with all the raincoats and rubbers. A schoolroom on a rainy day, steamy with wet raincoats in the closet and wet rubbers. The windows fogged with steam, the rain dripping down the outside of the windows. The hot lunch program. The hot soup. To each other the teachers spoke Yiddish, which was ridiculous because nine tenths of all the children were Jewish and they understood Yiddish from the mothers and fathers, from their grandfathers. The maps that pulled down like shades. The watercolors of Washington and Lincoln and Coolidge framed in glass high on the walls.

All societies indoctrinate their children. The marvelous Mrs. Goldstein in total innocence taught us the glorious history of our brave westward expansion: our taming of the barbaric Indians, our brave stand at the Alamo, the mighty railroads winning the plains. Thus I must understand the nature of the conspiracy against me: it is mounted in full faith and righteousness by the students of Mrs. Goldstein.

He begins to feel better. His stomach is settling. The long drawn out process of picking jurors has begun. He sits with his hands clasped on the edge of the table. He does not stare too intensively at each of these people who may decide his fate. His personal manner will offend no one. His mind is working, and he is no longer stunned. He feels the satisfaction of a soldier having done everything necessary to prepare himself for battle. It is a moment of clarity and exhilaration.

My darling, whoever is looking will think I am writing a note on some legal aspect to Ascher. I will pass it to him and he will pass it over to you. You look so pale, my sweetheart. Don't be afraid. Don't you know your girl longs for you with a love that is indestructible? Look up and you will see me smiling at you.

R.

It is as she says. He smiles, and at this moment all the fear backs up on him and the treacherous muscles of his smile mean to betray him and cause him to cry out. He swallows this dreadful feeling, swallows the terror, tastes it, gulps it. Oh Rochelle! Oh my darling. Do you know what? There is no one behind us. I have checked. Not a face we know. Neither Frieda nor Ruth. Nor anyone from the Concourse Jefferson Club. We are absolutely alone.

Who is the higher authority? Who do I call? Who saves me. The muscles of let me out. The muscles of they can't do this to me. When the cell door first closed I thought it would open if I tried it. They actually locked me in a cell. They actually do that, put someone in a place so that he can't get out. It is done. And the same people who have put me in here are trying me. What can I expect of a trial conducted by the same people who have arrested me and put me in their jail. The wish to get out. It is a terror that makes rigid the muscles in your arms, your sphincters, the cords of your sex; your body winds up on itself, it all tightens and begins to radiate this tremendous fearful energy that attaches to nothing. You smear electrons on the cellblock. You melt the palms of your hands on the bars. The more insane and infuriating and ridiculous the fact that you must stay here in this cage, the more it is true. With every minute that passes it becomes more terrifyingly insane and more true. And finally you reach the point when you realize that the situation is contrived to make you realize you are your own enemy: the muscles of let me out will destroy you. You have to untangle them, unhitch them from the rage in your throat, loosen them from the mind. Slack your ropes. At the moment you slack your ropes and begin to breathe you begin to do time. That is the name the inmate community gives to this adjustment. Doing time. You begin the process of outlasting the animosity of those who have put you here. You destroy the time in your life, the minutes and the hours, scorch them with your own indifference, make them valueless to yourself before they do it for you. As the Red armies retreated before Hitler, burning the earth behind them, their own earth, their own crops, their own fruition, so that it would not fall in its living ripeness to *them*.

This morning, when they came to take me to my trial, every man in the cellblock wished me luck.

WHILE YOU WERE OUT

Mr. A, a Mr. Feuerman called, left no number or message except that he had a matter of mutual interest to discuss—wouldn't talk with anyone else. Have a happy.

Joanne, 515pm

"I don't understand, Jake. You mean they even now have the power to call it off?"

"There are ways. He goes on the assumption that whatever it is you confess to generates a new legal situation that must be studied."

"You know what you're saying? You are saying that he punishes us with our own trial."

"Please, Paul, we haven't got that much time. I'm simply telling you what Feuerman said. It's a routine matter. Let's forget it and go on."

"My God, the implications!" Paul laughs. He is flushed. "The uses of your precious law, Jake!"

"Please—do me a favor. No analysis."

"That is why they arrested Rochelle, to make me talk. What do they want me to say? Whatever it is, they know that even under the threat of my wife's arrest I did not crack. Why should I change my mind now? What do you think, Rochelle?"

She says nothing, holding his hand tightly in her two hands as they sit across from Ascher. Her shoulder touches his shoulder. Under the table her thigh touches his thigh.

"What do you think, Rochelle? Is this a tacit admission that they know they can't win? That's it, isn't it? They're trying to bluff us before we call their hand. That's it, isn't it?"

"They are not without resources in this trial," Ascher says.

"What did you tell him—Feuerman?"

"Oh honey, please," Rochelle says. "What do you think he told them?"

"No really, Jake, what did you say?"

"I said no deals. We make no deals."

"Tell him to ask Selig Mindish!" Paul cackles. He laughs. "Mindish knows all these marvelous stories! Maybe he'll confess a new and better one. Tell them to ask the dentist."

She hears the cry of terror. She worries about him. When they are together like this he becomes agitated, he colors easily. He affects a toughness that frightens her because it is so hysterical. He is very thin! She knows he does not eat. He tells her the jail food is specially prepared to have as little nutrition as possible. To dispirit them and depress their alertness and energy. He lives on candy bars from the Canteen, and advises her to do the same. They don't have his cigars so he smokes Camels. He smokes too much and is too thin. Dear God, does he really look for justice? Dear God, grant him foresight. Make my terrible burden lighter.

Don't worry, Jake has said over and over. Everything will be all right. When he says this he sometimes places his large heavy hand on my shoulder. He does not understand its weight and that what I feel from it is the opposite of what he says. Jake, dear Jake, you cannot know. You distinguish yourself from the burning righteousness of my husband, but look at you, my Jewish gentleman, with all your education and wisdom: you shine in the faith of the individual practitioner. Yet he himself has told me what to expect. Under the charge against us the normal rules of evidence are suspended. For us they don't exist. We are charged not with committing espionage, but with conspiring to commit espionage. Since espionage itself does not have to be proved, no evidence is required that we have done anything. All that is required is evidence that we intended to do something. And what is this evidence? Coincidentally enough under the law the testimony of our so-called accomplice is considered evidence. Am I a fool that I can't see what this means? Do I have to be a lawyer to understand that this allows them to put Dr. Mindish on the stand and by Jake's own precious law anything Mindish says against us has the weight of evidence. As surely as the gun convicts the murderer.

She carries the odds with the instinctual knowledge of a keeper of books. In the courtroom her face is impassive. She composes herself into attitudes of forbidding dignity. She thinks of her husband. She thinks of things to say to him. This is one way she can survive the ordeal without illusions—to pretend to his. For if she reveals her fatalism he will be hurt. But this is emotional embezzlement. If she is right, and how can she not be, the bill will come due—and then what can she say to him? And then what will she be able to do to protect him?

By the rules of evidence in this trial the verdict is fore-ordained. If the testimony of Mindish is admitted as competent, the conspiracy is proved. Because it would not be admitted except under the assumption that a conspiracy existed. She smiles. Here in the country where she was born a defendant can be found guilty of being brought to court as a defendant.

I lie in this cell and Mama's voice of her curses comes to me down the corridor. The cholera, the Cossacks. Wait, my child. Wait just long enough and you will have what I have. For your sins a womb as dry as dust, to ashes your lifespring miracle, to the dust of the furnace and you will taste it on your tongue who have dared to challenge God, and call upon him his obligations. Wait, wait, my child.

The night before their appearance in court she writes the following letter:

My Darling Pauly,

Need I say that I'm looking forward to our trial? Not only that we will be exonerated and the children* re-

(*changed by an editor to "our beloved children" in the printed version—so that everyone would know whose children she meant; by this time there were very few people left in the C.P. who knew anything about writing)

turned to us. Not only that "every dog has his day" in court. But at the lowest level, of simple temporary release from this imprisonment that is so barbaric.

At the trial we will sit at the same table, my precious love. Can you understand how difficult I will find it to concentrate on the legal goings on! Just as in our meetings with Jake I have to pull myself away from the contemplation of you, which each time is like drinking water after a long thirst. But oh my darling, am I too bold? that water only leaves me more parched!

As ever, in love,
Rochelle

I ask the question of Professor Sukenick: Under what circumstances do we suspend criticism? Note the clear instance here of the paradox of the literary sensibility—that it is formed by the previous generation. But there were moments in these meetings with Ascher that were so painful to everyone, the old lawyer stealing a minute for them, standing in front of the safety-glass panel in the door with his eyes closed, his head bowed, prop papers in his hand, but unable to block from his ears the sips of salt water, the suckings of it, the bussings and suckings, the hands quickly dipping into the clothes, and that is a sound too when you don't want to hear it—for don't all bodies obey the laws of physics and share the properties of inanimate things, so that to our profound embarrassment cocks uncork loudly and piss pours like water from faucets, and the asshole is a musical instrument—so painful to everyone these quick horny thefts of each other's feel and smell, sudden sharp incense of unresolved sexual sentiment, that they agree for the sake of everyone's feelings—and Ascher sighs—it is less painful to meet in restraint. And that recalls to them their first chaste days of glances when the understanding was I would if I could, and that was enough, that and the excitement of the rally was enough. "Everyone is waiting for us to confess," she writes later. "Suppose I confess that I love my husband, and confess as to how I fell for him on our first 'date'—a Loyalist rally on Convent Avenue!"

FALLING

A hill, a long hill rises from the valley of 125th Street, in the darkening and cold compact of clouds coming in like fleets of Hindenburgs over New York, and they are war clouds drawn by the bourgeois cartoonists, clouds too heavy with rain of death and fire for the thin taut umbrella of Neville Chamberlain. And the trolleys pull themselves up the tracks of that hill, magnetized to the rails, jerking and gliding up the hill of rails on spurts of current sucked by the pantograph from the overhead wires; and these trolleys, in parade, carry students of the City College of New York up from their jobs through the darkness to their nighttime classes. Fences of planted spears and buildings of grey and black stone, it's not Yale but it's free and its academic standards are high, if you're a bourgeois romantic you can dim your eyes and pretend it's a real collegiate campus, like Michigan, or Brown, and the grubby municipal accommodation for the sons and daughters of immigrants, poor people, largely Jewish. Why, at Lewisohn Stadium an actual football team practices in the dark, although the lavender jerseys do not all match and the football pants are black on some and brown on others, and Notre Dame will never worry or Tommy Harmon. But if you're one of us, Lewisohn is a place for rallies, if that can be managed, or the Philharmonic in the summertime—John Barboroli for thirty-five cents on seats of stone, and two of these night students of tenuous connection to the football team sit there, known to each other less than a year, and for both of them thirty-five cents is a not inconsiderable investment. It is a feverish time, a summer of peculiar chill, and he woos her in their consanguinity of belief. Of course they cannot marry. He makes six dollars a week, part-time, in a radio and record store on Sixth Avenue, and lives with his older sisters on the Lower East Side; he is thin and fortunate. She is more fortunate, making fourteen-fifty as a bookkeeper, taking it home to her mother in the Bronx, her sole living relative. But both of them religiously hold out portions of their wealth for the Scottsboro Boys, or to free Tom Mooney, or for the Loyalists. LIFT THE ARMS

EMBARGO! And their nickels are for carfare and they carry their lunch in paper bags, rolled up when empty to be used again. An interlude at Lewisohn Stadium is a grand luxury, a dwelling in the mutuality of taste, for Benny Goodman does not move their feet, nor any of the popular numbers of the day, from the top ten of the *Lucky Strike Hit Parade,* which he hears over and over again in the Sixth Avenue store where the old Hippodrome used to be. *I've Got My Love to Keep Me Warm.* These songs show the cultural degeneracy of the bourgeois with their rhythms stolen from the southern Negro, cheapening a people's music. But Beethoven, Brahms, Rachmaninoff, these are the stirrers of the heart. When there is time. There's an important workers' rally downtown in Union Square and New York's finest Cossacks rear their horses into the crowd and swing their sticks. Or Paul stands at the gate distributing the mimeographed leaflet protesting—what? The rape of Ethiopia, the giveaway of Czechoslovakia, Georgia chain gangs, the D.A.R., the A.F.L. The President of City College is said to support Mussolini. OUST ROBINSON! Rochelle is active organizing the union in her office. The people are uniting, offering a common front against the spread of Fascism. COMMUNISM IS THE TWENTIETH CENTURY AMERICANISM! We go to the rally. We are the revolutionary heirs of Jefferson and Lincoln and Andrew Jackson and Tom Paine. The philosophers have only interpreted the world; the point is to change it. Endless arguments in the cafeteria of dark tables. The trolley cars wind up the hill, buzzing and whining; the wind blows the overhead wires. The lights in the streetcar flicker. He shifts his books and paper bag from one arm to another. She smiles at him, her hand barely reaching the leather strap. She fell for him at a Loyalist rally on Convent Avenue. Men still sell apples on the corners, and chestnuts from stovepails of coal lumps in the winter, or hot sweet potatoes for three cents. People sleep in doorways all over Harlem. At three a.m. the subway cars are filled. Mama, I want to invite him home to dinner. And who do you think you are—Lady Bountiful? For one year he feels her up not even thinking the words to himself, but it is all one can do in the park, or in a hall. He has never had a woman and she has never had a man. They are aware of the distance between their verbal sophistication and the actual facts; between their friends' view of them running hand in hand to the corner to catch the trolley, ragged coats trailing, the easy swing of their rhythm, envy of the world, the new life-style, young fighting Communists with tears stung out of their clear eyes by the wind, with red cheeks, a wadded handkerchief pressed to her nose, a sniffing in, a remark he makes, their laughter, their books bought used, the pages blackened along the edges—between this vision of them gliding off within darkness lighted by the interior lights of the streetcar (snap it quick, snap it) and their knowledge of themselves, unliberated, clothed, shy, scared, spiritualized by necessity. When you're poor you don't take chances. When each nickel counts and the world needs every able hand, you don't have sex. Besides, you have no place to do it. The truth is you would if you could. You learn the art of companionship, the heavy meaning of an arm taken, the way she can glance at you one merry moment and make it go right to the root of your heavy blue balls, or when you have an idea think of it in terms of telling her, or her small beautiful mouth, a familiarity with her limited wardrobe, and in bad moments alone condemning yourself, cursing yourself for thinking of her centrality, this lady, this soft revolutionary girl, and wondering with red ears and hot ears how to get it out of your worthless degenerate mind and by will alone projecting that energy into the revolution—you do not think of her strength, only of her softness. Or loving his wiry hair, his lean boyishness, his innocence, the endless play of his mind upon the world, inexhaustibly engaged, with a passion for justice and liberation of the poor, and his shoes worn down at the heels, the way he adjusts his glasses with his middle finger, with his passion for the theory of surplus value, and the transition from capitalism to socialism, and the dictatorship of the proletariat, and how the state will wither away. And the problem of Father Coughlin and shall we consider him as different in kind or degree from Henry Ford, or the mine owners. Big words from a six-dollar-a-week clerk, much arrogance from this skinny boyfriend, and intimations of a passionate nature, so naïve beautiful powerful, a passionate nature, and she thrills to contemplate holding all that power of passion, that intellectual arrogance innocence in her arms in her body.

She fell for him. Perhaps she knew then he was not to have a brilliant career in the revolution. Perhaps it didn't matter. He was not a practical fellow and his practical political understanding of the necessities of daily revolutionary life had been fused by the heat of too much belief. They were members of a party, after all. Russia was the only socialist nation, after all. They sat the next summer around a campfire in Connecticut, and understood that Poland and Latvia and Estonia had been socialized, and that the pact was to buy time, and Stalin knew what he was doing, and the Popular Front was over; but Paul sat in the light of the fire, chemically transformed in his anti-Fascist purity, and he didn't seem to hear. The day-to-day intricacies of strategy and tactics did not command his attention. The issues commanded his attention. The ends in view. They met an older man, Selig Mindish, and his wife, they met many interesting people in that progressive camp, they listened to marvelous lectures, they went to square dances, they were the youngsters in this crowd, shining college students who waited table, youngest of the grownups, apple of everyone's eye, and one warm night, with the stars shining and the blackberry bushes, and the crickets' fiddle and the frogs' jug band, they knew each other and it was good.

Sunday

Dearest Rochelle,

When we were downstairs during the recess Thursday I glanced at a copy of the Daily News one of the marshals had folded to a review of a new Marlon Brando picture: about a gang member who decides to brave the wrath of his comrades and testify in court against their criminality which he has come to see is wrong. Thus is promulgated for the millions the ethic of the stool-pigeon! Does this strike a bell in view of the prosecution's private remarks to Ascher?

P.

What else is to be expected of a Hollywood long since purged of its few humanitarian filmmakers? And what is to be expected of a jury picked however partially from a depraved culture? It is frightening.

8th day

Rochelle— Amazing the strong sense one gets of Judge Hirsch and Prosecutor Feuerman working together like a team. It couldn't be my imagination, Hirsch makes no effort to disguise where his sympathies lie. Their collusion is quite shameless—they are like bricklayers methodically sealing us up. But their arrogance will destroy them in the end. Feuerman's assistant is an ass licker if I ever saw one, an unctuous little b—. I recognize his type from the army.

My darling have you noticed how many of the characters in this capitalist drama are Jewish? The defendants, the defense lawyer, the prosecution, the major prosecution witness, the judge. We are putting on this little passion play for our Christian masters. In the concentration camps the Nazis made guards of certain Jews and gave them whips. In Jim Crow Harlem the worst cops are Negro. Feuerman in his freckles and flaming red hair, this graduate of St. John's, the arch assimilationist who represses the fact that he could never get a job with the telephone company—Feuerman is so full of self-hatred HE IS DETERMINED to purge us. Imperialism has many guises, and each is a measure of its desperation.

P.

I have to laugh about that testimony re the radio.

(undated)

The floors are made of marble, there's a guard at every door . . . Just like a bank. An altar for the judge, a lesser altar for the lawyers. Like some kind of church. Banks and churches and courtrooms all depend on the appurtenances of theater. On illusion. Banks, the illusion of stability and honorable dealings to hide the rot and corruption of capitalist exploitation. Churches the illusion of sacred sanctuary for purposes of pacifying social discontent. Courtrooms of course designed to promote the illusion of solemn justice. If there was true justice why would such trappings be necessary? Wouldn't a table and chairs and an ordinary room serve just as well? What are they whispering about up there? Trial by tedium, that's what this is. Rochelle, why do I feel so elated? Is it possible I believe this whole thing will collapse of its own absurd weight and we can simply walk out and go home? Let us write a musical comedy, my darling, and call it Foley Square!

Brushing her thick wavy hair, brushing it back from her temples, brushing it clean, maintaining herself in this cell with fastidiousness. She suffers most the shower rule. They will let her shower only twice a week. The humiliation is intolerable. Brushes her hair clean, brushes it, fires the scalp and learns to bathe at the sink in her cell. A matron, a woman like herself, with children, a clean decent woman who is sympathetic and becoming her friend, allows her to hang her blanket for a few minutes with borrowed clothespins over the bars each morning; and she removes her clothes and stands at the sink laving herself with the cold water, washing her body with soap and cold water, drying her body with the thin starched crusty prison towel and then washing the sink, and then washing her underclothes, and then washing the sink again. Enjoying the tensity of her coldness, the tightening stippled skin, the nerve thrill of coldness warming in its own blood. Walking barefoot on the stone floor of their prison.

The women in her cellblock have enormous respect for her, and though they call each other by their first names, they address her as Mrs. Isaacson. They ask her advice; they are hookers and addicts and thieves waiting for trial. She under-

stands that part of the respect she is due derives from the seri-
ousness of the charge against her. To herself she has to smile.
But green shoots of concern go out from her to these women,
and in the exercise yard she might explain to this one what she
understands of the value of psychotherapy, and where, in what
city agencies, it can be arranged for at no cost; or to that one that
the burning feeling during urination is probably cystitis which is
like a cold in the urinary tract, and that it should be attended to
by a doctor, even a prison doctor, and can quickly be cleared up.
They also like the way she plays volleyball, awkwardly, but with
absolute determination to win. When her trial comes, in the tradition of this place she is offered different items of clothes out of
different cells, so that she will make the best possible appearance
before the judge. In the privacy of her bed that night, she cries;
it can be heard, but at this time of night, before sleep, many of
the women cry, and because it is not uncommon it is private.
She cries not because she is so terribly moved by the generosity
of the other inmates—that alone would not cause her to cry—
but because she is so clearly one of them and the cellblock has
so unquestionably become her home.

ASCHER & LEWIN
Interoffice Memo

12.14.53

Mitch, according to Mrs. Isaacson she believes Selig
Mindish was born in Poland and came here as a young
man sometime after World War One. One assumes he
would have been naturalized in the twenties. This is easy
enough to check out unless there is some change of
name in the process.

JA

Jan 28 1954

FILE: Isaacson Case

Today I finally got what I demanded, the government's list of witnesses, attached. They have gotten

around this by listing nearly a hundred names, knowing I have no facilities for preparing cross-examination for such a number. Feuerman smiled as I was given the list. I am to understand that imbedded somewhere in the list are the real witnesses he will call.

JA

In her mind it is a ritual defense, a ceremony. Once Pauly took her to the theater, a workshop theater on Houston Street down at the bottom of Manhattan. There were these students on a stage without a curtain, and it was a Greek play with girls in togas doing this slow arm-waving dance to symbolize their fear their wish that what was going to happen would not happen, and they pushed themselves away from the terrible action, they pushed the air, ceremoniously putting their hands up to the sides of their faces and pushing away air. Nevertheless, what they feared and abhorred came to pass.

She has no doubt about the outcome of the trial. But the penalty is unknown and she listens to the testimony, she looks at the faces and listens to the language so as to fathom the penalty. But the way she receives this knowledge is unexpected: she receives it not from what happens in the courtroom but in the light of the increasing intensity of her hatred for them, for the people in this court. Her hatred intensifies day by day and she gradually surmises that the punishment will be measured in comparable intensity, and that what she wishes for them will be given back to her, a sharp and penetrating reflection of her own incandescent hatred.

Only then does she begin to understand, in the light of her instinct, how this punishment shall be justified. It is no mean feat in this highly textured trial with witnesses examined at length whose testimony is incidental, and with legal hassles that take half a morning, and with the recesses, marching back and forth to the elevator, and in the necessity for concentration, so physically demanding that she is exhausted at the end of the day's session.

At a moment when she can talk to Ascher alone, she asks him what is the precise meaning of treason.

Ascher tells her treason consists of making war against your country or giving aid and comfort to an enemy at war with your country. It is defined in the Constitution.)

She hands to Ascher a piece of paper with some words in her own handwriting, and behind each word vertical pencil strokes, crossed diagonally every fifth stroke:

traitors
traitorous
treacherous
treasonous
betrayal
treachery

"You are a very astute person, Rochelle. You have a mind for the law."

"Why don't you tell the jury what Feuerman is doing, what they are all doing?"

"I have once recorded my objection, which was overruled. Emotionally I do not think anyone sitting in the jury box is capable in the present atmosphere of understanding such a distinction. The appellate, however, is capable of understanding the abuse of such a distinction."

Once the pattern is perceived it fulfills itself continually to something in her that is satisfied by the exercise of order, in whatever cause. Implications of treason are fed like cubes of sugar to the twelve-headed animal which is Justice. In Feuerman's opening remarks. In the way questions are asked. In support of lines of questioning where cases of treason are cited and the judge endorses the relevance of the citation. Ascher trusts only a trained judicial mind to understand in the leisure of a study of the transcript, the abuse of due process in trying someone under one law as if he had broken another.

They have been characterized in the press as traitors. While the legal charge of conspiracy deprives them of the safeguards of the ordinary rules of evidence, it will not protect them from the punishment that can be meted out to those convicted of the worst possible crime against their country. It is clear that although she and Paul will be found guilty of conspiracy to commit espionage, it is for the crime of treason they will be sentenced.

I give this all to her. It is not the radical analysis of the Red visionary; it is the bookkeeper tallying accounts receivable, accounts disbursed.

Now only one question remains, and she needs Mindish for the answer. She has her suspicions, but she has to look at the man's face. In the meantime she has concurred in a defense worked out by Paul and Ascher, even to the sexual motivation. It is a distasteful defense. It is an exaggeration, and therefore it is not true. It is not true because it makes too much of the truth. But she doesn't care. It is only ritual. She looks forward to Mindish's testimony. She finds herself in a state not unlike pleasurable anticipation as she waits for the man to look at her or not when he climbs up in the witness box, like a prize dog who will bark and point and sniff on command and find her in her guilt. Suspense as to her own instinctive response to the sight of Mindish is her only interest. She no longer bothers to condemn him. We have all changed in seven months. All the cells of our brains are changed and our beings are no longer what they were. If by some strange and unforeseen mercy we were to be released, found not guilty and released, our lives would have to begin again and I don't know if that is possible. Our children are different children. I no longer know what they look like. I no longer remember what it is to lie next to my husband. Our trial brings out in me a self-knowledge that I might never have had to suffer: I am made of stone.

But I have had months to think about him, this erstwhile dentist with hands so lacking in skill that even his low fees could not retain his patients; a butcher in the mouth who could not make a bridge that fit, a filling that would not fall out. With all the delicacy of boxing gloves. You walked out of there and your jaw ached for days. And he was not clean either. Some sore, some kind of mouth ulcer always followed a visit to Dr. Mindish. Yet he was our friend. We laughed about his dentistry and we went to him and he charged next to nothing. A comrade's discount. It is possible with his practice that he stood in the center of a ring. He was a dentist to all of us. It is possible. He was already in the party the summer we waited table, Paul and I, at Paine Lodge. A dentist lives a public life and sees many people in privacy. At Paine Lodge he pretended with what we thought was his continental charm a paternalism which I thought led only to small privileges—his pleasure in our youth and in our minds, Paul's especially, his fondness for walking in our door unannounced, his frank admiration once or twice expressed with his hands, of my physical features—and always with his eyes. It was harmless. At its worst it wasn't even offensive, merely pathetic. He enjoyed us so. He did us favors. He took us to the beach, he drove us where we had to go. Always on hand. A loyal dull man who seemed to want no more than sparks from our life. With his poor graceless innocent wife. A crude mind, lacking in understanding of the finer things. He took his culture from us and his ideas from the meetings. Yet, and yet, he felt entitled to one further privilege beyond all these, in our friendship, and in his clandestine lechery for his friend's wife, never courageously expressed, an essential sneak in his mentality, he took one more liberty for the low fees and comradeship: he took our lives.

My God how I hate them all, how I despise their pompous little egos and their discussions and resolutions and breast-beating; with their arrogance as they delivered to us each week the truth, the gospel according to 11th Street. Always they treated Paul like a child and with his mind! a mind so fine, so superior to theirs except in the grubby self-serving politics of the Party. He was always being censured, he was never quite in step. All he did was slave for them, believe for them. Communists have no respect for people, only for positions. It is as if we never existed. Someone not Mindish, Mindish hasn't the brain, someone told him to do this. I can't understand it as anything else. Except that after years he learned in this thick Polisher way the impudence that permits you to use people for your own purposes if you speak in the name of the Party. You blind them with your ideals and while they are looking up you stab them in the belly for the sake of your ideals.

But he is so stupid, they are so stupid, he never properly

became a citizen. (He is legally vulnerable, sexually frustrated, a spy who saves himself by convicting his friends.) This is what Ascher will say. It is possibly true. It is conceivable that all these years a secret spy with his dental x-rays he never managed the practice of dentistry too well because he was not by nature a dentist but a spy. A man with two lives. A man with friends to be used in case of emergency. It is possible. I will know when he walks into the courtroom and I look him in the eyes.

BETH DAVID SYNAGOGUE
Grand Concourse and 175th St.
Bronx 57, New York

February 4, 1954

My Dear Robert,

I am not writing this at the office but wanted quickly to let you know I don't see what purpose your coming up to NY would serve. It is impossible to defend in this trial. Hirsch has ruled that my clients may be questioned about their political associations as establishing their motive for the crime they are accused of. Therefore no matter what strategy I employ by the inversions of logic of these times a conclusion will be derived that makes them guilty. Whether they declare their communism or take the Fifth, communists they are shown to be. And if they are communists they are liars. And if they are liars this dog Mindish must be telling the truth. That is because even if he is a communist he is a witness for the United States Govt. All I can have the Isaacsons do is deny Mindish's testimony. But if Mindish testifies he met with the famous Thos. Flemming, who is known in certain circles as Talkative Tom because he has been used by the govt in three trials already, and Flemming who is brought from his prison cell to the courtroom testifies he took orders from Kusnetsov of the Soviet Govt, how, not being there, can my clients deny that? Yet they are held to account for it. They are held to account for the Soviet Union. They are held to account for the condition of the world today. And all the indictment states is that they met with Mindish in the kitchen of their own house.

I don't think it is advisable for you to leave your classes. Please don't. If I think you can help I will call on you. I expect to lose the trial but win on appeal. I am saying yiska for your father. God forgive me, in one sense I am glad Samuel is no longer on earth—that he would have to see in this case the sometimes terrible power of his beloved law.

My sincerest regards to you and your lovely bride.

Jake Ascher

VERDICT

The Isaacsons are convicted of conspiracy to give to the Soviet Union the secret of the atom bomb. No—the secret of the hydrogen bomb. Or is it the cobalt bomb? Or the neutron bomb. Or napalm. Something like that.

One day after a rain, a young man trying to interpret and analyze the awful visions of his head makes an ordinary visit to his sister in her sanitarium. It is the autumn of a really great year. He stands outside her window, his cheap boots darkening in the wet grass. He searches for her first on one wet foot, then on the other. She's not in the bed, she's not in the chair, she's not in the corner near the door. If she is in the room she is somewhere along the window wall beyond his line of sight. A face appears in the safety-glass panel of the door. The door opens and he ducks. He hears a voice, cheerful, patronizing and solicitous. It is a voice for addressing pets.

The sanitarium is built to look like a series of connected garden apartments. It is located in a quiet residential street of Newton, not far from Boston College. Behind it is a professional building for doctors and dentists, also built to look like a series of garden apartments. The sanitarium and the professional building share a parking lot. One day in the previous week, this young man hunkering here in the shadow of these garden apartments, rushed out of the sanitarium and across this parking lot, his fleece-lined jacket flying from his upraised hand like a battle flag. He was screaming incomprehensibly, making hoarse guttural sounds of rage, he was really behaving quite poorly. Behind him trying in vain to call him to account, his foster father came out of the door of the sanitarium, just as the young man disappeared through the doors of the professional building. Behind the young man's foster father came the young man's foster mother. Behind the foster mother came a nurse. They were quite alarmed. Somehow the young man had gotten it in his head that his sister, a patient in the sanitarium, was being considered for shock therapy. A strong electric current is applied by means of electrodes fastened to the scalp earlobes shoulders nipples bellybutton genitals asshole knees toes and soles of the feet, to the nervous system of the patient. The patient does a rigid dance. The current is stopped and the patient relaxes. The current is applied again and the patient dances again. The current is relaxed. The young man was going after one of the doctors with an office in the professional building, a psychiatrist named Duberstein. He was going to kill this Doctor Duberstein. In his zeal he forswore the professional directory in the lobby and simply went down the halls, flinging open the doors of the waiting rooms and treatment rooms and x-ray rooms, banging doors and scaring mothers and their babies, old men with the shakes, and boys with severe cases of acne. It is just as well. Had he been a killer he would have moved quietly. But preceded by his shock waves he alerted the supposed victim, sending him a signal of the ritualistic nature of his fury. Not that Duberstein picked this up. His chair was warm and a manila folder lay open on his desk and his pipe smoke hung in the air. He was GONE! A lucky thing too, I would have killed him.

But you see I was learning. I was learning how to be an

Isaacson. An Isaacson does things boldly calculated to bring self-destructive results. It is a way of making the world do your bidding. My face now bearded, my hair longer than it has ever been, I career through my changes at an accelerating pace. The sense is of running too fast downhill. But why not, why the fuck not.

In the aftermath of my assault on his office Duberstein told the Lewins he would withdraw from the case unless they guaranteed to keep me away from her. I said I would guarantee to keep away from her if they would guarantee to have him withdraw from the case. My father, a lawyer with some knowledge of arbitration, suggested this compromise: I would guarantee to keep away from Duberstein's hospital and his person if they guaranteed to keep his miserable hands off the voltmeter. The agreement was made.

At the same time I initiated discussions with the Lewins with the end in mind of becoming Susan's sole legal guardian, an idea I view with warmth on days of sun, and coolly on days of rain. Today is chill. My feet are getting wet. I raise my face above the window sill and I see that the competent nurse has placed Susan back on her bed. The door is just closing. I watch my sister. Slowly her legs spread, her feet slide over the sides of the mattress and her toes hook into the crevice between the mattress and the spring. Her arms move outward; her hands curl over the edge of the mattress and find the same ledge. She holds her bed in her hands and by her ankles. Her tunic has risen above her knees. Her legs are skinny and have not been shaved. Her face is gaunt. She writhes gently on her back, swaying like something underwater, staring intently with her DP eyes at the ceiling. Finally the pillow is dislodged and falls to the floor. She presses her head back and peers at the junction of ceiling and wall directly over the headboard. And now firmly attached to the bed she does not move.

Today Susan is a starfish. Today she practices the silence of the starfish. There are few silences deeper than the silence of the starfish. There are not many degrees of life lower before there is no life.

Daniel raises the window, hoists himself to the sill, and

climbs through. He has a document which he puts with the others in the drawer in her bedtable. But that is not the main business of today.

He stands at the foot of her bed. To be objective, she is learning to rest upon what is designed to be rested on. From here I can see that the sanitarium does not require underwear. Look at that. A wave of hot guilt breaks over Daniel's ears. He moves aside, out of the beam. That is the last thing to go. More than once I have asked myself if I'd like to screw my sister. I mean I have not asked myself, I have examined myself to see if that was what I wanted. But in our history I don't think I have ever wanted that. My involvement with Susan has to do with rage, which is easily confused with unnatural passion. My interest, my raging interest is higher up, somewhere in the heart's canyons with their clear echoes up into the throat: it enrages me that anyone, let alone my kid sister, could have characterized my actions, could have found in what I was doing and the way I was acting enough consistency, enough of a pattern, to make a confident moral judgment.

Mrs. Madge Green, with one prosthetic breast, drives her Buick Riviera to the S&H Redemption Center. Her Pontiac Bonneville. Mr. Leopold Bloom ate with relish the inner organs of beasts and fowl. Look at her lying there making a fool of herself. Teach her to play her stupid games. Look at the actress. Isn't she something else! Look at how just lying there, not saying a fucking thing, not doing a thing but lying there and picking up bedsores she can still be morally preemptive. What character! To be truthful, Susan, I can live with your death. I will make a fuss because it will be expected of me. But I can live with it. I know how to do that. I'm not saying I won't hang sad, but at suppertime I'll be hungry, right? I'll want a hamburger with everything on it.

You know I'm not shittin' you, man. I can live with anyone's death except my own. You know it. Everywhere in my life people have been trying to die and lots of them have made it. As it is I've done too much for you—and for what? You don't talk, you don't reinforce their sense of you. All they have is my word. I remember your voice, but how can I expect them to remember your voice. You can't write out voices. All I can say about your voice is that it is so familiar to me that I cannot perceive the world except with your voice framing the edges of my vision. It is on the horizon and under my feet. The world has always been washed in Susan's voice. It breaks where her voice breaks, under declaration, or late toward sleep, or at moments of love—only to more fully characterize itself. It is the feminine voice that passes solidly through ontological mirrors. It lies at the heart of the matter, the nub of the thing, the core of the problem, in the center, on the bull's-eye, smack in the middle. We understand St. Joan: You want to fuck her but if you do you miss the point.

Susan, the other night I dreamed that with someone looking on I lifted my heavy scalloped gourd of a face with its eyes closed and affixed it to my head. It was not a funny dream. The eyes were closed. The thing weighed a ton but it wasn't the whole head, just the facial edifice, curled like a bent-penny head of Lincoln, or the Roosevelt side of the dime or the Kennedy half dollar, curvilinear, like a watermelon. I felt the flesh with my fingers, with the tips of my fingers down my temple and cheek and it felt like dead flesh. I noticed its imperfections, this skin. It was cold, like clay, which is to say not cold but without warmth. A touch of a smile tipped its lips in sleep. Was that you with me in the dream, looking on?

To be objective, the weaker her signals the stronger mine become. We know the art of that. But what is happening is that as my signals grow stronger she has to move further and further away to hear them. Attentively, she will back off into nothingness.

To be objective, she is dying.

To be objective, they are still taking care of us, one by one.

Life recedes like the tide going out, the waves of life shrinking back, and over her forehead and down through her eyes a dryness, a loss of life. And she looked so pale, my God, she is dying and there is nothing Daniel can do. She is washing up on the beach, and when the last moisture sinks below the sand, and the sand dries in the sun, she will be dead. And my whole family will be dead.

When I picked her up there was no weight to her. There was no heft of ocean and slide of salt dune, no ocean of seabed shifting. Her arms hung down from the shoulders, her skinny legs from the knees. I felt her backbone against my arm, the bones of her thighs across my arms. Her head lolled back as if her neck were broken. *Susan*, in her ear, *Susan*, whispering, *Susan* hugging her bones and her dry weightlessness, *Susan* kissing her eyes. Only the warmth of her bones told me she was not dead.

When I laid her back down the shock of what I had done distributed itself through her body, and her feet twitched and her hands twitched. And her head rolled on the sheet and her eyes closed and opened and closed and opened. Then slowly the tremors slackened. And once again her arms moved out slowly and her feet hooked the mattress and she fixed herself to the bed, sucking to the bed with the vacuum pores of her shrinking bone marrow, and she stared once more at the ceiling and listened to the slow ebb of the sea.

We understand that when St. Joan led them into battle none of the soldiers watched the way her ass moved. We understand that Churchill found it of immense value to have played with toy soldiers as a child. Every line of every novel of Henry James has been paid for. James knew this and was willing to accept the moral burden. We can accept our moral burdens if our underlinen is clean. That is why we have toy soldiers. Susan digs all this. A starfish is not outraged. We must preserve our diminishing energies insofar as we direct them to the true objectives. A certain portion of the energy must be used for the regeneration of energy. That way you don't just die like a bird falling, like a rock sinking, you die on a parabolic curve. You die in a course of attack. Susan knows this. To be a revolutionary you need only hold out your arms and dive. It is something like the sound barrier, there's a boom when you break through, a concussion of space, a compression of the content of space. An echo ricochets through the red pacific twilight all the way over the ocean.

We understand Churchill found it of immense value to have played with toy soldiers as a child. We understand Truman found it of immense value to have commanded artillery as a young man.

From under his jacket Daniel pulls a cardboard tube. From

this he withdraws a poster which he smoothes flat. Standing on a chair he tapes the poster as high as he can on the wall facing her bed. The ceiling would be better but even on a chair he can't reach it. The poster is a black and white photograph of a grainy Daniel looking scruffy and militant. Looking bearded, looking clear-eyed. His hand is raised, his fingers make the sign of peace. It is a posed photo blown up at a cost of four ninety-five.

JACK P. FEIN
Ny Times
229 West 43rd Street

Fein is the reporter who did the reassessment piece in the *Times* on the tenth anniversary of the execution. He's a robust bald-headed guy with grey sideburns.

"Do you remember the trial?" he asks me.

"We weren't allowed to go."

"It was a piss-poor trial. The case against them was nothing. Talking Tom's word as a convicted spy wasn't worth shit. All the government had was Mindish's accomplice testimony that to believe you'd have to believe it's possible that a radio repairman was trained and educated enough to draw intricate plans of the most sophisticated kind, and that he would reduce them so that they would fit on dental x-ray film—I still don't understand why anyone would have to do that. It was too much. And that this stiff was valuable to the Russians. Insane! The Russians had everything they needed. They had all that stuff. They had professionals right there, they had their own men right on the spot. Anyway, the day after the *Times* ran my piece I was having lunch downtown and just as I'm leaving the restaurant Red Feuerman walks up behind me, the chief prosecuting attorney. He's now Judge Feuerman of the Southern District, it was a career-making case, baby, everybody did well. Feuerman grabs me by the elbow, like this, you know how some guys grab your elbow like it was a tit or something, and he says, 'Jack, you let the wrong guys get to you, I can't believe you'd buy their story.' 'What story, Red, you're not gonna stand there and tell me without smiling that you had a case!' 'Someday when you have the time,' he says, 'come up to my office and I'll show you some things.' "

What things, I asked Fein.

"Oh, it's a lot of bullshit. That's the way they all talk. Even before the execution, when the heat was on to commute the sentence, they dropped these hints about evidence they had and couldn't use in the interest of national security. Like there's this big report in the Justice Department that they've never released because of security, and no one can see it, and it's supposed to have indisputable evidence. But a friend of mine in Justice told me if the report has evidence like they claim they would have released it. There's a report all right, and the reason it's classified is because it favors the defense. Shit, between the FBI and the CP your folks never had a chance."

Jack Fein is a chain-smoker. He slid his Camel cigarettes out of the pack and laid them on the table in a row like cartridges in a belt. He drinks black coffee. He does not carry a camera or a pad. We were in this luncheonette. It was warm there but he kept his coat on and leaned all over the table with his coat sleeves flopping.

"You're a tough baby," he said. "That's good. I'm glad to see that you're hangin' in there. What's the *name* of your Foundation?"

"The Paul and Rochelle Isaacson Foundation for Revolution."

"What's it gonna do?"

"We're, um, funding publications to develop revolutionary awareness. We're going to finance community action, um, programs. We're going to assert the radical alternative."

"Great. You want to tell me where your Foundation is getting its money?"

"Sure, man, it's no secret. It's my trust money and my sister's trust money. It's a lot of money."

"The thing the old lawyer put together, Ascher. From that committee."

"Right."

"What does it come to now?"

"Well, um, I haven't been counting."

"Beautiful. You're a beautiful baby. Are you in SDS?"
"No."
"PLP?"
"No."
"Where do you live now?"
I tell him.
"What about your sister?"
"Well, see, I don't think she wants to talk to anyone right now. She's recovering from the trial."
Wicked.
"Yeah." He lights a new Camel with an old one. "Yeah, I heard something like that. Yeah. She would be how old now."
"Susan is twenty."
"And where is she?"
"Out of state, that's all I can tell you."
"What about your foster parents. Could I talk to them?"
"Look, I don't care about blowing our cover. I don't think any of us care anymore. Anyone who was interested could have traced us up to Boston. But I mean there are certain family things to be settled by all of us, not me acting alone. We've all got responsibilities to each other."
"I understand. Don't worry, I don't fuck around."
I do not like the sudden sympathetic turn of things. Here I'm laying the Foundation on him and he wants to talk to the responsible adults. It occurs to me that I am dealing with a professional. *The son of Paul and Rochelle Isaacson, who were executed a dozen years ago for crimes against the nation, has established a Foundation to clear their name.*
"Of course it can't be done," Fein assures me.
"But that's not the purpose," I tell him.
"Listen, kid, a radical is no better than his analysis. You know that. Your folks were framed, but that doesn't mean they were innocent babes. I don't believe they were a dangerous conspiracy to pass important defense secrets, but I don't believe either that the U.S. Attorney, and the Judge, and the Justice Department and the President of the United Sates conspired against *them*."
"I thought you said the evidence was phony."
"That's right. Those guys had to bring in a conviction.

That was their job. But no one would have put the finger on your parents unless they thought they were up to something. In this country people don't get picked out of a hat to be put on trial for their lives. I don't know—your parents and Mindish had to have been into some goddamn thing. They *acted* guilty. They were little neighborhood commies probably with some kind of third-rate operation that wasn't of use to anyone except maybe it made them feel important. Maybe what they were doing was worth five years. Maybe. But that would have been in the best of times, and in the best of times nobody would have cared, nobody would have cared enough to falsify evidence. No one would have been afraid enough to throw a switch."

FANNY ASCHER
570 West 72nd Street

Fanny Ascher was curious to see how I'd turned out. That's why she agreed to talk to me. There was also a repugnance or fear of me, and what I came from, or of my name, and that's why she sat on the edge of her sofa with her ankles crossed, with her chin high, in wary widowhood. She is a thin lady with very fair skin, finely wrinkled, and grey jeweled eyeglasses, and hair tinted blue. It is difficult to clasp fingers painlessly around a diamond ring and a wedding band on that fourth finger. The crookedness bothered me, the distortion in that hand's form the arthritic form

"You are a student still?"

"Yes."

I have been trying to keep up with what you people are doing with your long hair and strange clothes. I am an enlightened woman and I like young people. Nevertheless I am disappointed that you look this way. It does not inspire confidence.

"And married, with a baby?"

"Yes."

She shakes her head.

"And your sister?"

"She's getting better."

"Still?"

"Yes."

The woman's head oscillates left right left right left right. Her eyes are fixed on me.

"I don't want to take up a lot of your time."

"My time? What do you think I do with my time?"

"Well, I only came to ask if there were any papers, any letters you know about. Any files."

"There are none. Robert has all the files. I gave him everything I found. How is Robert?"

"He's OK."

"You go up there?"

"Yes, when I can."

"They are busy people."

"Yes."

"I hear from them every year on the high holy days. A card."

"Yes."

Photograph of Ascher on the baby grand. A younger man than I remember, smiling in soft focus in a leather frame.

"Well, that's all I came to ask you."

"Jacob saved everything. For over a year every day I went to the office to go through his papers. Bills, letters, notes to himself—he threw away nothing. When I sold the practice and closed the office I had to clean up the garbage of thirty-five years. But it was all filed. There was no confusion. He was a man with an orderly mind."

"Yes."

"It was very difficult for me. I made myself ill."

"Yes."

"Robert did not want the practice." We consider that for a minute. Daniel fears his boots have dirtied the carpet. This is wall-to-wall carpeting, rose beige, on 72nd Street.

"Would you like something, a glass of milk? There was a point Jacob and I seriously discussed adopting you ourselves."

"I didn't know that."

"Well, it's true. How we would have managed at our age I can't tell you. It was his idea, of course, not mine. I held my breath and he talked himself out of it. I was frankly surprised.

Only after he died did I think maybe he knew he hadn't long and that was why he decided he couldn't. Otherwise, who knows. Jacob made the decisions. It was characteristic. He didn't know when to stop for people. The poorest client, he was meticulous."

"Yes."

"We were not the same in that respect. He was generous to a fault."

"He was very kind to us."

"Your parents should have been so kind." She is startled by her own remark. She looks as if about to apologize, but she pulls herself together. "They were not kind people—to any of us. What do you want papers for?"

"I don't know. I guess I think they belong to me."

"I see. I'm sorry there is nothing I have to give you. Talk to Robert."

I got up to go.

"I don't know what to tell you," she said. "I have no love for the memory of your parents. They were Communists and they destroyed everything they touched."

"You don't think they were innocent?"

"They were not innocent of permitting themselves to be used. And of using other people in their fanaticism. Innocent. The case ruined Jacob's. health."

She rose from the sofa. "They were very difficult to deal with. They were very stubborn. He would come home furious, he would want to do something and they wouldn't let him. He would want to do something for their sake and they wouldn't let him."

"Like what?"

"He wanted to call certain people as witnesses and they wouldn't let him. All sorts of things like that."

"Who?"

She walks with care—she is showing me to the door. "What?"

"Who did he want to call for a witness?"

"Who knows who? Jacob was a brilliant lawyer. And today when people write about the case or talk about it, it is Jacob they criticize. He should have done this, he shouldn't have done that. Do they know what he had to put up with?"

Her hand is on the doorknob. The bones growing around the rings, the pain in the fingers

Interviewed by Daniel
for the Foundation.

ROBERT LEWIN
67 Winthrop Road, Brookline

Daniel pulls up to the house. They are used now to his abrupt appearances. His inconsiderate departures. They hear the rage in the way he uses his brakes. In the patches he leaves on Brookline hills.

The chilly winds have dried the streets. The corner light comes on.

Now they are into specialists. The great faith. We had a specialist in to look at her. They're doing some tests. He wants to consult with another specialist. With enough specialists man can be made immortal. What do all the specialists do here on Saturday night? They come for the big look at Susan.

"Where have you been," Lise says. "Why don't we hear from you?"

They have turned strange. They are visibly shrunken, both of them. Their use of specialists is turning them into old Jewish people. What has happened to the fighting liberal the students love? My father lights his pipe with a slight tremor in his hands. My mother has turned grey overnight. I have the sudden intuition that their lives have become too sorrowful for sex. "When did you last eat a decent meal," Lise says.

Upstairs I clean up. I pass the back bedroom where I used to live. When my sister was twelve or thirteen she used to work her tentative saucy sex on me, and coquette and comb her hair for hours, and droop her lower lip and put black stuff on her dark eyes and accidentally graze her small breasts across my arm. And act cool. It was a high old time and it made me laugh. And she knew the humor of it: one day in this doorway she stopped when she saw me looking, raised her arms, and saluted me with a flick of her ass.

It is furnished now as a guest room, it's a neat empty guest room. From the window you can see the lights of Boston eight or ten miles to the east. What am I feeling, what awful need? In the late afternoon the sun burned on the windows of downtown Boston as if someone was flashing signals with a mirror. This was my window. I pretended the signals were for me. I didn't have to decode them because it was enough that they were being sent. What gave me immense satisfaction was the thought that anyone who tried to intercept the signals, and decipher them, would fail. No matter who, the FBI or the Nazis, nobody not standing right here in this window could read the signals exactly as they were sent or understand them as they were meant to be understood.

Daniel tried to leave the window. He stared at the evening skyline, Boston's lights glowing into the heavy atmosphere like the light of a furnace. It is a feeling with no bottom, no root, of no locus. It pulses out of him like a radio wave, out of all parts of him at once, and it *needs*. It disseminates, it is diffuse; and one moment he thinks it is something his heart wants the fullness of, and another that his arms want to hold, and for another moment it is something his cock wants to get into. But if he could accommodate any part of his body the feeling wouldn't leave, it would still be there in all parts of him at once, each cell of his body radiating its passionate need.

But the worst of it is that he hadn't remembered what an ancient friend of a feeling it was.

"I've got to talk to you."

My father sighs. We have talked before. He sits at the dining room table, a stack of blue exam books before him. His *New Yorkers* lie about still in their mailing wrappers.

"Do you know of anything my parents did to hurt the case Ascher was putting together?"

"What do you mean?"

"Testimony, evidence, anything they wouldn't let him use?"

"Who have you been talking to now," my mother says.

"What difference does it make?"

"Fanny Ascher?"

"Yes."

Lise snorts. "Of course. I made a kartoffel. Would you rather have pot roast or steak?"

"I don't care. I'm not hungry."

"Daniel, I'm making supper anyway."

"Anything, it doesn't matter."

"It never matters—"

"Jesus," Daniel shouts, "anygoddamn thing!"

"But when you sit down it matters!"

"Shhh, calm down, everyone," my father says. "We'll have the pot roast. All right with you, Dan?"

"Yeah, all right."

"Thank you," Lise says and frosts through the door.

My father clears his throat. "Let's go in the living room. The thing is, you see, Fanny Ascher's feelings are well known. And it's understandable. She's very bitter about Jake's death."

Daniel sits down. He grows very still. "Just tell me if you know anything about it."

"Jake never said anything to me along those lines. On the other hand I wasn't up there with him in the day-to-day handling of the case. That was my first teaching job at Virginia. I only got involved in the later appeals. I helped him a little bit. But lots of lawyers were involved by then. It was all very public by then."

"What does that mean?"

"Just what I said. I don't know any more than you do. Have you looked through everything in the file?"

Not a useful reply. They are stung and swollen about the heart. They have not forgiven me for Jack Fein's piece in the *Times*. The threat I made on Duberstein's life is fresh in their minds. A pattern of being denied their rights in Susan, their rights in me. They were not consulted about the changes in my appearance: the beard, the climbing downward of my hair, the newest recklessness of attitude which colors the face, sinks the eyes. A suspicion of having lived their lives to no effect.

The house itself seems to have shrunken, and lost its gleam. The furniture looks out of date and shabby. The walls are yellowed. There is a smell in the house of something less than assured life. A sense in the way my father sits with his arms on the armchair that he has passed the line across his life at which whatever was success is now understood to be failure.

"Dad, I can recite that file by heart."

"Do you ever drink?"

"What?"

"I'm going to have a drink before dinner. Would you like some scotch?"

He goes into the kitchen for glasses and ice. "Of course, a man tells his wife things he wouldn't tell anyone else. Who knows? Your parents were Party members and possibly they felt they had to consider aspects of their defense with an eye out for the Party. Maybe there's something to it. I don't know. Of course the Party made no effort to help them. It was only later, after the sentence, when the propaganda value became obvious to them."

"Well, would it be something important? Something that could make a difference?"

"You mean about their testimony?"

"Yes."

"I doubt it. You've got to understand Fanny. She lost a husband and she blames the case. That means she blames the Isaacson family. And to make matters worse in her mind Jake is remembered for this sacrifice by critics of the trial who find fault with his handling of it. She's very sensitive to that. She resents criticism of him. It's natural."

"He had emphysema. He had a bad heart."

"That's right. He was not a well man. But there's no doubt it helped him along. He was like my father. They only stopped working to eat or sleep. They were both that kind."

He puts the ice into the glasses. "It was a good partnership."

"She wanted you to take over the practice."

"Yes." A small smile. He keeps the scotch in the cabinet with the good dishes.

"She was always insensitive to Robert's ideals," my mother says.

"Try this," handing me a drink. "It's what we older folks use. Yes, Fanny was shocked that I didn't want the practice. Something was always shocking her."

"They never had children," Lise says.

"The Aschers and my parents were very close. They always brought me a present for my birthday. When my mother died Fanny started to give advice. For years she tried to get my father to remarry. Introduce him to Hadassah ladies who'd lost their husbands. But Sam was interested in the practice of law. He said he never had the time."

"She dislikes people not taking her advice," my mother says.

"L'chayim," my father says raising his glass.

"The judiciary today is more sensitive—the trend now is to stringent protection of the trial's integrity. There's no doubt in my mind that if they were on trial today the government couldn't do what it did then to get their conviction. During the trial the FBI arrested that fellow as another spy in the ring, and said he would testify in confirmation of Mindish's confession. They never put him on the stand, and he himself was never brought to trial. Long before their trial the Isaacsons were tried and found guilty in the newspapers. Also in my opinion a charge to the jury like Judge Hirsch's would today be ruled prejudicial. A judge today would be more sophisticated in his conduct. He'd have to be."

"You mean they'd beat the rap?"

"Well no, not necessarily. I mean it would have been a different trial in the way it was handled. It would be tougher to convict them. The federal conspiracy laws being what they were the indictment would still be the same. That hasn't changed. It is still the way to find someone guilty who you cannot prove did anything."

"You were at Susan's?" my mother says.

"Yeah."

"I washed her hair today. I bought her a lovely robe but it's too big. I'll have to get the smaller size."

"When it began I'm pretty sure the FBI didn't know what they had or where it would lead them. They knew they had to bring in something. In those days, this was years before the sputnik thing, it was customary to downgrade the Russians' science. People who know something about these things didn't make that mistake. But at the level of *Time* magazine the joke was how they copied everything and claimed it for their own. Well, of course the corollary of that is that it's our bomb they have and that means we were betrayed. After the war our whole foreign policy depended on our having the bomb and the Soviets not having it. It was a terrible miscalculation. It militarized the world. And when they got it the only alternative to admitting our bankruptcy of leadership and national vision was to find conspiracies. It was one or the other."

"Sometimes I used to think about the odds against it."

"What?"

"That it would be laid on us. A particular family in a country of millions of families."

"Well, if you're the Bureau you have on hand a resource of files, especially of known left-wing activists. That is what you go to first, your own files. It's like at the local police level, a crime of a certain kind is committed, say of sexual deviation, so you question your known deviates. And when he's brought in he knows he's vulnerable. He'll take pains to establish his innocence, or to distinguish himself from who is guilty. But say he is apprehended when no crime is known to have been committed, well then the distinctions he makes reveal to the police the sense he has of his own vulnerability. And they go to work on that. They go to work on it with the sense of being justified in their original decision to question him."

"You mean Mindish?"

"They questioned him for weeks before they arrested him. And after they arrested him they kept questioning him. And he became their case."

"Robert, I wish we wouldn't talk about this."

"He became their case because he named your parents."

"Well, first Paul was arrested."

"Yes."

"And then not for a few weeks, Rochelle."

"Yes."

"Well, what, did he have second thoughts about my mother?"

"Well, more probably they arrested her as a means of persuading your father to talk. He was not proving as cooperative as Mindish. This was their procedure, this was investigative procedure. And even after her arrest, if your parents had named other people they could have become prosecution witnesses like Mindish. But they didn't do that. Therefore they became the defendants of the case. The government tried to take it as far as they could. That was their interest. But it stopped with Paul and Rochelle. Even after their trial and sentence, the government let them know that if they confessed the sentences would not be carried out. That indicates to me they didn't know right to the end if they had the mastermind criminals they'd gotten a death sentence for. The idea of a confession was not to make your parents penitent, or to exonerate American justice. It was to make them name other people. So you see the death sentence itself was used as an investigative procedure."

"What is this family's continuing desire for punishment?" my mother says. "I can't understand it." She lays down her knife and fork.

"Lise, the boy asked me a question."

"Does he have to be told these things? He doesn't know?"

"I'm establishing for him the reasons Jake defended as he did."

"You are going to tell him now, with the Isaacsons a dozen years in their graves, how you would have conducted the defense. That is hardly comforting."

"Hey, Mom, did I ask for comfort? Did I say I needed comfort?"

"Lise, you'll forgive me: I never felt it was a good idea to talk to Susan about the case."

This remark brings us together. The air is clearing. Redness is in our cheeks. Around the kitchen table for one rush of an instant it is possible this son and his parents are having dinner together.

"So Mindish was their case. And Ascher chose to defend by discrediting Mindish. That was his defense. It seemed at the time the only possible defense to make. God knows I probably couldn't have come up with anything better. The pressure was enormous. So he worked on Mindish's self-interest. You see the theory for admitting accomplice testimony that is uncorroborated is that conspiracy is by its nature secretive and that only the parties to it can know it occurred. But in practice this means the accomplice's guilt is modified to the degree that he can convict the defendant. Mindish confessed and was severed from the trial; he wouldn't know what he was going to get until your mother and father were sentenced. For the same offense, they received the death penalty and he got ten years. Ascher developed the motivation. The jealousy theme—you remember that. Then the revelation that Mindish had never been properly naturalized and that his citizenship was in doubt. There was a question anyway but it seemed enough to show that Mindish might conceivably feel threatened by deportation, and therefore testify to anything the government wanted him to say. Ascher worked out an alternate scenario to show Mindish as guiltier than he himself confessed to being. His fear of deportation, his malevolence, his thwarted lechery. You remember that statement in the summary. You can just see him point his finger. Here is your spy. He and he alone is responsible."

"Right."

"Well, you see terrible error in that argument. It admits there was a crime."

"What?"

"By arguing this way Ascher grants the government the one premise he shouldn't have. That any crime was committed at all."

"But Mindish confessed!"

"Yes. And Ascher's one chance was to discredit the confession. I've thought about it a lot. It's not what you'd call ordinary procedure. But everything was loaded against them and something extraordinary was required. There was a very slim chance —for all the massive righteousness and fear of the time, and the relentless federal machinery—there was still a way to bring in the other verdict. And that was to prove the Isaacsons innocent by proving Mindish innocent."

Technology is the making of metaphors from the natural world. Flight is the metaphor of air, wheels are the metaphor of water, food is the metaphor of earth. The metaphor of fire is electricity.

"I know, I know. It goes against the grain. But the more Ascher attacked Selig Mindish the more he led to the government's strength. After all it finally boils down to which testimony the jury is going to believe. If the defense tacitly joins the prosecution in assuming a crime of espionage was indeed committed, where shall the distinction be made as to who was and who was not involved? Do you believe the prosecution witness who confesses or the defendant who denies? You see, in this light even testimony developed by the defense, Mindish's questionable citizenship, operates for the prosecution. If he is not a citizen, he is a foreigner, with foreign loyalties. His own testimony tends to be supported. You see my point? Ascher was asking an American jury to believe that a man would be evil enough to put the finger on his innocent friends of fifteen years, practically a father to them by his own characterization. Closer than family, as he also described the relationship. They were closer than family. It is easier to believe in an offense against the state."

"But why would Mindish confess if he was innocent? What would his motivation be for that?"

"Well, it's hard now through everything that's been written to remember some of the facts about Dr. Mindish. But he was an ignorant man. He never learned to speak English properly. He got his degree from some second-rate dental college when dentistry was not a full-fledged branch of the medical profession. Mindish was a simple mechanic. He affected a continental sophistication that could not stand up under five minutes of conversation. I feel about him that he was not a man given to political passion, but a very ordinary, very crude man perfectly capable of joining the Communist Party for no more than a satisfying social sense of himself, a kind of club life for a lower middle class Bronx dentist. So you ask what is the motivation for an innocent man to do what he did: Well, one motivation is to believe or to have been persuaded to believe in his own guilt. And to live in mortal fear of the consequences. Another is to believe in his own innocence but to believe or to have been persuaded to believe in the guilt of his friends. And to live in mortal fear of the consequences."

om om om omm omm omm om om ommmmmm
ohm ohmm ohm ohm ohm ohhmm ohm ohmmmmm

what is it that you can't see but you can feel
what is it that you can't taste and can't smell and can't touch
  but can feel
ohm ohm ohm ohm ohm
what is it that you can't feel but you look as if you do
ohm
what is it that can't move unless you put something in its way
What is it that moves through others, comes from the sky
    and is invisible, can only be detected after it's gone—not
    God, not the Lone Ranger.
ohm ohm ohm ohm
What makes you smell when you touch it, blacken when you
    feel it, die when you taste it.
ohm
What is it that lightens the life of man and comforts his winters
    and sings that he is the master of the universe; until he sits
    in it.
ohm

Interesting find is a review of the trial record by law
students at Univ Virginia pub in their review in Apr 54, or two
months or so before the end. Adviser of these students none
other than asst professor Lewin. The law students find no less
than seventeen abuses of due process as grounds for retrial. The
assumption is that the original trial was exceptionally and not
structurally inadequate. Yet we may ask how after a judicial
process of three years, involving the highest levels of American
jurisprudence, if these students were able to find these errors of
due process, no one in the judiciary was capable of this minimal
perception. Or to phrase the issue differently, if justice cannot
be made to operate under the worst possible conditions of social
hysteria, what does it matter how it operates at other times?
Robert Lewin is still at work on a way to reverse the verdict.
I am beginning to be intolerant of reformers. Ascher depending
on the appellate courts. I am beginning to be nauseated by men
of good will. We are dealing here with a failure to make con-

nections. The failure to make connections is complicity. Reform is complicity.

It is complicity in the system to be appalled with the moral structure of the system.

I have before me on this table the six books written about my parents' trial. Two support the verdict and the sentence, two support the verdict but not the sentence, which they find harsh, and two deny the justice either of the sentence or the verdict. All possible opinions are expressed, from Sidney P. Margolis famous Hearst philosopher (SPIES ON TRIAL) to Max Krieger liberal bleeder (THE ISAACSON TRAGEDY). Here is a statement from each. "For all the hysteria drummed up by the commies, their fellow travelers, and their dupes, the Isaacsons received a fair trial. . . . Who but the very ideologues committed to overthrowing our democratic way of life can dare claim in view of the defendants' use of every legal dodge available under due process, that justice was not done?" —Margolis. "History records with shame the persecution and infamous putting to death in the United States of America of two American citizens, husband and wife, the father and mother of two young children, who were guilty of not so much as jaywalking, for their proudly held left wing views." —Krieger. There is no substantial difference in these positions. To say nothing of their prose.

I am prepared to accept the idea that to the extent Ascher bought the premises of the cold war he made mistakes. I am prepared to accept too the idea that Dr. Selig Mindish was innocent. It is an idea they themselves were not prepared to entertain. I hated Mindish long before there was any trial. I hated his smell, his smirk. I hated his accent, and the merry death in his oyster eyes. Nevertheless I am prepared to accept the idea that he too was innocent. But only because he would have suffered more at the time. But only because he has suffered more since.

Innocence is complicity.

After the sentence was passed there was a big party. At the party, drinking champagne, was Judge Barnet Hirsch, defense attorney Jacob Ascher, Robert Lewin the son of Ascher's former law partner, the writers Margolis and Krieger (who got drunk and sang the *Internationale*), the Jewish prosecuting attorney Howard "Red" Feuerman, the President of B'nai B'rith, Thomas Flemming known as Talking Tom because he testified for the government at no less than four different spy trials, Boris Brill the famous anti-Communist expert, Mindish, and my parents. A late arrival who came to pay his respects was V. Molotov.

The Judge called Ascher to the bench. He conferred with Ascher, standing up from his chair and propping himself on his forearms. From his black robe his two hands extended like the claws of a bird from its black feathers, and gripped the edge of his desk. He was leaning into Ascher's ear, like a great bird pecking at the old lawyer's cheek. Ascher nodded vigorously. Then he shook his head and turned, looking up, to dispute what had just been told him.

The bench was of light varnished oak, like the chairs and the spectator benches. It was school furniture. A round-faced school clock with large black hands ticked on the wall. A flag grey with dirt stood in its stand in the corner of the courtroom. There was a picture of the President behind the bench, and a New York State flag in the other corner.

The courtroom was almost empty. A cop stood under one window with his arms folded. He was unarmed and wore no hat. He yawned. A woman with thick legs and low-heeled shoes who was dressed in the same blue color as the policeman's uniform sat directly behind the couple. There were for this momentous occasion no reporters present. The few people in the spectators' section were there on their own business with the Judge. They were nervous and sharp with one another. They whispered urgently and told each other to be quiet.

Ascher came back from the bench and addressed his two clients: "Stand up, please, come up here with me. The Judge wants to ask you some questions. Come, come, he won't hurt you."

Daniel and his sister Susan stood up and slid along the pew and came out into the aisle. Susan held his hand tightly.

"Come. Quickly, this is a busy place."

They stood in front of the bench looking up at the bird on his perch in his black feathers and white crest. "Is this Daniel?"

He nodded.

"And this is Susan?"

She stared at him making no sign of having heard.

"Isn't that who you are? Susan Isaacson, don't I have that right?"

"You must answer the Judge," Ascher said.

Susan swallowed. He could see her swallowing. He shook her hand, attached to him as if glued, shook it till she nodded.

"Very good. Now I want to ask you children a question, and I want each of you to answer. It is a very simple question, it is an easier question than any you have to answer in school. All right?"

"All right," Daniel said.

"My question is this: Do you like living at the Shelter? Don't look at Mr. Ascher. You will have to answer this question for yourself."

The boy was terrified. He didn't know what to say. The little girl continued to stare up at the Judge. She was not capable of making a sound.

"Well, surely you can tell if you like a place or not. Are you well treated there? Are you happy there? Or would you rather be somewhere else."

"Somewhere else," Daniel said. "We want to go home."

Ascher was shaking his head. He said something in Yiddish and then he and the Judge began to argue. The Judge's eyes were brown but around the circumference of the pupils was a rim of light blue. His eyelids lay over the tops of his eyes like hoods. As he talked to Ascher he looked at the children. And they looked at him.

Suddenly, he disappeared.

"We'll go into the chambers," Ascher said, holding us before him and shuffling us forward to a door.

We were in an office that had a soft grey carpet and a big desk and black leather chairs and a black leather sofa. There were books in bookcases that had glass doors. We sat on the big leather couch, Ascher sat in one of the chairs facing us, and the Judge sat in another. The Judge had taken off his black robe and he looked smaller. He had a white tuft of hair that stuck out of each side of his pink head. He wore a light tweed suit with a vest that was too tight so that it pulled away from its buttons and made elliptical gaps that showed the white of his shirt. He was a tiny man, and when he crossed one leg over the other, he helped it with his hand, lifting his leg under the knee and pulling it over his other knee.

"Ah, here we are," he said.

A grey-haired lady had come through another door and approached us with two bottles of soda in her hands. Eyeglasses hung from a chain around her neck. She handed the bottles to us and then put some change in the Judge's hand. Then she left the room. The Judge had to unfold his legs again to get the change into his pocket.

It was Coca-Cola. My father had once told me that it rotted the teeth. That if you put a tooth in a glass of Coca-Cola it would rot away. At home we never drank it.

"Now this is better, isn't it? Where we're all talking together like this instead of out there? Now has Mr. Ascher told you my name?"

"Judge Greenblatt," Ascher mumbled.

"That's right, Judge Greenblatt," the Judge said as if we had said his name. "And I am appointed by the State to be the Judge of the Children's Court to see to it that children in difficult straits for one reason or another have the best possible chance. You know that."

"They understand," Ascher said. "They are both intelligent children."

"I can see that," the Judge said. "I can see that very clearly."

The bottoms of Susan's thighs were sticking to the leather cushion. She kept lifting her legs and the sound was like adhesive tape coming away from the skin.

"So we have this problem," the Judge said. "And it is whether, in view of the present cicumstances, it is better for you to stay at the Shelter facility, or to be placed in a private home to live privately with a family the way children are supposed to live. And to be as fair as possible I wanted to know how you children feel about the matter."

"Excuse me," Ascher said. "They should be told, Your Honor, of their parents' opinion on the matter."

"We will not lead them, Mr. Ascher," the Judge said, staring at me with his hand tucked between his crossed knees.

"I agree to that," Ascher said. "To tell them neither how anyone thinks they're supposed to live. Not even justices of the Federal District," he added after a moment's thought.

"Well, children, I am waiting for your answer," the Judge said. "You understand," he said turning to Ascher again, "my sole concern is here in this room. There is in your attitude what I detect as a presumption of my brotherhood with a certain Justice of the Federal Court."

"Oh no, not so," Ascher said. He seemed genuinely aghast.

"I do not feel obligated to defend the judiciary for that man," the Judge said. "And I resent the pressure I feel from you."

"It has been a long and frustrating trial," Ascher said. "I'm not well. I would like to hear one ruling out of all of this that favors a defense motion."

"My dear Ascher, these children are not on trial!"

"They most assuredly are," Ascher said, rising to his feet. He began to pace the room. "Their parents are still alive. They have hope. They have hope of being all together again."

"I am merely asking a question."

"It has been answered. May God in Heaven forgive me, if you cannot give these children their mother and father, do not force on them other mothers and other fathers."

"According to your own words a dozen families have offered their homes. They are all presumably sympathetic?"

Ascher sighed and slapped his arms against his sides.

"Do you know what life is like in a public facility?" said the Judge. "Do you think it can be any good in a city barracks for children for not months but perhaps years? At best? And there is a history here of running away."

"Once."

"It is enough. No, you are being melodramatic."

"The parents—"

"I am not concerned with the parents. Their mental health is not the province of my court. It is the children I must consider and it is for the children's welfare decisions must be made. You have to make that clear to them."

The Judge closed his eyes and pinched the bridge of his nose. "There is such a thing as too much hope," he said.

TRUE HISTORY OF THE COLD WAR: A RAGA

Cold War is a phrase given to Bernard Baruch, a non-officeholding adviser to presidents and one of the architects of the Baruch plan for the international control of atomic energy. This plan, which was presented to the UN in June 1946, proposed that for the sake of mankind, the United States—the only country that had atomic bombs—would continue to build its stockpile and sophisticate its bomb technology until a system of foolproof international inspection and control had been established to its satisfaction all over the world, including internally in the Soviet Union. While its plan was under discussion the United States exploded another atom bomb in the South Pacific, on the island of Bikini. We may tentatively define *Cold War* as a condition of incipient bomb-falling hostility by which the United States proposed to apply such pressure upon Soviet Russia that its government would collapse and the power of the Bolsheviks be destroyed. Citations available from Kennan (also known as Mr. X), Acheson, Dulles.

■

As is well known the senior man in the cabinet, Henry Stimson, believed that the diplomatic use of a temporary bomb monopoly to ultimately change conditions in Soviet Russia was a terrible miscalculation that could lead to disaster. Let us look at Stimson. A long life devoted to the interests of his nation. A professional life not without its flush of patriotism, and a hot error or two. A member of the ruling class, as they say. But thirty-five or forty years of high governmental service polishes the skull to a wisdom that is almost oriental in its translucidity. At the level of international relationships life is not complicated at all, but polished by the large simple facts of national self-interest it can shine in simple beauty (and as all the sages of the East point out, the truth *is* simple and beautiful and unnecessary even to articulate). Perhaps Stimson feels that like genetic change induced by radiation the sole possession of this crackling nuclear energy is changing our national character— or fulfilling it. Either way, he sees with the polished eyes of an old man soon to die. We are at a moment when we have the power to alter human history or confirm it finally in its ancient awful courses. He writes a memo to Harry dated September 11, 1945. It's not Lao-tzu but for a diplomat it's not bad at all. It is not bad at all shouldering these concepts as only an old man could have the strength to do in the ultimate flush of youth the spirit blossoms, the last extrudescence before death: "If we fail to approach them now but merely continue to negotiate with them having this weapon ostentatiously on our hip, their suspicions and their distrust of our purposes and motives will increase. . . . Unless the Soviets are voluntarily invited into the partnership upon a basis of cooperation and trust, we are going to maintain the Anglo-Saxon bloc over against the Soviet in the possession of this weapon. Such a condition will almost certainly stimulate feverish activity on the part of the Soviet toward the development of this bomb in what will in effect be a secret armament race of a rather desperate character. There is evidence to indicate that such activity may have already commenced." Harry, listen to me. This is the moment for remaking the world.

■

Harry, at dawn, walks briskly through the White House grounds. Someone, Byrnes, has told him what terrible shape the Russians are in—at a moment when the United States is the most powerful country in the world. Stimson is losing his grip. He wants to negotiate a treaty directly with Russia whereby we would impound our bombs, cease their development provided she (and Britain too) would do the same, and that the three nations would agree not to use the bomb unless all three decided on that use. The idea is to cede a military edge that he thinks is temporary anyway to strike an international bargain that has some chance of being kept and saving civilization—not for five years, or twenty years, but forever. Harry at dawn walks briskly in the White House gardens. Stimson has been around an awfully long time. The President, I mean Franklin, was around too long too. The both of them. Of Stimson the suspicion leaks through that he has lost his usefulness to us. Instead of thinking of our interests he's thinking of humanity. Let him get Joe Stalin to think of humanity.

To confirm how wrong Stimson is, the Russians themselves propose at the UN a treaty close to the Stimson model. The memo of Sept. 11 is filed. The Honorable Secretary is filed. Harry and his Sec. of State, Byrnes of So. Car., will use the bomb the way it ought to be used. War-weakened, man-poor, Russia is seen as a tottering bear who can be brought down. Simply don't give her anything to hold onto. A month after Roosevelt's death all Lend Lease shipments and finances to the Russian ally are suddenly and without warning canceled. Leo Crowley, Harry's Foreign Economic Administrator, tells Congressmen the theory behind this move: "If you create good governments in foreign countries, automatically you will have better markets for ourselves." With that honeycunt staring you in the face, you'd forget your grammar too.

■

There is no evidence that even before the end of the war against Germany and Japan a policy of coexistence with the Russians is seriously considered, let alone put to the test. The false popular view of Yalta. The profound confusion of diplomacy with appeasement. Diplomacy in the formulation of Truman, Byrnes and Vandenberg, is seen not as a means to create conditions of peaceful postwar détente with the Soviets, but as a means of jamming an American world down Russia's throat. Historian W. A. Williams' analysis is that recalling the Depression the American leaders are worried about a postwar economic slump. The solution is to secure foreign markets for American goods. This is the traditional solution to ensure American prosperity. It is called many things by many people but by the State Department it is called the policy of the Open Door.

■

We may prefer a more primitive analysis: that when you defeat an enemy you are required to eat his heart. In this way is your victory recorded with The Gods. In this way too do The Gods ensure the continuation of their amusement: You consume the heart of your enemy so that it can no longer be said of him that he exists—except as he exists in you.

■

Horowitz in THE FREE WORLD COLOSSUS quoting Blackett, another historian of the cold war, demonstrates that the Soviets make comparable reductions to our own in land-army strength: With her potentially hostile borders in Europe, the Middle East, and the Far East, she drops to 25 percent of her strength in 1945. We, with the bomb, and no threatening borders, reduce to 13 percent of our strength in 1945.

■

At Potsdam Russia tells the Americans they need reparations from Germany, preferably in the form of heavy industrial equipment so as to get her shattered economy going again and also to lessen the chance of future German incursions, Germany being now a nation of whom she has historical reason to be morbidly suspicious, deathly afraid. The Americans reply that this is out of the question. At this point the bear has nothing. The art, however, is not in giving your adversary nothing, for with nothing he has nothing to lose by going to war. The art is in giving him nothing while making him think that you're giving him something. James Byrnes of So. Car. knows this. Here is one of the great moments in international relations. Molotov and Stalin sit impassive in their badly tailored suits. They do not permit themselves the luxury of rage. They are the rulers of a vast violent multination bound in ice whose major industry is death, whose only plenitude is violent death. Byrnes opens his carpetbag. He understands that all the aides, translators, guards, microphones, headsets, ranks of negotiators around the table are nothing. He understands the coals of the fire are growing cold in the lodge. And as Harry next to him drums his fingers in miniature representation of artillery fire, clouds of sparks and smoke glinting on Harry's glasses, he removes with loving hands from his carpetbag for the eyes of these savages a sample of glittering cloth. This has always been the way to deal out savages—with bits of glitter and tasteless design. And what is this, they inquire as he bows his Southern aristocratic neck and begs of them to feel the texture.

> Mr. Molotov: My understanding, Secretary Byrnes, is
>   that you have in mind the proposal that each country
>   should take reparations from its own (occupation)
>   zone.
> The Secretary: Yes.
> Mr. Molotov: Would not this suggestion mean that each
>   country would have a free hand in their own zone
>   and would act entirely independently of the others.
> The Secretary: That is true in substance.

Byrnes closes his valise. We've got them on the reservation, now let them realize we own it. The trouble is the Russians assume differently. Did we or did we not exactly mean a free hand? Having reluctantly accepted Byrnes' proposal as a poor substitute for German reparations, the Soviets are determined to make the best of it. This is not according to the American plan. In March 1946, Churchill makes a speech in Fulton, Missouri, with Truman on the platform applauding vigorously. Churchill finds provocative menace in the "iron curtain" the Soviets have dropped in front of Eastern Europe.

■

A MESSAGE OF CONSOLATION TO GREEK BROTHERS IN THEIR PRISON CAMPS, AND TO MY HAITIAN BROTHERS AND NICARAGUAN BROTHERS AND DOMINICAN BROTH-

ERS AND SOUTH AFRICAN BROTHERS AND SPANISH
BROTHERS AND TO MY BROTHERS IN SOUTH VIETNAM,
ALL IN THEIR PRISON CAMPS: YOU ARE IN THE FREE
WORLD!

■

The Russians are portrayed as aggressive, devious, un-
trustworthy, and brutally single-minded. Yet according to
Williams in THE TRAGEDY OF AMERICAN DIPLOMACY, as late
as 1946 Russian postwar policy has not been decided. Russia
has backed down on many issues and has shown indecision in
many others. In Moscow a conflict has existed between those
who subscribe to friendly relations with the U.S. and those who
don't. There is evidence that Stalin favors the former view
particularly as expressed by the economist Eugene Varga, who
argues that Russia can recover from the war by concentrating
internally on domestic problems rather than by expansionist
policies. Varga also calls for a reassessment of American capitalism. Not until 1947 do Varga and his mush-headed gang
disappear and the hard-liners under Molotov take over. This
happens about the time Henry Wallace is fired from the Truman
cabinet for making this statement: "We should be prepared to
judge Russia's requirements against the background of what we
ourselves and the British have insisted upon as essential to our
respective security."

■

A Congressional Committee in 1947 reports on the unprecedented volume of anti-Soviet propaganda coming out of the
U.S. Government. It turns out to be absolutely necessary. On the
one hand America considers itself the strongest nation, the first
and only nuclear nation, the wealthiest, the most powerful nation in the world. On the other hand it must live in fear of the
Russian. Secretary of State Acheson will testify some years after-
ward that never in the counsels of the Truman cabinet did
anyone seriously regard Russia as a military threat—even after
they got their bomb. Bipartisan Senator-Statesman Vandenberg

tells how the trick is done: "We've got to scare hell out of the American people," he says.

■

The Truman Doctrine will not be announced as a policy of providing military security for the foreign governments who accept our investments, but as a means of protecting freedom-loving nations from Communism. The Marshall Plan will be advertised not as a way of ensuring markets abroad for American goods but as a means of helping the countries of Europe recover from the war. Russia has had the effrontery not to collapse. We are faced with an international atheistic Communist conspiracy of satanic dimension. Which side are you on? Russia moves into Rumania, Bulgaria, East Germany. Russia rolls over Czechoslovakia. Here is NATO. Here is the Berlin Blockade. And behold, it came to pass, just the kind of world we said it was—

I don't remember who drove the car. It was not Ascher, Ascher was sitting next to me in the back seat. I was in the middle. Susan was on my right—I had given her the window. I could see over her head anyway. We were going up the Saw Mill River Parkway. The road was dry but snow lay in banks along the side. It was old snow covered with soot and dirt. This was the same way, I knew, that you went to Peekskill. The wheels hummed on the road. The hills were turning green.

"What?" said Ascher. "What is it?"

"The gas fumes. I want to open the window."

"Fumes? There are no fumes."

"Just a little." I was having trouble breathing.

I can't remember who drove. Ascher sat in the back with us. I was between Ascher and Susan. My stomach hurt. My fingers ached. I held a package wrapped in brown paper, a gift for my father. I had made a pair of book ends in school in the woodworking shop—they were slabs of wood nailed together at right angles, with the edges beveled and the surfaces sanded. Then we carved designs with the woodburning tool and then stained the whole thing walnut. For my design I had burned a large "I" into the vertical face of each book end.

Susan's gift was for our mother—a sheaf of her crayon drawings tied together with a hank of yarn in a bow.

Susan kept shifting and squirming. She wouldn't stop even after I asked her nicely. I punched her in the arm and she tried to scratch my face.

"Children," Ascher said. "Please, children, no nonsense."

It was a long trip. We had left just after lunch. When you are traveling to see people the sense of them fills your mind. Their voices and their attitudes. But I couldn't see them clearly—only their shadows. I was not feeling well. I was afraid to be going to see them. It was a long trip. I didn't know what they would say. I wasn't sure they would be glad to see me.

"Is this the right day?" I asked Ascher, not for the first time.

"Yes, Daniel."

"Do they know we're coming?"

"I told you yes."

"They expect us this very afternoon?"

"Yes."

"They're dead," Susan said.

"No, my little girl, that is not true. They are alive."

"They're not alive anymore, they were killed," Susan said. "It was in the newspaper."

"How do you know, you can't read," Daniel said.

"I can, I have learned how to read."

"You're a liar," Daniel said.

"Please," Ascher said.

"I'm a good reader," Susan said. "I can read everything."

"What newspaper?"

"In my class."

"And what did it say?"

"It said that my mother and father were killed. Bugs killed them."

"Please, children, enough."

"What kind of bugs?"

"Bugs and death."

"You're a dope," Daniel said. But it bothered me that she sounded so sure of herself.

We got to the prison in the middle of the afternoon. It was

cold although the sun was shining. I was glad to be out of the car. We had parked beside a wall of yellow brick. The windows in this wall were enormous—arched, like cathedral windows, but striped with bars. I stepped back for a better view. It was a big building. Rising from the corner of the building was a hexagonal tower topped with glass, like a lighthouse, and a roof of its own, like a Chinese hat. At the far end of the building was another tower.

We walked along a fence like the kind around the school-yard, except that along the top of it were three parallel strands of barbed wire.

I heard a whirring sound and turned to see a man shooting me with a multi-turreted movie camera. Another man appeared who ran backward in front of us, popping flashbulbs at our feet. We held up our hands. I can't describe this. I am tired of describing things. We are clients of a new law firm, Voltani, Ampere, and Ohm. If you've seen one prison you've seen them all. We had to give up our packages, over Ascher's protest. We were in this office and the man was dressed like a policeman. Ascher grabbed my book ends and tore off the paper. "Gifts from children to their parents!"

"Can't take 'em," the man said.

"The things of children!"

"Sorry, Counselor."

Ascher argued vehemently, and then suddenly stopped and pretended to us that it meant nothing. "It's all right," he confided to us, "I'll speak to someone."

We went to the Death House, a place that lacked the hum of the rest of the prison city. Elsewhere you could hear voices, or the rumble of machinery under your feet. Here, it was absolutely still. We were in a room bare of everything except a wooden table and some chairs. The bottom half of the walls were painted brown. The top half of the walls were painted yellow. No one was in the room. Everything was quiet.

"They have to bring them now," Ascher said in a lowered voice. "First your mother, then afterwards your father."

We waited and no one came. We stood in our coats and waited. I went to the window and looked out between the bars. We were high up. I could see the Hudson River. Ascher sat down at the end of the table, pushed his homburg back on his head, put his hands on his knees, and sighed. I heard the door open. I turned but it was a guard. He stepped inside the door, closed it softly, and stood against the wall with his arms folded. I went over to him and raised my hands.

"What are you doing, Daniel?"

"He has to frisk me," I explained without lowering my hands.

" 'At's all right, kid," the guard said. He cleared his throat. He had terrible acne, great red eruptions all over his face.

"No, go ahead, search me, I might have a gun."

The guard looked at Ascher. He cleared his throat again.

" 'At's OK, kid, I'm satisfied you don't have a gun," he said.

"How do you know if you don't search me."

"Me too," Susan said.

"All right, children," Ascher said. "They haven't seen their parents in over a year," he explained to the guard.

"Yeah, well they're here," the guard said.

"Search me," Daniel insisted, his voice louder now.

"OK, kid, I said it was OK," the guard said. He acted as if he was afraid I'd wake someone.

"SEARCH ME!" I screamed. I could feel my face turning red.

The guard looked at Ascher, who had stood and walked up behind me. Ascher must have nodded, because he quickly leaned over and patted the pockets of my mackinaw.

"Now her."

He lightly touched the hem of Susan's coat, and then stood up straight against the wall and folded his arms and ignored us.

Still nobody came. Susan began to walk around the edges of the room, measuring each wall with her footsteps. When she came to the guard she merely went around him as if he were part of the wall. I took up my vigil at the window. I wondered why they built this prison within sight of the river, since it would only want to make people escape. If I had long enough time here I'd find a way to get or make a rope long enough and to saw the bars so that no one would know, and to climb the fence. I'd learn all these things with enough time. I would let myself down the wall and climb the barbed-wire fence and run down to the river. Once I reached the river they'd never catch me. I could hear my own breathing as I ran. I could feel the cold water rising around me as I waded into the river, and then warming as I set out downriver with powerful strokes made more powerful by the current. The chill of late afternoon was touching the hills. The sky was growing imperceptibly darker. I would swim to New York. The river had turned black. The scene through this barred window was absolutely still. Nothing moved. It was frozen in the absolute stillness of the dirt-crusted window.

For some time I had been observed by my mother who had quietly come into the room. She had been as noiseless as the Death House stones. She did not speak but watched Susan in her walk and me in my revery. I have the letters between them—how for a week they wrote back and forth in anticipation of the visit and constructed the proper way of presenting themselves. They would be calm, composed, cheerful, matter-of-fact. They would answer our questions honestly and with no alarm. They would teach us, by example, how one lived in the Death House.

What happened was that Susan ran over to me and took my hand. Then I saw her too. We stood near the window and looked at our mother.

She was smaller. She had on a grey sack dress and house slippers. Her hair looked shorter. She was thin, and she was very pale, almost waxen. She stared at us with an expression on her face either of joy or terrible pain, I don't know which, but of such intensity that I couldn't meet her gaze. My eyes squeezed shut and when I could open them again I saw that she had pressed her fingers to her temples and applied such pressure that the corners of her eyes had slanted.

Susan was crushing my fingers.

"Look at you two," my mother said. "You're so big I don't recognize you."

"We sent you pictures," I said.

"I know, I know. And I love those pictures. I have them taped to the wall where I can see them all the time, even when I'm going to sleep."

"In your cell?"

"Yes."

"Can we go there?"

She glanced at the guard who stood there as if he saw and heard nothing. She smiled. "I'm afraid they wouldn't allow it," she said. But the feeling I had was that she ruled this place, and that the guards were like servants who took care of her.

"Aren't you going to give me a hug?" my mother said.

Susan and I looked at each other, and shuffling across the room, we suffered ourselves to stand before her as she kneeled and hugged each of us in turn. We were as stiff as boards. She did not feel in a hug the way my mother used to feel. She didn't smell the same.

"You're so big. You're beautiful. You're my beautiful children." She had red lipstick on that made her face horribly pale. Her eyes were sunken, burning very brightly from pits deep in her face.

"When are they going to kill you?" Susan said.

"Oh, they're not going to do that. It's just their way of talking. I'm sure Uncle Jake told you about appeals, about other judges who have to reexamine the evidence. It all takes time, you see. We're in no danger of that right now."

"But what if they kill you anyway?" Susan said. "How will they do it?"

"Well, darling, what they do is called electrocution, and it's very painless. It's very fast and it doesn't hurt. But let's not talk about that. Aren't you warm? Take your coats off, let me look at you. You're very nicely dressed. How lovely you look. Here, I have something for you."

From her pockets she took two bars of candy, a Milky Way for each of us.

We sat at the table and ate the Milky Ways while she sat on a chair between us, touching our heads, our legs, our shoulders. "Look how broad-shouldered you're getting," she said to me. She seemed quite happy now.

I tried to think of things to tell her, things to make her feel good. I said I liked school. I said I enjoyed math. I said I had lots of friends. These were the lies of my letters, and to my disappointment she seemed to believe all of them. It is the same way you lie to very sick or old people to make them feel good, and let them believe that their pain has at least brought some order to the world. But it is a measure of the unreclaimable distance from you that they believe what you say.

"Where is my daddy," Susan wants to know.

"Well, he'll be here soon. First I get a visit with you, then he gets a visit with you."

"Why not together?"

"I don't know. It's one of their rules."

"Why?"

"I don't know, my sweet girl. Look how long your hair has gotten. It's so pretty."

"Where is he?"

"Not far from here. In another cellblock. It's not far."

"Do you see him?"

"Oh yes. We get to talk once a week through a screen."

"We went home," Susan said.

"Yes, I remember that."

"But it was gone," Susan said.

It seemed to me vital to dissociate myself from my sister's remarks. I told my mother that I was planning to become a lawyer so that I could get her free.

"So?" Ascher said from the other end of the table. "This I haven't heard before."

"You'll make a good lawyer. Won't he, Jake?"

"Of course."

"I won't let them kill you," I swore. "I'll kill them first."

"Oh now," she chided. "Where did you get that expression?"

My mother took a kleenex from her pocket and wiped the chocolate from the corners of Susan's mouth. Susan hadn't finished her Milky Way, but stood up now, restlessly, and began to walk around the table with her arm outstretched and her fingers lightly brushing whatever they touched—a chair, my back, Ascher's back, my mother. I had a terrible sense of illness, of my mother's illness. It was as if she were a patient in this place rather than a prisoner. It was as if she was already dead. She was so unlike herself that I became discouraged about the possibility of communicating with her.

I found her looking at me with a sad half-smile. "It is a little hard to make up for all the lost time. A strange feeling, isn't it."

"Yes." I blurted out what was on my guilty mind: "We're going to live with a family in Westchester."

"I know."

"It's in New Rochelle. It's not far. It's closer to here than the Shelter."

"I know. I've exchanged letters with them. They're fine people, the Fischers. Don't worry, I know all about it."

"The Judge made us. When the term is over."

"Danny, you don't understand. It's with our consent. We want that for you. We chose them from all the people. It will be some time, and that's too long to live in the Shelter."

Susan was now back to her race along the walls of the room. My mother turned to watch her. She couldn't keep her eyes off Susan and I was embarrassed to see the expression on her face. I realized she was no longer pretty to me.

A few minutes later I saw the guard look at his watch; and almost at the same moment a matron in the same blue guard's uniform opened the door and told my mother her time was up.

We said goodbye. She hugged us again. "You'll come back soon, won't you?"

"Yes."

"I love you, my sweetest angels. I love your letters. I love your faces. Soon this will all be over and we'll have peace. It's a terrible thing to do to people, isn't it? But don't worry. We'll get out of here. We will have fun again. All right?"

"Yes."

We stand leaning backwards into her hands which hold us in the small of our backs, as she kneels in front of us as if she wants to bury her face in our children's loins.

"In all of this I never forget you for one moment. I'm so proud of you. Do you know that?"

"Yes."

She kissed us and stood up and left without taking us with her.

What is most monstrous is sequence. When we are there why do we withdraw only in order to return? Is there nothing good enough to transfix us? If she is truly worth fucking why do I have to fuck her again? If the flower is beautiful why does my baby son not look at it forever? Paul plucks the flower and runs on, the flower dangling from his shoelace. Paul begins to hold, holds, ends hold of the flower against the sky, against his eye to the sky. I engorge with my mushroom head the mouth of the womb of Paul's mother. When we come why do we not come forever? The monstrous reader who goes on from one word to the next. The monstrous writer who places one word after another. The monstrous magician.

When my father came in he was wound up in a parody of good cheer. He shouted a greeting, he was effusive. They had given him different glasses, with colorless plastic frames. His hair was very short. His ears were prominent. He wore grey pants and a grey shirt that was too big for him. Slippers and no belt. He looked very young. Smaller than I remembered him. Red of face. Insane.

It caused me terrible anguish, when I thought about it later, that they had to wear those grey uniforms. Why did they consent to being dressed that way?

"How are the two best children in the world! How are my favorite children in the whole world. Look at them, Jake. A million dollars. A million dollars. I bet they don't know what I've been doing while I've been in prison. Do you? Do you know what I have in this box?"

"No."

"Well, I'm going to show you. Watch carefully."

He took from under his arm a cigar box held together with a rubber band, the paper hinge having torn in the way of cigar boxes. With a great flourish, like a magician on a stage, he placed the box on the table and removed the rubber band and slowly lifted the lid.

"See this? It's my collection."

In the box were dead moths, roaches, spiders, beetles, flies and at the bottom, under everything else, an enormous brown water bug with its legs curled up. "The insect world is truly amazing. If you just look at it you discover marvelous things."

"How do you catch them," I said.

"With a paper cup, that's all the equipment I need. I hold it over them till they suffocate. That way they're not damaged, although I can't keep them from drying up. I can't mount them properly," he said. "They won't let me have pins or cotton or the killing fluid. But I've petitioned, I've petitioned. Some of these moths are beautiful, look at this one."

He held one brown and black moth up on a piece of paper. His hand was trembling and it seemed as if the dead moth were shaking, trying to take off.

"I hate it," Susan said. "I hate dead things."

"Now these are my roaches—I can usually find all the specimens I need." He laughed. "But they're very hard to catch. You have to trick them, you have to trap them. Sometimes it takes hours."

He was alarmed at Susan's reaction. He closed the box in the middle of a sentence. He stood up and walked around. He was flustered. He suddenly didn't know what to say to us. He sat down and held his head in his hands and looked at the floor.

When he looked up he had composed himself. "You know, your mother and I figured it out—as the crow flies we're not more than twenty feet from each other. I'm one floor below and one block over. And of course there's a lot of stone and steel between us, but we're that close. Poor Mommy. There's no one up there with her, you know. She is the only lady. I at least have murderers to talk to." He laughed.

He seemed to look at us for the first time. "You're getting to look like me," he said to his son.

"Am I?" Susan wanted to know.

"Ahh—you're luckier," he said with a smile. He held his arms out and pulled her toward him. "You're the image of your mother. You're beautiful like your mother. Jake!" he called over his shoulder. "Is that not an ideal situation? What could a father ask for but that his son take after him and his daughter after his wife. Is that not ideal?"

"Absolutely," Ascher said.

"We are an ideal family," my father cried.

He took some Baby Ruths out of his pockets and pressed them on us. "We just had candy," I said.

"Save them for later, then. Save them for the ride."

I asked him if he was ever allowed out of his cell.

"Oh yes, oh yes. Fifteen minutes a day I have exercise in the yard. I play catch with the guards. Or I run around. I find specimens there. I find my best moths there. You want to know all about it, don't you?" He laughed and mussed my hair. It was the first time he touched me.

"Also I play chess with some of the other inmates. We make our own boards and paper men marked with the pieces they are. And we shout out our moves. You remember how I taught you to notate on the chessboard?"

"Yes."

"I always thought chess was a waste of time. It is! It's a terrible waste of time. I look forward to the baseball season. They've already broadcast some of the exhibition games of the Dodgers and the Giants. Over the loudspeaker. Are you still a baseball fan?"

I shrugged. It was a taste I felt guilty for having. He thought all sports a means of keeping people subjected. He felt loyalty to a baseball team was the worst kind of working class gullibility.

"Well, they'll make one of me yet!" he said with a laugh. I was looking directly into his face, at his eyes made large and rude by his eyeglasses. He sighed, pushed us away, and got up to pace the room. He took a pack of cigarettes out of his shirt pocket and jerked his hand upward so that a cigarette came out of the pack. He put the cigarette between his lips and lit a match to it and replaced matches and pack in his shirt pocket. He did all this with a practiced economy of motion. Yet I had never known him to smoke a cigarette.

"Time," he said. "There's so much reading you can do. So many exercises. You have to find ways to make it go past. To fill it. You know what I mean? Time which is so valuable— in jail you've got to kill it. But I'm writing a book. I'm making notes for it now. Lenin wrote when he was in jail. All of them. They knew how to make the best use of it. As in everything, model yourself on the masters."

He sat down and grabbed me by the shoulders. He held his cigarette between his fingers and the smoke curled up past my eye. I noticed the ash was about to fall—if it did it would fall on my shoulder.

"They can put a person in jail, but they can't put his mind in jail."

I squirmed away. I brushed at my shoulder.

"What's wrong? Did I burn you? No, look here, it didn't fall, the ash is still here, you see?" He laughed.

"They are the ones whose minds are in jail. But don't worry. Don't worry. Already things are happening. This outrage will not happen. I have it on good authority—public sentiment will gather for us. You cannot put innocent people to death in this country. It can't be done. The truth will reclaim us. You'll see. You'll see, my big handsome boy. Am I right, Jake?"

"Of course. But calm yourself."

"Before our trial even started we were found guilty by the paid hirelings of the kept press. There was no possibility for a fair trial. On that ground alone."

"Paul." Ascher stood up. He was looking at the guard. "I don't think this ought to be discussed right now," he said.

"It's all right. I want my son to know. An organization is being founded to fight for our freedom. To tell people the truth. He should know that. He should know we're not alone, the Isaacson family. Soon the whole world will be behind us in our fight to regain our freedom. And he can help! You want to help, don't you?"

"Yes," I said.

"That's my boy, that's my wonderful boy." He held my face in his hands and pulled me toward him and kissed the top of my head.

Why hadn't my mother mentioned this? Without her endorsement I couldn't tell if it was true. Nevertheless, on the drive back to New York it was his voice I heard in my mind. I had felt the humiliation of having to leave them there. But as I thought about it it seemed less degrading to my father to be in prison than to my mother. It was his voice that rang in my ears outside the prison, in the car, on the way back to New York.

Probably none of this is true. There's a lot more I can't remember. But the first visit was the worst. The other visits were easier. We had things to tell them. We played games. We drew pictures. We settled into a regular routine. We shared the joys of a number of stays of execution. And toward the end they were allowed to see us at the same time. And the four of us in that room in the Death House, the family, back together, at last. And the four of us were together in that room. And we were reunited. And at last we were reunited.

Before the famous Egyptian adjustment of the Chaldean calendar, in 4000 B.C., judicial astrology proposed thirteen signs in the Zodiac of approximately 27 degrees each. The thirteenth sign was Starfish. We do not today know where it was located in the Zodiac. It is believed that as the earth's axis gradually altered, an entire chunk of the night sky, including this constellation, disappeared. But until that time Starfish was considered one of the most beneficial of signs. A Starfish ascendant suggested serenity and harmony with the universe, and therefore great happiness. The five points of the star lead not outward as is commonly believed, but inward, toward the center. This symbolized the union of the various mental faculties and the coordination of the physical faculties. It referred to the wedding in the heart of the five senses. It implied the unification of all feelings. Belief was joined with intellect, language with truth, and life with justice. Starfish in opposition to Mars usually meant Genius. Under the influence of Venus it suggested Peace. For some reason astrologers today don't mention Starfish and there is a common superstition that it means bad luck. This is undoubtedly because modern man can conceive of nothing more frightening than the self-sufficiency of being of the beautiful Starfish: he mistakes it for death.

LOOKING FOR STERNLICHT

I had not wanted to take Phyllis with me. There was an element of danger, crowds, confrontation. And since I was going to do what was being done, perhaps without grace, perhaps with flagging resolve, perhaps failing, perhaps shitting all over myself, I didn't want her there. But she began to feel the old torture, she said I was excluding her. It wasn't true but I didn't want her to feel that way. And then I thought of driving into the heart of darkness alone, across borders, across checkpoints, and the thought of being able to talk to her appealed to me. So there we were, all of us driving down a crisp sunny morning late in October 1967. I had put a hundred and eighty dollars into the trip. Brakes, front end, two new tires, new plugs, a tune-up. It was a tight smart little Volvo. There were other cars on the road with recognizable people in them, cars with five and six passengers, and horns blew on the Turnpike and people in little cars scooting around the trailer trucks waved at each other and held two fingers up to the windows. Nevertheless a sense of driving across borders. Across checkpoints. A sense of driving into the heart of darkness.

In this capital city of wide streets and white marble monuments and public greens, a sense of foreign country.

"Is it just me?" I said.

"I think everyone must feel it who's coming for the weekend," Phyllis said.

Great caution is required. You drive slow. You hug the wheel. In one public building is a famous crime museum. In the famous crime museum are pictures of the Isaacsons in handcuffs. A shortwave radio from Isaacson Radio, Sales and Repair. A dental x-ray mounted like a Kodachrome against a light screen. Tourists stroll by. In another public building is a file no one has ever seen.

We drive to the designated church, park the car, and join the others. It is a quiet beginning on the Friday afternoon of Pentagon Weekend. A few hundred only, marching from the basement of a church to the doors of the Justice Department. We string out for a quarter of a mile. Movie cameramen walking backwards photograph our faces. I do not see Sternlicht. Washington cops on motorcycles with sidecars purr alongside in the warm sun. It seems to be an academic gathering. Many poets from the universities. Middle-aged publishers in tweeds. Academic wives and sexy church ladies wearing loafers. Long-haired college boys in denim who chant Hell No We Won't Go. It is a peaceful, orderly march. The sun is out. I carry Paul.

Phyllis, beside me, smiles and hugs my arm. The self-conscious sense of doing something animates the marchers. Old friends gossip. The line strings out.

We chat with Professor Sukenick who has also come down. Possessed of a delicate sense of occasion he does not ask me how my work is going. We stroll to the Justice Department. There on the steps a microphone is set up for speeches. Cops guard our right of assembly. Cops stand in the doors of the Justice Department to ensure that we stay outside. Photographers take pictures of our faces. Four young American Nazis in swastika armbands are there to hurl taunts. They are taunt hurlers. As the speeches begin I find a place for us to sit down. Phyllis feeds the baby. I walk around the edges of the crowd, from sun to shadow, from shadow to sun. Dr. Spock is there. The Chaplain of Yale is there. The demonstration today is an act of civil disobedience. The young cats turn in their draft cards, the older cats aid and abet them. Arrest is invited. Sitting on the steps listening to the speakers is Norman Mailer. He wears a dark suit and vest. He leans forward, his left forearm on his left knee, his right fist on his right knee. Behind him, festooned in the deep stone sill of the ground floor Justice Department window, is Robert Lowell. Lowell is arranged cherubically. I watch Lowell smoke and press his eyeglasses to the bridge of his nose. I watch him making up his poetry.

The point of the drama is reached and the draft cards of hundreds of college boys across the country are dropped in a pouch by their representatives. There is applause. Others in the crowd are invited to add their own cards. Many do. I make my way through the crowd, and drop my card into the pouch, and say my name into the microphone. Daniel Isaacson, although the card is in the name of Daniel Lewin. My ears glow from an inner surge of righteousness and fear. What a put-on. But I have come here to do whatever is being done.

The pouch is delivered to the Justice Department, the demonstration ends, and nothing seems to have happened except the demonstration.

That night a crash committee set us up at the home of a sympathetic lady who had opened her house for "the Movement." It was an old, well-maintained house in a quiet neighborhood. The lady showed us to our room. "I can't physically march," she said, "but I can support those who do." She was a frail, gracious lady whose soft quavering voice seemed to transmit itself through her hands which shook with a slight palsy. Her house was very still. It was brimming with silence. Thin white curtains hung across the window of our room. There was a large oversoft bed with a cathedral headboard of mahogany. The baby was placed in a wooden rocking cradle. The floor was constructed of wide planks fastened with pegs. On an old splintery hope chest stood a white bowl and inside the bowl was a large pitcher with fine fractures in its glaze. Phyllis was charmed by the room. She ran her fingers along the glass curtains, and inspected the old pitcher and washbowl. She rocked Paul to sleep in the cradle and took off her clothes and brushed her long hair sitting crosslegged in the middle of the soft bed. She was serenely happy suspended in this quiet room in the absolute stillness of this house.

The last time I had been in Washington, D.C., the occasion was a vigil at the White House. Susan and I held candles in our hands and rested our foreheads on the White House fence. That is a famous news picture. It appears as if we're looking through prison bars. Washington was our town, I played Washington when I was a kid.

The next day, Saturday, is the big event. We sit for hours in the grass at the Lincoln Memorial and listen to the speeches. All around us people with signs on placards, on poles. Young Christian men and women, veterans, radicals with long hair. Self-conscious professors, older women in walking shoes and red noses of pert participation. Guitarists. Freaks with painted faces and gendarme capes waving broom handles crowned with boxes decorated with pictures of flowers and Joan and Bobby and Allen. Scuba divers with white bones painted on their black wetsuits. Priests. Members of organizations with hand-painted banners. It is a beautiful day. All the happy freaks of cold war have poured out of their chartered buses, climbed out of their sleeping bags, each life famous, and come to march on the Pentagon. The crowd is enormous. At the steps of Lincoln Memorial hoarse speakers shout into their microphones. I feel the concussion of crowd assent. I come under the awful conviction of everyone's greater right to be here. I feel out of it. It seems to me that practically everyone here, even Phyllis listening past the point of normal attention to the endlessness of the droning speeches, has taken possession of the event in a way that is beyond me. I feel as if I have sneaked in, haven't paid, or simply don't know something that everyone else knows. That it is possible to still do this, perhaps. Or that it is enough. In the heat of midday it is suddenly time to rise and form up in the march. Lasers of sun spear at the eyes of camera lenses. Bodies rise. Heat rises. Banners are raised, unfurled, the equipage of the picnic army clanking and groaning and creaking into rank.

In the jamming crowd I feel the first whispers of death by suffocation.

"This is where it begins to get heavy," I tell Phyllis.

She looks at me in alarm. I take her arm to get her out of there, walking away down the green, walking the other way.

"But this is what we came down for!"

"I don't want to have to worry about you, Phyl. I want you to go back to that lady's house and wait there until I'm through."

She was very unhappy.

"Phyllis, you didn't really intend to take your baby into that. Troops with bayonets. Tear gas. Did you? You can't be sure what's going to happen."

"But I want to go!"

"All right, you go. Give me Paul and you go." She doesn't want that, and I feel acquiescence to my logic—to the logic of my right and need to come here to do what is being done—in the sudden lack of resistance to my hand of her arm, the consent of her hurried steps as we go looking for a cab somewhere in the direction of Washington.

All day I looked for satisfaction. At one point during the squeeze on the bridge from the Lincoln Memorial across the river, I thought I caught a glimpse of Sternlicht in a three-pointed hat. But I was pretty far back from the front line where he would have been. There were more speeches in a parking lot across the highway from the Pentagon. Then I followed some people running toward a break in the fence: you ran up an embankment, across the highway, and you were on the Mall at the mouth of the Pentagon itself.

It still wasn't clear what was going to happen. The mood was festive. There were rumors that achieving the Mall was meaningless because it had been permitted by arrangement between the organizers of the march and the officials of the Pentagon. Then, as it began to turn dark, lots of people began to leave. There was room to see where the MP's and the marshals stood in rank at the steps of the front entrance. There was room to move up front. One could examine the mandarin faces. God was on their side. No matter what is laid down there will be people to put their lives on it. Soldiers will instantly appear, fall into rank, and be ready to die for it. And scientists who are happy to direct their research toward it. And keen-witted academics who in all rationality develop the truth of it. And poets who find their voice in proclaiming the personal feeling of it. And in every house in the land the muscles of the face will arrange in smug knowledge of it. And people will go on and make their living from it. And the religious will pray for a just end to it, in terms satisfactory to it.

It was now dark and getting very cold. It was possible to find a bonfire and be with others. There was a lot of dope to smoke. The feeling was good. Here and there, ceremonies of burning draft cards. Constant heckling of troops, singing; diggers coming around with loaves of bread, and baloney, and beer, and Pepsi. Still I am exhausted with this striving. It is as if my presence—none of them knows—but my attendance has robbed the day of genius.

But here in the chilling night a very thinned-out crowd is beginning to insist on itself in the night shadows of the great black looming walls of Pentagon, and the people are younger in this growing stubbornness, they are not polite, they are not particularly nice, many of them, but in changing wind flurries intimations of tear gas establish skirmishes hidden from the eye and the meaning of distant shouts. And their manners are not fine but they have to get through many levels of not particularly civilized let alone cool behavior in order to make clear to themselves and to the soldiers the true value of the occasion, which is to say its real nature. And yes, my brothers, war sucks, and american imperialism doth suck, and I'm beginning to feel the imminence of satisfaction. And here most of the older people are gone, and the reporters are gone, and the cameras are gone, and what the later hours of evening find —perhaps it is already midnight—is an accidental community of hard-core Quakers and rads and new boys and new girls of the new life-style and also one pusillanimous adventurer now crept and climbed to the foremost rows of disputants in order to do what is being done. And suddenly he is there, locked arm in arm with the real people of now, sitting in close passive rank with linked arms as the boots approach, highly polished, and the clubs, highly polished, and the brass highly polished wading through our linkage, this many-helmeted beast of our own nation, coming through our flesh with boot and club and gun butt, through our sick stubbornness, through our blood it comes. My country. And it swats and kicks, and kicks and clubs—you raise the club high and bring it down, you follow through, you keep head down, you remember to snap the wrist, complete the swing, raise high bring down, think of a groove in the air, groove into the groove, keep your eye on the ball, eye on balls, eye on cunts, eye on point of skull, up and down, put your whole body into it, bring everything you've got into your swing, up from your toes, up down, turn around, up high down hard, hard as you can, hard as you can, harder harder: FOLLOW THROUGH!

Daniel drank his own blood. It was Pentagon Saturday Night. He swallowed bits of his teeth. And he was lifted by the limbs and he was busted on Pentagon Saturday Night.

And I will tell now how one boy in the big cell, in this grand community of brotherhood bust, how this one boy is unable to share the bruised cheery fellowship of his companions or care for the gossip that Artie Sternlicht has topped everyone by landing in the hospital, or feel this group-sing spirit of gap teeth and seventy-six handkerchiefs dried crimson around the head; but sits in the corner, unable to stretch out full length, a spasm of wariness bowing his spine, knotting his fingers to his palms, his knees to his chest, his head to his knees. He cannot enjoy such places. They are too familiar. He knows how far they are from home. He cannot survive such places in careless courage. He is sensitive to the caged air rubbing his skin, the night of this place nuzzling his ears. He sweats in a chill of possibilities knowing now what it means to do what is being done, and sweats every minute of just one night only one night, every second sweating it, a twenty-five-dollar ten-day suspended trip INNOCENT, I'M INNOCENT I TELL YA, eyesight skating up and down the walls like flies, interpreting the space between the bars, and Daniel discusses the endless reverberations of each moment of this time, doing this time in discrete instants, and discussing each instant its theme, structure, diction and metaphor with her, with Starfish, my silent Starfish girl

The next morning I paid my fine and was released. It was another lovely day. I got back to Washington and found the car and drove to the neighborhood of old American houses and found my wife in the quiet white room of the quiet American house. Phyllis immediately began to cry. My right eye was closed. My lips were crusted and swollen and I couldn't open my mouth wide enough to eat. It hurt me to breathe, but I found I could ease it somewhat by holding my arms against my ribs. Blood was dried all over my shirt.

I didn't want her to go on and on. "Listen," I said, trying not to whistle through my teeth. "It looks worse than it is. There was nothing to it. It is a lot easier to be a revolutionary nowadays than it used to be."

Book Four
CHRISTMAS

Early in December

Daniel Isaacson boarded an American Airlines 707 bound for Los Angeles. He wore his fleece-lined jacket, prison shirt and pants, and sandals. His beard was full, his long hair tied around with a headband of red cloth. His steel glasses shone. His teeth were large and white and shining and his toes, always rather large, looked immense in sandals—they were crude toes, prominently knuckled with thick yellow nails not entirely clean. He waved a big chilled toe at the fascinated lady across the aisle who looked up at him, blushed, and turned away.

A good many of the passengers believed Daniel was there to hijack the plane. He considered the possibility. Two business-men conferred on the length of his hair. The stewardess found it difficult to maintain her smile when she passed him the lunch menu. In fact she seemed to be angry with him. But she gave him that practiced eyeflick.

After a lunch of sliced steak and small green peas and apple cobbler Daniel received from the stewardess some sort of stethoscope in a plastic bag. For which The Foundation paid a dollar. It is to listen to the fantasy breathing. *The Spy Who Came In from the Cold,* with Richard Burton. Burton, an English intelligence agent, or spy, is manipulated and finally betrayed by his superiors in an involved plot designed to protect a double agent in East Germany. His innocent girl friend Claire Bloom is killed on the Berlin Wall and Burton chooses to die with her, standing up in turn to be shot. Life is never this well plotted but the picture is meant to be appreciated for its realism. It is photographed in black and white, always a sign of sincerity. Burton walks around like a man with a realistic load of shit in his pants. And The Wall itself is there, with its guard posts and striped gates and floodlights. But is it realism to show the Berlin Wall as a wall? The Berlin Wall is not a wall. It is a seam. It is a seam that binds the world. The entire globe is encased in lead, riveted bolted stripped wired locked tight and sprocketed with spikes, like a giant mace. Inside is hollow. Occasionally this hot lead and steel casing expands or cracks in the heat of the sun, and along the seams, one of which is called the Berlin Wall, a space or crevice appears temporarily that is just big enough for a person to fall through. In a world divided in two the radical is free to choose one side or the other. That's the radical choice. The halves of the world are like the two hemispheres of Mengleburg. My mother and father fell through an open seam one day and then the hemispheres pressed shut.

Daniel stood at the curb in Los Angeles International Airport waiting for the Low Dollar Rent-A-Car Courtesy Cab. Looking down on the traffic the fringe tops of scrawny palm trees. Here he was in Southern California. The air a strange drink of balmy poison. The sky hazy blue overhead, solid phlegm toward the horizon.

Daniel thought renting a low dollar rent-a-car was a good idea. The courtesy cab came along with its big low dollar sign on the roof and a young black guy got out and came around to the curb and looked for the customer.

"It's me," Daniel greeted him. "I called."

"You? Just you?"

"Yeah."

The black guy took off his hat and put it back on. "Well, no offense, but they're not going to give *you* a car."

"Oh shit," Daniel said. He scratched his beard.

"That's right. I mean I'll drive you down there, it's all the same to me, but I'm just saying what's true."

"OK, I appreciate that."

"They'll just hassle you, you know. Till you get the idea."

"Right. Well, can you give me a lift someplace where I can thumb a ride?"

"Sure, which way you going?"

Daniel stood at Century Boulevard just before the turn to the San Diego Freeway. He stood with his bag between his feet and his thumb out. His chest hurt. Finally a VW camper pulled up. The driver was a blond kid with long mustaches and no shirt. The kid had a bed in the camper, a mattress with a sleeping bag on top of it, curtains on the windows, books in a bookshelf.

"Where you goin'?"

Daniel looked at his map. The wagon sped down the Freeway whining its way in the grey sun past oil refineries, billboards, power plants, industrial parks, furnaces, trailer parks, junkyards, storage tanks, ramps, cloverleafs, shopping centers, tract housing pennants flying, and on south into the country.

I don't know what to write to convey the temperature change of the book. Take your coat off, it's warm here. A headache passes through the eyes. It has to do with the atmosphere, the light. The light burns you. The sun warms you tans you but doesn't burn you. The light burns you, chars the back edges of the vision. The sun has to be out in this part of the book. It is a chemical sun. It shines through a grey haze. It shines through a balmy stillness of air which lacks all natural smells. And to think all this was once only orange groves.

It was all together so much of itself, so completely what it was I reveled in it. I was exhilarated, I took deep breaths of the balmy air. Power lines were strung through the sky. Sulfurous smoke rose over the flatland. Steel cities vibrated the earth. It was the country of strontium children.

LOVE IT OR LEAVE IT

Daniel realized that though he'd come three thousand miles to a place he'd never seen before he felt right at home. That is the way it is. Everyone who lives there has just arrived. It's a place you recognize immediately. On the Freeway we pass a convoy of army trucks. Helicopters cross the highway overhead. Gnatty jets loop in the sun high over the ocean. Electronic plants nestle in their landscaping. A highly visible military-industrial complex. Everything in the open in the wide spaces and bright light of California.

I sit in a trailer in a great plain surrounded by hills. In the great plain below the hills of the south a dark green helicopter rises and beats across the sky. It passes over the trailer, its compressions beating the white air till it's thick. The helicopter flies down the sky toward the hills to the north. There, in the great plain, it sinks to a landing. It is a marine helicopter. I'm told all day and all night it rises and flies and sets in the great plain. Nobody knows why. All the students here look ragged and wizened. They wear shredded pants held up with rope and no shoes, and torn shirts and coolie caps of tented straw, tied with a string under the chin. Water is beginning to fill the plains. We are abandoning cars for bicycles.

The trailer belongs to the kid who gave me the lift. He's a teaching assistant, a TA, and he shares this stationary trailer with three other TA's. He has western ways of quiet self-attention. In the new life-style you value yourself and your feelings. You don't ask questions. You don't even ask a dude's name if he doesn't tell you. It doesn't matter. There is a counter-world for us all to deal with. Let him use your office. This is the new University of California at Irvine, in Orange County. It is a ring of great concrete egg boxes with roofs of orange tile, recalling Spain. It is still under construction. Lesser faculty have offices in trailers.

"Hello?" A feminine voice.

"Phyl?"

"Are you there?"

"Yes, I got a lift from the airport."

"Are you all right?"

"Yes. It's hot as hell out here."

"How weird. It just started to snow."

"What's the story?"

"She's holding her own."

"Come on, no bullshit."

"It's not bullshit. I saw her myself. She looks the same."

"Are the Lewins still there?"

"Just your father. We came home to fix dinner. Then your mother's going back to the hospital to pick him up."

"Is the baby all right?"

"Yes. We're all fine."

"But?"

"What?"

"You said we're all fine as if something's the matter."

"Well, your mother keeps asking me what you're doing. She wants to know why you aren't here."

"Did you tell her?"

"It's not easy."

"You think it's weird, don't you?"

"No—you know I don't."

"Well it is. The whole trip is insane. I don't know if it can do any good even if I get what I'm after. But what else can I do? Can you tell me what else there is to do?"

"I'm not criticizing, Daniel."

"What did she say?"

"She said: 'Is the truth something you can give someone for pneumonia.' "

"Oh shit. No. The answer is no. But what the fuck does she expect me to do—sit the deathwatch with her?"

"You want to talk to her? She's in the kitchen."

"No. Tell her I called and that I'll be back as soon as I can. It's very rough for them. Do what you can."

"I am."

"Don't let them wait on you."

"I'm trying not to. But I think she wants to keep busy. She doesn't confide in me, Daniel. Your father barely talks to me. He barely pays attention to the baby."

"Well, their own baby may be dying, Phyl."

"You don't have to tell me that."

"All right—I'm sorry. Don't you lose your cool. Do I hear crying?"

"No. But I'm doing the best I can."

"I know you are. I hope to be back late tomorrow. I'll call you. OK? Phyllis, OK?"

"OK."

2ND PHONE CALL—NOT COLLECT

"Hello?" A feminine voice.

"Is this the Mindish residence?" A silence. "Hello?"

"What?"

"Is that you, Linda?"

Another silence.

"I'm afraid you have the wrong number."

"No come on, listen, this is Danny Isaacson. This is Linda, isn't it, Linda Mindish from Weeks Avenue?"

A hand covering the phone. A silence. A sense of someone listening with her hand over the mouth of the phone. Here is this sudden connection, this sound-hole. She's falling.

"Hello? Hey, are you there? Isn't this you?"

"This is not the Mindish residence. You have the wrong people."

Daniel smiled. "Well, what residence is this?"

"I'm afraid I can't tell you." She is hanging up.

"Wait! I've got your address, 1099 Poinsettia, right? See? I've got your phone. You might as well talk to me."

"It's nothing," I hear her answering someone, hand muffling the phone.

"Linda?"

"Who are you? What do you want?"

"Hey, Linda, you remember the way you used to poke me in the ribs? You remember how we used to bend each other's fingers? Only you usually won because you were older. You were a strong girl, you had strong hands for a girl."

"Goodbye."

"Hey—if you hang up I'll dial again. Or I can bang on your door. So what's the point?"

"You better learn there's a law against bothering people."

"But we know each other. Can't you talk for a second, is it going to hurt you to talk?"

"I have nothing to say to you. Just stay away. Leave us alone."

"I happened to be in the neighborhood."

The soft cup over the phone. "It's nothing, a friend," he hears her muffled voice.

"Linda?"

"What?"

"I happened to be in the neighborhood. I mean no harm. Honestly. I've known where you people were for a long time. I'm seeing friends at, um, UCI and I decided to call you. Is that so terrible?"

"We read about you in the paper. I know what you're trying to do. If you think I'm afraid of you, you're wrong."

"I don't think that. That story exaggerated, the guy misunderstood the purpose of the Foundation."

"We have friends out here. We have loyal friends who know our real name. We don't have anything to hide. So don't think you can scare me."

"I just want to talk to your father."

"Well, he doesn't want to talk to you."

"He used to like me."

"I'm going to hang up now. If you bother us anymore I'll call the police."

"Linda, be civilized. What's wrong with my talking to him?"

"He's an old man and he's sick. He wants to be left in peace. Do you understand?"

"Well, of course. I'd like to come by and pay my respects. I'll only stay a few minutes."

"You must be crazy."

"I was a kid when it happened, Linda. You think I can carry a grudge all my life? That's a waste. I've got my own thing."

"Oh God, that figures, a hippie. I believe that."

"We were all hurt. OK? It was terrible. But it happened to all of us. None of us can forget it, but we were all very close. I feel the need to see you people. Is *that* so very hard to understand?"

She has begun to cry. "How did you find out where we lived?"

"I don't know. Some guy told me a long time ago."

"Who?"

"I don't even remember who. What difference does it make? I haven't told anyone, not even my sister. I didn't even ask him, he just told me. I was sorry at the time. But Linda, things change. What seems clear isn't so clear after a while. What seemed a matter of right and wrong."

"I see." Silence on the line. She sniffs. "You think you're privileged to forgive my father, is that what you're saying?"

"Not exactly."

"That's arrogance, all right. That's the arrogance of the Isaacsons. So high and mighty—"

"Well look, it's not that way and I don't think the phone is the place to talk about it."

"How dare you call us! How dare you!"

This time I was silent. Let her think I thought I'd blown it. She pinches her nostrils with a Kleenex. She swallows. She listens at the other end. She waits.

"Of course there are resentments, different viewpoints. How can I deny that? I don't even know why I called you. I guess I hadn't considered that it might be a shock to you to hear from me. I'm sorry. Maybe I should have thought twice. But I'm out here and it suddenly seemed to me the thing to do. I wanted to see your father, that's all. How is he?"

"How is he? Fine. As well as can be expected."

"Good, good. And your mother?"

"Fine."

"I'm glad to hear that. Is there some way we could make an appointment? I'll only be out here through tomorrow."

"I don't know."

"I have to go back east. I came out on a job interview but I don't think they want me."

"You teach?"

"Yeah. I just got my Ph.D."

"I see. Congratulations."

"Well, it was a struggle."

I laughed with a wry note of self-deprecation. I let the images settle. Jack P. Fein really delivered. "Don't mess me up," he said when I told him thanks. Then he broke the connection.

In 1949, the year the Russians got the bomb, C. G. Jung spun three coins and asked the *I Ching,* a book of ancient Chinese prophecy, what it thought its reception would be in the United States. The *I Ching* was just about to be published in the United States and nobody here besides Jung and a few Sinologists knew much about it. The *I Ching* answered that it thought it would make its way very nicely.

I'd concluded the phone conversation with a sense of having triggered in Linda Mindish the beginnings of joy. I would describe it this way: You live for many years, certainly for as long as you can remember, in a menacing state of unfinished business. The phone rings. You realize your intimacy with what you fear. Or this way: Suppose the person who has been fucked is calling on you to ask no more than to be fucked again. A new life proposes itself. You are aroused to that purring eroticism that comes when you understand you're going to get away with something after all.

The house was a small pink stucco model on a palmy side street of cottage-cute houses. It was a half-block off the Pacific Coast Highway, which is a kind of Boston Post Road of the west, a thoroughfare at this point in its journey of gas stations, real estate offices, portrait photographers' studios, supermarkets, taco drive-ins and ivory-white mortuaries. I rang the bell. The novel as private I.

Linda greets me with a thin smile of distaste. She wears

a blouse with ruffled sleeves and a high ruffled neck. Her skirt stops just above the knees. She's a thin girl with pale hair cut very short and feathered up, the kind of fair skin that blotches with emotion, her father's grey eyes set too close, a big nose, a long face. Flat-chested but with surprisingly good legs. Not as tall as I thought she'd be. On the other hand she's more mature. More grown-up than she sounded on the phone.

I am led into a small living room, everything neat as a pin, modest and well cared for, the Sears American Maple series with selected bric-a-brac from other shores. A room that has never seen the likes of me. A man in a dark suit and tie stands up from the couch. His hair is cut like a brush and flat on top. We are introduced, and shake hands. He hands me his card. His name is Dale something and he's a lawyer.

The thing is people don't experience revelation. Linda had had too many years to adjust and conform her life to the demands of her father's career. He'd been let out of prison in 1959. They had taken him to Orange County. The mother, Sadie, was an ignorant woman. Linda, at eighteen, had picked out the place, chosen the new family name, talked to the lawyers. She had worked, gone to school, gotten a degree in dentistry, and now had her own practice in a shopping center in Newport Beach. I learned this from Jack Fein. She supported the old people. She ruled the roost. It is not something you give up easily.

"Linda did the right thing," the lawyer tells me. "You can't expect people to see you under circumstances like this just because you call them on the phone. She had no way of even telling if you were who you said you were."

"No, it's him," she says. "It's Danny Isaacson."

"So your father isn't here," Daniel said.

"That's right."

"Does he know I called?"

"Let me ask the questions," the lawyer said. "What do you want? Why are you here?"

Daniel sighed. "Does he?"

"I decided not to tell him until I made up my mind if he should see you or not. So if you think for one moment that he's afraid of you, you're wrong."

"I don't want anyone to be afraid of me," Daniel said. He seemed offended. He sat down on a tweed armchair, leaned back, and stuck his legs out and crossed them at the ankles. He massaged his forehead. I looked at Linda Mindish and saw the premature middle age at the corners of her mouth and under her eyes. She is five years older than I am. She is ten years older than Susan. She has worked hard. She looks at me and waits. In her eyes perhaps the recollection of our strange relationship of rib-poking, pushing, touching—she, her menses attained, and an eight-year-old boy. Always trying to break little Daniel's hand, twist his fingers, dig nails in his arm. Why? As Selig her father precedes her into the Isaacson house without knocking and sees what's in the icebox. As he laughs and makes a joke in his Polish accent. As he patronizes the child Paul. As he covets in his low-grade chronic coveting Paul's wife. How did my thing with Linda begin? Imposed on her face in this moment is the thirteen-year-old girl with the terrible misfortune to look like her father. Drop dead. That was a favorite expression of Linda's. Daniel, will you do me a favor? What? Drop dead. Followed by a fake smile, a mirthless flash of teeth, turned on and off, to illuminate the second stage of my wisdom—I was entitled to nothing but deeper and deeper levels of her alienation. She had gotten that line from some play or movie very big in the Bronx at the time. Do me a favor: drop dead. She exercised on me, bringing from what jungles of girl society in the upper grades I could only imagine, every shitty verbal abuse of the day.

"Linda, I think we ought to get down to business. After all you do have appointments this morning," the lawyer said. Image white coat hands in the pockets chew on the other side for a day or two. Kind of woman at her best in an office.

"I recognize in you the same look, the same look I see in the mirror. It's very familiar to me."

"I don't know what you mean."

"The look of the same memories. We walk around in the same memories. It's like a community."

She sat down on the couch next to the lawyer and their hands met. They held hands sitting facing me on the couch.

"Linda's a big girl and I can only advise her what to do,"

the lawyer said. "Tell us what you're getting at. There is nothing Linda or her father has to fear from you. There is no legal issue here. We're not obliged to discuss that case with you." He says "that case" as if he's dangling someone's pair of dirty drawers. "Do you need money? What's your problem?"

I said: "What did you say your name was? Dale? Why don't you shut up for a fucking minute, Dale. I'm trying to tell her something. You weren't there, were you? I don't remember seeing you there."

The lawyer glanced at Linda, struggled to his feet. He was white. "I want to warn you that as a lawyer I'm in a position to advise you on intimidation, threatened or implied, and on assault or threat of an assault in the state of California." He is pointing his shaking finger.

Daniel waited, like a public speaker, for silence. His eyes were closed. He had seen enough of the lawyer. He understood more of Linda by her lawyer: a fellow with brown shining eyes, Disney-animal eyelashes, square clothes, skinhead haircut. Emanates passivism. To be kind. Maybe it's his chin which in a few years will be completely engulfed in itself. Yet he's blandly good-looking. Thirty-seven, -eight years old. A dangerous wide-hipped whitey.

Daniel opened his eyes. The lawyer had sat back down. I think he had only wanted to show Linda that he could act commendably. Daniel said, "What I mean is both of us, we both live lives that accommodate an event neither of us was responsible for. Can you agree with that? Is that a reasonably fair description?"

She stared at him. Almost imperceptibly her head dipped, as if in assenting she wanted him to know how small how shallow the space they could both stand in. And even that she had to recant: "You, however, are the one who's bringing it up. You're the one who's come here to dredge things up."

"I'm hoping your father can help me settle some questions."

"What questions? Are there still questions? As far as I knew all questions were settled a long time ago."

"Do you really want me to talk in front of this guy?"

"Dale and I are going to be married." Their entwined hands lie between them on the couch. They stare at me attached in identical poses, feet flat on the floor in front of them, knees together, the dentist and her fiancé, a professional couple, and my heart sinks in the blank stare of their insularity and rises in rage as I realize whatever I mean to do I need them and rely upon them and have come three thousand miles to see them.

But there are certain things I am pretty sure of. It is not likely that Linda Mindish and her parents are prepared to reclaim their identity. I can assume the loyal friends she mentioned on the phone consist only of this guy. He is their big breakthrough. Therefore I am still a threat, I am potentially the public exposure of what neither of them right now wants exposed. On the other hand, although they have something to protect I'm sure that he, at least, feels his knowledge of the law and the fact that he practices here where he lives gives them leverage. I am a transient. He would want to persuade her that he can handle me with ease.

Yet it might have occurred to her after my phone call, granting her now a shrewdness far beyond my own, that an approach such as I made is essentially one of diplomacy. And that although she should of course anticipate something even as stupid as violence on my part, it is not likely. And that it might be worth the cost of a few tense moments to see what I want to trade. And an intuition, perhaps, that whatever it is she can take me. And be rid of the last possible connection. *They had children. Someday we'll have to deal with the children. I am good at dealing. My parents suffer no winters. They lack real friends, but so does everybody. Everybody here comes from somewhere else. Their neighbors nod to them in the morning. Once a week a Japanese gardener trims the little yard. I have my practice. I have Dale. There is more money in the Mindish family than Selig ever dreamed. Why should I think this bearded misfit is more of a test than my whole life has been since my father was arrested.*

"I am interested to know how you and your mother supported yourselves after your father went to jail."

"What?"

"Linda, it's none of his business."

"You were fourteen or fifteen. Your mother was not the kind of woman who could go out and get a job. Savings don't last six, seven years. And when you moved out here with your father he never resumed practicing, did he? I mean he hasn't practiced since his jail term, as I understand it. And you were able to get through college and dental college."

"Linda, don't feel obliged to explain—"

"No, it's all right, Dale. I see what he's getting at. In the first place there's no tuition if you live here," she said to me. "And I had scholarships besides. I carried extra course loads and I held down jobs. And in the second place my father worked in a lab until just a few years ago."

She sat up at the edge of the couch with her hands folded in her lap and her ankles primly together. "It's true what you say, Danny, neither you nor I was responsible for anything that happened. But we've borne the brunt. When my father went to prison my mother and I suffered terribly. But something else was good about the experience—I discovered all sorts of resources in myself that I otherwise might not have. From what I can see, and from what I've heard, neither you nor your sister have been that fortunate.

"In many ways I had it worse. Your parents after all were heroes to some elements. Today I understand you can find Isaacson Streets all through Eastern Europe. But Selig Mindish was a hero to no one, to say the least. What my father did brings no honor to himself or his family. You lose friends for something like that. You go to jail, where your health breaks. And afterwards you make no new friends. So you see in many ways it has been worse. I'll tell you something: there used to be times when I wished strongly, very strongly, that my father might be executed, that we could change places, the Isaacsons and Mindishes, and that I would be glad to stand in your shoes if only you could stand in mine. Let me have your hanky, Dale."

Daniel watched her. He folded his hands under his chin and rested his elbows on the arms of the chair. A surprisingly cool and objective eye glanced at him as Linda blew her nose.

"You call up with all this phony hippie humility and the minute you're in the door you start getting nasty."

"I didn't bring my lawyer," Daniel says.

"Perhaps you should have."

"I didn't hide my father somewhere."

"You take me for a fool? Should I have believed you? I owe you nothing. Your whole family have always been liars. All full of high ideals except when it comes to other people. Except when it comes to ruining the lives of friends."

"What does that mean?"

"They led Papa down the garden path. From the day he met them. They were always too good for him, but not too good to let him chauffeur them where they wanted to go, or run their errands, or fix their teeth, or turn into a spy for them. He wasn't an intellectual. I was a child but even I understood how little respect they had, and how they took advantage."

"Linda, honey, calm yourself," Dale said.

But she was calmer than he was. The way an actor is calm as the audience takes his emotion to heart. For one moment I experienced the truth of the situation as an equitability of evil. This is what happens to us, to the children of trials; our hearts run to cunning, our minds are sharp as claws. Such shrewdness has to be burned into the eye's soul, it is only formed in fire. There is no way in the world either of us would not be willing to use our sad lives; no betrayal impossible of our pain; no use too cheap of our patrimony. If Susan had only had a small portion! But nothing Susan did ever lacked innocence: no matter how loud, how demanding, how foolish, how self-destructive, nothing Susan did lacked innocence. This bitch was another matter. I imagined her in bed. There was no question in my mind that she wouldn't refuse. That's why she had called her fiancé—not to protect herself from my violence, but to keep intact her planned recovery from the life of Linda Mindish. She could take it on back very quickly. With just a small push. It would not be uninteresting, it would not be without blood, an incest of blood and death and jism and egg more corrupt than any I could have with my real sister. There was enough hard corruption in Linda Mindish and me, flawless forged criminals of perception, to exhaust the fires of the sun.

And then that moment passed and I saw her as locked into her family truths as we were locked in ours. Were these her formulations, or her mother Sadie's? Hadn't Sadie and her husband built them over the years of visiting hours? Wouldn't they do that? I saw myself as having provided Linda the opportunity to say out loud the righteous complaint that this family had had in rehearsal for fifteen years.

"Well, the awful Isaacsons are dead, Linda. All you have to worry about is me. And what can I do? Expose you to your friends and neighbors in Orange County, California? But you moved here for a reason. It was a shrewd place to come. If your cover is blown there's always room for an ex-Communist in Orange County. Right? After all, your old man helped bust a notorious spy ring. He was not without his part in the execution of the infamous Isaacsons, was he?"

Linda was looking grim. The lawyer said, "His testimony is a matter of record."

"Right, it surely is. But there are still questions to be answered." Daniel thought a moment. "For instance, have you ever discussed with him why he confessed? You're a lawyer, Dale. Don't you have a professional interest? It's one of the great cases."

"That's a naïve question."

"Why—because he was caught? And he purged himself and confessed and told the truth? To make *that* penance, right? Is that why he did it—because he was caught and had no choice? Or did he do it to save himself, to save his own life. My parents thought so—they thought he implicated them to save himself. They thought he was a spy. Or they pretended to. It's all very puzzling."

"What are you talking about," said Linda.

"Shit, I don't know. I wanted to tell your father I think he was innocent. I wanted to lay that on him."

They looked at each other briefly as if an idea they had considered before my arrival—that I was a madman—seemed now brimming with prescience. Linda crossed her legs, adjusted her skirt. She picked a cigarette out of the box on the end table and held it before her in that stiff-fingered way of lady smokers, as Dale got out his lighter.

"You make me very sad."

"Yeah, well, it's hard to get it down, I know. I had trouble myself. But start with the idea that there was a spy ring and the whole thing was just as he testified in court. You've got to ask yourself why. There was no evidence except his confession. If he had not confessed there would have been no case against anyone, including himself. My father, I mean my foster father, thinks that he was hassled by the FBI. He thinks Selig just couldn't hold up under the questioning. They had him for a long time. They had something on him—maybe citizenship. That he's not a, um, sophisticated man and didn't know what could and couldn't be done. But I disagree with that."

"You do."

"Yes. It's possible he realized every value in the situation beautifully. My father's interpretation lacks a knowledge of the old Left. The life of embattled Communist Party members in those days. That's what's missing from his analysis. There was another couple everybody in the Bronx membership knew about who had dropped out of Party life some years before. Did you ever hear of them? It was commonly rumored in the ranks, because none of our families or their friends were anything more than rank and file, that the other couple went underground, into espionage work. They took on a certain heroic mystery, that other couple. Do you know their name? Did your father every mention them to you? Has he ever said anything about this?"

"No, Danny."

"Well, this other couple had two children. They were about the same age as my parents. A lot of mythology grew up about them. You didn't talk about them without lowering your voice. Who knows how many children they had? Or what their age was? But they were supposed to have been fairly young, with kids, and they were said to live just a few blocks away, up on the Concourse."

Think about it a while. Look at me.

"Is that all?" the lawyer says.

"Well, that's the gist of it."

He shook his head and smiled sadly. "It is highly speculative, to say the least."

"That's right. That's why I want to talk to Selig."

"Stop calling my father Selig," Linda said.

"I have his fillings still in my mouth," Daniel said with his palms in the air.

"Let me see if I understand this."

"Oh Dale, it's insane."

"No, honey, just a minute. Now you're saying that Dr. Mindish lied about your parents in deference to another couple who looked like them?"

"I don't know if they looked like them. To protect another couple everyone thought was working under cover. To keep the FBI away from people of real value. They were closing in. To divert them. To get the heat off."

"And that Dr. Mindish, who was innocent, made this story up about himself and your parents?"

"Well, actually Selig doesn't have to be innocent for the theory to work. He might have been involved marginally. He might have been told to do it. But all right, let's say innocent."

"And that this mythical couple, these other people, were the ones who actually stole the secrets?"

"Well, not necessarily, because it's never been proven that any secrets were stolen. It isn't what really happened or was going to happen. It was what Selig and or some of the others *thought* had happened or was going to happen. It was as much fantasy as what the FBI thought had happened."

"I see. And have you come up with any facts, or any information in support of this?"

"It's just a theory, man," Daniel said with a smile. "It's my theory of the other couple."

THE THEORY OF THE OTHER COUPLE

Shannon, in THE DECLINE OF AMERICAN COMMUNISM, shows us the immense contribution made by the American Communist Party to its own destruction within a few years after the war. They had all the haughty, shrewd instincts of a successful suicide. It is no wonder in this club of ideologues of the working class, self-designed martyrs, Stalinist tuning forks, sentimentalists, visionaries, misfits, hysterics, fantasists, and dreamers of justice—no wonder that a myth would spring out of their awe for someone truly potent. It is ironic that such a myth would arise without planning or intent from their laboriously induced collective mythic self. But they were helpless before it. *We have our daredevils too. We have our cat burglars and laughing caballeros. Our George Rafts flipping coins. Our masked riders of the plains. We have them.*

The mystery couple of the Grand Concourse, and their two children, walked out of their apartment one Sunday as if for an outing. They carried no luggage. A camera over his shoulder. A tote bag in her hand. Leaving an apartment intact, with dishes in the drain, they were never seen again. This happened soon after my father was arrested. They were later reported to be living under another name in New Zealand. They were reported to be traveling through Britain on Australian passports. They were reported traveling through France on British passports. They were arrested in West Berlin, held for six months without trial, and exchanged for two Englishmen held by the Russians in Moscow. They were last reported living in Leningrad.

When Selig Mindish was called to the stand, my mother sat up in her chair and folded her arms and lifted her head. There he was. He looked shrunken. He was a physically big man but she was shocked now to see how different he had become, all collapsed, all fallen in on himself, with his neck sticking out of his collar and his suit that seemed to slide over him as he moved. But the fat nose was still fat and the little pearl-grey eyes shone their dog intelligence at Feuerman's assistant, the greasy one, who began to lead him through his testimony.

It was at this moment in the trial that she nearly lost her composure. Jake had told them what to anticipate. Still, to hear the treachery spoken with the emphasis of a nodding head in the familiar accents of their friend of many years was too much to be endured. She felt with her arms folded that she was holding herself together. Tears filled her eyes and flowed down her throat. She did not move a muscle. An electricity of rage flowed into her body. She wanted to leap out of her chair and catch Selig Mindish by the throat and tear out his tongue.

And he would not look at them. Even when he was asked to point them out he did so only with his hand, pointing to their table with his eyes fastened on the prosecutor. He would not look in their direction. Writing on his pad, Jake broke the point of his pencil. Mindish continued to talk, giving names and dates, recalling conversations. She gazed at him fixedly. Her tears passed. Her rage passed. She continued to look at the witness, looking up to the stand, arms folded, in unwavering attention. It had become more important to her than her life to make Selig Mindish recognize her presence in this courtroom. She willed it. She wanted to extract from that miserable deathface an acknowledgment of her real existence. She could reconcile her persecution, her death, but never a delusion so monstrous that it did not grant her the truth of her own life. Look at me, you pig! Look! I will know why you have done this. You cannot dare to ignore me. You owe me a glimpse of your rotting cowardly soul, you murdering Cossack! Pig! Look at me. I defy you to look at me.

At this point in his testimony the dentist was describing how certain drawings were stored in the darkroom lab he'd made out of the closet in his office. The drawings were scaled down and scratched on dental x-ray films. Among the files and sanders and plaster jaws. The little assistant prosecutor went over to his table and came back holding between his thumb and forefinger a dental x-ray mounted as a slide.

"Is this what you mean?"

"Yes."

"Will you please examine it and tell the court what it is."

Accepting the film and holding it up to the light, Selig Mindish actually began to smile—it was the kind of thing that happens to children, ballooning their cheeks and escaping in snorts through their nose, when the secret is about to come out. The man was an idiot. But before he said the words that put them in their graves he turned and looked for a moment at Rochelle, looking for one fraction of a second into her eyes with the same moronic smile dying on his face and the absurdly significant dental x-ray slide in his spatulate fingers; and in the little grey pig eyes of the dentist was the recognition she sought. A wry acknowledgment of this moment in the courtroom, in their lives, and she was stunned to read in it the message not of a betrayer

the novel as a sequence of analyses. But what of the executioner? A quiet respectable man, now retired. He is in the Yonkers phone book

no not as betrayer begging forgiveness, there was no appeal for forgiveness, nor did she see the rationalized hate that would permit him to do this, and justify it, no, nor the hypnotized stare of a programmed amnesiac, nor the actor's look for the court's benefit of a fellow conspirator—none of these: he presented the private faith of a comrade, one to another, complicitors in self-sacrifice, one to another, and I cannot communicate beyond this but by now you must know why and what is happening. She saw the comrade's life of terrible regret, of sad determination, one to another, and the assumption of their shared knowledge, the sexuality of it. And then she turned to look at her husband. Ascher was hunched over his table writing furiously. Beyond Ascher's shoulder, a sculpture of the burden of man, her husband Paul sat upright with his eyes closed and pain that had caused the corners of his mouth to turn upward. And they were not on trial but back at the summer camp, at Paine Lodge, Mindish and Paul and Rochelle, lifting their joined hands to the blackberry night of crickets' fiddle and frogs' jug band, spinning in intricate devolving patterns, diving through the arches of their own arms, and dazzling the brothers with a folk dance of infinite beauty, of eternal grace. And there swept over her now the horrifying conviction that Paul did not have to return this look of Mindish. That while she had been shielding him from her dread he had withheld from her his one crucial perception. And that what in this moment overwhelmed her was something her husband already knew in himself and for himself.

There is a line in one of her last letters to him. *The gambler has no rights.* It is a non sequitur. It is a line that makes no other sense. Its context is one of those miserable conversations they were allowed to have through the wire mesh once a week, a marital spat, low-voiced, urgent, full of fever and humiliation and nausea; as he tried to get her approval for what he had done alone, for the complicity he had forced upon them, for the defense they had offered, for the gamble of her life and his. She suspended all communication with him after the third appeal failed. This is usually attributed to her well-known mental problems, the court having supplied a psychologist once a week for therapy. *They want me to adjust to the idea of dying,* she wrote Ascher. But she would not write Paul the last month of their lives, and it is not clear if they saw each other the night before their execution although it is commonly believed they did. And possibly they did, for a dance before death, a reconciliation in heat and love and terror, while the jailers fled the corridor and the stones groaned and the bars rattled; and they rippled and spasmed and shook and trembled as if electrocution was something people did together.

"You're out of your mind," Linda Mindish said. Furiously she stabbed the cigarette into the ashtray. "I feel sorry for you. Is that why you want to see my father?" She laughed. "Oh my God, oh my God." She stood up and smoothed her blouse and skirt.

"You don't buy it."

"You poor tormented boy. I knew that's what he wanted. Some way of squirming out of it. Can you imagine?" She has turned to Dale. "Have you ever heard such a tenuous, fragile piece of nonsense? My God. Listen Danny, you'll get no satisfaction from my father. My God, the more I think about it! Let me tell you something, because I've got to go. I've wasted enough of my time. And keep in mind I'm not afraid of you or what embarrassment you can cause me. We're established here—you start something and you'll be sorry. Papa didn't tell the half of it. They were into all sorts of things that never came up at the trial. They had their hooks into space research and missiles and germ warfare—everything. Your parents were the head of a whole network. They ran the show. They planned things and they paid people off. Lasers—years before anybody heard of lasers. Everything. So don't come to me with this worm's-eye view and tell me my father sacrificed them. Or that my father was in a position to sacrifice anybody. You can't squirm out of it that easily. Your parents were what they were and nothing you can do can change that. Another couple. My God, that's pathetic."

"Linda, I've just come three thousand miles. I want more than the family line. That's the whole point. Can I have a drink of water?" I stood up. "Just tell me where the kitchen is and I'll get it myself."

"You stay right there," she said. "I'll get it. And then I want you on your way."

When she was out of the room I said to the lawyer, "Where's Selig?"

He looked at me and said nothing, as if without her hand in his back he was just a piece of wood. "Selig!" I shouted. "Selig Mindish, are you here!"

Linda came back with a glass of water in a plastic green tumbler. "You're wasting your breath." The lawyer stood up and they both watched me drink the water.

"Ah Linda," I said, feeling as if we were standing close quarters at a crowded party, "what has happened to you? You're not the little hipster I used to know. When the Russians got the bomb, what happened? There were changes, right? The situation stabilized, the superpowers cooled it, and that gave the rest of us a little time. And the bomb took Russia out of the revolution. She was dragging it down, man. She was dumping on it. So that was a good thing too. A whole new possibility of action, the guerrilla, guerrilla warfare, the restoration of ancient revolutionary possibilities—that's what happened, man. The revolution went back to the people. And look at the world today. It is aroused to its own education. It is aroused, man, the whole world is sticking up like a hard-on. Now if my own parents did their thing in their day, and that is the result of the thing they did—do you really think I'd be trying to talk myself out of it?"

She was shaking her head. "There's something the matter with you."

"No, Linda. You've turned your back on history. Look at this." I spread my arms to indicate the house. "This isn't the chick I knew. I am aghast, really aghast. I mean even if this is a cover it's in bad taste. Your father really go along with this shit?"

"Dale, I want him out of here."

"Are you really a dentist—I mean with a chair and every-thing?"

"It's a put-on. That's what they call it."

"Please, Dale, he's crazy."

"It's time to leave," Dale said. "If you don't remove yourself from these premises I'm going to call the police."

"Don't do that, Dale. Just tell me where the old man is. I'm not going to hurt him. Is he really not here?"

"No."

"You see, Linda, look at Dale with his nice expensive suit and tie. Look at his haircut. If they were *his* parents he'd want it to be another couple. But they're my parents. And do I look like Dale? Look at me. You see what it is now? I have to hear from Selig what you just told me. I want to know the guys he put the finger on were the guys who did it. I want to hear it from him, that's all."

At this moment it probably occurred to Linda that I was truly dangerous. I smiled and toasted them with the water glass. The Daniel she called pathetic was her Daniel. If her own assumptions had betrayed her, who in fact was I? And what did I really want? If you change your life you lose the connection. If you take a stand you lose touch. She became frightened. Possibly we can give her this as long as we don't ask her to act on it: all she has accomplished is to fortify her fear. One sharp poke of the finger and the fortifications totter.

I'm familiar with the phenomenon—Susan, tell her your brother who lives in the library knew at this moment what the daughter of Selig Mindish was going through. If she was now without confidence in her judgment, she was safe only in assuming the worst. And I could see it in her face, the recognition, at last, that I had come here to wipe out her family.

"I've got rights too, don't I, Linda? Think about it. Isn't anything coming to me? Not even a minute to talk to your dad. Think about it."

"Danny, I swear to you it won't do any good."

"It'll make me feel good. And then I'll leave and you'll never see me again. I have a plane out of here this afternoon."

"He's an old man. He's not what he was. I honestly don't think he can help you."

"Let me decide that."

She looked at me. I can only speculate on her reasoning. Perhaps I had set off some fuse of recklessness; perhaps we all live with the desire for destruction, Linda no less than my sister and I. Perhaps she hated her father as well as she loved him and in some weird way was only persuaded of our community of interest in the sudden sharp perception of personal danger. If I was insane and killed Selig Mindish, would that not free her for the rest of time from all inherited guilt? She was so controlled, this Linda. What an urge to let go is in such control. Or perhaps she wished that what I said was true; so that she could discover herself as the daughter of no disgraced informer, but of an architect whose cunning had not only taken the measure of the arrogant Isaacsons but had also fooled the eye of the most powerful government in the world.

Or perhaps she only realized the vulnerability of my radical affections and thought the final cruelty would be hers.

She called her office, canceled her appointments, and with Dale at the wheel of his Oldsmobile Ninety-Eight, and Linda in the middle, and me next to her, thigh to thigh, they drove me to Anaheim, a town somewhere between Buchenwald and Belsen, where Dr. and Mrs. Selig Mindish were spending the day at Disneyland.

DISNEYLAND AT CHRISTMAS

This famous amusement park is shaped like a womb. It is situated in a flatland of servicing motels, restaurants, gas stations, bowling alleys and other places of fun, and abuts on its own giant parking lot. A monorail darts along its periphery, in a loop that carries to the Disneyland Hotel. A replica 19th-century railroad line, the Sante Fe and Disneyland, complete with stations, conductors, steam engine and surrey type cars, delineates its circumference. Within the park itself five major amusement areas are laid out on different themes: the American West, called Frontierland; current technology, which is called Tomorrowland; nursery literature, called Fantasyland; and Adventureland, which proposes colonialist exploration of wild jungles of big game and native villages. Customers are invited to explore each area and its delights according to their whim. In the center of the park, where all the areas converge, there is a plaza; and the fifth thematic area, an avenue called Main Street USA, a romantic rendering of small-town living at the turn of the century, leads like the birth canal from the plaza to the entrance to the park.

As in all amusement parks the featured experience is the ride, or trip. The notability of Disneyland is its elaboration of this simple pleasure. You will not find the ordinary roller coaster or Ferris wheel except disguised as a bobsled ride down a plastic Matterhorn, or a "people mover." In toy submarines with real hatches, the customer experiences a simulated dive underwater, as bubbles rise past the portholes and rubber fish wag their tails. The submarines are said to be nuclear and bear the names of ships of the American nuclear fleet. Disneyland invites the customer not merely to experience the controlled thrills of a carny ride, but to participate in mythic rituals of the culture. Your boat ride is a Mississippi sternwheeler. Your pony ride is a string of pack mules going over the mountains to where the gold is. The value of the experience is not the ride itself but its vicariousness.

Two problems arise in the customer's efforts to fulfill Disneyland's expectations of him. The first is that for some reason while the machinery of the rides is impressively real —that is to say, technologically perfect and historically accurate—the simulated plant and animal and geological surroundings are unreal. When you take the jungle river cruise the plants and animals on the banks betray their plastic being and electronic motivation. The rocks of the painted desert or grand canyon cannot sustain the illusion of even the least sophisticated. The second difficulty is that Disneyland is usually swarming with people. People are all over the place in Disneyland. Thus the customers on the Mark Twain Mississippi steamboat look into the hills and see the customers on the mule pack train looking down at them. There is a constant feedback of human multiplicity, one's own efforts of vicarious participation constantly thwarted by the mirror of others' eyes.

Within the thematic unities of Disneyland, there are numbers of references, usually in the form of rides, exhibits or stores, to figures or works of our literary heritage. Some of these are Alice in Wonderland (Mad Hatter's Teacup Ride), Peter Pan (Peter Pan Flight), Life on the Mississippi (Mark Twain Riverboat), Wind in the Willows (Mr. Toad's Wild Ride), Swiss Family Robinson (Swiss Family Tree House), and Tom Sawyer (Tom Sawyer's Island Rafts). In addition there are implications of proprietary relationships with various figures of history, myth and legend such as King Arthur, Sleeping Beauty, Snow White, Casey Jones, Mike Fink, Jean Lafitte, and Abraham Lincoln. It is hard to find a pattern in the selection of these particular figures. Most of them have passed through a previous process of film or film animation and are made to recall the preemptive powers of the Disney organization with regard to Western culture. But beyond that no principle of selection is obvious. It is interesting to note, however, that Walt Disney's early achievements in his original medium, the animated cartoon, employed animal characters of his own devising. The animated cartoon itself, except for Disney's subsequent climb into the respectability of public domain literature, came to express the collective unconsciousness of the community of the American Naïve. A study today of the products of the animated cartoon industry of the twenties, thirties and forties would yield the following theology: 1. People are animals. 2. The body is mortal and subject to incredible pain. 3. Life is antagonistic to the living. 4. The flesh can be sawed, crushed, frozen, stretched, burned, bombed, and plucked for music. 5. The dumb are abused by the smart and the smart destroyed by their own cunning. 6. The small are tortured by the large and the large destroyed by their own momentum. 7. We are able to walk on air, but only as long as our illusion supports us. It is possible to interpret the Disney organization's relentless program of adaptation of literature, myth and legend, as an attempt to escape these dark and rowdy conclusions of the genre—in the same way a tenement kid from the Lower East Side might have grown up with the ambition of building himself a mansion on Fifth Avenue. Yet, ironically, many of the stories and characters chosen by Disney for their cultural respectability are just as dark and just as rowdy. The original *Alice in Wonderland* is a symbolic and surreal work by a benign deviate genius. Mark Twain was an atheist and a pornographer, and his great work, *Huckleberry Finn,* is a nightmare of childhood in confrontation with American social reality. In this light it is possible to understand the aesthetics of cartoon adaptation as totalitarian in nature.

It is clear that few of the children who ride in the Mad Hatter's Teacup have read or even will read *Alice,* let alone the works of Mark Twain. Most of them will only know Alice's story through the Disney film, if at all. And that suggests a separation of two ontological degrees between the Disneyland customer and the cultural artifacts he is presumed upon to treasure in his visit. The Mad Hatter's Teacup Ride is emblematic of the Disney animated film, which is itself a drastic revision in form and content of a subtle dreamwork created out of the English language. And even to an adult who dimly remembers reading the original *Alice,* and whose complicated response to this powerfully symbolic work has long since been incorporated into the psychic constructs of his life, what is being offered does not suggest the resonance of the original work, but is only a sentimental compression of something that is itself already a lie.

We find this radical process of reduction occurring too with regard to the nature of historical reality. The life and life-style of slave-trading America on the Mississippi River in the 19th century is compressed into a technologically faithful steamboat ride of five or ten minutes on an HO-scale river. The intermediary between us and this actual historical experience, the writer Mark Twain, author of *Life on the Mississippi,* is now no more than the name of the boat. Piracy on the high seas, a hundred and fifty years of harassment of European mercantile exploration and trade, becomes a moving diorama of all the scenes and situations of the pirate movies made by Hollywood in the thirties and forties. When the customer is invited then to buy, say, a pirate hat in one of the many junk shops on the premises, the Pavlovian process of symbolic transference to the final consumer moment may be said to be complete.

The ideal Disneyland patron may be said to be one who responds to a process of symbolic manipulation that offers him his culminating and quintessential sentiment at the moment of a purchase.

The following corporations offer shows and exhibits at Disneyland: Monsanto Chemical Co., Bell Telephone, General Electric, and Coca-Cola. Other visible corporate representation includes McDonnell Aircraft, Goodyear, Carnation Milk, Sunkist, Eastman Kodak, Upjohn Pharmaceuticals, Insurance Company of North America, United Air Lines, and Bank of America.

Obviously there are political implications. What Disneyland proposes is a technique of abbreviated shorthand culture for the masses, a mindless thrill, like an electric shock, that insists at the same time on the recipient's rich psychic relation to his country's history and language and literature. In a forthcoming time of highly governed masses in an overpopulated world, this technique may be extremely useful both as a substitute for education and, eventually, as a substitute for experience. One cannot tour Disneyland today without noticing its real achievement, which is the handling of crowds. Coupled open vans, pulled by tractors, collect customers at various points of the parking areas and pour them out at the entrance to the park. The park seems built to absorb infinite numbers of customers in its finite space by virtue of the simultaneous appeal of numbers of attractions at the same time, including not only the fixed rides and exhibits and restaurants and shops but special parades and flag raising and lowering ceremonies, band concerts, and the like. (At Christmas time Main Street residents in period dress sing Christmas carols at the foot of a large odorless evergreen whose rubberized needles spring to the touch.) In front of the larger attractions are mazes of pens, designed to hold great numbers of people waiting to board, or to mount or to enter. Guards, attendants, guides, and other personnel, including macrocephalic Disney costume characters, are present in abundance. Plainclothes security personnel appear in any large gathering with walkie-talkies. The problems of mass ingress and egress seem to have been solved here to a degree that would light admiration in the eyes of an SS transport officer.

One is struck by the number of adult customers at Disneyland unaccompanied by small children. One notices too the disproportionately small numbers of black people, of Mexicans, possibly because a day at Disneyland is expensive. There is an absence altogether of long-haired youth, heads, hippies, girls in miniskirts, gypsies, motorcyclists, to the point that one gives credence to the view that Disneyland turns away people it doesn't like the looks of. This particular intelligence occurred to Linda Mindish as Dale rolled into the parking acreage. The day was hazy and smog indicated the outlines of the sun. When we parked and boarded one of the tractor trains, the clean-cut girl conductor looked at me in what I thought was a regretful manner, her knowledge of my fate conflicting with the natural attraction she felt for my shoulder locks and fuck-everyone persona. Linda obviously did not know whether she was happy or distressed that I might not get in. I don't think she thought I would quietly go away.

I decided that if I was hassled I would break the line and jump over the turnstile. Dale bought the tickets and I noticed significant looks between a guard and a ticket-taker. A man approached me. Dale headed him off and talked to him for a moment. The thing was I was a freak, yes, but he would take the responsibility. Our tickets were presented and like a foreigner going through customs I was accepted into Disneyland.

Linda and I and Dale walked briskly down Main Street USA. We passed a horse-drawn trolley, an old-time double-decker bus. We passed a penny arcade with Charlie Chaplin flipcard Movieolas. Giant music boxes that make the sound of the whole band. We passed an apothecary. A red and white striped ice cream parlor. People sat smiling in beerless beer gardens. People filled the sidewalks and the street. People strolled past the bay-windowed shops. People stared at me.

"How do we find him?" I asked Linda.

"They'll be in Tomorrowland," she said. "That's what he likes best." In the Plaza at the end of Main Street we go through the gates of Tomorrowland. The whole world turns colorfully modern. Linda leads us to the Richfield Autopia.

People wait to board the little gas cars of the Richfield Autopia, a tracked ride that offers the illusion of steering to the person behind the wheel. Little snarling Autopia convertibles pile up at the freeway stop, drivers jump out, and drivers waiting their turns at assigned and numbered places jump in. Cars stream by, the air is filled with the droning of kicky toy engines. Linda points over the fence. There he is. With Sadie next to him, sitting straight and proud. In the toy car. She has a whole book of tickets. She hands another ticket up to the attendant and they don't get out. Selig grips the wheel waiting for the new run to begin. His arms are bare, he wears an Hawaiian shirt. He is incredibly old. His chin moves up and down, his lips flap against each other, his mouth opens and closes and there flashes across his face a moment of astonishment, a moment of pugnacity, astonishment, pugnacity, in alternating palsies of the nerve. He is white-haired. His hands shake as they grip the wheel. A car bumps them from the back, a child laughs, their grey heads look up to heaven, and they lurch forward on the journey into Autopia.

My heart was beating wildly. I found myself needing more air than I had. I was aware that Dale and Linda were on either side of me and were watching me closely.

"I want to talk to him, Linda."

"You still do?"

"Yes."

She was very grim. In a few minutes Selig and Sadie came into view and pulled up again. Sadie prepared another ticket for the attendant and for a moment did not hear her daughter calling to her.

"Mama! Mama!"

But the car shot off again, Sadie looking back over her shoulder to see who had called her.

It was decided that Dale and I would retire to the shade of the Coca-Cola Tomorrowland Terrace while Linda waited for her parents and prepared them for meeting me. I felt as if we were making arrangements for a burial. At the Coca-Cola Terrace a rock band was just finishing a set. The rock musicians had short hair. They waved and their stage sank out of sight to the applause of the matrons.

"He's senile," Dale said to me as we sat waiting. "She tried to tell you that. There's nothing left up here," he said tapping his temple.

People stood on line for hamburgers and Coca-Cola. Embossed on the edges of my vision were all the errant tracks of the overhead rides and rocket spins, the sinking submarines and the swiveling cars; the starting and stopping of strollers, the ruthless paths of careening infants. I sat with my arms folded at the formica café table. In the middle of my eye, out in the sun the Mindish family was about to deploy itself. Linda beckoned and Dale went out to join them.

Sadie Mindish was being stubborn. She believed if she came any closer some terrible contamination, or sudden death, would befall her. She kept peering in my direction and then giving Linda hell. Linda spoke to Dale and Dale held the old lady's hand and talked to her. Sadie pulled her hand away and waved her arm in my direction. The lawyer stood in front of her to block me from her vision.

Linda came toward the terrace leading her father by the elbow.

I sat across the orange formica café table from Dr. Selig Mindish. His daughter kneeled beside him asking him if he'd like a chocolate milk shake. Her knees were blanched in her sheer stockings.

"Chocolate milk shakes are his favorite," she explained to me. Then in a louder voice she asked her father again if he wanted a milk shake.

I leaned forward with my hands on my knees so that he had to see me. The whites of his eyes were discolored. He needed a shave. Brown spots and moles had attacked his skin. His white hair was thinned out. His eyes were sunken in age sockets of fat and skin. His jaw moved up and down, his lips made the sound of a faucet dripping as they met and fell apart. But there was still in him the remnant of rude strength I remembered.

I said, "Hello, Mr. Mindish. I'm Daniel Isaacson. I'm Paul and Rochelle's son. Danny?"

Linda was kneeling beside him holding his hand. He struggled to understand me. His head stirred like a turtle's head coming out of its shell. He smiled and nodded. Then as he looked in my eyes he became gradually still, and even his facial palsy ceased, and he no longer smiled. I was sickened to see water well from the congested yellow corners of his eyes. Tears tracked down his face.

"Denny?"

"It's all right, Papa," Linda was saying. She patted his hand. She had begun to cry. "It's all right, Papa."

"It's Denny?"

For one moment of recognition he was restored to life. In wonder he raised his large, clumsy hand and touched the side of my face. He found the back of my neck and pulled me forward and leaned toward me and touched the top of my head with his palsied lips.

Recently in Houston, Texas, surgeons implanted a new heart in the body of a fifty-four-year-old car salesman whose own heart was killing him. Two weeks after the surgery the salesman rejected his new heart. In Brooklyn a seventy-year-old grandmother divorcee with acute heart disease received the heart of a seventeen-year-old girl killed just hours before in an auto accident. The grandmother lived only three days before her body rejected the new heart. Heart rejection is a problem. The body attacks its own new heart as it would any foreign object. The heart is attacked by the body's antibodies. It is destroyed. In Los Angeles a young woman who had been bedridden for years and whose natural color was blue received the heart of an eighteen-year-old basketball player just minutes after his death by cerebral hemorrhage. Two days later, pink and lovely among her pillows, she was smiling to photographers. In a week she was walking around. In six months she was married to a young doctor who had interned on her floor. Within the year she was dead of her heart's rejection. Doctors still have a lot to learn about why we reject our hearts. Yes, doctors have a lot to learn. An old peddler from Delancey Street received a new heart at Mt. Sinai and spit it out minutes after regaining consciousness. That's what we call heart ejection. A black postman in Pittsburgh, Ohio, received the heart of a white steelworker killed in a bar brawl. The black man died immediately. That's what we call heart dejection. Medical Science has a lot to learn.

In Atlantic City, New Jersey, doctors put a new valve in a blood-pumping machine. The machine rejected its new valve and the man attached to the machine died.

There was some question about the signs. People were confused. Everyone was milling around and we were sitting on somebody's old desk waiting to be told what to do. Mr. Fischer had dropped us off and said he'd be back. People were on their knees on the floor drawing signs with paintbrushes. It was an empty store. A man was sawing lengths of lumber and stacking them against the wall. Then there was a flurry of excitement at the door, someone cheered, and two people came in laughing and dropped stacks of big cardboard signs with pictures of my mother and father in the middle of the floor. Susan and I sat on the desk with our legs crossed, facing each other, trying to keep some sort of fortress against the scene. Every once in a while someone would come in and we'd know without looking that we were being appraised. In all that noise you could hear some things very clearly. *Is that them? Those poor kids.*

We knew whoever said that was not one of the inner circle. The people who knew us thought of us as weird and demanding. Just before an appearance we'd suddenly decide we wanted malted milks or hamburgers. Once Susan insisted on chicken chow mein. We blackmailed anyone who made the mistake of befriending us. We were always a threat. By not cooperating we could ruin the best plans. Our public appearances were heartstoppers. The image was of two good, fine children. Those who were close to us knew better.

The Fischers disliked us intensely. They were always rushing us to rallies and meetings and hurrying our supper. We hated them. They lived in a big house and we had two rooms on the third floor. Mrs. Fischer left an old vacuum cleaner up there so we could keep the floors clean. There was a laundry bag for our dirty clothes; when it was full we brought it to the basement. Sometimes we'd find new clothes from Alexander's laid out on our beds. Our schedule was on the bulletin board in the kitchen. The house, a dark Tudor-style mansion, was well back from the street; and the entire property was surrounded by tall hedges. We often looked through the hedges but saw nothing but another Tudor house. We went to a private school in a station wagon, and a station wagon brought us home. We had no friends.

One day we hid in the basement behind the oil burner. We stayed there all day and missed a rally. I was growing hair around my penis and I showed Susan. We talked about that for a while. Susan read *The Enchanted Garden*. I took a nap. We could hear the phone upstairs ringing every few minutes. Finally we got hungry and went upstairs. It was ten o'clock in the evening. Mr. Fischer's tie was pulled down, his collar was open, and the points of the collar were turned up. He yelled at us. Mrs. Fischer looked pale and kept lighting cigarettes and almost immediately mashing them out in the ashtray. She was a thin blond woman with bulgy eyes. "Do you think we're doing this for our health!" Mr. Fischer screamed. "You rotten kids! They're your parents! You miserable brats!" Yet one week when it was time to make our visit to prison there was no one to take us.

Then Jacob Ascher came to the house. We hadn't seen him in a long time. He drove us back to Judge Greenblatt's Children's Court and the Judge removed us from the custody of the Fischers. "No more of this," he said pointing a finger at Ascher. The old lawyer laughed bitterly and shook his head.

What more is there to say? YOUR CAREER IN ELECTRICITY. Electricity is a form of energy. It is generated by various power sources driven by water, steam, or atomic fission. The leading electric-power producing countries are the United States (987,432,000 kilowatt-hours per year), and the Union of Soviet Socialist Republics (379,096,000 kwh per year). The theory of electricity is that atoms lose or gain electrons and thus become positively or negatively charged. A charged atom is called an ion.

I suppose you think I can't do the electrocution. I know

there is a you. There has always been a you. YOU: I will show you that I can do the electrocution.

First they led in my father. They had rightly conceived that my mother was the stronger. All factors had to be considered. They wanted the thing done with as little fuss as possible. They wanted it to go smoothly. It is not a pleasant job, executing people, and they wanted to do it with dispatch. His legs were weak. He had to be held up. His eyes were red from crying, but he was drained, and now they were dry. He wore slippers, grey slacks and a loose shirt with the sleeves rolled. A round area on the top of his head had been shaved. His right pant leg had been slit with a scissor.

There were a number of people in the room with him. The warden, the executioner, three guards, the rabbi, two doctors and three reporters chosen by lot to represent the press corps. One reporter was from the *Herald Tribune,* one was with Associated Press, and one was from the *News.* My father's hands were shaking and his breathing was rapid and shallow. He had been advised that a phone with a direct line to Washington would be in the execution chamber. He did not look for it when he entered the room. He made no sign that acknowledged the presence of any of the onlookers. He had to be helped into the chair, gently lowered, like an invalid. When he was seated his breathing became more rapid. He closed his eyes and clenched his hands in his lap.

Nothing had gone right. No cause had rallied. The world had not flamed to revolution. The issue of the commutation of the sentence, their chance for life, seemed to have turned on the quality, the gentility, the manners, of the people fighting for them. The cause seemed to have been discredited as a political maneuver. As if there was some grand fusion of associative guilt—the Isaacsons confirmed in guilt because of who campaigned for their freedom, and their supporters discredited because they campaigned for the Isaacsons. The truth was beyond reclamation. The President of the United States had called in the Attorney General of the United States just before he announced his decision on the Isaacsons' petition for clemency. It is believed that the Attorney General said to the President, "Mr. President, these folks have got to fry."

My father's hands were raised, and separated, and his arms strapped at the wrists to the arms of the chair. The arms of the electric chair are wood. The frame is wood, although a metal brace rises from the back of the chair and the chair is bolted to the concrete floor with metal braces. His ankles were strapped to the chair. The chair straps are leather. A strap was tied across his lap, another across his chest, and another, like a phylactery, around his head. A guard gently removed his eyeglasses, folded them, and put them aside. A guard came over, dipped his fingers into a jar, and with a circular motion rubbed an adhesive and conduction paste on the shaved place on my father's head, and then kneeled down and did the same for the place on his calf that had been shaved. Then the electrodes were fixed in place.

Electricity flows in circuits. If the circuit is open or incomplete electricity cannot flow. In electrocution the circuit is closed or completed by the human body. My father's lips were sucked up between his teeth as the hood came down over his face, every last tremor of his energy gathered in supreme effort not to cry out. The hood is black leather and is offered in respect for the right to privacy at the moment of death. However, it is also possible that the hood is placed on the head to spare the witnesses the effect to the musculature and coloration of the face, and the effect to the organs of the face, the tongue, the eyes, of two thousand five hundred volts of electricity. My father's hands gripped the wooden chair-arms till it seemed as if they could squeeze them to sawdust. The chair would kill him but at this moment it was his only support. The executioner took his place behind a protective wall in a kind of cove. On the wall in this cove was a large handled forklike switch. The switch is thrown from an up position to a down position. The executioner looked through a glass panel, and observed the warden observing my father. Waiting a moment too long the warden turned to the glass panel and nodded. The executioner threw the switch. My father smashed into his straps as if hit by a train. He snapped back and forth, cracking like a whip. The leather straps groaned and creaked. Smoke rose from my father's head. A hideous smell compounded of burning flesh, excrement and urine filled the death chamber. Most of the witnesses had turned away. A pool of urine collected on the cement floor under the chair.

When the current was turned off my father's rigid body suddenly slumped in the chair, and it perhaps occurred to the witnesses that what they had taken for the shuddering spasming movements of his life for God knows how many seconds was instead a portrait of electric current, normally invisible, moving through a field of resistance.

A few minutes after my father's body had been removed on a stretcher, and the floor mopped, and the organic smell of his death masked in the ammoniac scent of the cleanser, my mother was led into the chamber. She wore her grey, shapeless prison dress and terry cloth slippers. She knew that my father was dead. On her face was a carefully composed ironic smile. She calmly gazed at each of the witnesses until he turned away. Some, seeing her glance nearing them, simply would not look at her. Then my mother's eyes lighted on the prison rabbi. It was the same man whose ministrations she had refused for the last forty-eight hours. "I will not have him here," she said. The rabbi in his tallis and yarmulke walked toward the door. Before he was gone my mother called after him: "Let my son be bar mitzvahed today. Let our death be his bar mitzvah." The rabbi said later he didn't hear this remark, her voice not in this moment at its strongest.

My mother turned her back to the chair, disdaining any helping hand. She hugged the matron who had guarded her alone in the woman's death cell block for two years. They had become dear friends. The matron wept and ran out of the chamber. My mother, still with her peculiar smile, sat down in the electric chair and observed the strapping in of herself like a passenger in a plane getting ready for the journey. When the hood went over her eyes they were open. When the switch was thrown she went into the same buzzing sputtering arc dance. The current was turned off. The doctor came over to the slumped body and listened for a heartbeat with his stethoscope. He expressed consternation. The electrocutioner came out of his cove and they conferred. The warden was highly agitated. The three reporters communicated in urgent whispers. The executioner went back behind the wall, and again received a signal, and again turned on the current. Later he said the first "dose" had not been enough to kill my mother Rochelle Isaacson.

THREE ENDINGS

1. THE HOUSE. For reasons Daniel cannot explain, a week after he's back in New York he returns to the old neighborhood in the Bronx. It has changed. The Cross Bronx Expressway runs like a deep trench through what used to be 174th Street. The old apartment houses, rank upon rank, street after street, stand in their own soot like a ruined city filling with dirt. But people still live here. Great plastic bags of garbage are piled like sandbags against the sides of the buildings. The garbagemen are on strike. Garbage spills over the sidewalk. Empty milk cartons blow across streets. Newspapers stick to the legs. Coffee grounds drift across the schoolyard like sand across a desert. The old purple school still stands. It is not as big as I remembered. I rest my forehead against the fence and raise my arms above my head and hold the fence. Behind me, across the street, is my house. On the steps of the house, below the splintered porch, two black kids sit playing casino. A black woman opens the front door and calls to them to come inside. The night is coming on. The wind is beginning to blow over the schoolyard. I would like to turn and ask the woman if I can come in the house and look around. But the children gather up their cards and go inside and their mother shuts the door. I will do nothing. It's their house now.

2. THE FUNERAL. It was a huge funeral. The cortege stretched for miles—buses, cars, even city taxis. Policemen directed traffic. Policemen directed the funeral traffic. Police stood at the entrance gates of the cemetery. Not everybody could be let in. Graves might be trampled. It was a long stifling day, but not without its social aspects. At the funeral chapel

Jacob Ascher had introduced us to many people, including a young couple, the Lewins, who would be proposed as our parents. The weather was unseasonably hot, even for summer. Susan and I rode in the first black limousine behind the hearse. Aristocracy. We had the whole back to ourselves. But we sat close with our legs touching and we held hands as if we were sitting squeezed together between others. Faces peer in the windows.

We ride in a black Cadillac behind the hearse. It is one of those peculiar days of warmth with spring leaking through, escaping with a hiss into the winter like oil in water, like blood in milk. It is the kind of day the crocuses get fucked, exposing their petaled insides of delicate hue, yellow and white, lavender and flesh, to the spring. And it is too soon. It's a miscalculation. Crocus, first flower, dead flower, flower of revolutionaries.

We stand at the side of the graves. An enormous crowd presses behind us. The prayers are incanted. Everyone is in black. I glance at Susan. She is perfectly composed. She is neat and trim in a sleeveless black dress. A black lace handkerchief rests on her head. She looks beautiful, and I am enormously proud of her. She is getting to be quite a young lady, with her hair parted in the middle and combed over her ears and tied at her neck in a very grown-up way. I feel her warm hand in my hand and see her lovely eye cast down at the open earth at our feet and an inexpressible love fills my throat and weakens my knees. I think if I can only love my little sister for the rest of our lives that's all I will need.

The Lewins ride in the rear seat, Phyllis and I in jump seats at their knees. My mother wears a black hat with a veil over her eyes. Her eyes are swollen and red and her mouth is turned down in ugly grief. My father wears a dark suit and tie. He is demolished. He did not shave well and I can see patches of grey stubble that he missed under his chin and at the corner of his mouth. Phyllis's face is pale, drawn. It is a sunny day and her weeping eyes are blue. She wears a pea jacket and dungarees.

In the cemetery we wait behind the hearse while the drivers smoke and talk on the sidewalk and the funeral director goes up to the office and deals with the cemetery people. This is a small funeral and he will have others today.

My sister is dead. She died of a failure of analysis.

Last autumn's leaves scuttle across the plots. The plots are separated by pipe fences or planted borders. We drive down the straight narrow streets of the cemetery. It seems to me ridiculous that a cemetery should have street names and that one place rather than another is designated for a person's burial. It is a city for the dead, in their eyes, a holy place of rest for the dead, in urban grids, with stones and markers like buildings, and upper-class neighborhoods of fashionable crypts, and cooperative apartments in the name of this lodge or that. Some stones are so old they are brown, and very close together, as in ghettos. Fashions change, even in gravestones. The newer style is to have the family name unadorned on one large stone, and individual members' identity declared on footstones. Poems and biblical quotations seem to be out. Occasionally brief cryptic phrases in stylized Hebrew. The new stones are white and grey, and polished on their face and rough hewn on their sides.

Susan's grave is under a tree very near my parents' graves. I arranged everything. A green carpet covers the earth where it has been dug up. Three gravediggers move off and wait at a discreet distance as we get out of the car. They are young guys, not much older than I am. They will never lose their curiosity for the varieties of grief. Around the corner on the little graveyard street is a yellow trench-digger. Susan's coffin rests in its grave and the funeral director looks at me. I have refused the company rabbi, and it's now time to say the prayers and throw the shovelful of earth on Susan's coffin. I tell him to wait a minute. I run through the cemetery and hire little old Jewish men, the kind who always come along for a fee to say the prayers the younger Jews don't know. Little bearded men who make their livings in cemeteries—shamuses, scholars, bums, misfits, who make it begging people to say prayers for their newly dead, their recently dead, their long since dead. They are usually shabby, their heels run down. Some of them are drunkards. I run through the cemetery, hiring one after another, directing them, and by the time I get back, half a dozen stand there, ignoring each other and racing through prayers for Susan in their singsong rituals, rocking back and forth on their heels with their eyes closed, chanting and simpering their nasal prayers. It's a bonanza. Other shamuses come running, like pigeons, when they see the crowd. I accept each blessed one. I have a roll of bills in my pocket. I am bankrolled. My mother and father go back to the car. The funeral director waits impatiently beside his shiny hearse. But I encourage the prayermakers, and when one is through I tell him *again,* this time for my mother and father. Isaacson. Pinchas. Rachele. Susele. For all of them. I hold my wife's hand. And I think I am going to be able to cry.

3. THE LIBRARY. For my third ending I had hoped to discuss some of the questions posed by this narrative. However, just a moment ago, while I was sitting here writing the last page, someone came through announcing that the library is closed. "Time to leave, man, they're closing the school down. Kirk must go! We're doin' it, we're bringing the whole motherfucking university to its knees!"

"You mean I have to get out?"

"That's right, man, move your ass, this building is officially closed."

"Wait—"

"No wait, man, the time is now. The water's shut off. The lights are going out. Close the book, man, what's the matter with you, don't you know you're liberated?"

I have to smile. It has not been unexpected. I will walk out to the Sundial and see what's going down.

DANIEL'S BOOK: A Life Submitted in Partial Fulfillment of the Requirements for the Doctoral Degree in Social Biology, Gross Entomology, Women's Anatomy, Children's Cacophony, Arch Demonology, Eschatology, and Thermal Pollution.

> *and there shall be a time of trouble such as never was since there was a nation . . . and at that time the people shall be delivered, everyone that shall be found written in the book. And many of them that sleep in the dust of the earth shall awake, some to everlasting contempt. And they that be wise shall shine as the brightness of the firmament; and they that turn*

*many to righteousness, as the stars for ever and ever.
But thou, O Daniel, shut up the words, and seal the
book, even to the time of the end . . . Go thy way
Daniel: for the words are closed up and sealed till the
time of the end.*

About the Author

E. L. Doctorow was born in 1931
in New York City and was educated
at Kenyon College and Columbia University.
His earlier novels are *Welcome to Hard Times*
and *Big as Life*. Formerly editor-in-chief
of a prominent New York publishing house,
he was most recently writer in residence
at the University of California at Irvine.
He lives in Westchester County
with his wife and three children.

$$6 \times 8/06$$
$$9 \times 1/10$$
$$9 \times 1/10$$
$$9 \times 1/10$$